...acifico has written for a number of Italian publications, as well ...or *Rolling Stone* and *GQ*, and has translated into Italian the works of Henry Miller, F. Scott Fitzgerald, Dave Eggers, Will Eisner and more. He lives in Rome.

Stephen Twilley is associate editor at the online review *Public Books* and assistant editor at New York Review Books Classics. He is also the translator of Marina Mander's novel *The First True Lie* (2013).

THE STORY OF MY PURITY

FRANCESCO PACIFICO

TRANSLATED FROM THE ITALIAN

BY STEPHEN TWILLEY

PENGUIN BOOKS

PENGUIN BOOKS

Published by the Penguin Group
Penguin Books Ltd, 80 Strand, London WC2R 0RL, England
Penguin Group (USA) Inc., 375 Hudson Street, New York, New York 10014, USA
Penguin Group (Canada), 90 Eglinton Avenue East, Suite 700, Toronto, Ontario, Canada M4P 2Y3
(a division of Pearson Penguin Canada Inc.)
Penguin Ireland, 25 St Stephen's Green, Dublin 2, Ireland (a division of Penguin Books Ltd)
Penguin Group (Australia), 707 Collins Street, Melbourne, Victoria 3008, Australia
(a division of Pearson Australia Group Pty Ltd)
Penguin Books India Pvt Ltd, 11 Community Centre, Panchsheel Park, New Delhi – 110 017, India
Penguin Group (NZ), 67 Apollo Drive, Rosedale, Auckland 0632, New Zealand
(a division of Pearson New Zealand Ltd)
Penguin Books (South Africa) (Pty) Ltd, Block D, Rosebank Office Park,
181 Jan Smuts Avenue, Parktown North, Gauteng 2193, South Africa

Penguin Books Ltd, Registered Offices: 80 Strand, London WC2R 0RL, England

www.penguin.com

First published in Italy as *Storia della mia purezza* by Mondadori 2010
English translation first published in the United States of America
by Farrar, Straus and Giroux 2013
First published in Great Britain by Hamish Hamilton 2013
Published in Penguin Books 2014
001

Copyright © Arnoldo Mondadori Editore S.p.A., Milano, 2010
Translation copyright © Stephen Twilley, 2013
All rights reserved

The moral right of the author and of the translator has been asserted

Printed in Great Britain by Clays Ltd, St Ives plc

ISBN: 978–0–141–39950–8

www.greenpenguin.co.uk

TO MY SISTER

THE STORY
OF MY PURITY

1

Napoleon. Nineteenth-century mental asylums were overrun with men convinced they were the Emperor of the French. Roaming about in crumpled, ungainly tricorne hats, they gave orders to invisible troops in their institutions' English gardens. These men weren't aberrations, just outliers on a spectrum of absolutely normal human behavior. We all have to believe we're somebody. If we don't give ourselves a face, if we don't occupy some position, all action becomes impossible. At times we go too far and end up in an asylum, but generally speaking, we can't do without imagination.

For instance, I was at my parents' house, Christmas dinner 2005, and I had to ask my father for a loan. What kind of person was I? A Sergey Brin? A Julien Sorel? A Trump? Someone who, given a hundred-thousand-euro loan, could move the world? Or was I one of those sons of successful men, their faces swollen from seaside vacations, with childlike smiles and the lumpy bodies of unfinished men? One of those aristocrats who drown in their own pools, or the Kennedy kids, the Agnelli kids, with their vices, their complexes? Because my father was rich. And not even excessively so—he was happy rich, without serious obligations to the world. And not only was he happy rich, he was also the master of his own destiny, because when he was young he'd used his considerable talent to rescue his father-in-law's fortune and make a name for himself. In the late seventies, when the furniture market threatened to tank, aggressive new dealers started coming out of nowhere and

3

selling off their stock at ridiculously low prices, but my father saw it coming and advised his father-in-law to get out of the business in time. So my grandfather cut a deal with these new low-cost entrepreneurs and diversified. What he lost from one pocket was returned to him in the other, and the damage was limited. My father became Achilles, Hector, an unblemished hero.

It was none other than this charming and self-confident man whom I had to ask for a loan, I who was the soul of drab. My belly strained against my sky-blue tailored shirt, my stooped back ached, and as if that weren't enough, I always kept my eyes to the ground. Just like Jesus when he looked down and prodded the earth with a stick instead of facing the crowd baying for the adulteress's stoning: I followed his example.

What with my stoop and my belly, my wife had lost interest in me and my body, and I in turn had lost all confidence in myself. She didn't show the least interest even though I was tall and had the broad shoulders of a champion—prevailing over it all were the two startled little folds beneath my butt cheeks, excesses of fat, of physical resignation. And on that Christmas Day as well my thighs swelled the pants of my suit, the suit I was married in. Why an elegant suit for Christmas dinner? As everybody knew—because I took every opportunity to explain—it was my custom, on holy days, to set aside my usual shabby dress, my unlikely argyles and gray corduroys, and put on my good suit so everyone would understand that I cared only for the Lord; only for Him did I get dressed up, and certainly not to please women. With the anxious and contrite air that always clung to me, especially at my parents', where I insisted on saying grace before meals even though it had never been the custom in our house, with that anxious and contrite air and my gray English-style suit, it was impossible for me to make allies when I needed them. A good Christian should be more accommodating but, I told myself, the times are what they are, and if you speak softly, people won't understand that

4

the Lord is their shepherd. The state of things really bothered me, and everybody knew it and gave me a wide berth, refusing to take me into their confidence, denying me their loving touch. I gave anyone who found fault with the opinions of Pope Ratzinger a mouthful, and turned up my nose if anyone made dirty jokes; in short, I was totally committed, in my own way, to becoming a saint. Go and read the lives of the saints; they didn't mess around.

Now, even a saint, when asking his father for a loan, has to decide what kind of son he is: one with balls who knows his own mind, or nothing but a big baby who'll live in the shadow of his parents forever and die still soft. That's why saints don't ask their parents for loans and instead choose a life of poverty. But I wanted to change jobs. I absolutely had to change jobs, I was going crazy. I had to give up my position as an editor at the Catholic publishing house Non Possumus and look for something less stressful. But as you'll gather from the conversation in which I ask Daddy for money, at the time I had just the sort of job to make people shake their heads and say, "You made your bed . . ."

I was difficult. And if you're a difficult person, you'll agree that even if your obstinacy at times just seems to others like a bad habit, being difficult in fact prevents you from living well. In my particular case, I should add that before the conversion that struck me blind with the love of Jesus, I was a good-looking kid. Many people were dismayed by my voluntary transformation into a homely and unsociable man. I may have had my father's and brothers' sallow skin, but what with my height, my good shoulders and slim legs, my way with words, my tendency to philosophize, a nose somewhere between Jewish and Imperial Roman, I'd been able to take my pick before becoming engaged to Alice.

So now people would say, "How did Piero Rosini ever come to this? He's become ugly and even more insufferable than before. A lousy philosopher he always was, but now you won't even get a laugh out of him." They stopped calling. And I would think, Blessed are those who suffer for His cause.

I remained seated at the table, waiting to find the courage to approach my father. The others had already moved into the living room behind me. The two large, unequal rooms were separated by a pair of short partition walls that made them seem like mirrored stage sets. There I was on one stage, pure Harold Pinter: hunched over the table, my shirt cuffs resting among the crumbs on a battlefield of white linen, the gold-thread-embroidered tablecloth strewn with dessert plates smeared with Chantilly cream and the remains of *pangiallo* and *parrozzo*. Across from me, my little five-year-old nephew, wearing a red vest over a blue-and-white-striped shirt with an unbuttoned and crumpled collar, his fine brown hair parted to one side, was enraptured by the task of filling a page with alternating upper- and lowercase *H*'s. No doubt certain family members—my wife, for instance—had understood, knowing my temperament, that I remained there out of spite. I couldn't stomach the fact that my father had given the order to break ranks before coffee, before Mamma had even turned on the machine, just to cover up my older brother Carlo's dirty tricks. As Carlo nibbled on a crumbly slice of *parrozzo*, his cell phone gave a short ring; seconds later it gave another, longer this time. He'd checked the display and, after a second's hesitation, eyebrows raised, answered with a "Hey there!" and disappeared from the room, leaving his lobster-colored sweater on the back of the overstuffed chair. His mistress, obviously. And Papa, ever faithful to his sons, especially the two oldest, Carlo and Fausto, who had always accompanied him on his work trips and got up to who knows what together (I'll never know), had proposed, "Shall we move into the living room? Dear, will you bring us the coffee in there?"

Mamma had stood up, asking, "How many?"

Papa, big and tall, had shuffled away like a grizzly, dragging his leather slippers. Coming in for landing on the turquoise velvet easy chair, he asked for his cigarettes, which Mamma presently provided.

Christmas dinner *should never* be interrupted by a mistress. I remained at the table with my little nephew—"Uncle Piero, how many words do you know beginning with *H*?" "*How* is a word beginning with *H*." "It . . . it's at the start of the word. How many do you know?" "*How* is a word starting with *H*." "Whaat?"—and in the air between us, among the dessert plates, glasses, and silverware, hung the memory of the linguine with lobster, the turbot covered in thinly sliced potatoes, the prawns in cocktail sauce, and all that Piedmontese and Apulian wine we'd befuddled ourselves with as we talked about A.S. Roma, potholes, makes of scooters, the lengths of scarves.

At that point my father's heart must have ached with joy: the phone call already ably forgotten, he rested behind me, basking in the meal's success. What did it matter to him if two of his three daughters-in-law were suffering, scratching up the doorjambs with their cuckold's horns? If he had raised two older children (the younger ones, my sister and I, were Mamma's creation) as second-rate pleasure-seekers, uninspired, slaves to material needs, so what? In any case, the grandkids would be the ones to pay, the sons and daughters of mothers and fathers who didn't love each other in the light of Christ.

As you can see, my extravagant mind transformed familiar faces into ugly brutes and wretched victims, and well-known houses into inhospitable deserts where I was at the mercy of the Tempter. Such images may well suit Jesus of Nazareth as the Devil leads him up the mountain to offer him the riches of the world—for him reality truly is threatening and sinister. But for me? Well, I needed money, and it's hard to ask for money from someone you regard as the Devil Incarnate.

Yes, that's what I thought my father was. The last of the devils, like Al Pacino in *Donnie Brasco* is the very last of the Mafiosi, but still part of the hierarchy, Evil's lackey. Because he'd cheated on my mother (*I know even if I don't have proof*, as Pasolini had it), because he didn't approve of my ultrapapist religious turn, because ever since I set my sights on becoming a modern saint, an intellectual martyr, he no longer knew how to deal with me or even, literally, how to talk to me.

From another point of view, he was just an old man, a sentimental old man, easily moved to tears, who wanted nothing more from life than to enjoy his family gathered round the table for a four-course dinner, and afterward, Super Light Camel in hand like an orchestra director's baton, to watch his grandkids scampering about on the rugs, popping out of one door and immediately dashing through another, raising hell, while his three lovely daughters-in-law and his daughter, Federica, vestals of the household religion, conversed happily in groups of two.

And this was the scene on the other stage, which I took in at a glance as I turned, slice of panettone in hand: the custard-colored living room, the pin-striped wallpaper; Carlo in shirtsleeves and Fausto in a pea-green cashmere-blend sweater, smoking on the terrace with the rain and the pines shaking over the avenue behind them; their wives dressed in black with pearl necklaces, sitting on a satin settee, coffee in hand; three children, a girl and two boys (the one with the *H*'s had deserted me for his cousins), who scurried away from and then returned to their mothers, one dragging a plastic fire engine. On a pair of armchairs sat my sister, Federica, and my wife, Alice, all animated hand gestures and bright orange stockings, both women (Federica's stockings sporting three bright stripes of color, her legs brushing up against Alice's) a sharp contrast to the daughters-in-law in black. Federica, with her rounded shoulders, her knee-length chestnut-brown wool dress and ice-blue angora shawl, was a honeyed, unsettling pet of a woman with lots of wrinkles—she was thirty-six years old, seven years older than I was. That left Mamma behind the scenes in the kitchen, the barrista set to appear with the tray every two minutes to serve coffee, and my father center stage in his easy chair, meeting my gaze as he reached over to turn on a table lamp. With the light, the yellow pin-striped wallpaper suddenly lost its luster, as if oxidized; outside, intermittent rain stained the window ledges and tickled the glass.

Piercing the fourth wall, I went to join their performance, my gray suit in that composite chaos à la De Filippo making me the intruder in a coup de théâtre, the civil servant, the gravedigger, the bearer of bad news.

"Listen, Papa, I'd like to talk to you about work."

"With me? What an honor."

He'd taken his slippers off. He tapped a cigarette against its silver case. Placing the cigarette in his mouth, he brushed back the sparse white hair over his ears. He was wrapped in a blue cardigan like a sumo wrestler, tall and big-bellied. The cardigan took me back to my childhood. In his fifties he used to wear it under his jacket when he went to dinner with a bunch of yuppie socialists from Monte Mario, big fans of basketball and sailing.

He lights his cigarette, blows smoke, and stretches out; then with one hand he catches a passing grandkid, tells him, "Go and get us a chair, *amore*." The child gives his cousin and sister a superior look and runs into the dining room, where he begins to grapple with a chair like a dockworker. I walk over and grab the chair from him; the child looks at his grandfather, who, cigarette in mouth, slips a hand into a cardigan pocket and pulls out a fifty-centesimi piece. The child runs to his grandfather's hand, seizes the golden doubloon, and flees into another room, followed by the other two little ones, dumbfounded at the appearance of money.

"So, then, what's on your mind? Cigarette?"

"No, I don't smoke, no."

"What do you mean, you don't smoke? I thought you did."

I didn't like watching him smoke, him sucking on the cigarettes as if they were oysters.

9

"I wanted to tell you that . . . , to tell you about work. The thing is, I'm starting to look around, and I wanted—"

"Of course, of course. Rightly so."

"Rightly so?"

"Look, as I see it, Fede is keeping an eye on you." He leaned forward with a confidential, knowing air, the tip of his cigarette glowing like a precious stone. "As I see it, Fede is trying to figure out what you're up to at that . . . eccentric publishing house of yours . . . and as soon as she thinks you've got the right experience, she'll introduce you to the right people, understand? It's a matter of months, I'd say."

My sister Federica was a writer whose books were brought out by a big publisher. The original plan, hatched when we were still close, was for her to get me into publishing as well. Before Holy Scriptures swept it away, literature was my life. My father had failed to pick up on this change in me and listened only to what he wanted to hear, the way winners do; he overlooked certain details because he was always looking ahead. In the Anglo-Saxon managerial language that he had cheerfully made his own, for him a *problem* was an *opportunity*. Papa was a true believer.

"You know very well," he explained, "that before entrusting your brothers with paying jobs I made them toil *for free* until they showed me they really had the balls for it. Fede is doing the same thing with you; she's waiting for you."

Federica and I were no longer on speaking terms. Fede went out with married men, wrote about clitorises and theatrical salons; she thought I was a bigot. The bigot and the whore, that's what our literary alliance came to. Ever since we were little, Mamma had endeavored to make us better than Carlo and Fausto, whose overly bourgeois and paternally influenced upbringing (tennis, five-a-side soccer, girlfriends from Parioli, not much reading) she had come to regret. Federica, the pedagogical masterpiece, had turned out as Mamma had hoped, becoming a relatively famous writer of newspaper articles, exhibition catalogs, and novels full of declines of the West and wet crotches. Who knows what she and my wife had to say to each other whenever they met.

"Leave Fede out of this, Papa. There's something I want to talk to you about. It's the publishing house. Recently, I've been feeling I can't get behind it anymore."

"Only recently?" He was trying not to laugh.

It pained me to have to say this, but money is money. "It's become pure paranoia. I don't think it's doing me any good, spiritually."

He puffed his cheeks and snorted, unable to resist: he now had to scoff, "Do you have any idea what you sound like, Piero?"

"No, I don't, please let me speak. Alice and I are leaving soon."

"Why?"

"We have to go, and anyway I don't feel like staying and playing the fool for you with my work problems."

"And what would be so wrong with giving your old father some amusement?"

"Papa, will you just listen to me for a minute?"

"What would be so wrong with playing the fool for your father? You're so serious. Well, don't get me started."

"Fine, what is it you have to say to me, Papa?"

In my pocket I clutched the little tin cross and ten cherry-wood beads of my mini-rosary. My white boxers were slipping around inside my pants. A year and a half earlier my father had taken me to his tailor, perhaps the only time in more than ten years I had done something with him and in his style; but it was for a sacred occasion, my wedding outfit.

He stubbed out his cigarette in the ashtray, pressing down hard with the tip of his index finger, crushing it. As he spoke, my heart sank.

"You don't realize how much fun it is to talk to people about you. Whatever it is, their eyes always get big, like this!

11

Once, someone told me that from what I said, you were like someone running toward a burning city while everyone else was trying to escape."

"Something I might have learned from you . . ."

"Of course, my dear fellow, of course, but you also have to know which abandoned city to choose. I only run in if I know they've left their safes open."

"Very funny, Papa, so you're better than me, way to go." I'd been shaken but had to remember that the money was still in his pockets.

"Anyway, the story I love telling, usually at dinner after the dirty jokes, it goes like this: 'One time those crazies from the publishing house had him do some research for a book. He's good at what he does, you see, so they have him rewrite the books, make them better, get the subjunctives right, stretch out the material.'" He looked at me, extended his large hand toward my large hand, but I had broken out in a cold sweat and he noticed, hesitated, then continued: "I'm painting you a picture of the situation from the outside, you have to learn to see things in perspective. 'They had him rewrite a book about subliminal pornographic messages. In our family we renamed it the Book of Cocks.'"

I wanted to ask him if it was true about the name, but some great weight prevented me from speaking up.

"'Piero analyzed a series of advertisements and cartoons and Disney movies in which hidden cocks appeared. That is, a skyscraper with a round penthouse. A mountain cave full of shrubs. *Subliminal cunts*. A lamppost.' 'And why?' my friends asked. 'Because in the world according to Ratzinger . . .'"

"Papa." I tried to smile but I really wasn't the smiling type. "That's enough, leave the Pope out of this."

"And I told them: 'According to righteous, hard-line Catholics like my genius of a son, there are secret, hidden powers in the world who control the newspapers and TV and movies and comic strips and they insert cocks everywhere in

12

order to corrupt children.' Because let's be clear here, my son whom I love, this is what you all think."

I clutched the rosary and tried silently to recite a Hail Mary, but immediately made a mess of it.

"And do you know what people do? They buy me dinner. Because the story is just too good to be true. Nobody can believe people like that exist, let alone one of my own, my flesh and blood. Now listen to the end—"

"They don't really buy you dinner—"

He stopped me with a gesture. *"Listen to the end of my story* and see if they don't buy me dinner."

My father must be a Mason, I thought, otherwise he wouldn't be waging this war against me. Mazzini reincarnated. My imagination was running wild again and I found it telling that he and Mamma lived in Prati, the neighborhood of the liberal, anticlerical elite, of elegant nineteenth-century boulevards and apartment blocks, a little slice of Paris in Arcadian Rome, the Catholic village—Prati, the neighborhood constructed in such a way that St. Peter's could be seen only from one or two streets. My father the Mason. Ever since I became a great Christian of the saturnine Russian stripe, the city drove me crazy. Mazzini and the *non expedit* Pope, the soubrettes on their coffee breaks behind the RAI building, the civil servants, gaudy Neapolitans or gloomy Turinese, corrupt souls. I belonged to the Pope, not to newspaper publishers or bustling undersecretaries with flakes of croissant between their teeth, and I certainly didn't belong to my father.

"So how *does* your story end?"

" 'And my son,' I tell them, 'comes to me one day and says, "Papa, Papa . . . *I see cocks everywhere* . . ."' And everyone dies laughing. And they buy me dinner."

I looked at him, perplexed. "Did I really say that to you?"

Nodding, he says, "No, you didn't say it to me. Irregardless, if you had, I'd have died laughing. And let's face it, you might well have said it."

"*Irregardless?*" I reply.

"Yes, irregardless, so what?"

What a poker face. He probably said "irregardless" on purpose in order to force me into being a pedant. A businessman's tricks. "Should I get up and leave?" I threatened.

"No no no, c'mon, stay, let's have some fun. Are you trying to bury me alive? Laughing's good for my heart condition."

Unfortunately, he was right, I did see cocks everywhere. That book was the beginning of my nightmares. The author's thesis was that postwar sexual liberation didn't arise spontaneously, but was *induced* by esoteric strains of Masonry intent on establishing a new world order based on pleasure as religion, on nonreproductive sex. To this end, corrupt producers had inserted nudity into children's movies and cartoons in the form of photographs or drawings of breasts, vaginas, and penises, as new single frames or montaged into the existing ones. After three months spent reviewing the illustrations, I'd seen enough penises and vaginas to last me the rest of my life. The skyscraper with the glans-shaped penthouse on the cover of a Duck Avenger adventure was lodged in my head forever. Likewise, anything long looked like a cock and anything round and concave looked like a cunt. Wine bars, with all those bottlenecks on the shelves, were scenes of perdition. I told myself: This is why working women on the pill go drink wine at cocktail hour. Bottles in rows on the shelves, red and turgid, sheathed with labels. They surround themselves with cocks, they drink from cocks. I had an immoderate imagination. I always went too far.

"All right, let's not argue. So then, *amore*, what's your idea?"

I tried to keep my mind on the money. "I'm thinking of opening a publishing house."

"A publishing house. Good grief. But aren't they all going over to electronic books?"

"No, no," I explained (he always thought he knew everything). "What does that have to do with anything? It's been a flop, no one ever talks about it."

"But in the long run?"

"What the fuck, Papa, listen to me. A publishing house that's a bit less about taking sides than Non Possumus, and more literary. That's the idea."

"And who would help you?"

"Alice would do the covers."

"Uh-huh, and what about somebody who understands the market? Pardon me, but do you have somebody who understands books and isn't distracted by cocks—do you have that?"

I made to get up.

"No, don't, please, I'm only kidding. Don't get so upset."

"Papa, I'm talking to you about my life and you just can't help yourself."

"No, now hold it right there, we're talking about my life too." He leaned toward me and once again reached for my hand. He was about to get sentimental, I could tell. "First of all, if it's an investment, you can't expect that I won't have my say—but let's forget about that for the moment. What I really want to know is, how much fun can I still expect to have with my son before I go? My darling Piero who's always in church and never visits his father. It makes me ill just to think about it. How many more Christmases with my wonderful, bat-crazy son? Well, *amore*? The mathematics of it, Piero!"

He gave me a wrinkly smile full of love. What was I to do? I rejected him, withdrawing my hand. An unforgivable error. He decided he needed to teach me a lesson.

"You're always so unhappy, Piero. So serious. Why? Why doesn't the story of the subliminal messages make you laugh? Don't take yourself so seriously, for God's sake. I swear"—and here he tried to laugh as inoffensively as possible—"if the cock story doesn't make you laugh, you're in a bad way."

"So you're not convinced?"

"Why don't you have some fun once in a while? You're so

15

unhappy. We pay for our children's education, waste all this time teaching them to talk, send them off into the world while we learn how not to worry ourselves to death, and then they turn out so unhappy. When you're happy you seem crazy, and the rest of the time you seem unhappy. Why don't you have some fun? Why not go somewhere? You never leave Rome, never stop talking about priests . . . go on, take a trip somewhere!"

"You're not convinced."

"Okay, have it your way, we'll talk about you another time. Tell me, why should I be convinced? You want me on the board?"

"Well . . ."

"You want money? Is that what you want? Let's hear it then, how much?"

He was smiling. I was confused. Was he going to give it to me or not?

"Just, you know, to understand what kind of guy you are. Give me a number. How much do you want to extort from me?"

I had to be swift. Although I hadn't even come up with a budget, this was my moment to convince him I was Napoleon in charge of a vast army of euros.

"Twenty-five?"

"Thousand?"

"Hmm."

"And how did you come up with this number?"

I had no idea. I said nothing.

"How did you arrive at exactly twenty-five thousand? As a number, it doesn't seem either big or small."

"Well . . ."

"How? Tell me."

"I don't know." I bowed my head. How did I come up with the number, Papa? I was just tired of cocks and tired of how afraid I was of everyone. I wanted to get away from Non Possumus, but where do you go with a résumé like mine?

"Well, my dear boy, it would have been better if you had known. This way you look like an amateur, and somebody in your situation can *never* afford to look like an amateur. When Roman Abramovich was a poor young man, selling plastic toys on the street, he lived in a room that was completely empty except for an elegant suit on a hanger. In order to look serious, to make a good impression. All right, so you've already got the elegant suit covered . . . forget the example, it doesn't work. My dear boy, your proposal is one of the most delusional . . ."

From "delusional" onward I stopped listening as the black veil of defeat settled over everything, making the present seem like a bad memory even as it happened. Most likely he talked about his company, about what I was made of, and about Federica. Afterward I thanked him for listening to me and went into the kitchen, where in the meantime my brothers had holed up for another coffee. Having finished that, and inspired by what they found in the fridge, they had dug into an aged cheese. I found them dipping pieces in honey and talking about food.

"Here, try some," they said to me, "this honey is amazing."

"No, thanks, I'm not hungry."

"It's acacia honey. It's sublime."

Seeing them eat like that, bent over a silver bowl of sticky nectar, busy with their basic needs, bumblebees with human clothes and shaved chins, I felt a violent sadness overcome me; I left the kitchen and closed myself in the bathroom for a few minutes. Rosini, I tell myself now, you had truly delicate nerves.

2

When I come face-to-face with Saint Peter, the great bearded saint from the Lavazza commercials who waits with quill pen and register before the gates of Heaven, I won't have much of anything objective to say. He'll invite me to sit down in a solid gold chair, very comfortable, and holding little Lavazza cups between our thumbs and index fingers, we'll discuss my fears and my fertile imagination. He'll ask how I came to make certain moral decisions, what guided my choices, what was going on in my head. I'll tell him, "I was an impressionable guy. Don't say you didn't know."

A few days before Christmas, the tension I'd been building up on account of Non Possumus's recent ideological escalation had brought about a strange effect. My imagination, usually bogged down in trench warfare against nonbelievers, had, for the first time in my life as a newly devout Christian, launched itself full bore after a Catholic sister. And not just any sister, but someone I loved, someone whom I had for some time considered a spiritual ally: my wife Alice's sister, my sister-in law, Ada.

Twenty-four years old and a virgin. A beautiful girl with nunlike ways, quietly proud of her coyness, her ascetic interpretation of feminism. Hooded sweatshirts were her nun's habit; it was impossible to imagine her in a lascivious pose. Both she and her sister had inherited beautiful big breasts from their mother, whose own bosom was turning to dust in a cemetery just as her daughters' were blooming into existence. Upon these enticing fruits preceding Ada wherever she went, no one, as far as anyone knew, had ever laid hands. They were two pricey mink coats allowed to slowly degrade in storage, mothballed by friendly claps on the back and kisses cheek to cheek; you might fall in love with them, but eventually you fell out.

The week leading up to Christmas we were in a bar in the Africano neighborhood, Ada, Alice, and I, and some others from the parish group we called the Teste Parlanti, about fifteen of us. We never went into the city center in the evenings, or to fashionable neighborhoods like Trastevere, Testaccio, San Lorenzo. We loved this area, loved hiding away from the restless, sweaty masses. We were all between twenty-five and thirty-five years old (I was twenty-eight and wished I was older), happy to consider ourselves men and women rather than big kids. We shunned our generation's unserious ways; more than half of us were already married, with kids; earnest fathers who never made eyes at the babysitter; wives grown fat; people of goodwill in Windbreakers, shapeless overcoats, fleece.

By that stage, they were the only people I could talk to. We'd spend a couple of hours saying the usual things to one another, and then everyone would head home. Educated, sophisticated people. Coming out of the various neighborhoods' leftist high schools, teenagers in keffiyehs, we now found ourselves—in a future that we could not and would not have wanted to imagine—new conservatives, with the same idealism of back then and yet light-years away from the Young Communist–sponsored film clubs, from the student collectives where our sense of human destiny was born. We were highwire performers in the world of ideas, executing complex ideological acrobatics without a net; in the new century, each of us in our own way came to land on the Catholic crash mat. We shared a dream that the Church would win back the middle classes, reversing the process of general mental enfeeblement brought on by television and consumerism, and the glorious Christian Democratic middle class—stripped in our idealized vision of the usual compromises and egotism—would "return" to shine in modesty amid the joyous pandemonium of grandparents and children. We were organic intellectuals in stripes and loafers, and pictured ourselves as good salt-of-the-earth types, serious people who worked and raised their children. Helping us to remain steadfast in our faith were the books of Non Possumus, an articulate counterhistory that vindicated the Church so ill-treated by secular culture: revisionist essays against the Masonic Risorgimento, polemical tracts on the UN's contraception policies, on the apocalyptic drift of the Bush administration, on evangelical plots.

In our sporadic trips to the bar (more often we would gather at someone's home, parking the strollers in a corner, for fitful conversations interrupted by feeding breaks; the mothers would lift a bra cup to display breasts swollen with milk, and as they suckled the little ones we men would lose our train of thought, astonished by the miracle of life, a miracle that for us was also a political statement), beyond some small talk limited to practical matters—about dry cleaning, about government offices with the shortest lines—we spoke only about religion, about religion and its servant, politics. Other interests fell by the wayside. We were passionate about every aspect of the Church's role in the confused world of the twenty-first century. ". . . This friend of mine, they said to her in her office, 'You're not thinking of having another kid, are you? It's about time you calmed down'"; ". . . but is it true that the Washington elite perform pagan rituals?"; ". . . I read this book by a priest who says that any Catholic today who makes love using a condom places himself automatically outside the Church . . ."

Geopolitics, clashes of civilizations, policies promoting abortions, these were all worthwhile topics. But we all thought in the same way and there was never any disagreement. To talk meant to recapitulate and to recapitulate made sense; it was the mantra of our nonconformism. Nor, for the sake of distraction, could we get together as men and talk about women: we were all faithful to our wives and scorned low necklines. We didn't share secrets with one another and we followed the Islamic rule whereby to look at a beautiful woman in the street once is inevitable, but two times is a sin, because it's willful.

Ada was one of the most active members of the Teste Parlanti; she knew how to make two hundred sandwiches in a few hours for parish events and could remain on her knees saying the rosary for the four consecutive mystery cycles without ever once stretching her legs. Everyone knew she was a virgin. She herself talked about it openly, and people would say, "She's such a beautiful girl, the way she conducts herself is such a sign of the presence of God . . ." Meaning: "Those beautiful, still firm twenty-four-year-old tits, nipples more pronounced in winter, soft and lazy in summer, fragrant with the woods and scented deodorant, her marble eyes, large mouth, small nose, she could have anything she wants. Instead she saves herself for her future husband, be it Jesus in a convent or a fortunate honest man who one day will make her his in an even split with God."

To my eyes, Ada was proof of woman's vocation for purity, and I, the local champion of sexual abstinence in the years leading up to marriage, was her male counterpart. That Advent Sunday, in an abrupt reshuffling of emotional equilibrium, I unwillingly became her enemy, and at the same time—an awkward contradiction—her secret suitor. Seeing her dance was all it took. I was undone.

Elvis was playing on the jukebox. Ada, leaving her small mug of beer on the wooden table, got up to dance to "Heartbreak Hotel," in the space between the table and the stairs. I meanwhile was busy explaining to two fellow Teste my ideas about how the Evil One lays snares for priests high up in the Vatican hierarchies. Having intuited the form of her breasts under her gray sweatshirt—instinctively and without malice, as always—I tried to capture her in a single look, because once I'd turned away I wouldn't be able to look again. She started swaying to the words "I get so lonely I could die." With her honest smile and slightly upturned nose, stretching out her fingers so innocently, so free of the languid depravity of impure women, she cut through Elvis's nasal sighs and the fifty years of world history that came between the hunky Irish Indian Jewish Elvis Pressler's first Sun Records singles and this winter night in the bar. While the rest of us talked about the Devil roaming the halls of the Vatican, about priests hiding in their bedrooms, chanting the evening prayer or performing exorcisms, I was mesmerized by my sister-in-law's sterile dance. And in my effort to watch I lost the thread of my own argument, subsequently gathered up by my clean-shaven friends in checked shirts. I was enraptured by that dance, an inverse Salome, which for the first time brought before my eyes unhealthy images and negative thoughts.

I fantasized about my sister-in-law blaxploitation-style, standing in the doorway of a little log cabin in Faulkner's Deep South, saying to the still contractless singer in a down-home black accent: "Uh-uh, handsome, ain't no way I'm lettin' you in here." Crushed by this denial of favors so blunt it could only be innocent, he gives up, walks away from the cabin defeated: I haven't got it, I can't even talk a common negress into bed. So he accepts a job at a gas station and rock 'n' roll is lost to the world.

Alice stepped over me to grab her coat and cigarettes and go outside for a smoke. I remained in an absurd trance. With the awkward grace you might see in girls at an orphanage or an end-of-year dance recital, my sister-in-law's full hips shook; she offered up a parody of a moan against the brokenhearted voice of the King begging "ba-by," then, indifferent to the powerful forces she held at bay, she walked back to the table while the decapitated head of Elvis Presley rolled into a dark corner of the bar.

"You're not dancing?" she asked me.

And something inside me said, "What's the use of dancing

if we're all already dead?" I couldn't call it a fully formed thought, but, in the gradual way certain big thoughts come about, the doubts I had about my work at Non Possumus, having found their perfect objective correlative in that antisexual dance, were spilling into this new vexation: it's all my fault if these people are losing their own bodies and live as if they were dead, if I can't get it up and Ada is wasting away without even knowing it, it's all my fault; and if the merit in so much virtue on the part of us committed Catholics, who hang on the Pope's every word and despise the flesh according to the counsel of Saint Paul, depends on things like the Book of Cocks, and if on account of things like the Book of Cocks our imagination has pushed us to hate our bodies and those of others, then I am dead, Ada is dead, this whole scene is not happening for real, we are like souls recalling a life never really lived.

Who had conceived this thought for me? How was it possible that a stalwart believer like Piero Rosini held such things inside him?

"No, Ada, I don't know how to dance. Don't give me a hard time."

I extricated myself from my place on the bench and, having joined Alice outside, told her there was a change of plan, that on the twenty-fifth we'd be having dinner at my parents' place. Together we had decided that since the birth of Jesus was, if you had eyes to see, of no importance to my parents, we would celebrate it among believers. With, that is, her sister and her father. Christmas Eve supper at our place, with Ada and my father-in-law, the widower; the twenty-fifth, we four again, on a visit to some priest friends at the Lombard Seminary, perhaps with some lonely wretch from the parish in tow. I said I had changed my mind. A small anxiety attack. Alice was flummoxed.

"But we decided—"

I cut her short: "Look, I'm your husband, not your father, okay? Don't be morbid."

24

In response she delivered a kick to my shins, splashing my pants with muddy water. Afterward she smoked another cigarette, mumbling something under her breath, but then said finally, "Okay. You certainly could have told me sooner."

I loved her like a mendicant, although deep down I knew she always gave in to me out of a fear that I might die at any moment, and that the last words between us would be spoken in anger. She was, at the end of the day, an extremely pious motherless child, and the possibility of death was always on her mind.

Christmas dinner with my father-in-law and his two darling daughters in the refectory of the seminary, with Ada's friends from Milan? Eating off wooden trays? Under neon lights? I didn't want that. My father-in-law, Sergio, a good, humble, and gloomy man, was therefore obliged to spend Christmas alone with his younger daughter. Sergio has been unlucky several times over. In the nineties his wife died one evening at dinner, choking in front of him and his daughters on a thick-cut slice of fatty prosciutto (Was it you who sliced it? Or had she done it herself, or worse, the girls or a careless guy behind the *salumi* counter?). Now he was obliged to spend Christmas Day with priests and future priests, like the lowliest vagrant. I felt guilty because currently he was the one making our mortgage payments. I earned eleven hundred euros a month and Alice, working as a freelance decorator and tutoring high school students, made less than half that. Sergio paid for everyone, and in exchange got to spend his Christmas with priests. Life is beautiful, Pops.

When I went back into the bar, Elvis's "Baby I love you"s had been reduced to the stuff of sad provincial lounge acts, to the sinister simpering of someone you'd be disgusted to kiss. At this rate Ada, sheathed in the shroud of her living-dead undergarments, queen of an empire perched on the head of a pin, would have humbled John Lennon and Marlon Brando, Nabokov and Proust, John F. Kennedy and Bono: the whole languishing line of contemporary civilization. All because she refused to sleep with anyone.

After that Elvis evening my thoughts went back daily to those immaculate tits laughing in the face of the world, and I considered the fervent speeches of the first Christians, who, blinded by metaphysical fury, wrote, "The body is to be mortified. The body decomposes. The body stinks." In "All Shook Up," Elvis sings that his tongue gets tied when he wants to speak and his insides shake like a leaf: "There's only one cure for this body of mine / That's to have the girl that I love so fine!" Caught in this bind between Elvis and Salome, the only bright idea I had was to change jobs, to leave Non Possumus, and since I was at my wits' end, I became obsessed with the plan for a publishing house all my own. A plan that my father, hard to say he was wrong, would later call amateurish, ruining my Christmas dinner.

As far as tits go, it had been years since I had thought at such length and so intensely about the body of a woman who wasn't Alice. I know it's hard to believe, but before I got married I went long periods, even six months straight, without masturbating or getting anywhere near Alice—no intercourse, not even a blow job. After a first few months of passion, our engagement had been desexed, by mutual agreement. A priest advised me, in my torment, to stop thinking about women entirely. I followed his advice, but after the wedding, I'd started to masturbate again every once in a while. In fact, I suspected that it was *not* thinking about women, and the attendant lack of jacking off, that had made my erections so uncertain, putting me in the paradoxical position of not being able to fulfill my conjugal duties. So that occasionally I would close the bathroom door and indulge in the shameful practice, prey to many theological doubts; but on the principle of relative chastity and the lesser evil, I had resolved that the sole protagonist of my sexual fantasies would be my wife.

And now here I am in bed, in the nuptial bed, with my

wife, thinking immoderate thoughts about those tits chastened by frayed sweatshirts, by bras as stiff and ugly as wooden spoons, entertaining the outrageous idea that nature had taken millions of years to refine and perfect Ada's round, majestic breasts, and that in a few years they'd start to droop, and that, while there was still time, it was imperative that somebody should fondle them in their full glory and at their greatest extent, should weigh in his hands these perfumed bosoms, fragrant with lavender and fabric softener. And so I felt anger—no, terror, rather, a wild, unexpected terror—at the thought that it was not to be. To be clear: such thoughts did not give me a hard-on. I had spent so many years not looking at women that my blood sensed the peril and no longer descended to my groin, even there in bed with Alice. Poor unsatisfied wife! Who now slept on one side, with her back to me, the sweet hill of her flank lifting the Bordeaux-red duvet, a flaming bucolic sunset that I made out in the dim light of the bedroom. Nevertheless, even if it was an exclusively mental impulse, even if I could in no way call on my circulatory system, not even if I held my hand on my groin (something that I didn't in any case care to do), for once I abandoned myself to the thought of a female body and placed it at the center of my reflections.

3

Returning to work one damp, rainy morning after the holidays, I slipped into the building with my head down, an esoteric gesture that each day marked the end of a long bus trip from my suburban neighborhood to a cross street of Via del Governo Vecchio, the editorial office's new address. I kept my eyes on my feet, studying the area around them and rhythmically striking the tip of a shoe on the marble steps. My spirit sang a war song to this rhythm, against the tourists, the idlers, the lovers with their wheelie luggage breathlessly darting into boutique hotels.

Passing through the darkened foyer, out of breath, finding the door to our office open, I said hello to Alberto, the other editor, and sat down to review some book proofs without removing my Windbreaker. I opened it up a bit, sweaty from my bus ride, then unzipped. My bag still over my shoulder, I leafed through the pages without understanding a thing. It was pointless to busy myself with proofs anyway: we had a meeting with the publishers to pitch a risky book we were working on, and Mario, the editorial director, wasn't sure how they would react. I was overseeing the book and, given the dandruff paralyzing the metropolis of my hair like a Canadian winter, how badly I was sleeping, and the way my sister-in-law's innocent dance could look to me like a terrible omen, I evidently had a lot (literally and figuratively) to scratch my head about.

Alberto was a few years older than I was, married with four children, one of whom, having died in the second month of pregnancy, was in Heaven (in the way we Teste calculated lives, it counted the same)—all belly, beard, and eyebrows. His fingers were praying mantises at the keyboard, taking down the strangest ideas at high speed; the stranger the ideas, the more frenetically busy the pink mantises that sprouted from the sleeves of his wool sweater. Seated behind a white Formica table, free of clutter only because we had just moved in a few months earlier and he hadn't yet had time to accumulate kipple, he surfed Catholic websites in search of ideas, only breaking off to hastily roll up the sleeves of his black clerical sweater.

Sitting close to the window, I abandoned myself to the noises of the morning. Light rain multiplied the yellow lights and violet shadows on the cobblestones. Twenty printed pages in my lap, I exposed my sweaty forehead to the sticky breeze.

"I'm tense, Albè."

"Are you afraid?"

"I'm tense . . ."

"Say a prayer."

He got up to smoke at the window, apparently annoyed, but no, just wanting to look out. The cuffs on his pants were too high, and his socks showed—the cuffs of a handicapped person, someone dressed by others.

"I've prayed, but the fear won't go away."

"Well, I'll do it if you want."

"What, pray?"

"No, the book."

Alberto had already handled *controversial* books, as the Americans say, and not having been appointed to head up this latest undertaking must have seemed to him a sign that his career in the Catholic cultural underground had plateaued. Since my hiring three years earlier, Mario had seen in me something stronger, more desperate and sparkling, and faced with the new cultural challenge this book would represent had made me its editor.

When I hesitated, Albert added, "He came to bring a

sword." Meaning Jesus, Jesus who doesn't unite but divides. "It's normal to be afraid."

I could have left the job to him; I suspected I'd lost the courage. My obsession with Ada, and the vicious logic in which it had trapped me, said it all: Book of Cocks, fear of the body, Ada's Tits, the need for me to take an even more extreme position with these books in order to confirm that I was right to flee from the world. I was the editor to put these books together, to read them. I couldn't get it up and my wife, my beautiful wife, slept with her back to me—we were on our way to sainthood. Exactly as predicted by Saint Paul, in the condensed and impalpable New Economy of faith.

If I wasn't going to leave it to him, at the very least I could have enlisted his help, in the hope that to share my burden might alleviate my distress. The desire in his eyes was suffocating me. I left the room without saying anything, responding to the tremors of an irritated colon. I spent ten minutes in the bathroom. From my perch atop the loser's throne I heard the intercom, the buzzer, the sound of footsteps and greetings, and then these men, conspirators, settling into Mario's still bare office. Behind the scenes in the little windowless bathroom, I dried my forehead with toilet paper, struggled to catch my breath, and rehearsed my speech.

In the hallway I inhaled the scent of the varnished dark wood of the doorjambs; the rest of the office still smelled of cardboard boxes opened with scissors. I entered Mario's office with my arm raised in greeting, bucking myself up here with an Angel of God, my guardian dear, light and guard both me and the book entrusted to me.

The two publishers were seated in the wheeled armchairs facing the desk; Mario, at the command post in his old leather jacket, beneath a large unframed photo of Ratzinger. Alberto and I sat down on either side of the desk, on metal-and-clear-plastic chairs from the seventies. Mario, clean-shaven, black hair combed back to reveal a square face with vaguely Indian features, got things started. The meeting wouldn't take long, we all had work to do, but it was "a good thing to look each other in the eye before launching into a year in which we'd be taking some risks."

As soon as I noticed that I too, like Alberto, was nodding vigorously, I understood that I was back on the inside. As I rode the bus that morning I'd seriously wondered whether I should quit; Alice had made her feelings clear and she might have had a point; now here I was, hanging on to Mario's every word as if no doubt had ever crossed my mind.

"Non Possumus has to date played a distinct role in the internal debates of the Church. We are considered by many to be courageous truth tellers who don't pull any punches. Who else talks about the cultural power of the Jewish lobbies in Europe and America, their dechristianizing efforts? We do, it's always us. It's a difficult position to take, in a debate that is to some extent internal to the Church. And even here we are finding it tremendously difficult to induce people to follow our lead." Mario, for example, had contributed to the Catholic daily *Avvenire* for a year, before they made it clear that his publishing activities were looked upon unfavorably and thus so too was his byline. "The book on John Paul II will be completely different. We'll get more media attention. They'll be on our backs, not all of them but some for sure. 'Blessed are those who suffer for the sake of righteousness,' sure. But do we feel up to it?"

The two publishers were old friends and Non Possumus had been a shared dream of theirs until, in the mid-nineties, one of them had earned enough to invest in a sideline, and the dream had become a reality. From the beginning, it had operated in the red. They were a perfect couple. One tall and composed, the other short and nervous. The tall one's wife had left him twenty years earlier, and he had never remarried. About fifty years old, with speckled gray eyes, a prominent nose, and a wide, moon-shaped goatee like a nineteenth-century railwayman's. Handsome, well-proportioned, he must have had flocks of women ready to console him. Today he wore a well-pressed gray vest and a pale yellow necktie from a Neapolitan tailor. He'd made a fortune with a small consulting company and it was he who put up most of the money.

The other one—short, with a prophetic air about him—supplied the fighting spirit and the brains. A computer programmer, with round, dark brown eyes that bulged when talk became serious, he was the one with his eye on the ball. He dressed like an ex-radical professor, in beige or maroon corduroy; a shaggy beard, stringy thinning hair, four daughters. A pair of recherché horn-rimmed glasses and a pocket watch were the aesthete's only indulgences in a life sacrificed to household expenses.

Preparing my speech with the two of them in mind, in the days leading up to the meeting I had asked myself: Did these two have bodies? Did the tall partner have a lover? Was the short one happy with his wife? Did they have physical needs and desires? Did they have their own Ada's Tits? The expression "Ada's Tits" was becoming ever more solid and clearly defined. It was entering into the same class of concepts as "Achilles' heel" and "tennis elbow."

"Responsibility for the project has been placed upon the strong young shoulders of Piero Rosini, who will work hand in hand with the author, helping to organize the material and, let's be blunt, rewriting where necessary."

This was a variation on a running joke, a ritual tribute to a fixation on the part of the short partner, whose aesthetic sense, beyond its limited expression in luxury accessories, had imposed on the publishing house a particular attention to the language of its texts. The nonaligned Catholic publishers, in his view, didn't care much for beauty, privileging content and the instructive-informational aspect over reading pleasure, a kind of reverse snobbism that he found annoying and ultimately lazy. He had also fought for an aesthetic improvement of the physical books, coming around to more moderate recommendations once Mario showed him the balance sheet, crimson execution squad of every refinement. But then, in exchange, and as incentive and compensation for us staff, he had ordered that each volume's colophon should include the name of its respective editor.

This was the primary reason behind my success at Non Possumus—the short partner thought my books were better— and why Mario's pompous words had made him chuckle and nod. Encouraged by that little laugh, enough to feed my sense of superiority such that it triumphed over my desire to withdraw from the undertaking, I pulled from my shirt pocket a piece of paper folded in four.

"Greetings to all. I'll be brief. So far we have only touched on the theme of Frankism in our books, but Mario and I think the time has come to look at the problem more closely. Now, try to follow me here."

To introduce the topic, I recounted the story of Jacob Frank, the man whom we had identified as a great scourge of humanity, of whom few people were aware. I read from the notes I had printed out and added to with slovenly pen strokes, tall verticals running across the page in crooked lines. In short, Jacob Frank was an eighteenth-century Polish Jew who went around preaching the end of moral law and inviting his friends and followers to disregard the commandments of the chosen people. Frank's enemies had this to say about his band: "According to these people it's a fine thing to masturbate and cover one's body with semen. They consider it pious to sleep with their neighbor's wife, in the presence of ten men . . . and they recommend other abominations and horrors, such as fornication with persons of the male sex and with animals as well." Harsh words from an eighteenth-century rabbi. Frank proclaims himself the Messiah, saying, I bring you the end of the law, of moral law. "The secret annihilation of the Torah is its true fulfillment," preached Jacob Frank, the countermessiah.

"His Jewish followers," I explained to the two publishers, who listened with a serious air, hands in pockets, eyes wide open, "wanted to infiltrate high Polish society pretending to convert to Christianity. One hears of great Saturday night orgies. We're talking about people inspired by an incomparable *cupio dissolvi*, do you follow me?"

"It's sensational," said the short partner. As he removed the palm of his hand from his knee to stroke his beard, I noticed a faint circle of sweat.

"And how does the Pope come into it?"

"I'm getting there. So, the Frankists don't lack for idealism—abolishing moral law is in certain respects an exalted undertaking. Their objectives are not too far from those of . . . I don't know, John Lennon." My mind had gained a newfound agility; I listened ecstatically as perfectly formed sentences flew out of my mouth. "Take 'Imagine.' The song mocks everything that is important in human civilization. Identity, rules, religion. It's a hymn to liberation from everything that determines our identity. And without identity, who are we? The method at work is the demolition of moral law. The dream is to be able to live free, enjoying everything without taking anything from anyone. Let's see . . . to possess all the women in the world without upsetting your neighbor, if you follow me. The idea that abundance resolves conflicts, that the heart is not a black abyss, that man has need of pleasure. Through the dissolution of morals they hoped to achieve harmony for everyone, without stepping on each other's toes. The same vibrations coming from Coca-Cola commercials, from the 'Summer of Love.'" I was effortlessly molding ideas from my progressive childhood to my new conservative imperatives. "What was 1968 with respect to morality? The ability to perform mass rape with the approval of one's neighbor. All the girls who had their virtue taken in the name of Che or the Comintern, in the name of 'My Generation' and 'All You Need Is Love' . . . I'll rape you today, you rape me tomorrow. Ginsberg was calling for liberation with *Howl*, the homosexual's howl of *sorrow*. This is free love. Was Allen Ginsberg a Frankist?"

"Piero . . ." Mario called me back to order. "Ginsberg couldn't have been a Frankist. He was known to be a Jew, and he hadn't converted to Christianity."

"Listen, Mario, okay, but identity was a different problem in the eighteenth century. Maybe in the eighteenth century you had to convert to be accepted by a Christian society, but today?"

He looked at me in astonished admiration. And the short partner was nodding, turning his head three-quarters away in an attempt to read the face of the tall partner. Alberto stroked the end of his beard. As for me, vanity lived on even in the renunciation of pleasure and the emptying of the self, the petty little vanity of the cardinals' purple cloth. Fascinated by my own words and by the rising black tide of Alberto's attention, I continued to transvalue cultural values right under their well-disposed noses: "If they'd been the ones to film *La Grande Bouffe*, Michel Piccoli wouldn't have died from farting, Mastroianni wouldn't have smashed up his car as he escaped from the house. To them pleasure is not immoral!" I was so much more brilliant, more audacious than Alberto; even with my stooped back I was something of a seducer. "They are the greatest theorists of the happy ending! To them nothing should have negative consequences, not even sex! Legalize abortion!"

I drew a breath, accepting the glass of water Mario handed me.

"*Thank you*. From that eighteenth-century band, the Frankists spread across Europe and across the world, even supporting Atatürk in the anti-Islamic revolution in Turkey, pretending to convert to Islam in order to dissolve it from the inside. They're in Paris, New York, and Hollywood, they're poets, magnates, producers, journalists, they're everywhere, they want to liberate the world from moral law. They're Jews who won't admit to it, who change their own names!"

Like Lou Reed/Firbank, I thought, as my anger moved slowly, steadily ahead toward an enemy encampment just glimpsed on the horizon, identifying its targets, taking its time to attack. Those Jews who hide behind a false name like Richard Hell/Meyers, I thought, like Bob Dylan/Zimmerman. It was my Gettysburg Address, my March on Rome.

"Explain about the Pope," Mario urged.

"Okay. Wojtyła. And here we arrive at the subject of the book. Wojtyła." Magic word.

"Wojtyła?" said Alberto.

"The young Karol kept company with the twentieth-century followers of Jacob Frank, Polish poets and playwrights who, two hundred years after the death of their master, still considered the world a complicated thing conceived by some devil, a prison in which man was constrained by natural laws and, in his attempt to overcome them by means of moral law, found himself all the more in chains. The Messiah, a *true messiah*—Jesus had taken an entirely different path—could only liberate humanity by abolishing moral law and unleashing man, releasing him from the chains of morality. And it appears that it was these artists who pushed Karol to enter the Church, wanting to make of him a champion of liberalism in the Vatican. They introduced him to a cardinal through friends of friends, a cardinal born into a Catholic Polish noble family of Jewish origins. Frankists as well? Karol's father was old; his mother, Jewish, had died young. Karol's real family was the Frankists. The Pope was fed lies."

This sounded excellent and it had come out just like that. I kept an eye on Alberto and his envy gave me strength, but above all it made me forget that I had come into the office with the idea of giving up the commission. I found myself repeating, "He was steeped in lies. Is this why everybody loved him?

That's just what troubles us. That his 'Christianity with man at the center' may be nothing other than Frankism in disguise, nothing other than *liberation*."

The tall partner grimaced uneasily. For a moment you could feel the fear in the room, the pure, unadulterated fear of a child who wanders the halls at night in search of the bathroom.

"And if 'Christianity with man at the center,' the Wojtyłian payoff par excellence, his 'Just do it,'" I wound down, "was no less than *man* . . . who sits on the *throne* . . . and makes of *himself* a God? This is the Antichrist—this is Karol, the boy who frequented the Jewish communities of Wadowice and Kraków and could not be unaware of what people were saying about those converted Jews."

Alberto fretted with his hands, looking at the ceiling, probably praying. His many ticks were the crutches of an anguished mind.

"Very stimulating," said the tall partner after a moment of bewilderment.

"It seems unlikely that anyone could press charges against us," judged the other. "It will, however, stir up a hornet's nest. Do you feel up to it?"

I know what he felt, the short partner, when he said "stir up a hornet's nest." Words that want to explode, to leave a violent signature. If you see a mushroom cloud in person, don't you stand in awe of the power of man? And yet the power of man is as nothing before the Lord of Hosts, and while we may have wanted to leave a trace, it was only to the greater glory of God, a trace in ink to serve Him.

"As Mario says," I replied, "every time I raise objections concerning the timeliness of this book: 'In the beatification process there is always the need for a devil's advocate.' Everyone is saying '*Santo subito*,' but *subito*—immediately—has nothing to do with sainthood. Sainthood is an ordeal. Sainthood is a wound. Stigmata."

Mario tried to bring me back in line. "The story of the last name. Tell them about that."

"The last name could be the title." I really needed a cigarette. "The name Karol's mother hid, her Jewish name."

"And all these secrets . . ." said the computer programmer, "because it served their purpose to have a champion of humanism in the Church?"

I nodded.

"And notwithstanding," he pressed me, "his conservative positions on moral issues?"

"We're not concerned here with whether Karol understood and thus resisted the Frankist influences, or whether on the contrary he felt himself to be the mediator between the Frankists and the Church. We're concerned with what he kept hidden, and with the forces arrayed against us."

He nodded slowly and deliberately, like they do in mosques before a war.

"Well then, the last name? The title of the book?"

"Karol's mother, Miss Kaczorowska . . . was in fact Miss Katz."

"There are two possible titles," Mario said. "*The Jewish Pope*. Or *The Son of Miss Katz*."

"The former," I observe, "would make a stronger impression. The latter, well, extremely elegant."

The tall man said nothing—it must have sounded quite daunting to him. As for me, I was finally convincing someone to put money into a project. I had convinced an investor that I was the right man for the job while my more experienced colleague sat wringing his hands. To be sure, no man is a prophet in his own country, but how is it that to my father I looked like an amateur and to these people a kind of genius?

I mulled it over for hours, staying late at the office. I put off going home and being mocked by my wife for my anti-Semitic tendencies. Seeing me unhappy would have only provoked her further, because everyone is provoked by my type of unhappiness; she'd behave just like my father did at Christmas. Now, when normal people are upset, they humbly ask for a blow job from their wives, or from whomever, to calm their nerves. Or else they take tranquilizers. Me, on the other hand, I didn't ask for blow jobs. Sex was a remote, forsaken continent, and tranquilizers a plot devised by doctors (probably Jews) to maintain a grip on the spirits of us Western slaves and substitute chemicals for morality. A third possibility was pot, a nice big joint—but who was the first Westerner to promote the use of pot as a peacemaker? That third-rate Buddhist, Jew, and sodomite Allen Ginsberg, in those same 1960s that had taken a dagger to the heart of Christianity. Smoking pot meant setting oneself against the Church and joining the legions of dropouts.

And so anxiety held me in its grip, grew in my lymphatic system, threatened to explode. I tried to subdue it by saying the rosary, but the more I thought about the Virgin, so full of grace as to be assumed into Heaven, too luminous to die and decompose, the more her watery transparency took on the features of my wife, Alice, less saintly than Our Lady of Sorrows but in distress nonetheless thanks to the unresolved riddle of the book about the Pope.

Alice was less fanatical than I was but as a rule put up with my intellectual excesses for an odd combination of reasons: first, the loyalty she owed her husband; second, a vague suspicion that the Church is driven into the future by fanatics, visionaries, and the inspired, by *crazies like me* (even if at times our actions seem hard to justify); and third, the belief that there is a pattern to history, a tapestry interwoven with the gold and black and red threads of debatable or even incomprehensible individual actions.

Nevertheless, even if she indulged me, there were extreme cases when her good sense prevailed and forbade her from embracing causes that did not immediately present themselves as wholesome or just, and in these instances, she made her doubts and objections clear. In this particular case, the voice of innocence in stretch skirt and full-support bra, now the lawful consort of Piero Rosini, had brought to my attention, just before the Christmas holidays, that it was one thing to work at a far-right Catholic publishing house (the times being what they are, you don't turn up your nose at a chance to earn a living); it was another entirely to be identified as one of the creators of a book that "accuses" one of the most powerful men of the twentieth century of being Jewish. "This time it's not just your own obsession, this time you're putting your name on it, it's an official document. In twenty years, when your son is browsing the bookstalls on Corso Italia or in Pigneto, he'll come across this crazy little book with yellowed pages, and he'll find your name still on it. It's like throwing a plastic bag into the sea: it never goes away."

Around nine o'clock that evening, Mario came to find me. We were the only ones left; the office staff and Alberto had left hours ago. I was still dealing with the letdown that had come over me following my earlier performance.

He walked in without knocking or saying anything, a cigarette between his lips. He ashed out the window.

"Still here? You're not going home to your wife?"

As the day wore on he had seen how worried I looked, and he needed me to stay calm. This book was a big deal for him, the fruit of ten years of meticulous research into the dark plots threatening the current age. I suggested ordering a pizza. "I'm about to leave," he replied, "I'll give you a lift. Let Alice know you're on your way."

We walked along Corso Vittorio to the parking lot on the river where Mario rented a spot. From there, up Muro Torto, we cut through the most majestic section of Rome. Villa

Borghese and Porta Pinciana shimmered in a mist lit by yellow low beams and turn signals and red brake lights.

"What's on your mind?"

"Nothing."

"C'mon, tell me."

"Mario, I can't do a job like this job and be married. You know what women are like."

"What are they like?"

"They couldn't care less about what we do. At least Alice couldn't."

He shrugs his shoulders. "Maybe she has more faith than we do. Maybe she has less. Who can say?"

"Alice is not a rigorous thinker," I protested, neglecting to acknowledge that her passive resistance had to some extent gotten through to me.

Approaching the underpasses, we caught a glimpse of Piazza Fiume before we plunged below it and then shot out onto Via Nomentana. The nineteenth century and the baroque and the ancient monuments faded rapidly away in the neighborhoods beyond the old city wall. After the Art Nouveau high note of Corso Trieste came Viale Libia, dominated by the broad and solid facades of early-twentieth-century public housing. Beyond the Delle Valli bridge and the freak show of buildings thrown up by speculators during the Fascist and immediate postwar periods, we reached Val Melaina, where on the right rose up, like unsettling Pillars of Hercules, three gray public-housing blocks from the seventies, a lingering urban hangover from an age drunk on idealism: ten floors of science-fiction delirium hurtling into disrepair, stairs and elevators contained in colossal concrete cylinders looming over the rising thoroughfare just as Rome comes to an end and one might have expected to breathe. Beyond this vision, however, and after the greenbelt of a long meadow dotted with small playgrounds, began our new neighborhoods, fledgling little utopias responding to the maximalist errors of the recent past. These were modest beige four-story buildings, with the shallow terraces you see on beach houses, elegant solar panels on the roofs, zero totalitarian impulses. The only blemishes were the blue, white, or eggplant fences alluding almost tactfully to our national preoccupation with "perceived security." The neighborhood was called Porta di Roma and it was there, a year before we were married, that Alice and I had bought an eighty-square-meter house in which to raise a healthy family amid the green of Parco dell'Aniene. Tonight the avenues are dark, the construction sites cold and deserted, the cranes at rest like workers blind-drunk on beer, stunned into immobility above the stream of toy cars on the Grande Raccordo Anulare.

I say goodbye to Mario and walk through the rain to reach the glass door framed in electric blue. In the elevator, under the pitiless halogen lights, I see myself in the mirror: flabby, hunched over, with shadows under my eyes.

The house is dark, but at the end of the hallway a warm light spreads over the rug like spilt milk. Hanging up my Windbreaker, I head toward the light and inadvertently trip over a folder Alice has left on the floor. She is stretched out on the sofa, asleep, with her head bent so low that her chin almost touches her breastbone. Her computer rests on her stomach, the screen saver cycling through a collection of Victorian illustrations.

When I was a little boy, I could hear angels floating around in my room at night. Mamma would say her prayers seated on the edge of the bed, just like her own mother before her. I would repeat the words as my eyes, chin, and nose sunk into the feather pillow. The angels were impalpable, like the downy seed tufts of dandelions. That same feeling of milk-white angels pervades our own house. At bedtime, during prayers, the walls weep.

On the sofa, laptop on her stomach like a hot-water bottle, lies my wife, her small frame collapsed into sleeping-beauty slumber. Her feet are covered in cobalt-blue stockings, her entwined fingers move gently to the rhythm of a dream, she makes the sound "Hmmm."

"Are you sleeping here?" I say, picking up two sweaters and two jackets and placing them on a chair.

"Hmph," Alice says. "Why'd you wake me?"

I would like her to embrace me, would like us to make love, but I don't know how to ask. I turn to look at her: a large forehead with two damp strands of hair above and a body attached below.

"I'm unhappy," I say.

"Why are you unhappy?"

She fusses with the laptop to shut it down. It too stirs and gurgles as it settles down to sleep. Alice puts it on the ground from where, when she goes to brush her teeth, I will soon retrieve it and return it to the little desk in the corner of the living room. An unspectacular circus performance of seemingly random gestures.

"Why are you unhappy, my love?" she says, shaking off sleep.

"I don't know. I'm scared about the book."

"*The Jewish Pope*?"

"Yeah."

"You were so happy." Her voice cools. Then a burp escapes her. "Oops. Sleepy, *acid*. Bleah."

I rest my black briefcase against the bookcase and say, "Sorry I'm so late."

"I'm going to brush my teeth, can you tidy up a bit?"

She moves away. I do as I'm told, gathering into the palm of one hand the crumbs on the table beside the sofa; opening the window to air out the smoky room; making a pile of some of our books that ended up on the floor; finally, picking up her little princess shoes, with their wide, ultralow heels and rounded toes; and I ask myself: If Alice is the only sign that my life is not an instance of purely imaginary delirium—her tangible combination of small shoulders, double chin, and deep feelings—how long will this sign withstand the trials of Jewish Popes and Ada's Tits?

I organize some CDs, including the Velvet Underground's *Loaded*, into a pile, and I think about Lou Reed/Firbank when he says, "You know that women never really faint . . ."

Alice comes back into the room, toothbrush in her mouth. She's wearing a white shirt and black sweater, but she's taken off her skirt and now those ridiculous stockings go all the way up to her round hips.

"You're really unhappy, then?"

I say yes and sense my weariness preparing tomorrow's shadows under my eyes, tonight's bad dreams. I nearly ask her to give me a hug; then the moment passes. Afterward I brush my teeth while she turns out the lights, turns on the hot water, fills up the coffeemaker for tomorrow. Not long afterward we find ourselves in the same bed, a big double bed, our four legs intertwined. I look into one of her eyes, dusky with sleep; for a moment she holds it open, an immense, unseeing globe; her eyelashes brush against my face, eyelashes whose function is to warn the eye to close. Then she closes it, and we hold each other while one of my arms, as if at an agreed-upon signal, twists and finds in midair the lamp switch hanging from the bedside table. The light disappears into nothingness—and, at the end of our performance, we land into slumber, forgetting the Paternoster.

4

I'm woken up by a weight on my stomach. Alice is clutching me and asking, "Are you dead? Are you dead?" It's her joke, a reference to our first vacation together when, waking up, I feared her breathing was too shallow or imagined her heart was beating too fast, and woke her, saying, "Are you okay? I thought you'd stopped breathing . . ." We'd turned it into an exorcism, a bizarre routine that we performed with some frequency.

Having confirmed I'm alive, she vanishes. I get up, slip on a wool dressing gown, and go sit in the kitchen, where breakfast awaits. Broken melba toast, rindless orange marmalade from the discount store. If I look out the window, beyond the earth-colored buildings, I can see six cranes: they're building Porta di Roma. In a few years we'll have everything just outside our door. IKEA has already opened, an enormous LEGO brick the blue of Alice's stockings, the store's name spelled out in yellow toylike block letters; nearby, a home improvement store for motivated fathers. Soon everything will open, we'll barely need to go into Rome at all. It will be one of the largest shopping centers in Europe, with its own nursery school. The cranes are green and their arms each face in a different direction. They've split the work among them, six giants with their feet in the mud towering over the Raccordo, their mere presence an advertisement for the future that's impossible to misunderstand.

This morning Alice is going to the home of the boy she tutors in Latin. He asked her to shift the two-hour session to the morning because there's a school assembly today and he'd rather skip it (the truth is that in the mornings his mother's not there, making it easier for him to imagine he'll get lucky). My wife's sun-dipped blouse in a room in Parioli, fantasies delivered to his door. The forty euros from the lesson in her pocket, she'll stop by a designer's studio to show him her sketches; all she does is freelance, but she's talented, you can tell from the stockings she wears. She's never been fazed by the proverb "The devil is in the details." (It was incidentally that same proverb, cropping up in an agitated discussion about art years ago with one of the Teste Parlanti—"The truth can't be found in novels! The truth was revealed once and for all!"—that had made me stop reading novels, hotbed of sordid details.) She carried on, part pagan, part student of the Enlightenment, part Catholic.

I turn on the coffeemaker prepared the night before and wait for Alice to come into the kitchen dressed in her spice-market colors. I stop thinking about the boys lusting after her in Parioli and pour myself some coffee.

Our private daily circus proceeds with Alice's entry in a deep-purple herringbone overcoat, black skirt, and mustard-colored stockings. She sits down and eats a half slice of toast I've prepared for her, drinks her coffee and a glass of water with vitamin C that's still fizzing on its way up to her mouth. She drinks and her throat muscles go up and down. She sets down the glass.

"Have you cheered up?"

I say nothing. She licks the foam from her lips. I prepare my own vitamin C.

"He was really Jewish?" Alice says.

"Well, you know how it works, the line of descent—"

"You're really passionate about it, huh?" she interrupts as she gets up to put her unopened yogurt back in the refrigerator. "So then why are you unhappy?"

"It's a risky subject. And my name would be the only one on there, as the editor."

"That's good, right?"—as if we hadn't already discussed it and she hadn't already expressed her own ambivalent mix of repulsion and acceptance. To intensify the disembodying effect of her strategy she sticks her head into the fridge, disappearing behind the large white door, so all I can see is her herringbone behind.

"Look," I say, "if the Pope was Jewish, we're all fucked."

She closes the fridge without comment.

"Listen, *bella*, I'm sorry if you don't care about the health of your Church, in which you claim to place so much trust . . ."

"You're going to act superior?" She does up the last button of her overcoat and breathes a long sigh.

"And you're going to act inferior at all costs?"

"You're really an asshole," she says, and leaves the kitchen.

I hear sounds that aren't part of our regular circus programming; then the front door opens and closes.

I spread honey and orange marmalade on the toast. I've been sitting wrong, my back is killing me, and it's only eight thirty. IKEA, I think. I've ended up living across from IKEA. I've read all of Tolstoy, visited New York and Tokyo, slept in castles on the Loire, and now I live across from IKEA. It's been years since I've traveled, I don't go to the theater, don't read music magazines. But, as the Gospels teach us, to pass through the eye of the needle one needs to concentrate on the essential, to free oneself of every burden.

A minute later and the front door opens again. Alice walks into the kitchen, sets down her bag, and without unbuttoning her coat comes and hugs me from behind. She kisses the inner part of my ear, deafening me. She sits in my lap. I place the palms of my hands on her face and rub her fresh and lightly glowing cheeks, leaving only her nose sticking out. I would like to ask her to strip and take me to bed.

"On Christmas Day I asked my father for a loan and he said no."

"A loan?" She shakes her face free. "That's why my father was left all alone on Christmas Day?"

"Yes"—I give her a kiss on the nose—"for the money. And it's hardly as if your father was alone. He was with Ada."

"You're such a shit." She moves away slightly.

"And he didn't even give it to me!"

"What do you want money for? Are you buying me something special?"

"I wanted to start a publishing house."

"And how much money did you ask him for?"

"Enough for a publishing house."

She studied my eyes and hair. "Because one anti-Semitic publishing house isn't enough, you need to start another?"

"No, it was supposed to be a fresh start."

She shrugs, unconvinced, and gets up. "Strength and courage, my love!" Then she leaves, slamming the door, taking her colors with her, leaving the apartment gray and cold.

I called the office to say that I would be working from home that day. I went for a walk to clear my head about the Jewish Pope and came to the following tentative conclusion: If the publisher of *Lolita* is not a pedophile, the publisher of *The Son of Miss Katz* is not an anti-Semite. This work gave me my daily bread. I had a beautiful wife, and if I wasn't sleeping with her, at least nobody else was, and I was a source of envy regardless. Who would suspect I wasn't getting any?

I sunk my tennis shoes into the mud between home and IKEA. There weren't any sidewalks yet. Rome's newest streets were lined with construction sites, puddles, weeds, and mud. Light-years away from the city. Where was unattainable Rome now? In the middle of this open work site and under the vast sky of the Raccordo, I tried to retrace the passions that had pushed us to take out a mortgage before they had even turned on the power or finished the plumbing in our building.

So far the neighborhood had supplied me with a single memory: Sunday afternoon visits from Ada and my father-in-law. I'd play cards with him on the terrace or, occasionally, he and I and his two daughters—one dressed to kill and the other in a sweatsuit—would wander in circles through the wide, empty streets, stopping for coffee under the cranes' watchful eyes at the counters of newly opened cafés. Ada chattered away. I held Alice's hand. My father-in-law would pick up the check. The owners of the cafés complained about how difficult it was to recoup their investment in a neighborhood that was still half empty, but it was clear that one day they'd be telling their grandkids: We were here when it was all just a construction site, and there at the end where the park and the Roman ruins are, *it was nothing but countryside.*

Alice and I moved to Porta di Roma because it was respectable, no funny business, no aperitifs at seven or speed dating, no decadent vices or offices where bosses corrupt their women employees, weighing in on when or whether they should have kids.

As I passed a row of dumpsters a girl of about twenty walked by, with damaged, worn-out hair dyed ink black, pants slung low on her hips. Very easy to avoid looking at twice. At a certain point the girls in my new neighborhood ended up pregnant and put on twenty pounds or became dried-out old witches. This suited me down to the ground: Alice and I alone with the manger, our first baby soon on the way, no rivals, a man and woman outside history, with no past, no social class, no bourgeois parents. *Farewell, Father,* I had said to him, *I'm heading east, to the new neighborhoods.* But why? he asked in surprise two years ago, once we had set the wedding date. *Because there are signs*: we have found a reasonably priced house in a new location, we're close to Alice's parish, our parish. But it's forty-five minutes away from us . . . and what will you do

51

when you have kids? *The Lord will provide,* I responded, quoting the Scriptures as usual. I adored the Bible's off-kilter sound, the old-time expressions that would strike my interlocutors dumb.

I stopped at a café and ordered an espresso. The two owners, overweight like their two children, spread mayonnaise on bread in anticipation of lunch customers. I chatted a bit with the man behind the bar, then sat down at a table. I had nothing with me to read—I wanted to think. I felt lonely. I had lost all my nonbelieving friends, and the believers were always busy with their kids, with work, with parish activities. Megasize packages of tuna, urban planning, IKEA, Roman women, my sister, the Scriptures—each had played its part in shutting me up here. Walking in the clay-colored morning before returning home to shuffle the proof pages, I thought back to my religious initiation, not something I did very often, living as I did either in the future or in the constantly prayed-to hereafter, ostentatiously shunning the present.

Some of my literary friendships had come to an abrupt end. One day in 2003, a friend and aspiring poet, originally from Emilia, had confided in me; he couldn't get his girlfriend to come. I told him, "Maybe I'm wrong, but it could be that it simply comes down to the fact that you're not *open to life*." For a Christian, being didactic is a virtue.

"What do you mean?"

"One makes love in order to have God's children."

That was one of my last excursions into the city center after dinner, a little side street in Trastevere resounding with the hearty clamor of American tourists.

"Wait, wait"—my friend laughed—"you mean to say that she doesn't come because she takes the pill?"

"She takes the pill?"

"Of course she does, why?"

"Well, I have to tell you that we're really not on the same page here."

"Maybe I've just got a small dick . . ."

"What kind of talk is that . . ."

"I've always had doubts about my dick . . ."

"We should stop talking about this."

"I have nightmares about it."

"Stop it, please."

"Stop what?"

And at the end of our exchange I told him, "You're so confused!"

I enjoyed generating the tension that would sabotage conversations. And losing friends seemed to me a tragic touch, an initiation, the proof that coming to know God changed one's life and not just one's heart. Once my poet friend was gone I stopped reading poetry, stopped staying up late to play role-playing games on the computer, stopped getting high. There was another friend—now a journalist—whom I invited to a catechism session. He refused to enter the church, and we ended up talking on the steps out front. It was spring, all the trees in blossom, the dumpsters smelling ripe. I looked up at a neon bank sign as I listened to him: "I believe that beauty is truth, you believe that truth is beautiful. I want to seek beauty."

"You're fooling yourself," I chastised him. "When you masturbate in front of the mirror, all scrunched up like a baby, conjuring up orgies with that imbecilic grimace on your face, do you call that beauty?" I heard my words and found them true and beautiful—and prophetic.

"You've been brainwashed," he said.

"You're a conformist," I responded.

No more trips to Venice for the film festival; no more nights out at dub shows or conversations about how different ways of coming modulated pleasure, how you could expand or contract the spectrum of spasms according to the kind of receptacle you were using. I said farewell to my Warp and Lee "Scratch" Perry records, the Jarman or Greenaway marathons, and so many other experiences I came to belittle as "gaudy cultural junk" or "countercultural clutter." In line with these same principles, I got rid of not just friends but also the joy of remembering the experiences we shared, and since all the shared experiences in my life had to do with thinking about women and their breasts, I got rid of art, of the fine arts, books by Foucault, collections by Avedon, Mapplethorpe, Milo Manara, Eric Stanton, till I felt like I was no longer weighed down by all that junk, till I felt like a permanent missionary.

I arrived at the edge of the work site where they were building the western section of the big park, where my children would grow up, the children whom my wife, if it pleased God, would give me, as long as my sister didn't convince her to look for a house in the center. Federica had never come to our house when I was home, not wanting to hear me enumerate the advantages of Porta di Roma; she stopped by during the day when I was in the office, to chat freely with Alice and, it appeared, to encourage her not to bury herself in the suburbs and play mother.

Federica lived in the Monti neighborhood, that cradle of trendy wine bars between the rivers of traffic on Via Cavour and Via Nazionale. I had been to her place twice, against my will. They smoked pot there. The living room had a high ceiling with exposed wood beams and orange walls. Until that day in 2002 when our paths diverged, it was more or less obvious that having graduated from college and needing to come up with some kind of job, and having already staked everything on the world of culture, I would look to my sister as my Schindler, the one to rescue me from the gentle genocide of postbourgeois unemployment. This, however, was not to be, and all because it had been months since I stopped looking women in the eyes, the only effective remedy against temptation. Ovid said: "As many stars as are held in the sky, so many women does your Rome hold." Think about it, whenever you go to the theater, or the races, he said; you can sit hip to hip with a woman, brushing her arm, nobody even notices, you can guiltlessly look at her knees. The putative descendants of these women were conspiring to make me lose Alice. Soft and shapely creatures, cunning colors and textures, refined fabrics, all designed to trip a man up. My sister was a prime example, given her foulards and shawls. She had Etruscan shoulders and a seductively protruding belly, a little Monte Mario with her navel in place of the observatory.

One evening, she invited me out for dinner and a confession: "Pierino, dear, I've got myself into a fix."

"Tell me," I responded, immediately lowering my eyes.

"I'm in love. His marriage is ending and he's very unsettled, but I'm in love with him *now*, right?" She laughed. "Not in a year or in ten years, I'm in love with him now." She told me all about her new flame, about his son with Down syndrome, his weakness for Labrador retrievers, his wife's nervous breakdown. I let her speak. Our waiter, a scrawny, absentminded queen, wasn't bringing us our beer. I listened to her and kept my eyes on my pizza; I had the increasing impression that all the people in the pizzeria, except for maybe the table of German college students, were busying themselves with similar topics.

Suddenly I lifted my eyes from the runny sunset of my Margherita and said to her: "Please stop it, Fede, I can't fill my head with this shit."

She'd become absorbed in her account of a quarrel. She blinked and looked at me. "What?"

"Forget about him, he's married. Forget about it. You're talking about a marriage. Was it celebrated in church?"

"What does that have to do with it?" Without meaning to, she nodded yes.

"Then why break up a marriage and get involved in this mess?"

"What? Wait a minute, I'm in pain and you're lecturing me?"

"I know, I'm sorry." I put down my knife and fork and

continued to look her in the eyes. "I don't want to lecture you, but I have to tell you that that is a marriage and you have no business getting in the middle of it."

"I told you, they're separating."

"But it's a marriage, dammit, a sacrament."

I had caught her off guard. She wiped her mouth with her napkin and began again: "Don't be so sanctimonious. Can't I tell you about it anyway?"

"No, Fede," I sighed, "don't tell me about it. It's bad for me. You put images in my head that I don't want to have there."

"Please."

"I'm asking *you*, please."

"What do you mean, *you*? Please what?"

"*Please.*"

She took a breath. "I can't believe it."

"I know that much."

"Oh yeah?"

"It takes the Holy Spirit to believe it."

"You're kidding." The shadow of a malicious smile passed over her plump Renaissance face; she had given up the idea of having a confidant in front of her. "It takes the Holy Spirit to believe you don't want to sit and listen to me?"

Disheartened, I jumped straight to conclusions: "Evidently, if some of the Holy Spirit doesn't intervene and descend to this table, we can't talk about these things."

Federica stopped confiding in her little brother, her literary Sancho Panza, and no longer sought him out, and above all no longer considered him a protégé she could usher into the world of letters, newspapers, publishing houses. But hey, what a coincidence! All those newspapers and those publishing houses were run by Masons, antipapalist followers of the Enlightenment, probably Jews, and obviously—at least some, at least the best ones—*Frankists*, like our Holy Pope. No wonder my literary career came to such an untimely end.

Having reached the IKEA underground parking garage, I took the moving walkway that led up to the store and marched across the trapezoidal square like a king; the shopping center behind me was still a construction site. Entering the solid and rational environment of the store, I picked up a yellow bag and hurried to the house accessories floor, skipping the bedroom displays. It was a discount morning (IKEA rewards those who shop during the dead hours of the workday). I knew the store by heart, just as I knew the brand, its vision; the mirage of the blue parallelepiped the star leading us to Bethlehem, we serving as our own wise men. I'd first heard about Porta di Roma one Saturday morning in 2003. I was at Rome's first and only IKEA with one of the guys from the Teste Parlanti. He told me they were opening a second IKEA not far from our parish, in a new neighborhood with brand-new houses. He was acquainted in a roundabout way with someone who worked in the sales office. "It's a turning point, they're also putting in a Leroy Merlin and a huge shopping center with a multiplex *for families*, pizzerias, cheap restaurants, clothes, an Auchan supermarket, everything. They don't cost much. You should check it out."

I remember the first time I visited Porta di Roma's IKEA. It was identical to the one south of the city but its floor plan was a mirror opposite. One was right-handed, the other left. The Gospel came to mind, when Jesus says to the fishermen: Cast your nets to the right. Your fisherman's common sense tells you to cast your nets to the left; you do the exact opposite of what common sense tells you. At that point we had already signed the deed and were surveying the neighborhood like colonists. And now I knew the IKEA by heart; I went there every week and knew how to avoid the lines and take advantage of the discounts.

I bought a magazine rack for the bathroom and started for home. It was an overcast January morning and I thought: This walk is the result of certain choices of mine; all this has my signature on it. Had I chosen freely? The first mistake is to answer the question; but I can say that I had thrown myself into this completely, had in fact made the final leg of the journey toward absolute freedom alone, becoming the only member of the Teste Parlanti to don the intellectual hair shirt of anti-Semitism. And in those days I would say to myself that I had bitten off more than I could chew: if I hadn't followed my religious thinking to its extreme consequences, I wouldn't have run up against the Jewish Pope, and in that January of 2006 I wouldn't have had the infantile guilty desire to flee from my neighborhood. It's just that intellectual consistency, a characteristic value of the Italian left, remained important to me; I clung to it even as I became a reactionary. And in this light the following series of considerations—let's not call it a "line of reasoning"—had emerged: This age, this age in particular, seems to be, as the Pope says every Sunday, marked by egotism, solitude, frenzy, lust. If it's a sign of the times, and the times are particularly dark, the grounds for this appear to be philosophical, moral. If you listen to the Pope (and I listened to him with my heart in hand, as though it were a hat), those with the means to spread ideas and values (the means of intellectual production, newspapers, TV) were spreading the wrong ideas and values. Nothing new, but I wanted to dig deeper. In whose hands, exactly, lay this power? The answer murmured among Catholic intellectuals was threefold: Above all, it was the Masons who held the power, and then, maybe, let it be said among sympathetic ears, the homosexual lobby, and, finally, but no offense, let's be clear, no offense and not tarring them all with the same brush, the Jews, certain Jews, the rich and powerful Jews, those on bad terms with Christianity from the very beginning, like the Montagues and Capulets.

I arrived at Non Possumus with this appetite for burning truths. I had met Mario through some friends at a Latin Mass in a parish in the city center, and he understood my fever. I didn't have any problem with Jews back then; on the contrary, I loved them: Singer, Roth, Larry David, Bellow, Dylan, Lou Reed. What does it say about me that I'm endlessly fascinated by the ideas that upset me most? At the time, to find in Mario and Alberto two supporters of sophisticated anti-Semitism upset me a great deal.

The craziest Non Possumus book prior to *The Jewish Pope* had been edited by Alberto (the Book of Cocks paled in comparison). Basically, it was a collection of obscure passages from the Talmud in which Jews were invited to look upon Christians not as human beings but as beasts, to kill and to rob them. Newly hired, I picked up a copy from the storeroom. On the cover, two rabbis with sinister white eyes were reading the Talmud, wrapped in traditional heavy cloaks. Alberto had written a brief preface and edited the volume. Ours was the collection's third edition. The first came out in Russia toward the end of the nineteenth century, compiled by a Russian Catholic theologian. The second came out in Italy in '39, at the height of the racial laws. Mario had decided to retain in our edition the second edition's long introductory essay, in which a Fascist intellectual of unmistakably anti-Semitic intent condemned the "pietistic attitudes of many thoughtless or extremely ignorant Aryans with regard to the regime's sensible measures aimed at isolating the Jewish peril." It may seem strange to anyone who's never felt himself truly in the minority—a minority in the world of ideas, that is, and not a minority à la Nanni Moretti ("I will always be in agreement with only a minority of people," he claims in *Caro Diario*, but what do you know, those people run newspapers and film festivals)—but anyone who has felt like that (UFOlogists, conspiracy theorists, Cassandras) knows that once you've taken to the barricades, your own most abstruse and violent ideas can ultimately appear plausible. You get to thinking: If even we are almost scandalized by our own ideas, that just means we're in such a minority as to doubt ourselves. And at that point you can choose to put your faith in the absurd as a way to break with the majority. Like the punks who drew swastikas on their cheeks.

In the introduction to the Non Possumus edition, the long-dead-and-buried Fascist intellectual was left free by Mario and Alberto to express on their behalf, in a violent and outdated idiom, truly scandalous ideas. Thus in referring to the Jews he says: "a Hebraic horde exceedingly united in evil"; "the Jews scheme without surcease"; "the logic of Talmudists comes down to plays on words and inconclusive subtleties." The introduction sought to reveal the corrupting influence of the Jews in world history. During the Enlightenment, for example, Lessing had been "Judaized to the core by Mendelssohn" ("the shrewd influence of Mendelssohn made him into a champion of Judaism"). At Non Possumus they decided not to distance themselves from the tone of this introduction dated 1939. Albert's short preface, barely two pages long, gave the reader no indication that on the next page he would find himself immersed in the Fascist lexicon. They supposed that the reader would have known to take it with a grain of salt. Or maybe, as in the old days, they only wanted to provoke the bourgeois, unaccustomed as they were to strong ideas.

Alberto and Mario weren't Fascists; that much was clear. They voted for whoever pushed for the criminalization of abortion; a powerful, orderly, and prestigious state hardly concerned them. To put themselves in jeopardy in this way, I thought to myself at the time, they must have read some seriously subtle messages between the racist lines. Epic metaphysical battles.

What had put me in a state of mind so receptive to paradox? It's not clear. Certainly, after 9/11 my world of ideas, of pleasure, of books, had collapsed a bit like the towers. Out of fear of a general collapse or a dictatorial turn in the West, I had to put my trust in something solid; for me, "weak thought" wasn't enough. But tradition—in the generic Victorian English sense of the word—didn't exist in Italy, and the center-left had in ten years squandered the patrimony of the Communist left, its practical Bauhaus beauty; on top of that, although I'd consider it moral apathy more than anything else, I was tired of my individualism. When the Muslims arrived and began to complain, to point out that our Western showroom world was a colossus with feet of clay and they would see it fall, I asked myself: So they too have glimpsed the truth, but who is it that has stripped the Western world of its foundation? (Of its *Christian* foundation! I surprised myself by thinking.) I trembled as I spoke the words that certain books from the Catholic underground had put in my mouth, but the answer was: The Jews! The same Jews in the manifestos of Fascist propaganda three generations earlier, the greedy, rich, well-informed Jews in power, those who choose the government in Paris, newspaper headlines in New York, the cost of living in the Middle East, and strive for a mixed-up world without identity, where everything is relative, where the very earth beneath your feet goes missing.

I didn't get there right away. At first I believed in conspiracies in general, secret societies, the Americans' fake moon landing, the theories about Pearl Harbor and 9/11. Then, in an attempt to understand who was behind the conspiracy, the circle closed around our cousins in faith, the deicides, the chosen people, the blood of Judas and King David. The diabolical task of secretly influencing political power and public opinion fell to them. Having the Jews occupy the hot seat in my new cosmology represented not only a forbidden pleasure but also the opportunity to come to terms with those who had shaped me, a list of singers, writers, artists, philosophers. At any rate, if I could give up sex, I could also give up art and a nutritionally varied intellectual life.

But now, with the hypothesis that Karol Wojtyła had been planted in the Vatican by a libertine conspiracy, Pope Karol the prince of sexual abstinence, practically the prime mover behind my decision some years earlier to stop having sex, I had reached the *finis terrae*. If even *he* was part of it (and our thirst for guilty parties pushed us to believe it), if he was the instrument of a shadowy power confirming our most spectacular fears, it meant that the trail of gunpowder I had laid down to blow up the bad guys became a fuse leading all the way back to the match I held in my hand.

The minority report behind my recent dissent, my fear, my autorebellion, had not yet succeeded in overturning the deliberation of my interior parliament that permitted Mario and the two publishers to maintain my name in the colophon at the beginning of the book, under the austere term "Editor" (sufficiently severe to my ears, given the circumstances, to sound more Latin than English), as if in a parallel world with its own sacred scriptures, scriptures that nonetheless corresponded to our own: instead of Pontius Pilate, Praefectus, there was me, Editor, and instead of Jesus, his beloved son John Paul II, with INRI written on the cross—the King of the Jews. And like Pilate with regard to Jesus, I was obliged to ask, in my prayers, "What is truth?" Because if Christ is the way and the truth and the life, and if it was my fascination with his words that led me this far (to Porta di Roma, to Non Possumus, to the colophon of an excessively equivocal book), I could not fail to ask myself what kind of joke was this truth I'd set out in search of when still in my salad days. And what was the ultimate indignity? That it wasn't even possible to predict what the result of our publishing provocation would be. Thus I had yet to find out what role I would play by virtue of my active participation. In the face of a major literary event, of a media frenzy, I would become a knight of the faith, or a deputy hero, or an antihero. But if the newspapers, magazines, and broadcasting companies decided to ignore us, considering us irrelevant or outdated, with the passing of years it would become clear I was a mere petty clerk pressed into the cause not so célèbre of a racial-religious-intellectual hatred that was neither perspicuous, nor radical, nor chic, a sentiment neither interesting nor generational.

It should be added that the part of me that might have taken pleasure in the two possible outcomes—antihero or obscure scribe straight out of a Borges story—still held the majority, but from the chairs of my parliament rose up an irrepressible creaking: I was a country at war, destabilized from within by subversive, revolutionary, defeatist forces, just when times called for an effort requiring the greatest possible cohesion.

I stuck the IKEA receipt in my back pocket, the magazine rack under my arm, and headed home to return to work on the proofs with the certainty that with or without creaking chairs, the seat of my parliament would remain Porta di Roma. As I left behind the half-built shopping center, I tried to reconstruct some of my typical reflections, like this one: If Ground Zero is the West washed up, overfed and corrupt, this construction site, just as big, is its opposite. Ground Zero is antimatter, Porta di Roma matter, the clay from which to create not houses of cards propped up by Jewish banks but healthy Christian children.

I went up the elevator and, after having made tea and placed the transparent red magazine rack between toilet and tub, stretched myself out on the couch. My father didn't like us to shop at IKEA for reasons having to do with family history (low prices aren't everything; one should support the national economy), but as far as family history goes (or the national economy, for that matter), I didn't give a damn.

From the window came the dry bark of an old man complaining about something; his voice bounced off the buildings across the street, perhaps coming from our own, I don't know. Someone answered him, a younger, female voice. I didn't understand what they were saying. They were soon drowned out by a strange, intermittent squawking, a crow somewhere on one of the noise-filtering trees placed in order to limit the incessant roar of the Raccordo; the bird's displeasure resonated in the open space between the buildings, drowning out the human protests in volume.

Meanwhile, on the other side of the wall behind me, a young mother screamed at two obnoxious children: "Enough already! Enough! Enough screaming!" On a typical evening, when her husband came home, at which point my head was usually killing me, the children would desert their mother and rush over to him with rapid, percussive steps. I'd hear their impact against the legs of their father, who some evenings responded with "Hey there!" others with "Whoever makes Mamma mad is getting a slap!" and still others with "I'm putting you to bed right now if you don't quit!" He was a burly, ginger-haired man, whose firm voice and handshake I'd encountered every so often in the elevator, and I couldn't imagine what kind of job he might have in a postindustrial world, with his laborer's build and big FIAT minivan. His wife, thirty-five, tall and slim with straight dull blond hair and a hint of scoliosis (a slight defect with the appeal of a beauty mark or a mild squint), stayed at home with her one-year-old and her three-year-old. Why? How could she stand it, with the TV and radio blaring all day long? On the weekends sometimes they would take off in their minivan, and the wall we shared would go silent, cease to vibrate.

As for me, brought up like a little lord, what was I doing in this building with cardboard-thin walls? My brothers lived in Parioli and Vigna Clara, my parents in Prati, my sister in Monti.

Have you ever felt that the part of you insisting on your right to freedom is in fact your worst part? In my case it was the rich young man in me who had remained stubbornly alive, notwithstanding the fact I'd set aside even sex in order to feel poor; the rich young man from the parable who, incapable of giving up his riches, goes off dejected after his encounter with Jesus; the young man I had since high school tried to suppress with my political, ideological, and social choices—it was this same young man, the most hateful part of me, who roared back, imperiously pointing a finger and calling out: Faithful Catholics to the line, devotees of the hour of the end of the world, chaste self-exiled heroes with receding hairlines and shitty jobs! Get yourself back to the center, Rosini, flee the women in hair curlers and those nostalgic for the temporal power of the Church! In my fantasy, a movie camera set up among the solar panels on the roof of one of the buildings would film me Elio Petri–style as on winter mornings I wandered down a broad avenue, a courageous future father among the respectfully bowing cranes, the mud-splattered car hoods, the musique concrète of the IKEA cash registers. Me, hero of abstention, capable of self-denial in times short on moral fiber. Faith, charity, self-denial. Not much hope, lots of boredom.

5

But then, strangely, I simply swept away the rage from my neural pathways and carried on impassively for all of January; February; until March. To my eyes I seemed like a man on the verge of change, and yet for three months I remained docile and toed the line, engaged in a sort of work-to-rule action of the conscience—I restricted myself to doing my duty. I worked on *The Jewish Pope*, proceeding slowly because the author kept changing his mind. There was some problematic jerking off, problematic because my wife, in my bathroom fantasies, tended to turn into her sister even as she remained in my arms. I didn't speak in church, just put flowers in vases and hymnals on their metal shelves. At dusk, if Alice had gone to her father's for dinner, I would sit on the balcony and spy on the lives of those in the buildings across the street. My e-mail's spam folder was full of ads for Cialis and Viagra that said "Just fuck and don't think about anything else." From my wooden chair, elbows up on the railing, I evaluated the profundity of these messages, I superimposed them on the condominial panorama: little yards with children on red or green plastic minislides, living rooms, curtains pulled back, revealing the glow of televisions at the evening news hour.

Three months down the drain, making me feel stupid, even if maybe I'd just needed time to mull over my new ideas a bit, to impose some order on that bloodless, still undefined sense of disappointment. In the fog I opened my ears to all and sundry, and even though I pretended not to listen, not to change, many of the things I heard provoked strong reactions in me. I paid as much attention to spam as to the priests on Sunday. The junk e-mails had subject lines that wore on my nerves:

"Find out what makes your willie tick."

"Blondes will suck like crazy."

6

If there's a demon overseeing those turning points in life when a buried part of you asserts its right to exist, he's cunning. The great encounter that would change my life presented itself at the beginning of spring in the guise of nothing special at all—a young man with desperate, anonymous brown eyes and a manuscript to submit, an undistinguished member of the mass of Italians with a novel in the desk drawer. Normally we'd send them packing with replies like "Looking at our website, you will have noticed the absence of fiction titles in our catalog," but this time I felt the need for a distraction that would get me out of the office. The voice on the phone was young, tense, and innocent. I went to our agreed meeting place, a café in the center, with a clear idea in my head: to try to act the part of a real publisher. Not a Napoleon, but at least a great man of letters like Neri Pozza or Roberto Calasso, just to, let's face it, feel like someone important for half an hour. So that's why, on that sunny day, at the hour of afternoon coffee breaks, I turned up with an air of "Let's see what we've got here," or "I know talent when I see it." Around the corner from the Trevi Fountain, sunlight blazing in the interval between two thunderstorms, I cut across the streets feeding into Via del Tritone and sat down in front of this tall man, thinner and younger than I was, and began in a skeptical tone: "We primarily publish nonfiction; aggressive, popular stuff."

Rome's caricature, generated by the foreigner's shallow gaze: a precious village of marble and earth at the edge of

Europe, ivy-covered columns and Illy coffee. The supplicant's name was Corrado, a skinny Stan Laurel type with curly hair and narrow shoulders in an oversize sport coat, perched on the edge of a wooden chair. He laid out his idea: a novel about a gay couple obsessed with traditional family models, who want "a happy family fifties-style, a suburban town house."

"A polemical novel, I hope."

"Depends on what you mean by the term."

"Tell me what *you* mean, I don't have much time." My moment of glory would be over as soon as he figured out what Non Possumus was, but how could I deny myself this harmless pleasure, given how few pleasures I allowed myself?

"Well, my idea is to make fun of gay people a bit, nobody does . . . but I also have gay friends."

"I'm not the least bit interested."

He looked disappointed.

"Not the book," I clarified without losing my composure. "In who your friends are."

We ordered coffee. He added some plot details I didn't pay attention to. The Bangladeshi waiter interrupted him, swooping in between us with the metal tray. We added sugar; we stirred.

He kept his elbows tightly at his sides, his delicate hands, open like spiders, pressed fingertip to fingertip.

"I really don't know who I can ask, or who I should have read it, you know, in order to possibly . . . to publish it. There must be some crazy kind of mafia, you have to know people to get to the top, places like . . ." And here he named all the big Italian publishing houses, my sister's among them, producing a pang in my chest.

I picked up the little coffee cup, looked at the darkened sugar at the bottom, scooped it out with a spoon, and placed it in my mouth.

"Listen," I said, then stopped, pressing my lips together and leaning forward. "Italy is full of aspiring writers"—he signaled yes, yes, with his eyes, hanging on every word, my conspirator against an imaginary crowd of supplicants—"and you have to convince me. I've seen so many . . . illiterates who use too many ellipses . . . You know that you shouldn't ever use more than one question mark?"

He nods, enraptured. "Of course, just one at a time." One more up and down with his dreaming head, then he claps his hands together firmly.

Tourists with milk-white calves pass by in brand-new canary-yellow sandals, observing us from behind their sunglasses: my Windbreaker bunching up over my belly, Corrado's white dress shirt and bright curls.

"So then let's hear it, what kind of book is it, who are your influences?" I sit back in my chair. "I don't have much time, I've got other appointments. Five minutes."

He talked about the writers he loved, what his characters were like, what kind of circles they frequented. Distracted in his anxiety, he mentioned in passing that he hadn't finished his undergraduate degree and that he was twenty-five. For a moment, I speculated that a book making fun of gays could be just the thing right now, it would represent an attack on civil unions and as such would be sure to garner some reviews. These were my half-baked thoughts as I prepared to take my leave, checking the time on my cell phone; Corrado understood that the publishing window was preparing to close, then impulsively informed me that his mother was separated and depressed and worked as an accountant and had had breast cancer and a mastectomy; he didn't mention his father. He was still short several exams for his communications degree and didn't know whom to ask to be his thesis supervisor. He worked part-time as an assistant or factotum for an event-planning company, a job that "on bad days seems like it has no future in it; today is a bad day."

I now looked openly at his tubercular chest, the shadows under his eyes, the unbuttoned sleeves emerging from his

71

beige cotton jacket. He told me, with a smile drawn from the depths of his eyes, that he'd already handed copies of a story or two to publishing people he'd met through work, but no one had ever gotten back to him or stopped to listen.

I was ashamed not to have anything to offer him; when we got up I gripped his hand firmly and let him go in to pay for the coffees, standing there among the tables in my enormous sail of a Windbreaker, twiddling my thumbs. I shook his hand again when he came out and then pulled my hand away, thinking *poor guy*, but little by little in the course of the next week my sense of guilt disappeared. It was out of sight, out of mind, and anyway I had lost my feeling for human relationships unregulated by the Church, seeing as how I worked with Alberto and Mario and my life demanded a kind of cordon sanitaire, a state (the Church) within a state. When my wife heard the story, she said I was being silly and gently laughed: why throw away a potential new friend or companion just like that, when "it's been years since you met anyone new"?

The following Sunday afternoon I found myself sunk in a giant easy chair with lace-trimmed armrests in my father-in-law's living room. A widower, retired, he and I took turns boring each other, unable even to take refuge in the placid, benevolent resignation inspired by use of the formal manner of address, which acknowledges distance and makes wasting time among people who have nothing to say to each other more bearable. I was talking to him, using the familiar *tu*, about civil service examinations (Sergio was a retired civil servant), asking whether there was any way Alice might give up interior decoration and sit for an exam; he politely pointed out, three times in fifteen minutes, that he didn't see his daughter and the civil service as a good fit, and I, having set off after eleven o'clock Mass toward his house under the delusion that I was a country curate on a courtesy visit to my parishioners, now discovered in that living room abandoned by Alice and Ada that I wasn't the true victim of this torture: it was Sergio who couldn't take any more of me, who kept his hands on the arms of the chair as if about to get up and fussed with the fancy white armrest covers (knitted by my wife when she was a teen-ager).

The sky was overcast and the day muddled. I got up, to get out of his way—"Yes, yes, go ahead," he discharged me—and went into Ada's room to make a telephone call, to speak with someone.

I called the nicest member of the Teste Parlanti, a computer scientist and once a drummer in a New Wave band, with whom I'd always talked about Freemasonry. The phone rang but he didn't pick up. I called another friend, and after that a third, but clearly they were all at lunch. I pictured them with their wives in the homes of relatives, the young fathers grave and self-important, playing up their Roman accents to sound down-to-earth, toasting the seventh with the good glassware and enjoying a well-deserved rest *en famille*.

The fourth picked up: "How are you? Everything okay?"

I didn't know what to say: "Yeah, no, nothing much, I was just calling."

"Everything all right with Alice? We're just about to have dessert, talk later?"

"Up for a movie tonight?"

"We'll see, I don't know if either of our parents can watch the baby."

"Sure, no problem, we'll see you in church Tuesday."

"Definitely, that's probably better. See you then."

"Take care."

I sit down on the single bed, beneath a rose-petal rosary hanging from the lamp, and I really want to talk, but I truly don't know whom to call. Because this is what certain choices are made of, not knowing whom to call on Sunday.

"Hello, Corrado?"

"Oh, hi, I thought you'd never call!"

"Well, here I am."

"I forgot to give you the manuscript—I'm a total idiot, I can't believe it, I was too nervous."

"Indeed," I lied, "I waited for a while for you to send it to me, but . . . nothing."

My sister-in-law walked in. I was barefoot and lying on her bed and smiling as I talked; she looked me up and down and, in the weak light of the lamp, she too smiled. She had her hair tied back, a few stray wisps on her cheeks, a turquoise-green cardigan buttoned up over swelling breasts. I slapped the mattress beside me, inviting her to sit down. Meanwhile I agreed to meet Corrado again and wound up the conversation with some bonhomie (where did that tone come from?): "I've got my beautiful sister-in-law standing here like a spare part, looks like she wants her bed back . . ."

"Well done . . . in bed with your sister-in-law. Not bad for a Sunday afternoon!"

His comment spurred me on and I started to pat the bed again with my hand, but Ada ignored me. Once I'd hung up, she asked, "How many sugars?"

I wanted to make a joke about her sweetness, something like "You're the only sweetener I need," but the memory of my savoir faire had retreated into the fog of the 1990s and so all I did was stand and hold up two fingers.

Alice was right: a breath of fresh air, that's all I needed, and in fact Corrado turned out to be a charming person. My sense of him as a failure (*factotum?* I didn't know anybody who was a factotum) faded bit by bit, starting with our second meeting, which took place in the bar he went to for aperitifs and coffee breaks, a little world unto itself where he found refuge from the rigors of professional misfortune.

It was situated on a narrow street near Piazza Mattei, on the edge of the old Jewish ghetto. Until a few years earlier it had been one of those *salumi* and cheese shops run by old Roman guys who make their coffee with chicory and cover the walls with soda cans; the owners had sold it to a man named Roman, an unpleasant forty-year-old Parisian with Italian roots who played at being the host, and he'd turned it into an elegant café, a bistro with lots of iron and wood, salami hanging against stone walls, stinky cheeses stuffed in every corner and bristling with artisanal labels, old carriage wheels covered with a sheet of glass for tables. A lively place, frequented by Corrado's friends and colleagues. Roman's unpleasantness was like a minor handicap, no one paid much attention to his French sarcasm, and what's more he was a generous proprietor who made his customers feel they could camp out in his café, a rare thing in Rome. And the two of us camped out, we talked about novels, he read me pages of his unfinished manuscript and treated me to drinks as if he were paying off a debt.

Corrado truly refused to look this gift horse in the mouth: I told him about the publishing house, and even with me leaving out the anti-Semitic aspect, it was clear we were ultrapapists; I described my sentimental education and admitted that we had not yet published any novels but—a lie, *un pio desiderio*—we wanted to branch out. He told me not to worry, time would tell, for now we were working on it and it did him good to engage with someone in the know. He enjoyed himself in my company, he thought I was an eccentric and laughed at my stories of self-denial and all the odd personalities I described, and the fact that I had a virgin sister-in-law made me a half-decent comic character.

"I really should put you in my novel, your sister-in-law and you both. When are you going to introduce me? I'd get her to fuck."

Yes, it was clear I'd misjudged him at our first meeting; he'd been nervous only about talking to somebody in publishing. In fact, he didn't lack for self-confidence; women liked him and he possessed a sort of slipshod brilliance, inherited from an idiosyncratic tobacconist father, a devoted reader of scientists' and politicians' biographies. He was sure that sooner or later, he'd trade his position as factotum for that of personal assistant to his boss.

For the moment, he made photocopies, dropped off mini-pizzas and fruit skewers, waited in line at the bank and the post office, performed in short the trivial and logistically inconvenient commissions that keep an events agency going. He'd run through the rain to deliver information to museums, sit for whole half hours on vast flights of steps outside grand old foundation buildings. The company had plenty of connections with the center-left establishment; Corrado claimed that sooner or later he would stop shuttling sandwiches and bottles of prosecco in his moped's carrier case, and by dint of having coffee with the boss and learning the business's unwritten rules he would become, if not somebody, then something.

His logic reminded me of my father: it sounded idiotic but it was the postdated stamp of success—that is, when success finally arrives, it gets attributed to that logic.

Corrado: someone who gave social climbing the premoral glamour of an expedition through the mangrove forests of Borneo. He got along with everybody, not just with the bosses, but from the bosses, and from the rich in general, he knew how to win respect. Some of his friends were men of the world: English high schools, or French, wines, master's degrees and fiancées abroad. They'd have horrible car accidents in their BMWs—and survive. They had fathers working for RAI, Warhols in the living room, uncles connected to D'Alema. Who knows how he met them, probably at parties; but he had a gift for finding himself, the morning after, in the homes of people with whom he'd shared nothing more than a Cuba libre.

And it wasn't just the rich. Killing time at Roman's, at any hour of the day, knowing how to get people to like him, he had also made connections with the idle species of humanity who wandered the streets of Rome every morning: men who bet on horses and support themselves playing poker on the Internet; pensioners who repair boilers off the books in order to spend the day away from their obese wives; ex-junkies with good manners, ponytails, and the long faces of centurions in Asterix comics. There was room for me in this motley crowd too. I'd send Alice a text message to let her know I wouldn't be back for dinner; she was happy that I was in a good mood and took the opportunity to spend evenings with her father, trimming various objects with lace.

I was used to spending my time with people who made an effort to be alike, even interchangeable. Some of the couples among the Teste Parlanti had been formed, as it were, thanks to meetings organized, with the priest's help, by middle-aged parishioners, where young Catholic men and women could come in search of love—a pastoral-sexual production line. The sheer variety I found at Roman's had a calming effect on me; there was so much to observe and to be scandalized by here that I was obliged to suspend judgment.

For example, rumor circulated that the boss with whom Corrado was drinking coffee and white wine in an attempt to make a career for himself was cheating on his wife. Il Fassi, that's how they referred to him—definite article and last name, like in northern Italy—would show up at Roman's nearly every day after seven and, placing his thick fingers on someone's shoulders, shout: "Biancosarti: The Full-Bodied Aperitif," a twenty-year-old TV ad featuring Telly Savalas. Someone had told Il Fassi that he resembled Savalas, which pleased him (he was shorter and fatter), and he'd made the slogan both his trademark and his drinks order. He'd squeeze a chair in between two people, lean forward, and start nibbling from their plates. His jokes may have been cheesy but he told them with great conviction. He was an easygoing guy.

To my eyes he was exotic. Not much over a meter sixty tall, he favored red, orange, or green pants, glasses with pink sidepieces, neckerchiefs rather than neckties, white jackets. He drove an Alfa Romeo Spider with a permit for the city center. He lived around the corner with his wife in a cramped apartment because they'd chosen living centrally over having kids. One evening, as I replaced the manuscript in its folder, he explained: "In the city we all shut ourselves in. Like rich people. But without *fucking like rich people*. Understand? We shut ourselves in. I don't have a TV at home"—according to Corrado this was a lie, sublime in its superfluity—"I watch television with Pacini in the office. If you have a television in the house, when do you ever get around to fucking your wife?" His was a priggish giraffe from Lucca, she'd appear every once in a great while to drag him away.

"So now that depends on TV, in your opinion?"

"In my opinion, yes. Oh, but use *tu* with me, Pierone, you're always so formal . . . If I always shut myself up in the house, do you think I'd ever have met you? I used to live in Parioli, in a house belonging to my wife's family, on loan— they offered it to us, what are you going to do, say no? But Parioli, man, what a drag. Where do you live?"

I explained.

"Ah." He looked at me worriedly. "You eat like a horse, fall asleep on the couch with the TV on. How old are you? You're a bit, I don't want to say overweight, who am I to talk . . . but you're, you're not *compact*, you're . . . *expansive* is the word . . . Your wife doesn't mind? I bet she's always on top. Pardon me, eh? Like the Chinese with their sumo wrestlers . . . What are you doing here, anyway? Your wife needs a good fuck!"

He spoke at the top of his voice, to make sure someone turned around. ("No, not tonight," I replied.) In the meantime Pacini, Il Fassi's enormous right-hand man, entered the premises, unwinding a wool scarf. He made his way over to our table, chewing a truffle-topped crostino: "Are you still listening to this asshole?"

He was taller and broader than I was, with a Tuscan accent muddled by ten years of living along the Tiber; he had the Norman physique of the family's Lombard branch, poorly concealed under a haircut with a part that made him look like my nephew. I seldom had to look up when speaking with someone, but I did with Pacini, and it made me uncomfortable. He was glamorous, he knew how to dress and how to talk to women. His one handicap was that he tended to kill conversations. He was such a big deal for Fassi Events (if he had packed his bags, they would have lost all their best contacts) that he made everyone anxious as soon as he opened his mouth. He sought to fill the silence with tales of his PR bravado, like how he had fought with a supplier or local official. He loved to fight and make up with everybody. What endeared him to me was the fact that in addition to a wife, he had two children. He may have been Jewish, but I didn't have the courage to ask him to confirm that.

"When are you going to buy yourself a place in the old ghetto?" Il Fassi asked him.

"I like it where I am along the river. Where do you live, Chewie?"

At that point we had known each other for all of two weeks, and I already had two nicknames: the incomprehensible *Chewie*, and *Pierone*.

"*Chewie?*" asked Il Fassi.

"I live in Porta di Roma."

"Where the new IKEA is?"

"Yes."

"Jesus Christ. But I heard they're also going to open a Fnac there . . . maybe it'll turn out all right."

People on the move, with the roaming, expansive curiosity of those who have made it. There was also a cute flat-chested intern named Lavinia, about whom I'll say more later; other, less memorable colleagues; and, on the margins, Corrado's motley crowd of friends, rich and poor, who stopped by when they were in the neighborhood.

Everyone had time to talk to me, and no one even asked where I worked; I was a walk-on in their lives, a character actor; besides, Corrado had good taste in people and vouched for the likability and kindness of his friends, including me. He had a supple mind and an attitude typical of liberal Romans at the turn of the new century—an attitude I would call, a bit disparagingly, Veltronian, after the mayor Veltroni—that made it clear no difference of opinion could get in the way of the fraternal atmosphere inspired by our common membership of the human race.

As for me, thrust in among the unbelievers, I became a giant clown of a kid who made bizarre speeches with a logic all his own. They would greet my occasional rants about civil unions, abortion, or euthanasia with a "There goes Pope-boy again . . ." A strange way for an ultra-Catholic to behave in public. In Corrado's opinion, my reasoning reflected my own tortured brain more than it did the Church, which I might have found offensive if it weren't for how, in this light, for the first time in years, I came across as likable. Maybe I inspired pity. Maybe my body was saying something I didn't understand, something I wouldn't have known how to speak aloud. In any event I appreciated my two-dimensionality, found it restful; who wouldn't choose 2-D over 1-D? Returning home on the bus in the evenings, I said to myself: I'm not in such bad shape after all; I've made new friends; I'm not the dangerous anti-Semite with a telephone under surveillance by the CIA and the Anti-Defamation League. All of which made it possible to tolerate the long hours at work, the tension in the office, the looks I found myself exchanging with Mario, anxious looks about the martyrdom that awaited us on account of the Jewish Pope. What kind of martyrdom would it be, exactly? We didn't know and we were terrified. By day, fear and hidden forces at work; after sundown, aperitifs and Il Fassi's boasts, the gossip normal people engage in about women, and above all the sweet-smelling company of Lavinia, the intern whom Corrado liked and, according to the transitive property, was also liked by me.

Il Fassi and Pacini liked Lavinia as well. Il Fassi had taken her on as an intern because she was a family friend, and he knew he needed to keep his hands off her; in fact he treated her like a protégée, paternalistically, dealing out continual taps and pats. "Now, beautiful, those are colleagues, not suitors . . ." "Hey beautiful, come have coffee with us . . ." "Oh, beautiful, today you're dressed like a real woman, that's some skirt! Shall we send you over to the client and knock him dead?" As for Pacini, rumor had it that for some weeks his (possibly circumcised) penis had been "poking his chin."

Initially I didn't understand all this interest in a girl who appeared to be so ordinary. Her Pocahontas cheekbones were potentially one point in her favor, along with the classically Egyptian shape of her eyes, but she had anonymous, straight, slightly less than shoulder-length hair, sometimes tied back, other times not, and really appeared to be, I told myself, very ordinary. She spoke with a Roman accent with shades of the South. She was too candid. She almost always wore pants, and ever since low-rise pants became popular, short women look as though they've been driven into the ground with a cartoon hammer. She had a torso as long as her legs, stumpy little hands, tiny feet, and almost no chest.

It's true, there was something about her personal history. She'd taken two years off (two years can see you married with a kid already enrolled in nursery school) and traveled all around South America with a girlfriend, for which her parents came close to disowning her. With her exotic travels, Lavinia was trying to escape the fate of her older brother, who had become severely depressed after years of using cocaine to keep up with the broker lifestyle of the City (this detail turned my head— the brother didn't work anymore, he'd left London and gone down to Bari to live with his aunt and uncle). From stray words I picked up from friends I managed to piece together Lavinia's story; a few of the resulting combinations blew me away with their smell of danger. Twice she had gone an entire year without speaking to her father; and once in a while, when she was in London, she'd slept in a double bed with her brother. I embellished the story so much I started to suspect incest.

One evening I finally talked to her alone: "Even an ocean might not be vast enough to get away from my father," she told me. "And I needed time too. One year, an ocean: neither is enough. We started out in Miami, then went down to Mexico . . . We worked in Mexico City for a month, in a big restaurant all crooked from the earthquake. We had to carry trays, and the first few days I kept tripping on the loose tiles, enormous blue tiles that had come loose, and I would fall into the holes. We got together some money and left. I didn't really know what to do, you know. But travel can't hurt, right?"

In other circumstances I would have told her to honor her mother and father. I didn't care for her yet, but I didn't want to treat her like Federica. I encouraged her to talk: "You think that open-ended travel, the sort you did, is like surplus value?" I didn't know the best tone to take because up until a few weeks earlier the only kind of woman I regularly spoke with face-to-face was Ada.

"What is this, Pierone, a job interview? I have no idea. But better to have done it than sit at home and think about it."

"And when you got back you were reconciled?"

(I had a theory, but I didn't feel like formulating it. The theory was that two years away from parental control and any kind of value system had incapacitated her virtue.)

"Sometimes I don't understand the way you talk, Chewie."

"Why do you call me Chewie?"

She smiled, a smile for me alone, a promise of friendship. She set about folding a black cocktail napkin with her stumpy hands as she made fish sounds, smacks, with her lips. Then she continued: "One night on a bus in Guatemala I got scared by how fast we were going, downhill at a hundred kilometers an hour. I told myself I wasn't a total dropout, that this was just a phase, that I would give up travel and look for a job, if not in Italy, then at least in Europe. They were showing a Chinese martial arts film on two old TVs hanging down from above; the sound bored into my brain. It was raining and in the little net pouch of the seat in front of me there were some apricot pastries. Those apricot pastries, just seeing them made me feel like vomiting. You know, when you hallucinate? Industrial apricots had become humanity's enemy number one, what the end of the world smelled like, I swear. Not pollution, or war: apricot pastries. It was one of those moments, you know?" (How could I make her story last forever? I tried to check whether there were people around. I was on the alert and I vaguely remembered that being on the alert involved certain desires and expectations. The inner thigh muscle on a woman that engages when she moves her leg closer to yours. Delicate little flame, how to keep it alive?) "Do you know that when you're sick to your stomach, you should never think about your future? Otherwise you'll project your misfortune onto it. Anyway, I'm on this bus: I could see the road cones lit up by the headlights, the rain in the middle like swarms of tiny yellow flies. I had a vague sense of how the curves on this road were made and I thought, *At this speed we're all going to die*. In my future—in my future without chemically treated apricots—I saw reconciliation with my father and a real job. There are certain burdens you can't get rid of so easily. The whole trip I was asking myself if it was all an act, if I was doing it just to make peace; if I was starting my run-up to making peace from really far away."

"How old are you?"

"Twenty-five. I was twenty-two then. I wanted to go all the way, but I was afraid it might be an act. Playing the part of the runaway. And yet I was earning money, I was traveling around, sleeping in bus stations. It's hard to get rid of the feeling that you're pretending, pretending, *pretending* . . . I saw my father's eye in the sky, instead of the sun! That's why I had to go all the way."

"All the way where?"

"We made it to Patagonia."

"And how was it?"

"Fine. Then I came back."

She got up to go to the bathroom. Roman, small, thin, and compact, wearing a hateful combination of youthful curly hair and a gratuitous old-style white apron, came over to ask whether he shouldn't include me in the bistro's betting pool; then he disappeared, trailed by his knowing laugh. The whole place was dominated by Lavinia's presence, or by her absence, notwithstanding her resemblance to a worn-out espadrille.

A few days later, trying to make an impression, I told her that I had met my wife in the hospital. She had survived a horrible accident, the car had flipped over (my brother was in that car; I ran to the hospital and that's where I met Alice), and the first time we made love it was in the car. Not the car from the accident, nothing that outré, but my car, my mother's Clio. We did it at Forte Antenne, coming back from Sant'Andrea on the Cassia extension.

"That's totally sick," she said, lit up with enthusiasm to hear such things from the mouth of Pierone. "You were the type," she inferred, "who wanted to fuck, cry, and talk about death with the music on. You listened to the Cure."

Names and sounds that bring back from the bottom of my glittering ocean treasures, memories of girlish feet under a sheet, tickling your instep, clambering up further, a little expedition; a mouth talking about itself and half an hour later bending over the unzipped fly of your pants. "I knew it," you'd say when receiving permission to unzip, "I knew you wanted it, I figured it out by how you got closer whenever someone interrupted the conversation."

"Yeah, sure, I listened to the Cure. And New Order. And Joy Division." I breathed in happily those names from the past. "A month later she was sorry she'd started having sex again and asked me to stop. And I was in a very Tim Burton mood, fantasizing about the overturned car and two upside-down fairy

84

girls, and I don't know why I gave in. I know I was hanging on her every word, and before that her mother had died . . . it was hard to deny her anything . . ."

"Sure, it was totally goth, like fucking while talking about car accidents."

"Yeah, that kind of stuff. And deep down she liked men . . . she didn't seem repressed to me, I thought we'd be at it again."

"Having sex in the car . . ." She was still stuck on that. "Never take me anywhere in a car. For me now, car equals sex. How do you stay close without sex, though?"

I noticed she'd moved closer since my confession (*Never take me anywhere in a car*). I said, "The bond's even stronger."

"I'd never go without sex."

"Going without it is quite an experience."

"I knew there was something about you; you're no uptight priest."

"I love her to death."

(A few years ago I would have known what to do, but now it was too much for me. Over time you become accustomed to the cognitive effort involved in assessing the infinitesimal differences among intimate odors, those olfactory secrets, the musty smells that reveal so much about a person—at this proximity a woman reveals so many secrets; for me these secrets were now written in Cyrillic.)

"Of course you do, of course," she said, and moving closer she swung her legs over mine and put her arms around me, in a flash putting the finishing touches on the bibliography of memories I'd been furiously compiling. What came back to me in that moment was how I didn't used to be fussy about approaching something that, going by what people say, should smell of daisies, and instead its odor is only tolerable following repression and idealization and requires everyone's participation in a conspiracy of silence. Having overcome the obstacle of the odor, that transparent muck that sticks in your nostrils, overcome it multiple times with multiple people, you forget the real odor, the hormonal stench of unbalanced pH, you idealize it and forget. Chastity—these are all thoughts I had in the days that followed, but they got their start that evening and in particular as soon as she placed her legs on my left thigh—chastity is an effort to bring us back to the near side of that first contact with the odor, to promise to ourselves and to others that that odor will not be the fulcrum of our relationship with the future, with possibility. When you start having sex you discover new lifestyles and forms of art, entire continents and alternative vocations, new ideologies and ways of falling asleep, breakfast menus, combinations of amusement and mystery . . .

"But sex in the car," she said with her legs on mine, those precise words, *sex in the car* . . . "sex in the car is the greatest . . ." And then, surprise: "Keep this a secret, I have to tell someone: I'm fucking Corrado. In the car." She put her arms around me, this tiny woman, and forced me to talk about sex, to fill my head with shit.

"Corrado? You're with Corrado?"

"I fuck him in the office too. And in the car." She laughed. "I even fuck him in the park." Her mouth smelled of drink. "And also at one of my friend's houses. And in the car. Chewie, Corrado is such a hottie."

What sealed my feelings for her (and toward my own buried past life) was a minor event occurring two or three days later. I was in the bathroom at the café, two adjoining stalls in a tight space all black and gray with tiny round lights in the ceiling; the stall dividers didn't go all the way up and sound traveled over them. Lavinia had got up to go to the bathroom and two minutes later I got up myself, perhaps hoping to meet her as she came out and to speak privately with a view toward another embrace. Without making any sound that would give away my identity, I shut myself up in the stall to piss. After I closed the door and before I started to pee, Lavinia in the other stall held back; then, as if at my signal, as soon as she heard my pee cascading down against the ceramic bowl, she emptied the contents of her bowels and I smelled her shit, which sank smoothly into the water, immediately sprinkled by her intercontinental traveler's pee. I flushed and left the bathroom without washing my hands, unsettled by the comradely odor that had risen from the toilet and by that childhood sound that organic things make when they land in the water, and by the intimacy I now felt with the girl Corrado liked.

7

My fondness for Corrado was more cerebral. I first felt that tickling of the salivary glands that signals a new friendship one sunny, rainy afternoon, on a long walk down Via Nazionale to Piazza Venezia, along Via dei Fori Imperiali, all the way to the Colosseum. I began with a long, rambling monologue about how I couldn't live in this two-headed city of Mazzini and of the Pope. "Rome: Do you belong to Christ or to Garibaldi? Can we clear this up once and for all? Veltroni says we're all equal . . . but I am not equal!" It rained and then the sun came out and then it rained again. I tried to convince him that Rome before the Risorgimento was a dream, a Christian paradise.

We walked down the slope of Via Nazionale beneath winking clouds; when the sky darkened and warm drops fell, we ran under café awnings and entered clothing stores until it stopped. We went down to Piazza Venezia, talking about our literary sensation: Corrado's book and the scandal it was guaranteed to create. Our ideas ran ahead of us, along the sidewalk encumbered with cripples and their coin-collecting hats and office girls picking out underwear in the discount fashion stores. There was the usual pileup of taxis and articulated buses, blue government vehicles and big tourist coaches, all bouncing along on the pockmarked surface of the cobbles.

It was the first time I made my madman's speech to a nonbeliever. But in the era of Pierone, the all-too-human stain, every word that came out of my mouth sounded to me offkilter, pleasantly desperate, hyperreal.

"I can't stand this disorder."

"You're crazy, Rosini."

". . . Rome's unfinished business!"

I told him that Via Nazionale, at the time of Italian unification and Garibaldi's invasion, was a street leading up to the nowhere east of Stazione Termini. Rome was a broken music box. The Industrial Revolution was sweeping Europe, but Rome didn't have an economy, just a lot of landowners like the Ludovisi and the Filonardi, and the Roman *generone*—the two-bit bourgeois grandfathers of the handful of Romans who really do come from Rome and aren't immigrants in disguise— who fed the patricians and the Pope and provided other services the city needed. Everything was green, the people were thrown food from the windows of the nobles' palaces. Rome was just the home of the Pope and the ruined tomb of an empire.

"Ah, the Papal States," I would say to him.

And as he listened he would split his sides laughing. "Pierone, you're crazy!"

Then they demolished a couple of neighborhoods, built Corso Vittorio and finished Via Nazionale, splitting up Piazza Venezia, which immediately went from being merely the end of Via del Corso to the intersection of several new Paris-inspired boulevards. The Turinese had come down to work in the ministries. I had it in for the Turinese, Francophiles and followers of the Enlightenment to a man, for whom it wasn't enough to load us up with office space and new duties that our slovenliness could not tolerate: they decided to modernize everything. They built piazzas with arcades, thinking they'd be useful to us—and they weren't. They built boulevards because the Turinese are all rationalists. They stuffed Rome full of things to do, and Rome couldn't be bothered, so everything went downhill, the center filled up with automobiles as soon as they invented them, the Roman *generone* became middlemen for the new masters packing the ministry buildings that crowded out the little city of priests and pipers. Rome should never have been a capital city. Then I had a go at the Abruzzesi:

"The Abruzzesi came up these long, long roads from the east, they took days to cross over the Gran Sasso and push their way in to become laborers, and now they're part of our blood, them and their accent nobody can identify. We've got mixed blood without even having the satisfaction of being mulattos."

"I'm from Abruzzo," he says.

"See? And who even notices? If you were Tunisian, we'd know from a hundred meters, but the Abruzzesi . . . how do we pick them out? The Neapolitans came up here too, the Calabresi and the Sicilians. The Turinese came down, along with the Milanese and the Florentines, and they ruined our city." (My father's grandparents came from Campania. He was an accountant, she made dishes with fior di latte and complained you couldn't find good fior di latte on Via Nomentana.) "We're not Roman, nobody's Roman, nobody but the nobles who make others go hungry, and the Jewish merchants, who are the most Roman of all." That day I bought a dark green corduroy jacket for fifty euros. In my new jacket I cried: "Bring back the Papal States!"

I laughed a lot with him. I wasn't sure I liked his novel, but him I liked. The hypothetical possibility, a kind of running joke, of Non Possumus publishing a novel about gays had become a parallel life for me. At times I went further and fantasized about setting up a publishing house for real and bringing out the book myself; about showing up at my father's with the manuscript, having him read it, and saying to him: "So, you want to publish this little beaut of a novel about fags?"; and splitting my sides laughing like I had learned to do among normal people at Roman's, showing him that I knew how to laugh and then he'd have to give me the money.

"And the Fascists," I explained to Corrado, who had on impulse taken my arm, "the Fascists, not content with what Giolitti had done—and yet they hated Giolitti—really went all out: more boulevards around Piazza Venezia, and they knew it would clog up the center with automobiles; Via dell'Impero, Via del Mare. The upshot? Too much to do. What are all these people *doing*, scurrying to and fro? A thousand errands, shopping bags, official stamps, everything in triplicate, undersecretaries asking their drivers to pick up some pastries, and these are the ones double-parking their blue cars in front of the pastry shops and creating traffic jams, and you yourself get stuck in it, doing the slalom just to deliver some minipizzas. And then nothing fucking gets done in the offices, we're not cut out for work, we should just collect alms from the Pope. Why make Rome a modern city? Have you ever read Henry James? You can't ask a Catholic city to become modern, to keep records, to behave properly. Otherwise people stop going to confession."

"Henry James says this?"

"I'm saying it."

From Piazza Venezia, past the Arab bank, next to Trajan's Column and a pair of horse-drawn carriages, I said, "You see, we're nostalgic for the power of the Pope: horses that crap in the street."

But Corrado made it personal. "Pierone, I've been thinking about your sister-in-law . . . and about Christians in general. It's not just the Fascists; you also perform demolitions—eviscerations. Like Il Duce with Borgo Pio, when he razed the little houses of Borgo Pio to the ground, to create Via della Conciliazione. Now there's a boulevard that leads straight to St. Peter's. The troops from CNN can set up in the space around Castel Sant'Angelo and have a clear shot of St. Peter's when the Pope dies. Without the Fascists' evisceration of Borgo Pio they wouldn't have been able to do that. Without kicking out the residents of Borgo Pio, who had St. Peter's around the corner, they couldn't do it."

"Brilliant," I murmured. "Brilliant."

"Then there's moral evisceration, wiping out all kinds of things and . . ."

"And details too. You're a little devil, you know."

"Without the evisceration provided by faith, your sister-in-law would be a whole complicated jumble of things, like a traditional old neighborhood. And instead, faith has made her more linear. It's flung a drop of cement down on . . . on her desires. And how do you rebuild an old neighborhood that's been eviscerated?"

"It's impossible."

"They pour asphalt over the fucking hole!"

I let slip a laugh.

"But one nail drives out another," he concluded. "You've eviscerated Borgo Pio, in order to set things right you have to eviscerate your sister-in-law."

"Eviscerate," I murmured, and he burst out laughing.

He gave me a smack on the back of my head: "Don't think about your sister-in-law naked."

"No, no, who's thinking about her . . ."

"Look, even I have a conflict of interest here, because I'm only interested in you publishing my book" (here I felt a twinge of sorrow), "but you really should hang out with less depressing people, get out a bit more . . ."

"Corrado, you sound like my father." I gave him a big smile, and that's when I noticed the tickling beneath my tongue.

It seemed Corrado wanted to take over my imagination entirely, and one Sunday he succeeded. We met him by chance in Parco Nemorense after Mass and brought him to lunch at my father-in-law's. It was during Lent. Ada, Alice, and I were just leaving Mass when he burst onto the scene of our feast days.

Every Sunday following the *Ite missa est* we would head up from Viale Libia to Via Nemorense in the Trieste neighborhood, and walk in the park until the *sugo di pesce* was ready and Sergio called us back home. Lunch was a chore, but I loved the ritual journey from our parish church, in the African neighborhood, up to the park. Viale Libia, Fascist top to bottom, was soaring and monumental, flanked by enormous pale tetragonal condominiums. It looked like a boulevard in a colonial capital and led up toward the bridge, the Ponte delle Valli: a leap into the eastern void, in search of Lebensraum. Beyond the bridge, which spanned the railroad line down in the Aniene River valley, you had to be in a car to begin to see the rest of Rome, the periphery on the far side of the dry riverbed. We would take the boulevard in the opposite direction, toward the center, and climb the rich people's hill.

I liked the imperceptible transition from the middle-class Fascist neighborhood (Il Duce had built those houses for the great-grandparents of people my age) to that belonging to the modern bourgeois with his calf suede jacket, his understated dress shirt with a French collar, his wife carrying the newspaper under her arm. Past shuttered storefronts and climbing to the right toward Villa Ada, in fewer than one hundred meters Viale Libia—plastered with the leaflets and nostalgic posters of far-right political parties, crowded with all manner of stores, from men's tailors to Benetton, and with its center, in those days, eviscerated by excavations for the extension of the subway, which darkened the street even as it promised a second, radiant (but colony-less) future—gave way to the Trieste neighborhood, which soared higher and more nobly, with its rich, center-left-voting Romans, its coffee and expensive grappa from the Arcioni enoteca. Such wealth had to be the reason why Corrado, who spent time with the sons of millionaires and hoped to be important one day, had come from where he lived on Via Tiburtina to spend Sunday in the park.

He was seated at an outdoor café, pages in hand, pen in mouth, feet nestled in the pebbles, coffee and cigarettes before him on the table. Introducing themselves, the girls showered him with greetings, and we immediately invited him to lunch. En route I put my mouth to Alice's ear and implored her to tell her father that the Jewish Pope and my writer sister were off-limits.

Apart from that, I wasn't worried. Corrado could take any situation in his stride and Ada and Alice would treat him very well. I also knew he wouldn't talk about Lavinia—he was a man of the world and knew how things were done. At the table I stayed quiet, staring at his diamond-point cheekbones, gray eyes, and light yellow shirt, while my new friend, without betraying his emotion at meeting the mythical virgin sister-in-law and the wife of his editor in pectore, allowed himself to be interrogated about his work at Fassi Events.

"And what is it precisely that you do?" asked Sergio.

"Precisely? Events. Not too many on my own, not yet. For now I help out. But it's a good company, very well connected. We organize cultural events in Rome. Neorealism is dead, we need to look after Rome's image, unfortunately; to dedicate ourselves to futile things like culture."

Alice and my father-in-law rewarded him with a laugh. Who knows, maybe they despaired of finding a husband for Ada and he looked like a good catch. For a second I was sure he was going to end up as my brother-in-law. Dante and Manzoni may have created Italy, but to understand the Italian soul you have to look to Italo Svevo.

"And Rome," he continued, "has to say a great deal about itself, about Rome. It must represent itself, know what it is, what it was, where, for goodness' sake, it wants to go . . ."

"Certainly."

"A metropolis is sustained by what it imagines itself to be" (these were my arguments, he had made them his own and now I wondered where he was headed), "because in some ways, such a large collectivity is also a sort of collective illusion . . . I've understood this thanks to attending a lot of opening ceremonies for festivals of culture . . . Let's be clear, I'm just an errand boy, but the boss lets me take over sometimes . . . he sees himself in me, he likes me . . ."

"I get the impression everyone likes you," my wife says. "You're so cheerful, you even put Piero in a good mood."

"Well, I don't know about Piero in a good mood"—he played along—"let's say at least not mad as hell . . ." He had everyone's agreement, and then continued: "Anyway, every so often Il Fassi asks me what I make of an exhibit, what I think of it . . . So maybe one way or another, sooner or later, I'll become his assistant. I have this dream of doing an exhibit on the urban planning of Rome, it's something I want to propose to him. An exhibit on Italy during the Risorgimento and then under Fascism, on the *eviscerations* that shaped certain parts of the historic city center . . ."

"The eviscerations?" Ada asked.

"It's a wonderful idea," I said, and looked him in the eyes. "Is there any water in the fridge, Sergio?" I rose to retrieve it, and to be able to laugh a little alone in the kitchen, in admiration of my new friend, who had brightened my Sunday and created conditions such that my sister-in-law (who never went in for such messy stuff, as far as we knew) allowed the word *eviscerations* to come out of her mouth. I sat down on one of the wooden chairs at the table with the scraps from lunch, two sea bass bones, parsley, an empty can of tomatoes, to devote myself to imagining all the things my sister-in-law had never done on beds and couches.

A stroke of luck: in the middle of my reverie she appeared in the kitchen.

"So where's that water? I'm dying of thirst!"

"Yes, yes, beautiful, one thing at a time."

"Don't laugh! Hey, we should have your friend all the time if he makes you so cheerful."

"Yes, why not?" I took her hand.

"Give me the pitcher." She took back her hand.

"That's it, you take care of it."

"Oof, the little lord."

As she went to the sink, I looked at her rear. *Viscera*. To eviscerate. To open the stomach. Pagan stuff. She set the pitcher under the faucet; I came behind her and put my arms around her, pulling her to me and placing my hands on her stomach, gently on the material, so she wouldn't pull away like the last time.

"He's a good-looking kid, right?"

My whole belly was filling her arched back; she tried to move forward but couldn't. Not that I was pushing very hard.

"Are you crazy!"

I kissed her neck. I took a bit of her hair into my mouth.

"Corrado doesn't have a girlfriend. You noticed how cute he is?"

"What are you talking about!" She moved sideways and away.

"He's cute, c'mon, he's cute!"

So thanks to Corrado I was in Sergio's kitchen, with my sister-in-law in my arms and my pelvis virtually pressed against her rear. For once Sunday flew by without the apprehension of death, in fact it almost seemed to contain a promise, but it was better to describe the promise for what it was: the first spring in years that I allowed myself to think again about the past and about sex . . . kneeling in front of a woman backed up against a chest of drawers: she's still wearing a shirt but you've pulled her pants down to her ankles and then her panties as well, and face-to-face with that crooked fold and its mollusk scent, you implore the nondead thing to speak—you bring your mouth closer to bring it to life, and it's not the thing that speaks but the entire body that grows around it, the woman who until a few minutes earlier had, in another voice, told you an entirely different story, and that face perched up there atop her chest and neck is very far away.

This was spring, these were the thoughts: the reassuring honor of making a woman come; her socks warmed by steps taken that day; bras that fasten in the back, in the front, on the side, in pale green, gray, beige, light pink, faded from nervous perspiration; the woman as seen from the inside, stored away as packets of information: a heel, unfiled nails, stray hairs on a shin thanks to too hasty a wax, muscles that contract and relax, the paler skin of certain areas around the panty line. A sea of panties, slipped off while on her feet, on her back, on her belly, on her side, left at the knees in haste. Navels clumsily closed by the doctor at birth, underarm hair growing back, unsightly moles, perfectly shaped moles, backs buckling like inexpertly fashioned wardrobes, psoriasis behind an earlobe, mouths gone sour with wine drunken earlier. Reading the poetry of Gozzano from a paperback held open between two breasts, leaving a mark on the white skin; choosing what record to listen to as you both undress; deciding together in what order to undress; covering a mouth with a cupped hand; girls who tell you as you enter them, "Fill me up with your . . ." I remembered everything, but how could I call that feeling a "promise," if it was born not from my wife but from Lavinia?

In any case, whatever I was trying to get from Lavinia, our relationship didn't progress. When I tried to get her alone, her response was, "We'll talk later, just you and me," but in fact we never talked, or ever embraced again. I became impatient. I'd walk over and say, "Something to drink?"

"Don't get upset, Pierone."

"What do you mean?"

"Don't get upset, I can see you're getting upset, that you're waiting to talk to me."

"Sure, I'm waiting to talk to you because you're the best person in here." Even this from a married man was saying too much, and yet it didn't move her; actually, the solemn talk made things worse.

One day Pacini turned to me and abruptly asked: "Does she like you? I don't know. She calls you Chewbacca."

"Is that right?" *Chewie.*

"However, I wanted to know if, notwithstanding the unpromising nickname, something had happened between the two of you."

I took my time. That he thought me capable of such an enterprise was flattering. A conversation between men. Certainly, I would have been very embarrassed in bed (or in a car) with Lavinia. Thank Heaven I hadn't confessed my erectile dysfunction to anyone; they would have crucified me.

"And between the two of you?"

"Okay, I shouldn't have asked. Do you need a drink?"

I continued to bluff. He seemed worried. He seemed to respect me.

The Parisian playing the host, who that day seemed to me intolerably false, brought us drinks, accompanied by Il Fassi, who out of sheer horror vacui filled a moment of silence with "But all the same, dear Piero, you've got to fuck your wife." He thumped his solid hands down on my shoulders as if packing me into a suitcase. "It's your duty as a husband. Your duty—as a husband. Remember it well, and don't say I didn't tell you."

Pacini told him to get back to the office immediately, there was a meeting.

"Yeah? Who with?"

"With a delegation from your own fucking business." Then, to me: "Why don't you ever bring her here, your wife? Is she cute?"

"You don't bring your wife here either."

He looked me in the eyes, nodding yes, and I too nodded yes. I wanted to give myself the air of a man with secrets, with men's secrets. A man with aftershave and tweezers in his overnight bag.

A few days later, Lavinia terminated the internship ahead of schedule and disappeared into thin air. She was *making a mess of things*, Il Fassi confided. "And you didn't hear it from me."

"We should stay away for a few weeks," Corrado said the next day. "There's a bad vibe in the office."

One afternoon I went back without having arranged to meet anyone there, and saw no familiar faces. At the counter Roman brought me a glass of wine and a plate of cheese. I was wearing my dark green jacket, which was a little short for me in the sleeves but still by far the best thing I had in my wardrobe.

"Where is everybody?"

"She didn't tell you?"

"Who?"

"Your friend?"

"Who?"

"Lavinia."

"No, she didn't tell me."

"She left for Paris. A friend of mine up there found her a room. You know about the mess she made?"

"No."

Bartenders can permit themselves this role, seeing as how they always have their hands busy with glasses and dishcloths; I, on the other hand, leaning against the counter, I seem like a little boy ordering potato chips at the seaside snack bar.

"She finally fucked someone," said the Frenchman. "After having had everyone, *tout le monde*, sniffing around."

"Who, in particular?" I should have kept my mouth shut, shut!

"The big one."

"Pacini?"

"And the bald boss got angry. They threw her out."

"Really?" A trip to Paris . . . I'd take Alice and we'd go see Lavinia, see whether she's settled down all right, whether she needs anything, whether she's okay. A nice trip to Paris to relax and to help a friend in need. (What a complex sentence, this last one; it would take years to unpack.)

"Look around. They don't come here anymore. But they'll be back, one day they'll be back."

"You think they'll be back?"

"They had you sniffing around her too," he said.

100

"Ah, well, I'm married."

"So is Pacini."

The next day I called Corrado. He was tired and depressed. In person, later in the week, he told me that Lavinia hadn't told anyone about the two of them, which, if nothing else, kept him his job.

"This shitty job," he added. "Delivering sandwiches, basically."

"But now you'll become a great writer," I comforted him.

"She hasn't been in touch at all. Her parents are pissed."

"Because they pulled some strings to get her in?"

"Who knows where the fuck she is, she's turned off her phone."

Instinctively, I held back from telling him about Lavinia being in Paris.

"Your book will keep you busy now, you'll see."

He came to within ten centimeters of my nose: "Let's finish this book, I'm begging you. I can't stand it anymore not to . . . ugh . . ." and he didn't say.

A few days later, during Holy Week, I decided to speak with Mario to pitch him the novel. What little I had read seemed promising. His characters were bewildered and obtuse, straight out of Gogol or Grass. It was uneven, and since I hadn't read a novel in years, I felt like my judgment was impaired. But I'd discovered a new world in Piazza Mattei and I wasn't about to let it go, with Lavinia in Paris and Corrado discouraged—it was time to up the ante. I didn't know what forces were at work, or what my real intentions were; I only know that from then on things happened extremely quickly, and that these things only confirmed, in the order they unfolded, that my ideas were unclear.

The warm rapport Mario and I had enjoyed prior to the Jewish Pope was gone. I confronted him in his office and, in

101

order to introduce the idea of publishing fiction, appealed to our publishers' good taste while listing all the changes I considered necessary: I told him my wife should design our covers and that we needed to improve on the ugly font we used and that the publishing company should give me a lot more responsibility. Then I told him about the novel and who Corrado was.

He dismissed me in an instant. "No. I'd say no. It can't be done. It's not for us. Essentially, he's worked up a tendentious theory about the man–woman dialectic. However, having covers with the Miraculous Medal, that's a nice idea."

I had proposed updating our book covers, using simple images like the little tin medals from the Rue du Bac chapel in Paris.

"And I couldn't pay your wife, I don't have the money."

I tried to insist. Mario was listening to Vivaldi's *Stabat Mater* as sung by Andreas Scholl.

"Listen to Scholl," I said to him, "he could be a tranny! And Vivaldi was a priest! And we can't publish a layman?"

"We can't do it. Please, don't insist."

"Let me insist, please. Please. Let me try. I'll bring you the manuscript."

"Piero, I have to be frank here."

"Go ahead and be frank, then, please!"

"It's bullshit."

"It's not bullshit."

"Yes, it is."

"Then let me give this piece of bullshit a chance, maybe it'll turn out to be a good thing . . ."

"No, if it's bullshit, it's not a good thing." He dismissed me. "I beg you, please leave my office now, I have to work." He rose, crossed the office to turn off the Vivaldi, then returned to his seat. "Let this author go. He sounds disturbed, confused, nothing more. Don't get mixed up in things that are bigger than you."

The day drags on. I get back home when it's still light out, thinking the only thing bigger than I am is a Jewish Wojtyła and this neighborhood. I undress, turn on the radio, and get into the bathtub and sit on the edge. I rub my dry hair as the water sprays out of the handheld showerhead laid across my knees. A snowfall of dandruff and hair descends from my bowed head; the hairs are pine needles and they land on my belly or the bottom of the tub. The lukewarm water has brought out goose pimples all over my belly. Poor Corrado: first he loses Lavinia; now his publishing dreams are shattered.

Nevertheless, as a man I'm not all of a piece: the strongest images prevail, those most likely to become symbols of this or that, and I go where they lead me. Holy Week furnished me with just the scene I needed, a touching reminder of my duties as a husband, mocking my foolish, unchristian ambitions (to find favor with a young woman and dally with fiction). This same week, God gave my beautiful wife the flu, such that I understood unequivocally what my priorities were, at least for the present.

I nursed her back to health, preparing her meals as I worked from home, kissing her warm forehead before draping it with a handkerchief soaked in water. I ministered to her sneezes and her heavy eyes, smiled at her, scolded her when she threw the blankets over to my side. I slept beside her, saw the color her skin was taking on, opaque or translucent according to the kind of sweat, which I wiped away with an old T-shirt. Every once in a while, with the tip of my tongue, I would lick her lips and taste the salty fever.

On Holy Saturday I fasted almost all day long, drinking a shake with bananas and strawberries, milk, ice, and sugar at lunchtime, a cappuccino in the morning, and a few coffees during the day.

Alice said to me, "You fast the way Marco Pannella goes on hunger strikes." When he was protesting some injustice or other, Pannella would have four cappuccinos a day.

"I fast as I see fit. I weigh ninety kilos"—ninety-six—"I can't not eat, otherwise I'll pass out while I'm cooking for you!"

"*Pannella!*" she cried in the weakest of voices.

We decided that Alice wouldn't fast; she was already pretty weak on account of her 38°C fever. Saturday evening, for the first time in my life, I cooked the traditional baked fish all on my own. Her father would drop by to keep her company between ten and one, allowing me to attend the Easter Vigil.

I was really taken with it all: the fish has represented Jesus since the days of the catacombs. I held the fish, a sea bass, in my hands and stuffed garlic, lemon, and parsley into its belly. I thinly sliced the potatoes. The knife with the black handle from the wedding registry was dangerously heavy and my blood pressure, already on the low side, was at its lowest ebb thanks to the fasting (it's not easy to keep such a big man on his feet), so I was afraid of distractedly slicing open a finger, but I persevered. I added the potatoes and the cherry tomatoes, and the good olive oil we get from Sergio; I put the glass casserole in the oven. My stomach was gnawing on its own walls; I felt my arms and neck sucked toward a void there at my center; my stomach was salivating. All is full of love, I told myself; love is everywhere and everything is pure to the pure at heart.

When the cooking smells took over the kitchen, the sweetness of the potatoes and the tomatoes caramelized by the high temperature, this aroma, so common in well-to-do households, was utterly new. It wasn't like fish. It was like the edible version of a kiss between two girls who've just run a race.

The reading for the Easter Vigil, which I'd be participating in within the hour, spoke of milk and honey, of the succulent foods promised to Jews and Christians after death, at the end of all things, at their arrival in the Holy Land, and as I smelled the saturated air in the kitchen I prepared myself for a more practical immersion in Scripture. I removed the bones and the skin from the fish and served it on a plate with the vegetables. For a moment I put my open lips around the spatula encrusted with potatoes and tomatoes; a drop of saliva dripped from beneath my tongue and disappeared into thin air; my stomach contracted and gave a long rumble of discontent.

As I carried the tray into the bedroom, Alice's big forehead popped out from beneath the blanket. She managed to prop herself up (the fever was kept down by acetaminophen), she feebly pulled her arms out, but we didn't spare ourselves the grand finale, in which I fed her by hand and she extended her neck and said "Thank you" as if I were her resuscitated mother. The light in the room was dimmed by the lampshade. I fed her, brought the food to her mouth, and she met my hand with her tongue. After four or five bites, Alice slipped the fork from my hand, slowly, to continue on her own. The fish gave off the aroma of ambrosia; I saw it disappear bite by bite between Alice's infected lips and felt like a truly good husband, the kind you don't find very often, a courageous husband, capable of abandoning his dreams of glory in order to keep his job, out of love for his sick wife.

I liked myself like this, so tireless, faithful, humble, honest. To be so free of need is beautiful, an intoxicating, rarefied sensation.

The Lord giveth and the Lord taketh away. Lavinia was gone and Corrado's novel was a chimera, but my languishing spouse, feverish and idealizable to no end, a delicate thing in need of care, had been returned to me, in the best European spiritual and philosophical tradition. I exaggerated the symbolic weight of her fever—this is how I operate—and this is the poetry I needed in those circumstances, the poetry of sacrifice.

But there were other versions of me that pushed to play a role, however minor. The version of me that had become inflamed rubbing up against Lavinia and Corrado now became newly inflamed at every minimal contact. On the Monday morning after Easter, as I readied myself to tell Corrado that Non Possumus was a no-go, he caught me off guard with an invitation to a party that evening; naturally I replied that I couldn't go. Two hours later he had also invited Ada and at that point how could I tell him no? I left Alice at home to convalesce.

The party was in Garbatella, a recently fashionable neighborhood that I didn't know at all, full of old, elaborately designed housing projects and mini Gothic villas. A six-story building, the entrance hall multiplied by mirrors on every wall and embellished with plants with long leaves; the apartment on the top floor, submerged in loud music. Ada and I follow our cicerone; the entrance hall opens on the left into a dark drawing room. Leaning up against the threshold, two men are kissing, one in tight jeans, the other in camouflage pants beneath a raincoat; they're holding each other by the neck with a certain intensity. A man who looks about forty walks ahead, gives the lovers a caress, and plunges into the darkness.

A long corridor, then a hundred sparsely furnished square meters, white walls. In the kitchen, a souk of supplicants; all of humanity is here except for the middle classes: scruffy Indians with sweaty bangs, rich kids with pearl necklaces, Roman druggies, lots of red eyes. The French doors in the kitchen open out onto the terrace; there's a crowd and you can't get through. It's drizzling; clusters of people with wet hair occasionally reenter to take shelter. It seemed impossible to me, the idea that someone would bring all these people together into his house, people busy swapping cigarettes, suspicious packages, half-empty bottles with slobber hanging from them. "What is this?" I asked myself. "The avant-garde?" I was frightened and alert, disappointed but awaiting new developments, new Lavinias.

Corrado led us into the dancing room to say hi to a friend. Looking out over the boulevard and the minivillas, the room was really just a section of the terrace that had been illegally glassed in, with sofas to either side and piles of CDs on the ground. The source of the music was a DVD player under a

TV screen glowing electric blue, the only light in the room beyond what seeped in from the corridor and the pink reflected in the sky (all the brake lights of all the cars in Rome?). The friend was a woman around thirty-five years old, with a nondigital camera hanging from her neck. Short, curly hair and a showy white suit: a slim-waist jacket, bell-bottoms, a black blouse all ruffles. Black lace fanned out at her wrists. A meter away from me, two gay men with sweaty cheekbones and big pirate earrings were dancing and kissing, showing their tongues. One had curly hair, stuck to his forehead. The other, his head shaved, wore patent leather pants. A pretty, shapely young woman with a noble-looking oval face danced between two men in tight shirts. Her red wool dress centered on a U-shaped neckline that plunged from covered shoulders. She was an alabaster egg with straight hair, full and regal. After Corrado had greeted the photographer, the shapely woman went over to her, raised up her face, and allowed herself to be kissed. The white suit and the red dress met.

"C'mon, let's find somewhere to sit."

Three ragged-looking rich kids were walking out of a room; we walked in. A bedroom. A young woman was sleeping on a closed sofa bed; Corrado proposed moving her to an armchair.

"I know her. We can. She's not the hysterical type."

We lifted her up without waking her. I merely held a hand to her hips; it was Corrado who did the heavy lifting, holding her under the armpits. I was hypnotized by his arms being under those armpits. Corrado's hands sunk into the woman; I felt like I was dreaming. Ada moved some jackets and pillows to a chair and stepped back. Corrado laid the woman down on the armchair and, as he arranged her, touched her some more: her stomach, a bit of breast, the hips bound by the black stretch skirt. Then he slipped a hand beneath her rear and made some further adjustments.

We settled down on the couch, Corrado and I with Ada in

the middle, and shared a bottle of sharp-tasting wine we'd found on the bedside table. To be brief: half an hour later, softened up by talk, by a certain atmosphere of danger and solidarity, Ada and I were shoulder to shoulder, and at a certain point my sister-in-law, attempting to extricate herself, raised her arms and placed the palms of her hands behind her head. She was wearing a black cotton cardigan, unbuttoned, with a baby-blue polo shirt with a stiff white collar underneath, a bit like a tennis player's, where her tits surged, held in a cupless bra. In this way my nostrils were invaded by the strong smell of her left armpit; a few minutes later her left breast pressed up against my arm (sunk into the sofa) and ribs. I felt that mass of available flesh, female ribs covered by a bit of fat and the breast; I felt the soft contact, slyly obtained, and I didn't move a muscle, wanting it to last forever. For a few brief moments, everything was perfect, and then it ended and I was crushed. But a warm glow lit me from within and sustained me in my hour of need.

As we walked east we passed St. John Lateran, deserted and majestic, and Tiburtina Station, wedged in under the freeway. In the car our voices were soft, carefree, a bit murky and rambling.

After dropping Ada home, Corrado—Lampwick to my Pinocchio—and I headed back up north toward the suburbs and agreed on what a good time we'd had. Outside my house, for the first time in years I confessed something to a friend: "I really like my sister-in-law's tits." A new me, assembled from cast-off pieces discovered in the attic, was making its first appearance; a tone of voice, *I really like her tits*, a scandalous phrase to my ears.

"Oh, don't get me started," said Corrado, confirming the banality of my sin, "I would have stayed there on the sofa all night."

"I had them all over me as well," I confessed further.

"Eviscerations."

A few days later, the resolutions of Holy Week forgotten, I

boarded a train at Termini Station, bound for our printers in the Castelli Romani. I had a new friend—a real friend, a friend with *secrets*—and I had to fight for his happiness. The train passed small factories, industrial parks, clusters of trees, and the weathered wrecks of cars. They picked me up at the station; in the car I remained silent and resolute.

I entered the factory and greeted the printer and his assistants, all relatives of his. We wended our way among the blocks of paper piled up for the sextodecimos, past the printing presses, and reached his office, a room at the far end. As we were led past all that machinery, it felt as if we had returned to the nineteenth century, when ideas, to become strong, had to become physical, to knock down trees, be quantified in reams and sextodecimos and print runs; a place where the Internet didn't exist and blogs—proliferating, immeasurable ideas— were dismissed as the unprintworthy's delusions of grandeur. The artisans at work on the machines were humble people of Renaissance grace, with coarse Roman accents unknown in the halls of government or at the RAI, custodians of a secret knowledge.

I stared at the printer, a tall man with affable gray mustaches and a checked shirt.

"Listen, Franco, I need to publish a book on my own. Without Non Possumus. Something I'm doing. Will you print it for me? How much would it cost to do a thous— let's say, five hundred copies of two hundred pages each?"

"For you?" My fate was in the hands of a man in a checked shirt.

"Can we keep this between me and you?"

"And Non Possumus?" he asked.

With words of passion, with gestures, counting on his agnosticism, I told him my little secret.

When I'd finished speaking he said to me, "Honestly, Piero, I'll have to think about it."

We made a telephone appointment for the following day

and shook hands. His son gave me a ride back to the station, being kind enough to drive fast so I wouldn't miss the train that returned to Rome at lunchtime. I said goodbye and lit a cigarette, heading for the platform. A graffiti-covered express train chugged into view. I tossed the cigarette, stamped my ticket and climbed aboard, found a seat. As we reached the city gates, skirting the Roman aqueduct, I felt my cell phone ring in the pocket of my jeans. It was Mario.

8

I would like to be able to say that I was "fired on the spot" and forced to change my life against my will. Instead, looking back, I see that there was, the whole time and unbeknownst to me, another, more cunning Piero Rosini operating behind the scenes. Is it possible? Did I conspire against myself? Did I force myself, without knowing it, to lose the job upon which I was supposed to build a Christian family?

I was sprawled over my seat in the train car, fantasizing about the cover of the novel and about how I would go back to my father for money, convinced that the printer's scruple was merely pro forma, when Mario's call brought me crashing back down to earth.

"Perhaps you don't understand how this publishing house works."

But it took a bit longer for the train to pull in, then I had to take the 60 bus all the way to Piazza Venezia; in that anxious hour there swelled in me an anger against Mario and against the way he—I would like to have been able to tell him this in a high-pitched uxorial voice, disdainful and disappointed—*took me for granted*. I was furious as I entered his office and said, "Just because two slow-witted madmen put some money in your hands so they can play at being big publishers doesn't mean you're not an ex-florist." "Slow-witted madmen" and "ex-florist" were phrases I had come up with on the bus. "You don't understand a thing about the business and everything I propose to you, you don't ever want to do any of it. I don't see what's the problem for you if I publish a book on my own! I'm free to be a publisher too if I want to!"

"You're pissing me off," he replied softly.

"I make all kinds of suggestions, you always reject them. You insist on this shitty graphic design, you only want to publish books that are all the same, all just like you!"

He waited for me to finish venting. He got up to open the window. He poured himself a glass of water and grasped the gilded window frame in the pose typically used for author photos. He raised his other arm and drank three-quarters of the tall glass; a sweat ring stained his sky-blue shirt below.

"What can we do, Piero? *They*'re the ones who are divided. We can't be: the Church is one. What are you doing, going on about aesthetic concerns? You think we're a beauty salon? That book covers mean anything? And novels?"

He had narrower shoulders than I did and dressed like an ex-biker. His arms were covered in dense black hair. He breathed heavily, with his head held high. The Church brought us together, this ex-florist autodidact philosopher and me; but just now, I found it baffling to think that two guys like us shared nothing less than a mission. Everyone feels equal in the Church, but I was the rich kid who didn't want to leave his riches behind; Mario was the fisherman blinded by Jesus, who had given up his boat to follow him. He set his glass on the table and fell back into the stuffed chair:

"C'mon, Piero."

"C'mon, what?" I was calmer now, and about to apologize, but gritted my teeth.

"Now stay calm," he said more serenely. "Take a little walk, spend some time in church. It's already so hot. Think of your wife, pray a bit for your wife."

"Sure, sure, my poor wife. Always thinking about my poor

wife, who can't get herself a job and goes around dressed like a whore . . ."

He passed a hand over his face. "This is all so frustrating. Can't we do this without arguing? Can't you do it without insulting your own wife?"

Mario and I didn't even argue, really, as if neither of us wanted to show Christians in a bad light. For my part, however, I stopped working hard in the office, wasted time on phone calls and at the photocopier; finally, in an e-mail of which Alice was aware, as hastily composed as it was long considered, written and sent from one room to another of the office so as not to talk to my boss in person, I told him that I would no longer be "able" to work with him. We canceled my fixed-term contract and Mario contrived to get me a job interview with a right-wing bookstore in the Talenti neighborhood, not far from Porta di Roma. He was a good Christian, aside from his madness, or at least that's what his gesture seemed to indicate.

I arrived for the interview one Monday morning in May and spent a few minutes browsing the nonfiction section. It was a midsize bookstore on a busy, well-connected, lower-middle-class street, with display carts out on the sidewalk, a home appliance store, an optician's, all under a uniform gray sky. The bookstore had three spacious rooms and big windows. The books were laid out on tables; the panorama of small-press typography and covers confirmed that it was a right-wing bookstore.

I knew that it would be six pretax euros an hour, which would come to nearly a thousand a month; I was soothed by the idea that becoming the priest of this little temple of books was within my grasp. I saw myself already middle-aged, guru to the pockets of cultural resistance in the neighborhood. (Resistance against whom? Against the power of center-left dailies like *La Repubblica* and of my sister? Resistance is a vast and delightful concept.) I saw myself in the future, older, waiting anxiously for shipments; I advance-ordered books on the death of Pope Luciani, made friends with long-necked twenty-year-olds, gathered up the scattered energies of various right-wing social movements and brought them to church.

Perhaps I would be a cripple. In a cruel future in which the government's moderatism had provoked a new era of extraparliamentary chaos, the thugs from the *centri sociali* on Via Nomentana would kneecap me. Rosini: limping through the neighborhood with a wooden cane and bristly white beard; with bristly white eyebrows as well. I would hold meetings, strike up a friendship with the local parish priest. (They didn't carry my sister's books: good.) I would make liberals uncomfortable.

Coming toward me was a man of about fifty, with a thin, clean-shaven face and short, graceful wavy hair. His character a game of two opposites: white cashmere-blend sweater, iron handshake.

"Hello, Piero."

"Hello, how do you do?"

Emerging proudly from his V-neck was the large knot of a white tie, over a black shirt. One of those Roman Fascists with a booming voice, a coarse Roman accent, and no drawl.

"You're punctual."

He let go of my hand by quickly withdrawing his own, without lessening the grip, as if removing a clip from a rifle. In response he expected me to look him in the eye, which I did.

He led me toward the counter, through the fog of my future memories. The store was more or less empty; it was still early. We sat down on two small clear plastic chairs behind the cash register.

"There's not too much to learn. You know how books are made, what goes into them. You also know the kind of discourse we've established here."

114

I nodded.

"You could start the first Monday in June, I'd say. Let's do seven euros an hour. This you already knew."

"Yes." No, I thought it was six! That makes fifty-six euros a day, for twenty days a month: 1,120! It was practically as much as Mario was giving me.

"We have always had a dialogue with Non Possumus, always. Strictly speaking, we're not what you'd call a confessional bookstore, but there's enormous respect, friendship. And then the Latin Mass . . . the beautiful things, which we like."

I held my hands one against the other, rubbing them together. It was an ugly day, diffuse light from a low, flat sky. Here was my new job, and here in front of me, seated with his back straight, was my new Mario, a man with ideas, values, principles.

He explained: "There's a story that's made the rounds of the distributors and booksellers. They say that your editorial office is made up of people who met at the Latin Mass."

"Well, yeah, more or less."

"There are a lot of people out there who pride themselves on this kind of thing. Monarchists."

"Monarchists."

"Me personally, I'm ultrarepublican. That is, when I'm not a republican of Salò, ha-ha. But monarchists, monarchists don't mess around. We have monarchists among our customers. It's a family neighborhood, you'll see."

I listened with a vigorous, panoramic smile. These kids needed a guide; I had to lead them toward better things. I had found a job, for which I ought to have thanked Heaven: salesclerk in a right-wing bookstore. I was breathless. The dazzling career of Piero Rosini.

I left to get some coffee. There was an image of the Eiffel Tower on the sugar packet. With blackened breath I went back to the bookstore and told him I would definitely think about it. "It's a wonderful position," I reasoned, looking him in the eyes as if I were the one offering him the job. "A beautiful neighborhood. People who know their stuff. Nonconformist politics."

Committed Catholics and Fascists alike adore variations on this theme. The Left never expects to find the same short circuit—good people/nonconformism—on the Right. It's nice to think that the masses aren't conformist, it's a riddle that gives you faith in people. He rewarded me with a virile grin, all concentrated in his upper lip: "Nonconformist politics, we're always talking about that ourselves. You are welcome here."

And instead, a month later I was working in Paris, as an editor at the Catholic publishing house Éditions du Bac. I had made the move without Alice, who supported it but was unwilling to accompany me.

Since it's difficult at this point in the story to consider myself something more coherent than a first and last name, a body and a voice, for the sake of brevity I will lay the blame for everything on the sugar packet, which during that coffee break on the brink of a new career had set my thoughts spinning around one image after another as they tumbled from the Eiffel Tower. The first was Lavinia, driven around the boulevards in a city bus in search of life and in flight from her father; the second was Alice and I beneath the Arc de Triomphe, for once, after so much time, taking a trip purely for pleasure, without pilgrimages, spiritual retreats, or gatherings with the Pope; the third was Lavinia and I, seated at a café, talking about sex; the fourth, Alice and I as guests of my Éditions du Bac colleagues, whom I'd come to know in the past few months by telephone and e-mail because they had bought the rights to two books on the Virgin Mary from Non Possumus; the fifth, Alice, Lavinia, and I touring museums, churches, and dance clubs, in an all-reconciling Rosini World.

So much sugar in a single packet. Even more: the idea of a

trip with Alice was in a few short hours supplanted by the much stronger one of asking Éditions du Bac whether they were by any chance hiring at the time. And this was why, a week later, I had taken an overnight train to Paris and, unannounced, with the morning in full swing, had turned up in jacket and tie in their office in the Sixth Arrondissement, neighborhood of universities, lycées, and billionaires, explaining in my best poker face that I was planning a move to Paris and was feeling out the job market. A plan at least as preposterous as that of founding my own publishing house, you would say. And they hired me.

Now stir that sugar two or three times in the cup and enjoy the scene of Piero Rosini in a one-room apartment, alone, without his wife, with a job superior to his last (my new colleagues weren't conspiracy theorists). Don't allow the taste to be ruined by the thought of the four or five telephone calls from the republican of Salò, which I most ill-manneredly failed to return; nor by the thought of Corrado, left without any contacts in the publishing world; and not even, for that matter, by the thought of my wife . . . Alice, on the contrary, had taken it better than anyone. The day after the interview she had come home with a bottle of Mumm and toasted me. I had prepared myself for a dutifully mournful evening, for muezzinical laments about "brain drain," "the precariat," and "national crisis." My wife, however, was far removed from the issues of the day and didn't interpret the event as generational.

"So you did it, huh? You got the Jewish Pope off your back . . . ," she teased me. "It's so like you. I've been thinking about it all day. First you go all out, to the point of absurdity, for the sake of something absurd, and muck up everything else around you for good measure. Then, ta-da: 'Oops, I've lost my job, but I may have found another . . .' 'And where would the little prince be off to?' 'Paris.' 'You poor thing! And where, exactly? In the mines?' "

I listened to her, glass in hand, unable to add anything, delighted with her jokes.

"No, not in the mines, exactly; at a publishing house in St.-Germain-des-Prés," she continued playfully. "No no no, you poor little thing, you . . . such backbreaking work . . ."

She raised her glass and we toasted again; she was getting drunk, and so was I. Not that this was enough for us to find the energy to make love—half an hour later some kisses on the neck had led nowhere—but prior to the impasse we'd reached the highest level of harmony with this type of exchange:

"Well, not only am I down in the mines, my dear, but there's no contract and I'm paid under the table."

"It'll fly by, you'll be great."

"Of course, if you came with me I'd be much happier."

"I'm not coming, don't even try; it's your choice."

"It's true, you have to nurse your daddy."

She slaps me, I laugh, and she, slaloming between her demons:

"If I don't, he'll shit himself."

"But if he shits himself," I say, "Ada will clean him up; that way she goes to Heaven first."

"And what if I wanted to go to Heaven first?"

"Well, then, go ahead and wipe my ass, I eat worse than your father."

"You make me want to vomit . . . C'mon, I want more wine, you're so selfish . . ."

"In any event, if you want to come you can always decide later . . ."

"There you go: I'll decide later, for now be happy I didn't throw a jealous fit . . ."

Jealousy? Of whom or what? We were two little angels, incapable of jealousy, our souls separated from the body by an oleaginous film, the thin layer of slime that angels leave behind when we evoke them.

And so in the summer of 2006 I began living and working on a street in St.-Germain, a gentle slope between Boulevard Raspail and Rue de Rennes, winding down to the Avenue de l'Observatoire near the Port-Royal RER, where, to the left, Boulevard St.-Michel begins its descent toward the river. In the neighborhood were the famous lycées, the Sorbonne, the École normale, Rue Mouffetard, pleated skirts, bicycles chained to every railing, bad-tempered *boulangers* . . .

The apartment was located next door to the publishing house, at the preceding street number, on the third floor of a small building with cigarette smoke–infused carpeting on the stairs and landings of bare wood. Between me and the office the sidewalk was interrupted by a cross street, onto which looked both my windows and the office's. It was, in short, always before me; all I needed to do was look out the window and I could see it. The owner, also the owner of the publishing house, had bought the apartment a little while ago, just before leaving for Africa. I lived there rent-free in his place. A photo of a mountain landscape, a wire crucifix, two spartan white chests of drawers, one wide and one narrow, to either side of the door.

I placed my books in a small white bookcase. With me I had nothing on conspiracy theories and nothing revisionist. The wardrobe was made of cheap plastic. Papa would have looked upon it with a superior air, struck it with an open hand and dismissed it as junk. I put some clothes inside it, and some CDs, and some more books. Ovid and Tolstoy, Gogol, Wittgenstein, Scholem, Bellow and Philip Roth. Corrado's novel had renewed my love of literature, Lavinia my love for the human species, prompting me to reread the stories that had formed me. I bought *Les Inrockuptibles*, filled with a renewed interest in music and art and the photographs of women devoted to trends and subcultures unknown to me. I strolled through the center, hands in pockets, mumbling the choruses of songs by Dylan or Richard Hell. Trained to recognize temptation, I noticed a mild Bovary effect on my nerves: after years, I'd rediscovered (and at the same time discovered to have forgotten) the feeling of melancholy.

Which is a rather pleasant feeling, one that feeds off tender female figures only to produce a laborious emotional digestion that slows everything down except for the capacity to take long walks. For the entire summer, I did nothing but walk the streets of the city center, after work and on the weekends, in the faint hope of running into Lavinia. To do what? Nothing. To have found her. For the pleasure of pursuing her. For love of melancholy.

After work I would go down on a reconnaissance as far as Place St.-Michel, where the large fountain attracted Americans in 1.25:1 scale, just slightly larger than the Europeans. They spread the chewing gum of their accents over everything; I trod on it with my ears and it stuck. I left them to their aperitifs and headed straight over the Seine toward the Île, catching a glimpse of Notre Dame upriver; I abandoned the Île, and on the right bank of the city passed through Châtelet and the lines outside the theaters. I moved on, lifted my nose at the blue mock–exhaust pipes of the Centre Pompidou breaking up the procession of pale facades. If I had the energy, I kept heading north, toward Arts et Métiers and then farther up into a black neighborhood, where they offered manicures and African braids in large, dusty, neon-lit salons or clustered outside KFC, eating potato chips. I climbed higher, all the way to the Gare de l'Est, but didn't find her; I went into the Métro and returned home.

Weeks went by. The student protests against Villepin's first employment contract, which clogged the boulevards from time to time, hardly touched me; they slipped away along with the Italian World Cup victory over the French, a source of embarrassment rather than pleasure. Then a continental August, occasional rain. Daylight until ten, eleven. I looked for Lavinia at the Bastille, or near the Canal St.-Martin, where the local young people sat watching the river in cafés or along the walkways or on the little bridges, their gazes lost in the diminutive system of locks. Or else toward midnight I would walk along the Seine, heading west on the left bank until I spied the luminous spaceship-like vault of the Grand Palais appear against the great backdrop of the night. Among the girls sitting crosslegged on the pedestrian bridge, the Pont des Arts, where I'd wind up my tour before heading back toward the Odéon via the Rue de Seine, there was no one who was exactly Lavinia, only dubious approximations in open sandals. At night along the river the streetlamps shone in an endless sinuous line, their yellow reflections shimmering in the black water. The upright Gothic buildings, immense shadows pierced by faint lights, provoked fits of affection.

The Teste Parlanti had immediately smelled danger. The night before I left, the ex-drummer computer scientist, Nicola, had caught up with me at the neighborhood gelateria, to lay out a little speech full of Roman dialect, the language and accent that we ex-readers of Musil used when we wanted to call a spade a spade like preachers do.

"You're thirty, my man, and Alice is nearly the same age. You're on your way to getting old. If you split up, when you gonna start a family? Alice won't move . . . Let's be honest: Alice won't move, she's got her father here. You have to stay here . . ."

My father gave me his own little speech over the phone, containing a very different message:

"Your mother told me—well done! You've got guts! Getting rid of those good-for-nothings—and with a bang! Just imagine, Paris!" He added unrepeatable banalities about the city of light and of love, and: "So some paternal blood runs in your veins after all. Look, in Paris . . . what's done in Paris doesn't even show up in the black box . . . Ah, Paris! You can do what you want, it's the most beautiful city in the world and you can go into cafés and talk to all those extremely cultured, slim, very cold, cruel women . . . My, my, are they cruel!" Then some advice: "Behave like a man, naturally; don't mix your private life with your family . . ."

"Huh? What are you talking about, Papa?"

"Mamma and I have stayed together for forty years . . . It takes persistence, got it? You need to know how to stay quiet when it's time to stay quiet, got it? You need to develop some practical wisdom, got it?"

I wanted to hang up, to dismiss that exalted malefactor, who had, nonetheless, caught me off-balance: "I took the liberty of depositing a thousand euros into your account so you could buy some decent clothes. Don't imagine you can go around in your usual getup; it's a metropolis, a big city, don't embarrass me."

It was a big city, and I had hated it for years as the epitome of evil in Europe: the Enlightenment, centralized government, sexual liberation, high-profile careers for affluent young strivers. All qualities, I would say, dear to my father, whose bank-transfer beneficence I had accepted without batting an eye.

It was big and very beautiful, and I found it irresistible: so rational and pedantic, with its spiral of neighborhoods numbered one to twenty, established once and for all a hundred and fifty years ago, when Rome had two hundred thousand inhabitants; neighborhoods indestructible in their network of uniform boulevards converging in serene rapport. Paris is more majestic than Hong Kong or New York, where every skyscraper challenges its fellows in terms of color, form, height; here the buildings aren't rivals, one dissolves into the next, white and dirty, working together for the sake of urban-planning beatification. Paris is the Virgin Mary of cities, I told myself; at the end of the world it will be assumed into Heaven without dying, without its slate roofs being pulled down, the black railings of its terraces pulled up; it will be returned to its fathers, Haussmann and Napoleon III, as it was received from them: perfect.

I formulated these new thoughts in the course of my solitary, meandering searches for Lavinia. I didn't have to worry about staying in to save money on meals, Alice had told me to keep my salary; she had something left in her account but above all almost no expenses. Which meant—I knew it but didn't raise the question—that she was eating every day, lunch and dinner, at her sister's, at her father's. That probably, therefore, with the car the only option for moving between Porta di Roma and her father's neighborhood, it was more convenient for her to stay there between meals. And probably, therefore— and this was the most complicated *therefore* to admit—she spent many nights in her old room together with her sister, the four family tits brought together again in a pliant rosary offered up to their mother, to whom I imagined them dedicating prayers before getting into bed, probably on their knees, in nightgowns, regressing further with every passing month to what they were before, what I had hoped in vain, with foolish ambition, to free my fiancée from.

This doesn't mean that while my poor little wife regressed I became man of the year. If, on the one hand, in a suspension of intellectual coherence, I had "managed to get rid of the Jewish Pope," to put it in Alice's terms, on the other my work at Éditions du Bac wasn't a real job, my colleagues had turned out to be even crazier than the last bunch, and the company I kept in the evenings bored me: in short, I was lonely and it didn't look as though my association with Paris was destined to last much longer.

If I told everyone a tale of my great fortune, this job having descended upon me like a sign from God, Alice and I knew that wasn't the real story. A job like this one doesn't just materialize unexpectedly. The morning of my surprise visit, the deputy editor had at first appeared politely perplexed; he urged me to wander around the neighborhood while he thought it over (that is to say, while he called Non Possumus to find out what was happening), and when I got back he wearily explained that if indeed I was interested, they could find something for me to do. We agreed that I would start at the beginning of July: six months guaranteed with a handshake and paid under the table, something unthinkable in Paris. They were performing an act of charity on my behalf. The free apartment constituted part of the offering. The publisher was in Africa for a year, aiming to write a book about missions. In terms of monetary compensation they couldn't offer me much. I had returned to Rome with this still pending; they called to propose five hundred euros a month, and reaffirmed that come Christmas I would have to look for something else; I was only helping out in the editorial office in the absence of the boss, and in any event—they insisted almost without knowing what tone of voice to use—it was better if I didn't talk to anyone about our agreement.

"Forgive us if this seems like a lack of respect, but for now we'd like to see you as more of an intern."

When I got back to Paris they entrusted me with a pair of tasks: to verify the accuracy of some Italian-to-French translations—two or three books acquired from Edizioni Paoline—and assemble a sort of daily press review of what was being said about the Vatican in the Italian papers. As the weeks piled up and the work began to seem not just boring but downright useless, the conspiracy theorist in me had no problem imagining the entire operation had been orchestrated by Mario so that I could blow off steam, or because he understood that the Jewish Pope had put the fear in me (and then later he would welcome me back with open arms). Alice, via Skype at an Internet café just down the street from the apartment, teased me for what had developed into full-blown conspiracy theories. Mario called her a few times a week for news of me and to ask whether I had decided to come back; thus for Alice it made no sense for my former boss to have been behind the offer of a fixed-term position. As far as she was concerned—she reassured me in order to avoid any misunderstanding—she didn't care whether I returned to finish the book on the Pope; in fact she was relieved I was keeping myself out of it. (On this topic a number of things were left unsaid.)

As for my colleagues, I quickly bonded with the deputy editor, Robin (a skinny thirty-eight-year-old, married with four adopted children: three small Indians and one French child with Down syndrome). Sometimes after work we would head down the long and twisting street Rue Notre-Dame-des-Champs/Rue St.-Placide/Rue du Bac (it changed names), thumbing rosaries made from pressed flowers until we arrived at the shrine of Our Lady of the Miraculous Medal, the one behind my proposal for the new cover art for Non Possumus, the first one to appear in Europe in the nineteenth century. If in my solitary strolls I could feel like a cross between Belmondo and Dylan, with Robin I was unequivocally Piero Rosini at the height of his religious excesses. We spoke of Mary, for the most part, and of her apparitions. Robin was devoted to Our Lady of the Miraculous Medal and liked how the chapel rose next to one of Paris's oldest shopping centers, a massive and at the same time airy monument, still embellished at the entrances with signs made of stained glass. He liked to joke about the fact that for her first official apparition in Europe, the Virgin had chosen to open a stall selling little medals next to a shopping center, a nineteenth-century manger.

We went there almost every week. Once, on the way, Robin talked to me about the secrets of Our Lady of Fátima.

"The Virgin showed the three children an enormous sea of fire that flowed beneath the earth. A sea of fire, can you imagine? Demons and human souls were sunk in the fire like embers; some were black, others the color of bronze pots. Clouds of smoke gushed from their chests and the flames raised them up in the air. Then they fell back down, screaming. Lucia wrote in her diary that she and the other two children would have died of fright if Maria, before showing them Hell, had not promised them they would go to Heaven. And they must have believed it, because if Hell is frightening, if God had gone to the trouble of building *that Hell*, imagine what he can build that's beautiful, imagine what *Heaven* must be like!"

By and large I adore this kind of reasoning. To feel yourself part of the ultimate destiny of man is a thrilling sensation, it fills your chest, and to have metaphysical fears in addition to earthly ones (hunger, work, money, reputation) makes you less single-minded and animal-like, frees you somewhat from the struggle for survival. And then, a God who loves man, isn't that adorable? A Virgin who chooses some Portuguese farmer's children as helpers, like Cinderella dressed by the little mice . . . But who really wants to imagine, in the face of all that, that Hell exists, a sea of fire that flows under the earth? Obviously, this question has no intrinsic value; what counts is that it's being posed by Piero Rosini, someone who in recent years had almost boasted about his collection of inspired and even slightly unhinged Christian friends. Now, however, asking myself the typical questions of someone who didn't drink at the trough of spiritual exaltation, I put some distance, in a somewhat ventriloquizing manner, between myself and my usual ways of socializing.

Unfortunately, I didn't have much luck with laypeople. Through a colleague I had become part of a group of people who would invite me out three or four times a month, but the Chewbacca effect, the miracle by which I was taken for an odd but lovable character, didn't happen. The Parisians have different conversational rhythms and are more reserved than Romans. In Paris, once the bill is paid the whole thing is over, you don't linger by the exit to chat; the boulevards are windswept, you go your separate ways. The evenings never go any further. You never see each other two evenings in a row, not even twice the same week. I couldn't seem to build up any momentum. The women were twenty-two-year-old teachers, thirty-year-old publicists, bank employees, psychologists from Lyon in boots. Back in my apartment, I'd shut myself in the bathroom and think of them and my wife and Lavinia and my sister-in-law. I fixated on a threadbare gray angora sweater, the neckline against the delicate skin of a financial consultant. Into the bathroom with me I brought fine veins against white wrists and two tearful sailor's eyes, details of women I wanted: how they pulled their cell phones from purses; a Spanish girl with big breasts in a red T-shirt and enormous teeth that laughed all on their own between swollen lips.

I hadn't made such an effort since the 1990s. Slowly and with difficulty, one fantasy after another, I began to send blood to my genital area. One day toward the end of the summer I woke up with an erection; I couldn't even remember when that had stopped happening to me. Then every morning, with the chattering of the private-school kids in the street, I held it solidly in my hand, then got up to eat muesli with milk. To me the erection and the muesli seemed to be the same thing, the same life.

The room's old parquet flooring sunk in the middle; at night I was ashamed to walk across it, to hear it creak in the dark. I put out meat to defrost on the electric radiators under the two windows. The kitchenette, a hole with a door that couldn't really be called a room, stunk of unwashed dishes. I bought neither flowers nor plants. On the other hand, I was organized to a farcical extent, piling up the books on the table according to size. But the solitude of a man is a long day without pants, the windows closed and a hand constantly in his underwear, in front or behind, to liberate, to scratch, to shift.

Body odors reign supreme, along with those from the trash can and the sink, along with dust from the stairwell, unrelieved by the smell of anything pleasant, except maybe shampoo.

Beyond the room's sixteen square meters I had a tiny bathroom and the kitchenette, both the same size, six square meters between them, each with its respective tiny window. The water pressure for the shower was feeble. I had breakfast and bathed like the fairy-tale ogre in his cottage. Getting in and out of the shower, I knocked my shoulder against the frosted-glass panels; as I soaped up I examined the plaster where the wall met the ceiling, moldy and flaking. I ate my meals on a wobbly little table that folded down from a cabinet in the kitchen; you could return it to a vertical position to clean the floor. From the apartment I could see, on the ground floor of the building opposite, the publishing house's windows looking out onto the street. The office's floor-to-ceiling glass revealed both the employees and, on inclined display shelves, rows of books. The Pope gazed out at me from the book jackets.

Some mornings I went running in the Luxembourg Gardens, following the course of the long wrought-iron fence topped with golden spikes. Until the sun rose, the garden was dominated by the black Tour Montparnasse. People in tracksuits of various different ages, some of them very old, slowly practiced tai chi; young professionals or students, with iPods strapped to their arms, ran winding routes through the rows of trees flanking the Senate. On Sunday I would attend Mass in St.-Germain, where the organist, perched up on a balcony below the vault, played organ fugues full of augmented fifths and where the priests were lean, elegant, exclusive-looking. At the exit were homeless men my age kneeling on the ground, holding a sign—"*Pour vivre, merci*"—in the ineffable style of Mallarmé. I'd toss them an offering and cross the boulevard at the crosswalk like a real man, a baguette or free newspaper under my arm, hoping that Lavinia would see me pass—where was she? Where was Lavinia? I would return home without ever having found her. Back in my underwear, lazily scratching myself on the open futon sofa bed in the center of the apartment's single room, I thought of the women I would have been free to bring home. This was enough, this and knowing that I was once again a man, enough to send me to the bathroom with the usual scenes going through my head, enough to install myself on the poorly attached toilet seat, which every so often would slip over to one side and make me leap up just as, lost in thought, I was on the point of coming.

9

Considering the glass half full: finally, I was living in the center.

Topping up the glass: distracted by a series of dramatically new problems, I hadn't noticed that meanwhile Mario, Alberto, the Jewish Pope, the Teste Parlanti, Ada, my father-in-law, Federica, Porta di Roma—they had all been struck by the shrink ray. Was this what I really needed that summer? To breathe, to make some space for myself? The shrink ray struck Corrado and his poor dreams of glory as well; I'll never feel sufficiently guilty.

In my heart the stentorian voices of the past now spoke in falsetto. The chicks reproached me from their little cage: "When you gonna start a family?" "Find me a publisher . . ." "Damned Frankists . . ." Alice too seemed to have shrunk, not through any fault of her own; almost every evening, my pocket-size darling produced, from the cell phone or in phone booths on the street or via Skype at the Internet café, the voice she'd always had, the voice of my wife.

At the end of August she came to visit me for ten days, to see how I was getting along. She noticed I could keep it up for longer, but only took advantage of this fact once. Every so often I'd take the train back home, sleeping poorly in my couchette. Back in Porta di Roma, back in church, I'd once again become husband and parishioner, bat-crazy son and ungrateful brother.

10

You don't need to take drugs to be freed by them. I learned this one autumn night when finally, finally, finally, a quartet of female bourgeois bohemians contending with the generational experience of the "Friday night pill," illogically sent my way by the drug, came up to me at the end of an evening outside a bar.

We were near the Place de la Bastille, on a sidewalk crowded with foreigners. I recognized one of them from earlier that evening. She was the smallest of the four and was wearing a bizarre ensemble of short white pants reminiscent of summers in Cortina, a baggy white cambric shirt, and high-heeled yellow combat boots. The creases between her mouth and her cheeks assured her a minimum age of thirty-three.

"You!" She pointed at me. "You! You're Italian, right?"

They crowded around me. Their heads were thrown back; they blinked, whispered in each other's ears, swayed in their shoes. I had been outside, smoking with a Belgian who worked for the world glider association, but you could see that he was in a hurry, and indeed when the group approached he nodded his head and took off (laughing).

Benedetta—whom one of her friends, meanwhile, was watching with a smile traced on closed lips, caressing her forearm—was small but had a huge pair of tits who, suffocated by the fabric, seemed to say: "It's not our fault, it's the shirt." A gauzy black scarf encircled her neck. Her three friends, whom I'd never seen before, were not as striking and less pretty, their heights and thicknesses all wrong (one tall, one short, one flat-chested). Two of them swayed their hips, hands in their pockets, calmly euphoric, while the third checked her cell phone. When I confirmed I was Italian they became restless.

"You definitely have to come with us to Disquaires," said Benedetta, taking hold of my hand.

"Where?"

In English she said, "We need, er, a bodyguard . . ."

"A protector," said the tall Italian woman with black bangs, a ponytail, denim vest, pants an artificial-looking dark green color. "You have to defend us from the Italians."

"Those Italian football players!" said Benedetta in English. "It'll be impossible to lose sight of you!"

"What's your name?"

"I'm Piero . . . my name is Chewbacca," I offered.

"Chewbacca? How perfect! Nobody will bother us if we stay close to Chewbacca."

"Bodyguard!" the other short one said in English; she had even bigger tits and the Spanish *th*: "bothigarth."

"A huuuge lucky charm," said the flat one in English, a German with a harsh accent. And with this they gathered me up and made me theirs, just as Parisians gather up cast-off furniture left in front of their houses by their neighbors.

Back on the street, during our five-minute walk on the increasingly less crowded sidewalk, I let them talk, a continual "Ooh" and "Everything's okay" repeated in various languages. The bar was located on a long, narrow, straight street, untouched by the Sunday promenade crowds, an ex-garage now completely white, with iron chairs. The dance floor was a basin squared off at the bottom, reached via two short flights of stairs that began at either side of the bar and continued all the way around; the bar overlooked the dance floor, to which the bartenders turned their backs.

The women went off to dance without having told me

their names; the tallest one, the second Italian, stayed behind on the steps with me. They were playing funk music, new and old; the DJ was a good-looking Franco-Tunisian, tall, with a horsey face and straight brown hair down to his shoulders, black T-shirt with a stencil of a rainbow big rig in three-quarters view. Benedetta danced below him, all white in the white venue, showing off her yellow footwear. She must have dressed that way on purpose. The men—several big, tall North Africans, with their pale, slight Franco-French friends—were drunk and calm, doing little more than greeting each other solemnly and nodding. There were about forty of them, they all knew one another, a handful of them in the bathroom either throwing up or sniffing something, and Benedetta conspicuous in the middle of it all. The broadest-shouldered among the men went down to talk to her, submerging her with their attention.

Standing on the step, thinking (Could tonight be the night I come across Lavinia? Had the fateful moment arrived? Something told me these were the kind of guys she might like and, for all that I knew, DJ parties in garages could be in), I turned and asked the name of the woman next to me, who was almost as tall as I was.

"Clelia."

"Don't you want to dance, Clelia?"

"No."

"No?"

"No. If I danced I'd clear the floor."

"Because you're such a bad dancer?"

"Huh?"

"Are you deaf? I asked if you were a bad dancer."

"No, I'm the queen of the dance floor."

"Huh?"

"If I danced, then everyone would die, and I wouldn't wish that on anybody—they're so happy to be dancing. But even if

I wanted to dance"—she showed the palms of her hands—"I can't move away from the light, I neither *can* nor *want* to. Understand? Of course you do. *Can* and *want* are the same things. My father says so. My father is as tall as you. So why do we use two different words, then?"

"What can't you move away from?"

She sighed, continuing not to look at me, and stared out across the room. She looked like a man, like one of the countless Patti Smith clones you see walking around Paris. "If I dance, they all start to cry. It's my super . . . my super . . . power . . . and it's much, much better if I stay here with you."

"That's some responsibility." How was I supposed to talk to her?

"I cannot put a meter of distance between myself and your shirt, it's . . . something is emanating from your shirt. It's *so orange*. You're a . . . a walking sun, one of those Day-Glo night buses. Ho ho ho"—she laughed like Santa Claus—"Ho ho, Chewbacca, your clothes!"

"You like my shirt?"

"Absolutely. Absolutely. But . . . we saw you. From far away. You blinded us. It was *im*possible to resist you. But don't feel threatened." Without looking at me she delicately took my wrist and felt my pulse with her fingertips. "Don't feel threatened." Then she dropped my wrist, which returned to its place at my side, stupefied.

She sang in English: "This orange, orange . . . Mr. Chewbacca. You shine like a new penny, you reeeally do."

The orange shirt with thin black horizontal stripes was one of the purchases I'd made with the bonus from my father, the same man who had, in a recent phone call, declared that if I dressed well, I would find both myself and a real job: you find a real job by knowing the best people, and the best people know how to read body language, the language of movement and clothes. In fact, maybe these pretentious and intoxicated bourgeois bohemians were someone's daughters. According to my Catholic anticonformist prejudices, mildly lost girls such as these are always the daughters of rich and sophisticated people (the anti–middle class).

For now, however, I had no idea where to begin.

"Do you like the colors? Do you work in fashion?"

"What?" She leaned closer.

"You work in fashion!" I was hardly brilliant.

"Not always," said the big, strapping girl. "Look at the shoes on that guy with the shaved head over there."

I stretched my neck out, feeling increasingly excluded from the conversation.

"The shoes on that guy. They're a golf course. They're the most white-and-green thing I have ever seen." She ran her hands over her face in amazement. Standing on the other flight of stairs at ten o'clock from us was a man with a bottle of beer in his hand and giant green-and-white-striped sneakers.

"Why don't you ask if he'll sell them to you?"

Benedetta danced like a butterfly. She entered my field of vision. She caught my eye and blew a kiss in my direction from the palm of her hand. I went up to the bar and got myself a drink. I noticed that Clelia was looking at me. Casually, she touched her shirt and then wrapped her fingers around her neck to suggest a collar she didn't have.

I walked over to her, holding a big glass of vodka tonic.

"What?"

"Your shirt." She grabbed my bare arm; I'd rolled up the sleeves.

"What's up?"

She didn't answer, just stroked my arm.

"You want me to give you my shirt? You like it so much."

"No! No!"

She left me and slowly but inexorably flung herself down the three steps and over to the German woman (Jette, but we would introduce ourselves another time) to speak to her in her ear. Jette came over, weaving between two tall dancers with loose-fitting shirts, and said in English:

"Stop right there, you have to take care of us, not take your shirt off! You must not. Try to understand. We are lost."

She found her own words, *We are lost*, very funny and burst out laughing.

Clelia looked around her and echoed Jette's English: "We are now—lost. We, are, now, dust. Anyone? No? Dust. Anyone? No? Dust."

Jette returned to the dance floor and a languidly gazing Benedetta came toward her, caressed her cheek, and, raising herself up on the tips of her yellow boots, gave her a long kiss on the mouth, followed by some more dancing, then by another kiss, this one with tongues, I think. From that moment on I tried to drink enough not to judge those who had taken me under their wing, at least for a few hours, a few hours of nonsolitude.

And the hours did fly by; I may have even made it onto the dance floor. At the end of the night, around three o'clock, after having seen Benedetta also kiss Ana, the Spanish girl with the biggest chest, and finally even the DJ, but only as she passed him on our way out, I caught the night bus with Clelia, who got off with me at Port-Royal but then continued on foot past Boulevard du Montparnasse, where she lived with her uncle (when we were alone together, once the effect had worn off a bit, she gave me some information). They were Italians. She was born in New York and had been to school there. They had moved to Paris a few years ago.

I wobbled all the way home. The door closed behind me; I theatrically leaned back against it with all my weight and sighed. I was an enormous, hirsute Cinderella, a listless, sweaty insect. I washed my hands, kicked off my shoes, grabbed the roll of paper towels, and stretched out on the bed—which the alcohol and emotion conspired to make soft, even if it was only a seven-centimeter-high mattress over a few flimsy wooden slats, some already broken.

The next morning, expecting to be left empty-handed, I received an e-mail with the subject line *Chewbacca*. Benedetta, for all it appeared absurd and tortuous, expressed gratitude, also on behalf of her girlfriends copied on the message, for my participation in the evening:

> *dear chewbacca, in yesterday's dark and stormy night you were our beacon, our north star. tomorrow or the day after we have a social engagement. try to be free because the social engagement is once again unfortunately an evening affair and without your flashy colors we won't be able to find our way home.*

After a few drinks, I had written my e-mail address on Benedetta's arm.

A paragraph in English followed:

> *chewbacca we love you. you are a sexy giant. be our awe-inspiring bodyguard. dresscode: flashy orange shirt.*

I read it in the office, setting aside the proofs of a French translation of an Italian book on Ratzinger, pulling forward the screen on the laptop they had me using.

And so it was that after months of inertia came weeks brimming with activity: aperitifs at Barbès and Place Voltaire; dinners in overheated studio apartments covered in posters, with peeling stoves, peeling paint—the homes of women, I told myself, who slept with everyone. They took me to bars and clubs, to drink and to dance; I was introduced to friends as Chewbacca, and they in turn had their own nicknames, pet names, names they mispronounced. A good half of them were gay. They didn't talk about work, in fact they hardly talked about anything at all; they danced and smoked in the middle of their one-room apartments until they started to blather. I smoked their hash and grass, but I swore to myself I wouldn't take MDMA (responsible for the extra flashiness of my orange shirt that first night) or embrace a single homosexual. We got to know one another better; I told them things about myself. I started to call them the witches. They liked having a Catholic friend. I was attracted and repulsed simultaneously. We were having fun and messing around and I knew this was escapism. When they went out to clubs, they wore wigs in shocking colors, bobbed hairstyles somewhere between jazz age and drag queen, pink boas, loose-fitting shirts with animal patterns, platform shoes, occasionally corsets. They screamed.

Paris was now unmappable and subdividing, I was losing the overall view of numbered arrondissements in favor of individual streets and the wide-open spaces with trees in pots or benches where we smoked, and I began to save the four-digit access codes to my friends' buildings on my phone.

I'd eat dinner at Benedetta's studio in the 7th, or in the large apartment where Ana lived with five students in the Oberkampf neighborhood; they made me quiche with tomatoes and goat cheese, Ana mixed Coca-Cola and red wine, we got drunk, we smoked all night using transparent rolling papers made from cellulose, they talked about their sexual adventures and the colleagues they wanted to *do* or had done. In English their anecdotes were all about *cock, I need cock, he's some cock*. I accepted the betrayal of the unwritten rules of the Teste Parlanti—no smoking joints—deciding for myself that if, while smoking, I didn't suffer from tachycardia, it meant I was okay. If we were at her place, Benedetta's son would also take part in the evenings: a skiing teddy bear by the name of Hansel; the bear was her adopted love child with a man from Helsinki. They mailed him back and forth every three months, having decided on joint custody after splitting up. We kept him with us in our circle on the ground, on the coarse IKEA carpet, identical to the one at my house.

To fall asleep after having smoked spared me the difficult half hours of reflection that usually started with my prayers, prayers that called to mind the people I loved and those I hated, obliging me to think of them. With hashish I sank into richly seductive and wide-ranging thoughts, which at times gave rise to sudden spirals of reasoning, frictionlessly spinning higher and higher, thoughts that little by little became pure form. I fell asleep among soft masses of ideas, without thinking.

By day it was easier to establish what was happening to me, to get certain facts straight. Benedetta was thirty-four years old and didn't want children. Until two years ago she was a gallery owner's personal assistant; now she was a secretary in Renault's press office. I obtained these few bits of information with difficulty and not directly from her because she never talked about work. She kissed me close to the mouth. She talked with everyone, in English, Italian, Spanish, and German, as little as possible in French because she hated Parisians. Of the four, she was the only one older than me and I hung from her tits, figuratively speaking, which rivaled those of my sister-in-law in size.

Jette was an expert in solar energy, in Paris for a year on an internship, twenty-four; she hid her forehead and eyes behind superstraight dyed black hair, which she tended to take into her mouth and suck on. Jette had a fat woman's laugh, *Ho ho ho* (a laugh picked up by Clelia). She didn't know how to tell a story, they were always too long. She was androgynous, flat-chested, and dull. She couldn't dance to save her life. She had bad skin, three conspicuous moles, pimples, large pores. Whenever she saw me, I don't know why, she would make a big fuss and kiss me three times.

Clelia was tall, nearly a meter eighty, with broad shoulders and something imperfectly realized in her long face, her rounded chin. Her greatest asset was her beautiful, smooth

141

skin. She had a husky voice, but it wasn't as masculine as Jette's. She worked for the gallery owner that had fired Benedetta. A former ballerina, she danced with half-closed eyes and an economy of movement. Only in those moments did I think of her as a woman; otherwise she didn't interest me. She had too many complexes and she never looked me in the eye.

Worst of all was Ana, the busty Spaniard. I couldn't stand her because whenever she talked about some guy *qu'elle a niqué*, it always seemed like she'd only done it so she could tell someone. Consistently bleary-eyed, twenty-five years old, delightfully freckled lips, she was studying art history and was hoping to get an internship at the gallery where Clelia worked, and perhaps this was why she sought approval from her every time she told one of her stories. She spoke French poorly, maybe, or maybe she just preferred English for the vulgarity it added to accounts of her erotic exploits.

Every now and again, within myself, I drew a line; on the street I muttered entire sentences about them: *How can they live like this? When they gonna start a family?* I felt a need to talk to someone about them, to tell a friend what I liked and what repulsed me, and how happy I was to have found them.

My witches. A group of prostitutes straight out of *L'Éducation sentimentale*. They didn't have tuberculosis, they were healthy like every Western metropolitan bourgeois or postbourgeois with a family supporting her, but I considered them sick. To my eyes, their tuberculosis was an even subtler sickness than that infecting the lungs of those trollops of the sordid and brilliant Paris of the mid-nineteenth century: the sickness that is sterility, evolutionary suicide, rejection of the maternal vocation.

But whom could I talk to about my witches? In Lavinia's absence, the person most likely to be happy for me was my wife, and I ruled her out; in second place, my father, and I ruled him out; third—no, the third was really the first—Corrado, but out of embarrassment over our forsaken project, we were no longer in touch; in joint fourth place, kilometers away from the podium, back a stretch as vast as Siberia, a stretch of thousands and thousands of frozen versts: Ada, the Teste Parlanti, Mario, Robin, the parish priest, Mamma . . . In last place, on a little, isolated island in the Pacific full of palm trees and nude waiters, Federica, for whom any account of my autumnal divertissements would have provided a wealth of mistaken pleasure.

They hugged me, beat my head like a drum, fell down laughing—always somewhat artificially, striking a pose, but with genuine warmth. Then, alone in the bathroom, I would dedicate my visions of hot pink group scenes to them, drawing on the shocking sight of their promiscuous kissing, the irresistible details . . . one woman tickling another's neck with a fake feather . . . and then passing it over her own cheek for countless minutes . . . eyes hidden behind the teeming patina of one's own eyelids . . . soft backs and hips on couches, in bars, in apartments . . . the stupid smiles . . . those stupid bailout smiles . . .

11

The situation had not yet become clear to me. I wasn't apprised of all the facts. What I mean is that these women weren't just your average women: one of them had what I was to regard as a dark secret, and when I came to know the truth, my perception of the group as a commune of equals was set aside.

A bitterly cold, overcast evening in the historic Marais neighborhood, puffy down jackets, me at the center of the group in a duffel coat without a scarf, after a dinner of fried-onion soup at Jette's place. We'd been discussing how Parisian fags were the only people who were friendly toward other men, and thus how I, Chewb, should seriously consider taking a lover of my own sex. In Rome I was the perfect husband, which made it imperative for me to have a secret in Paris, a *drastic* second identity. Benedetta said:

"Excuse me, but you like blow jobs, right? They're a beautiful thing, right? So it follows that you'd want to suck someone off, right? I mean, you know it's a beautiful thing, so?" She didn't wait for me to confirm this before concluding: "And so of course you'd be curious to know what it feels like to have one in your mouth."

This is what it had come to in the fall of 2006: I allowed a stranger to ask me about things that, a few months earlier, I would immediately have drawn back from with a modest "I cannot fill my head with this shit." Those walks I'd taken with Robin, my fellow nut, to the shrine of Our Lady of the Miraculous Medal, had made me resolve to seek a change of scenery. But enough was enough and I had no desire to see myself kneeling in front of one of the rich fortysomethings living in the old neighborhood behind the Centre Pompidou, with their well-furnished apartments and hand-in-hand strolls.

Here I need to add some information about the neighborhood. After a wave of immigration at the end of the nineteenth century, the Marais came to be populated by a large community of Ashkenazi Jews from Eastern Europe. Now it's the center of gay life in Paris, brimming with lovers young and old, with affectionate middle-aged couples, smartly dressed men with foreheads smooth and bright, glasses with brightly colored frames, hands squeezing hands with grace, that pink, smooth-shaven skin that made me think of sodomy, bulging buttocks in tight pants, straight backs, attentiveness as they asked each other "How *are* you?" It made someone like me dizzy to see this *cowardly, womanish, and honeyed crew* file past the shop windows of bakeries, restaurants, and bookstores owned by fourth- or fifth-generation Ashkenazi Jews. Perhaps this was why, on an impulse of the moment, dispelling the image of me kneeling before a mature lover, at the words "what it feels like to have one in your mouth" I responded with my typically exaggerated brand of ambiguous compunction: "At most, *darling*, I would prefer to make an honest woman out of a nice Jewish girl."

At which Benedetta set about singing the wedding march. "Off to the synagogue we go! Find yourself a glass and I'll marry you right away!" She grabbed my wrist and drew me close to Clelia, the big, strapping girl, who had been walking behind me in her short black coat. "Forget about giving blow jobs to fags, I'll marry you right away!"

"Why a Jew?" Clelia, *the Jew*, asked me, after having taken my arm, playing the docile and chaste partner in an arranged engagement.

"Oh, better a Jew than a fag . . ." I replied. Up against it, but keeping calm, I risked the joke about homosexuals and blacks: "If you're Jewish, there's no need to tell your mother."

General laughter, fortunately, from my friends the witches, generous as always, and rising above this laughter, on my right, Clelia's *Ho ho ho*s, a laugh copied from Jette, which suddenly, however, became *her* laugh, Clelia's trademark, seeing as how a Jew could certainly never steal a way of laughing from an Aryan German. That laugh had to be a genetic or cultural treasure, had to have a story, a story involving dead great-grandparents, sweets made with almond paste, mispronounced German words, acumen, pragmatism, and other clichés on which I might endlessly improvise.

They left us behind and we, still arm in arm, languid from having drunk and smoked, chatted away. It was slightly awkward. The world is full of Jews, I thought, you have to be careful what you say; in metropolises, it's the law of large numbers.

But by now I'd committed myself with my fag joke, and so on I went:

"I dunno, who can guarantee me that you're really Jewish? You've got a shiksa's nose."

"It's not as if all Jews have big noses. You're into physiognomy, then?"

"You don't all have big noses?"

"No, we don't."

She was still Clelia, the same Clelia who fell asleep on other people's couches every time she smoked and then had to take a taxi home; but she was also Jewish.

"Well," she said, happy for the attention I was giving her, I believe, "to be honest, the nose isn't really mine."

"No? What do you mean? You stole your nose? You stole it from a Gentile?"

"No, Chewb, no, I had a nose job! *T'es bête ou quoi?* I swear I didn't steal it, I paid plenty! Don't call me a thief!"

"You got a nose job?" I burst out laughing, and without letting on what I was feeling, taking advantage of how strange and how comical some of my words sounded, I said, "You got a nose job because you didn't want anybody to know you were Jewish, *obviously* . . ."

"Exactly. Well done, Chewb," and she caressed my forearm. I felt her Jewish caress through two centimeters of material. "Ballerinas can't dance when they don't breathe properly, and I couldn't, so I had to have an operation . . ."

"Of course, for the Aryan corps de ballet of Paris."

"Exactly! And also because of three separate accidents I'd had as a kid, falling on my face while roller-skating twice, and then another time down the stairs (I was superclumsy when I was little) . . . so that in the end one of my nostrils had only thirty percent of its, I don't know how you say it, breathability, viability, whatever . . ."

"You couldn't dance without air."

"So I got a nose job."

"You eviscerated it good," I said, thinking about Ada's Tits and the Frankists, about my wife, about Mario, and then drove them all away and got back to her. "You razed it to the ground, huh?"

"Yeah, I bombarded it and this lovely little nose grew up in its place."

"You were a real dog before?"

"Huh?"

"You were ugly?"

"I had a cute boyfriend."

"This was when you still had your Jewish nose?"

"No, I admit it, the boyfriend came after the nose change."

"But before you had a great big nose? You had a Jewish nose like you see in the cartoons?"

"Uh-huh, I'll have to show you."

I was dumbfounded.

"I'll have to show you pictures."

"Oh, I thought you would have preserved the old nose."

But here Clelia, as always when she had smoked a lot, lost

her memory for a moment (or pretended to do so)—"Wait, which nose? Why?"—and afterward we changed the subject, and a bit after that we left off playing the couple arm in arm.

That walk, subsequently recalled and relived in every detail, provoked a breakdown in my imagination. The Marais was so Mitteleuropa it seemed like Prague, or Poland, with crooked, tidy alleyways, shop windows crowded with goods, restaurants displaying tubs of Eastern foods—rice wrapped in spicy leaves, pink fish-egg cream, blini . . . It was such a patently traditional neighborhood that at the onset of the late-nineteenth-century wave of immigration from the East, the Parisian Jews, assimilated generations earlier, ever since Napoleon had made them French citizens, had little patience for all that folklore, afraid that it could lead to a revival of anti-Semitism. The baker, the side curls, the dialect, the black clothes; the problem of collective character, of stereotypes, of the relationship between folklore and caricature . . . It's not surprising that after that evening I found myself reimagining the scene as something straight out of a book: the Italian and the Jew strolling along together, an interreligious couple unpopular with both communities, the eyes of the mysterious Jewish Roman New Yorker uncle aimed at my back. And in my vivid, false memory we forced our way through the crowd, the gaggles of faggots and Americans with light-colored shirts and brawny knees, of Italians with their plaid Burberry scarves, we, ancient and exemplary, an impossible love in the shtetl. I projected myself into a mythical European past, in the dangerous period between the wars, say, as in the stories of Isaac Bashevis Singer; or maybe in a story of immigrants coming ashore on Ellis Island before the First World War; or in Will Eisner's comics set in the Bronx. Oh wow! The Italian and the Jew, the Great Depression, Malamud's novels . . . I already felt like an unforgettable character in some classic five-page story.

·

We had so much in common, we naturally became friends. No, actually, not Clelia and I, but rather Clelia and the person I had been at her age. It was along this axis that our exclusive relationship took shape. She was twenty-three, one year younger than I was in 2001, when the fear of the Apocalypse, together with an immense need for love, restored me to the flock of the eternal children of Jesus. In the new century I had stopped keeping up with who the good writers were, with current music or film. I had explained to Clelia my recent aversion to culture and especially to subcultures; it'd been easy to say certain things while I wore heart-shaped glasses, impossible to be sure whether I was telling the truth, and my tirades came to seem like little more than a habit, like wearing a mustache. Clelia began to fill me in on what'd been happening in music, she dragged me along to exhibitions and openings, and when I picked her up in the evenings at the gallery where she worked, she'd take me around the show or introduce me to artists. She called me "Like a Virgin": "Hey, Like a Virgin, come here!" She wanted to seem more worldly-wise than I, and she succeeded. The story of the guy who had left her, for example: how could I know what it felt like to move from one continent to another, with her uncle, for love, and upon arriving put on weight and get tossed aside, what could I know? We spoke openly about our private lives, as it appeared everyone did in Benedetta's orbit. Clelia told me she had learned how to give blow jobs after being dropped, with the thought that there was no longer any future, she had to get someone to care for her *now*. She had "learned from Benedetta." I didn't have the courage to clear up this one doubt: she had learned from Benedetta directly, that is, in the same room? I didn't know a thing about life and I was envious of her, who at the age of twenty-three had the beginnings of a career in an art gallery, and even if she looked straight ahead as she spoke, like a tortured high-schooler, she knew how to divulge her sexual and romantic preferences, *at least she had some*, and she lived with an uncle she couldn't stand (like a Dickensian orphan). She took the stairs to the Métro with decisiveness, grasping the rusty handrail, plunging underground—a woman's decisiveness.

I didn't have the courage to ask her about any relatives who might have died around the middle of the last century, and she for her part didn't talk about it. Also because, while she did have preferences, sexual and otherwise, she didn't speak from the heart; instead she spoke ironically, as if acting or at least wanting to give that impression, as if playing an actor, and she quoted from films and songs and TV shows. Protected by her strong shoulders and upright bearing (a wooden plank of soft, inexpensive wood), she expressed herself by way of aphorisms characterized above all by their comic sense, their crookedness, and behind these she took refuge.

She gave me a lot of attention. She never had to be somewhere else; the afternoon would wear on and potential commitments would be canceled via text messages to shadowy third parties. We listened to surf rock on her iPod, with a splitter and two pairs of headphones, and that new dance music, all slutty falsettos and upbeat hi-hats. It was chic to head down Rue de Rennes after work, pick up something to eat with raisins en route, then take Rue de Seine to pick up my eviscerated-nose friend, who would recognize me through the gallery window and, without becoming flustered in the least, let me know with a nod that she was almost ready. She would come out and take my arm and, as if Flaubert were the only God reigning over the universe, we would set off together toward Odéon. We'd listen to music on our headphones in a café, and she'd explain in a loud voice who the groups were; then I'd give her a slap on the hand so she wouldn't scream so much. Then we'd go over to Benedetta's or else to Jette's, and afterward out dancing.

The day they decided to take MDMA again, about a month after the night of the orange shirt, they insisted I take part; I refused, but they still wanted me with them, they enjoyed me, even sober. Upon my arrival at Benedetta's they slipped over my head a large, suffocatingly synthetic dashiki in orange, yellow, and white, with purple stripes along its length. Two hours later I was seated in a small armchair and they were looking up at me from below, and in the course of disjointed blather about the meaning of life they would every so often caress one of my knees. The room was illuminated by a blue neon light, a meter-high stick leaned up on its end in a corner, and by a halogen lamp covered with green fabric for color, which made me sweat. I dried my forehead with the hair on my wrists and forearms. I too had had something to drink. But it was important to me to entertain them. They had explained the evening as a propitiatory rite: one of them had identified a certain überdick she wanted to possess, but the man already had a fiancée and would need to be convinced. Needless to say, to me all this seemed unreal, gingerbread houses and candy apples.

One afternoon with Clelia near the Les Halles shopping center, among the clusters of blacks and North Africans, she wanted me to buy an MP3 player so she could fill it with the latest music, and had brought her computer along. I was unaccustomed to places full of people, and at Les Halles a good percentage of these people arrived on trains from the *banlieues*.

Clelia was wearing a purple jacket made of nylon taffeta, a black T-shirt with a V-neck so deep her bra showed, and an insubstantial black scarf. The shirt was in fact a short dress that came down over her black jeans. In my capacity as the escort of a girl wearing a low-necked dress, I felt like I was in danger; they could have approached me and pestered me, made inquiries about her. I asked whether she felt like she was in danger, and following a few exchanges in which I disavowed my initial fears so as not to appear xenophobic, she came to say:

"Okay, so *these* are people who have real problems

adapting—no, seeing as how you're always asking me about Jews. These people have real problems, they really can't adapt to Paris . . . whatever *Paris* means, they come in from so far away. Just think, the Ashkenazi had the Marais, while instead these people go back and forth from where they live to here, what a nightmare. So these are the ones with problems. And sure enough, it's hard to find a Jew who will stab you in the street, because the Jews aren't suffering. *These* people are suffering."

"They stab you?"

"Sure, they stab you. They ask you for a cigarette; you don't give it to them, they stab you. But also, if you give it to them and you look at them in a way they don't find . . . appropriate."

The shopping center at Les Halles emerged from the earth like an aviary, a collection of transparent domes straight out of utopian fantasies like the Martian Renaissance (think 1980s, Schwarzenegger movies). It plunged down four stories into the center of the earth until it reached an underground railroad junction, where there was the Métro and the commuter trains that came and went from the outskirts. On the levels closer to the surface were shops with all the well-known brands. At the bottom, where everything was dirty, even the sounds of footsteps and clanking metal, anonymous stalls sold croissants, newspapers, and cell phone accessories to hurrying rush-hour commuters. Unlike Porta di Roma, which when it came to open a shopping center next to IKEA would populate it with strictly wealthy Romans, consumerists perhaps but solid people, here the grand aviary with its underground public square at the center hosted the least well-integrated groups. These beautiful black and Moroccan boys from the colonies, with their oversize hip-hop tracksuits and brash airs and the biggest and puffiest parkas in the world, were on bad terms with snobbish Parisian society, and they made that clear with the cigarette routine, which my friend proceeded to explain.

"They ask you for a cigarette and then get annoyed: 'You're

not giving it to me because I frighten you?' You can reply, 'I'm not giving it to you because I don't have one,' or even give them the cigarette, but they'll still circle around and enjoy seeing you afraid." She advised me to mind my own business and never meet their gaze, even if they spoke to me. "It's not like they stab you every time, I was just saying . . . Usually you just shit yourself and that's it, but sometimes they stab you too."

" 'You' meaning 'one' in this case."

Clelia, like many central Parisians, wasn't troubled by such contradictions, even just a few months after the quasi insurrection in the *banlieues*, the cars overturned and set alight—which ultimately, according to a law of current events derived perhaps from the internal logic of TV news schedules, had died down without ever really dying out. The problem of the Afro-French periphery's pressure on the center seemed like a matter of physics, a pure thing, provoking stress, at times fear, but not moral confusion—it was inevitable that such pressure exist. She changed the subject in the midst of my full-on anxiety attack—in my mind's eye I saw wave upon wave of the disenfranchised, throwing up barricades—starting instead to talk about *Irma la Douce*, the Billy Wilder comedy set in the open markets of Les Halles, on the ashes of which the current shopping center was born. The main characters are a prudish policeman and a prostitute. Was she saying I was the prudish policeman? Was she saying she was the prostitute?

Once inside Fnac, I calmed down. There the black people are security guards, and so their size and air of strength and importance are no longer a threat but a service. They stand like columns at the exit on each of the underground floors. Standing in front of a shelf of MP3 players, Clelia found me a nice inexpensive orange one with four gigs, placed it in my hand, and ordered me to go to the register and to wait for her for a moment if she was delayed. Before abandoning me, she promised dinner would be her treat; that way I wouldn't feel too bad about blowing a hundred euros.

I wandered through the computers and video games, my palms sweaty against the plastic package, then went down to the checkout. Twenty minutes later she still hadn't appeared. I stood there obediently, in front of the notice board advertising all the concerts, holding the golden-mustard-colored bag against my pants zipper. She reappeared after another ten minutes and with a sly air exclaimed "Ta-daaa!" She had put on green tights like the ones worn by Shirley MacLaine/Irma la Douce.

"All right," I said, "now you can hit the street."

"And you can arrest me."

"Ah, so I'd be that poor bastard?"

"Jack Lemmon is a lot skinnier. But you're sexier."

"Everyone's sexier than Jack Lemmon."

As we rode the escalators up and out of the shopping center, resurfacing among the Tunisians, Algerians, and dark-skinned blacks in the area with the Chinese restaurants and Pizza Hut, I hung back in hopes that Clelia would forget the plan to come to my place and load up my MP3 player.

"Your place?" she asked me, looking at the time on her white, sixty-gig iPod.

"Why, are you hungry?"

"A little."

"Pizza Hut?"

"Chewb," she replied, "let's eat at your place, otherwise we always spend a ton of money and then on top of that I can't go to the bathroom for days: too few vitamins, too few vegetables."

"And you said dinner was your treat, you cheapskate! If anything I should pay; we've already opened the coffers, might as well spend all the money." It was worth paying to save myself.

"The coffers? What are you talking about? Let's go to your place, we'll be more comfortable. I'll roll a joint. I don't feel like opening up my computer here in McDonald's, then they'll follow us and *brrr*," she teased, "those guys will stab us!"

For the subway we had to return to the shopping center, down several floors until we reached the bottom, a white-and-yellow-tiled square with shallow vaulted ceilings where the skein of trains tangled. Among the hundreds of people running to and fro, some stopping at the newsstand to buy chewing gum or magazines, every one more or less aware of his own destination, the will of Clelia appeared to me for the first time as a factor, as a tangible force. I reconstructed the unequivocal, glaringly real dynamic that went from her fanciful and inevitably intimate idea of buying green tights, to her decision to actually acquire them, to her entry into a lingerie store. A woman had entered a lingerie store with me in mind. On the subway we dwelled on how orange my orange MP3 player was and on the ruggedness of the plastic packaging they used for technological gadgets, all in order, I suspect, to avoid the topic of prostitutes and policemen.

A woman entered my one-room apartment, warmed by a pair of green tights, and found open before her, shamelessly, an IKEA futon-couch (a well-thumbed paperback, printed in sympathetic ink, full of sexual fantasies that included her).

My only edge here was that she wasn't beautiful. But was she so clearly not beautiful? They say half of beauty is height. On the other hand, she had small breasts, an equally flat ass, a giraffe-like shape I didn't like; my wife was much more attractive. Clelia moved well, though; her large, long hands did hold cell phone and wallet and glass with grace, and the contrast between her movements and her manly way of speaking . . . but honestly, her hands were intolerable, it was enough to focus on those to lose any desire. And she didn't have a beautiful mouth. Her lips were flat, lifeless, thick but not plump, always chapped.

In the changing room at the store she had taken off her jeans in order to show off the tights, and now, with those already looking loose on her hips, she also took off her shoes, Prussian blue ballerina flats, to sit down on the bed with her legs three-quarters pale green, placing one foot atop the other to warm them. So intimately posed there, on the bed, she brought her white Mac to her lap. With the fingers of one of her ugly hands, after having used the kitchen scissors to cut open the stubborn transparent plastic packaging, having unceremoniously tossed to the floor packaging, scissors, and shoes, she inserted the long and narrow object into the USB port with an elegant click.

I came and went from the kitchen, checking the pot I'd put on to boil, glancing out the window at the EBac display, at the sixteen Ratzingers in a row. The grave gaze of our Pope: intellectual, esteemed, feared, derided. The facile quips about the errors of his Hitler Youth, about his supposed effeminate manners, and about Georg, his handsome blond assistant. My position was as uncomfortable as Ratzinger's. We were both exposed to criticism from all sides, and perhaps in his day he had had to ward off the assaults of a woman as well, or of some other human being seduced by his pianist-theologian's Gothic charm.

And while I thought about the Pope, Clelia was infecting my little MP3 player with the languid, knowing songs of the past decade in bourgeois bohemian music.

I tried to distract myself by cooking. I took down the container of coarse salt from the high cupboard and tossed a handful in the pot. I cut the grape tomatoes directly on the plates. I had turned off the ringer on my cell phone and didn't want to check whether Alice had written to ask me to go down to the Internet café to chat or to Skype. I went back and forth from the room to the kitchen, a two-meter trip. I had already thrown the pasta in by the time Clelia put on "I'm Waiting for the Man" and it played through the computer's tiny speakers. Seated uncomfortably on my sky-blue bedspread, she started to move her legs, one awkward knee over the other, kicking them up in an unnatural manner. I went into the kitchen to strain the pasta; she interrupted the song halfway while I tapped my feet on the kitchen mat.

We ate at the folding table, very close together. Then, as she explained the recent history of rock music or what was left of it, Clelia rolled a joint, which we smoked, she on the futon, sitting and afterward lying down, I on the single bed against the wall, wrapped in its cobalt-blue cover between two cylindrical cushions. We fell asleep listening to American country; I woke up half an hour later and saw her flat on her back in the center of the futon, sleeping as if in her own home, fingers interlaced in a fist resting on her stomach, below her chest.

I lay and watched her after turning out the lights, the room illuminated by the streetlamps coming through the blinds. I didn't fall back asleep. I got up to check on the EBac display; I saw Ratzinger in the window and Clelia on my futon and I thought about the owner of the apartment, the devout stranger, and about the things that can happen in your house when you loan it to someone, which made me feel like a thief.

After ten minutes I woke her and asked, "Should I call you a cab?" (She lived less than half a kilometer away.)

"A cab? What are you talking about, Chewb? No, forget it. Let me sleep." She cracked open her eyes, squeezed with her index finger and thumb, and pulled out first one lens and then the other. She placed them in my hand, reclosing and screwing up her eyes with a grimace of pain. "Toss them for me?"

First thing next morning I looked out the window: the office was still closed.

"Clelia, I have to go to work."

She sat up. "Do you have a towel?"

How could I tell her she had to go home to take a shower? "It's really late."

"I'll lock the door behind me and bring the keys to your office. That way I won't have to stop at Uncle Leo's."

I was still at the window, struck by her abominable suggestions: Keys to the office? *Shower?* "No, you leave first."

"We're not having breakfast?"

"No, it's late."

She pulled the green tights on. "I'm hungry."

I didn't want to say it, I was already dressed and ready to go, without having taken a shower; I wouldn't under any circumstances remove my underwear while she was still there. Without replying, I went into the bathroom to wash my face.

When I returned she said, "You're not much of a host, Chewb . . ."

"You have to go, c'mon."

"Ah, okay, you think they'll fire you because you slept with me. Catholic Big Brother will fire you."

"I didn't sleep with you."

She rose with difficulty from the futon, yawned, and went to take a shower. Ten minutes later she reappeared in my white bathrobe.

"C'mon, fuck, Clelia, I have to go."

She sized me up from head to toe, leaving me scarlet with embarrassment. She had the hood up but she hadn't washed her hair. A woman in a bathrobe, Lord, you're making me stand here in a room with a woman wearing my white bathrobe (which I haven't washed for three weeks; it must be full of dried sperm). Lord, you should be more jealous of your lamb.

We looked at each other for a while, as if man to man; she was tall, with a long neck, and stood up straight; then she turned to go back to the bathroom, saying, "I'll bring you the keys tonight, we're going out anyway."

"Fine. If anyone buzzes, don't answer."

From the bathroom, her back still to me, she added resentfully, "Like a Virgin, you really have to get a new place."

12

A few days later, out of breath, having climbed up Rue Notre-Dame-de-Lorette in the Pigalle neighborhood, I passed through the street door of a large early-twentieth-century apartment building. Preceding me was Clelia's uncle, Leo, who made his living renting out the apartments he owned. The day before, he had called to confirm my interest and set up an appointment for Saturday afternoon. Beyond the street door, on the left before the gravel courtyard with potted plants, Leo stopped to unlock a four-panel glazed door.

"It's six flights of stairs. You see how thin I am, thanks to stairs?" In midflight he suddenly turned, his eyes wide, his broad forehead shining. "What an idea, eh? They kept the city this way, without elevators. Now they have a city of people with no circulation problems—not the city, and not the people's veins. Oof."

Leo the Jew was a short man, about one meter seventy, with a small frame, unlike Clelia, and furnished with a lovely Jewish nose, squashed at the tip, as if not permitted to exceed a prescribed length. Above the nose a pair of heavy-framed glasses, light brown and semitransparent, teardrop-shaped, almost as tall as they were wide; below an almost imperceptible double chin.

When we got to the top, we were both out of breath. The stairwell was topped by a glass cupola, slightly obscured with limescale, capturing what little light was left of the sunset. Green wallpaper, carpet runner of a darker green, golden handrails, and atop it all the glass dome.

With the key in the lock of the half-open door, he said, "I don't know what state we'll find it in, heh-heh . . . Just kidding! I came by last week."

The apartment didn't smell stuffy. It had parquet floors and white walls; a large bedroom, a living room, a bathroom that was long and narrow, just like the kitchen beside it. The right-hand wall of the hallway was convex, following the oval of the stairwell; in the kitchen, a high little window gave onto the same stairwell and received light from the glass dome. Molded ceilings, and a windowless bathroom with bathtub. A remarkable apartment, filled with dark old furniture and select IKEA reinforcements, white shelves and plastic chests of drawers. It even had a terrace, nothing more than a deep cornice with a railing, and as I stood there Leo pointed out on the right, standing modestly among the rooftops, the dome of Montmartre's Sacré-Cœur Basilica.

"Look, I just want to keep this place alive, keep it from rotting. Now and then it's empty because it's big like the Bastille place, but people like the Bastille neighborhood better, there're more stores, more bars, it's not so hilly. And I tend to rent to friends of friends. But Pigalle's not so bad, you know? It's just that not everybody is up for living around the corner from the strip clubs." He sought my gaze. "But it's gentrifying, I can assure you. The strippers' days are numbered. Go see 'em before they disappear."

He was talking to me as if I were looking to buy. In order not to break the rhythm, I replied, "Right away."

"I rent it for fifteen hundred euros, no broker fees. Usually two people are happy here, but it's also worked for three—this is a sofa bed." He indicated the red sofa facing the TV, in the living room.

I don't know whether I was nourishing any particular hopes, or whether I had gone there out of politeness or to put my renewed sense of adventure to the test, but on hearing "fifteen hundred" I sadly went back to thinking about the EBac display windows and the short trips between home and work I would be making between then and Christmas. Leo, however, hadn't finished:

"It's the apartment I expect the least from, even though the building's high-class. The neighborhood's not as gentrified as I'd like yet. It's getting there, though, so better to keep the apartment alive. You already see a few *bobos* around, the last few years, couples. No fees, fifteen hundred. Did I already say that? I have my own private circle, for a few of the apartments. With the others I do long-term rentals. How are you set for money? You came for work, right? How long are you here?"

"I don't think I can manage it, it's too big. It's beautiful, though, thank you . . ."

His bald dome was dominated by his forehead, which extended back into an ample tonsure anchored by two thick white sideburns. His head was covered with freckles, spots, and moles, light brown and pinkish stains. Protected by the sideburn as if by a trench, a majestic, pale, waxen ear dripped into a great hanging lobe. The great ears of a great Jew: the listening people, *Shema, Yisrael, with you I shall do great things* . . . Perhaps this was why, because he had listened to me with special ears, he interrupted me, waving his hands in the middle of the living room, and proposed an incredible price: six hundred euros a month in cash. He said it with the same docility with which, in my fantasies, women abandoned their reserve and allowed themselves to be touched. That evening with Alice, at the Internet café, I bragged about it to the point of forgetting how guilty I had felt about the irresponsible, decidedly frivolous step of giving up the free studio apartment and spending money for the pure pleasure of living in a less sleepy neighborhood and getting to know this family of Jews. The Teste Parlanti clamored in my head, "When you gonna start a family?" I had a little more than two months left in Paris with Éditions du Bac and the adventurous part of me wanted to play the bon vivant and make this move. I sketched out a plan of free dinners at the girls' places and hurriedly calculated from the receipts kept in my notebook that I still had more than five hundred euros from my father, therefore three thousand euros in total. I told myself: Just go out in this final blaze of glory and by Christmas you'll see you've been reborn. You'll find a good job—a job that will do you good, that you'll do well, because if you're doing well, you function better; you'll fuck your wife because the girls have restored you to the world by dint of dancing and wigs, you needed it so bad, and now every morning you wake up and the dashboard lights are saying "All systems go, *functioning* . . ."

"Listen, Leo," I'd blurted out when I heard the price, "I accept, I don't know how to thank you," and I'd shaken his hand.

"You've got to do a little good every once in a while, eh?" he replied. "Otherwise it's just nonstop debauchery every night . . . ha–ha, I don't mean that literally . . . Buy me a drink downstairs?"

I secretly moved what little I had, three differently sized suitcases and two backpacks, late one evening, an hour after Robin had left the office; with difficulty I dragged my things up toward the summit of Boulevard St.-Michel, leaving behind the Mona Lisa smile of Pope Ratzinger in sixteen copies. I fell asleep late, lost in thought over parties with my witches and moral dilemmas. The next day I explained to Robin, to the others, and to the Pope in the window that I was letting their apartment go.

Robin asked, "And how are you handling the rent? We thought you were in a difficult situation, that's why we . . . hosted you at EBac. You've put us in a difficult position."

The question annoyed me, but I managed not to get too worked up. Neither I nor the wedding ring on my finger, both so exposed between the front windows and the desk. "Look, I'm not paying them either," I lied, "and seeing as how I'm in Paris, I wanted to get around a bit."

Robin said to me, "Don't you think it would be better to return to Rome? Pardon me for interfering, but seeing you're here alone, maybe you haven't been able to discuss the decision *avec personne*."

"No, yes, I've spoken about it with Alice . . . Thank you, but let's honor the contract, then at Christmas we'll decide. I'm having a really nice experience here."

"Certainly. But have you discussed your future with Mario?"

Finally, he had dared to ask me about him and it gave me a great deal of satisfaction. Sometimes my conspiracy theories weren't entirely without foundation.

"My future? Yes," I lied again, "I'd say so. But we agreed that this stage should be seen through to the end."

"Are you sure?" If he was in contact with Mario, he knew I was lying.

"I'm sure."

"And you live alone, in the Barbès neighborhood?"

"Yeah, yes."

"The place belongs to friends of yours?"

"Yes."

"*Et bien* . . . You're a lucky man, eh?"

"Yeah, it's incredible. 'Knock, and the door shall be opened unto you.'"

"What does your wife think?"

"She's in seventh heaven. She likes the area."

"Ah, so she'll be moving in for the winter as well?"

"Looks like it," I lied again.

After work I felt a need for something to counteract Robin's diffident defeatism, so I called my father: "I found a beautiful apartment just south of Pigalle." I added that I was spending time with *notable people*. Who else could I tell this to? I didn't have any friends who were interested in beautiful apartments or notable people. My father was so happy, he got on my nerves.

"I told you so. Well done. You got married so early, what a relief! . . ."

By chance I ran into Leo again late one afternoon in Rue Vauvin, around the corner from the office, in line at the bakery. We started chatting (I was farther back in line; he lost his turn in order to keep me company), and at the register he paid for my pistachio *macaron* as well as his flan. We went out onto the sidewalk to devour our sweets and in the course of an hour, seized as I was by a sudden sense of familiarity, perhaps owing to how the Jew was alone and wandering the streets, I told him about myself. Touched in turn, he immediately responded like a good friend:

"No way, things can't be this perfect, you're hiding something from me."

"And you're not hiding anything from me? C'mon, tell me you've got something going on with Clelia . . ."

"Ouch, man!" he said in English. "Do you know each other well?"

"Eh, sort of."

"You're kidding, right? You didn't think that because of the way she talked about me, right?" He spoke again in English: "Gosh, this is creepy."

We met in Rue Vauvin after sunset on other occasions as well. I went to the area specifically to look for him—and I always found him, because he was a bachelor and a creature of habit. He'd be sitting in the little square or on the street that cut across the corner of the park, or at the intersection with Boulevard Raspail, and he was always dressed the same way, comfortable pants, untucked dark shirt, and a heavy light-colored jacket. An ascetic outfit, always ironed by the maid. And he wore immaculately white athletic shoes, which he obviously cleaned or had cleaned.

He was the owner of five apartments: in addition to the one between Port-Royal and Montparnasse, where he lived, and mine, he had two between the university and the Jardin des Plantes, just south of Place d'Italie, and one on Place de la Bastille. Based on what Clelia had told me, Uncle Leo was (for everyone but her) such an adorable person that at his parents' deaths (tumor '91, heart attack '94) he had been adopted by a rich Sephardic financier twenty years his senior, his former office head and bosom friend, a Parisian transplanted to America toward the end of his career; when the man—a whoremongering bachelor without kids—died, he left Leo the apartments.

He was approaching fifty and up to a certain point he must have hoped to become an intellectual. Like the remains of an old, never-completed city planning scheme, he lectured a few hours every week on American literature at the Sorbonne. Over the years he had also offered courses on Leopardi and Montale, translated from the Italian and from the English, but for some reason he had failed to become a fully fledged adult, and the apartment houses financed a lifestyle without rhyme or reason. To the question of whether Leo had a woman, Clelia shot back:

"That's the problem. Let's just say, there's more than one."

And, unusually for me, given how much I made Benedetta and the others tell me, this time I let the matter drop. My imagination was sufficiently stimulated by the improbable pair, Leo and Clelia, both come to live in Paris, she with the nose job and a guy just waiting for the chance to leave her, Leo with his mysterious women I didn't want to know about, a series of pretend jobs, and his apartments.

I let myself go in his company, which turned out to consist of a continuous walk-cum-conversation about faith, love, and moral life, a monotonous pilgrimage among his houses. It so happened that I started taking Monday afternoons off to accompany him on his tenant visits; we'd exhaust ourselves in monologues as long as the boulevards, in digressions like winding alleys, punctuated only by the need to pay up at a café, a bakery, a crepe cart. Approaching the apartments, we'd only stop talking once we reached the door, to hear how things were going (his customers understood immediately that he was an odd guy, overzealous; he'd show up without an appointment and more often than not they'd tell him, "The place is in great shape, if we have any problems we'll call you"). On the street once more, we'd start up again between a flan, a *macaron*, giant cups of coffee, idle dialogues on faith along the western palisade of the Jardin du Luxembourg, which was sinister and melancholy at sunset.

I was lumbering and hunched and he was small and quick, two well-matched characters. He the devil's advocate, I the impassioned young knight of faith:

"An intelligent guy like you needs a woman at his level. Who are you seeing?"

"Me? My wife."

"But your wife is in Rome. So you don't always go out with her."

"I'm going to go back to Rome."

"We don't know if you'll go back. You just rented an apartment . . ."

He might buzz my intercom midmorning to say:

"Rosenzweil, come on down! I'm buying you breakfast!"

What was he doing in my neighborhood? Had he spent the night in a strip club? Or had he come just for me? From Port-Royal to Pigalle just for a coffee? Were we so alone? As far as the nickname is concerned, it was one of the two he used for me, based on my obsession with the Jews, which Leo had picked up on even if not quite in its precise terms. He called me Frank or Rosenzweil. The former came from the Bernard Malamud novel *The Assistant*, in which an Italian character named Frank first steals from a Jewish shop, then gets himself a job, then converts (when he said "Frank," I thought of Jacob Frank and got a shock). The latter was a distortion of Rosenzweig, a Jewish philosopher; when he first called me Rosenzweig I misunderstood and mangled it, so after that the *l* stuck. (I called him Rabbi in return.)

In fact, Leo accused me of wanting to become Jewish. He was even convinced my passion for the Jews depended on the fact that, as a Catholic, I had the constant sensation of not de-serving God's love.

"*Good Father,*" he would begin in falsetto, mocking my religion, "*I am your humble son. I am unworthy of you but love you so much* . . . Who wants to have a relationship like that with a father? In terror of ending up punished!"

"I'm not afraid of punishment."

"No? Are you faithful to your wife, Frank?"

"Yes."

"Then you're afraid of punishment."

He constantly said I had run away from Alice. I counter-attacked:

"Look at your own life: what light do you offer to the world, what have you accomplished?"

And Leo: "Rosenzweil, the problem is, you mix up the higher needs—salvation, the contemplation of God—with the lower needs—the low and mundane needs of morality, of orga-nization. It's your Church's fault. It confuses you. Rosenzweil: contemplation of the stars and cleanliness of the hands and feet. It's a mess."

Me: "You made a mistake not getting married, Rabbi."

I kept coming back to this, and Leo:

"You're such a little shit . . . What do you have to teach me, going through life gritting your teeth?"

" 'Eunuchs for the Kingdom of Heaven's sake' . . ."

"Exactly, eunuchs for the Kingdom of Heaven's sake. Jesus was crazy."

"No, Leo, *you're* the crazy one, and you need a wife. You spend too much time alone and with Rosenzweil, your imagi-nary friend. Leo! Leo! I don't exist, Leo!"

"So this is how you defend your arguments, huh?" He made fun of me that time. "Look me in the face, Rosenzweil. You follow a religion based on a crazy man. This is why you're crazy, Rosenzweil. You're crazy, you're stressed, you're bitter, you're nasty, you're sad. It shows. Christ, you're thirty years old! You get on my nerves, you're totally spineless . . ." (And here he prodded me with a long, cold finger.) "Why do you spend all this time talking to me? Doesn't it piss you off?"

As the days grew shorter, he started to invite me to his house, a breathtaking apartment on the fifth floor, a high-ceilinged palace that, seen from the sidewalk, seemed all giant, spotless windows, through which shone triumphantly, like straight out of a magazine, his bookshelves and a white ceiling crossed by wooden beams. One hundred and fifty square meters, half given over to the living room; Clelia's room, which he never showed me; and his room, with an enormous bed, preceded by an antechamber-cum-study. A simple, uncluttered place, a place of books, embellished with a small series of Italian collectibles from the fifties. In the living room he had a Marshall Plan poster ("American help, helping us help ourselves"), one advertising the Rinascente department store in Milan's Piazza del Duomo, surrealist-style, and some smaller ones: Pirelli Tires, the digestif Antonetto (a man with white hand on black stomach, a laughing red face revealing white teeth), the poster for a Renato Rascel film. Among the sofas, a red Ico Parisi "egg" chair stood out. In the study there was a chestnut display cabinet containing a number of examples of Italian industrial design: a metal-and-porcelain Bialetti stovetop espresso maker patterned with chunky violet leaves; an electric coffee grinder; a Cynar wall clock (stopped). Atop the small filing cabinet beside the desk sat a green Olivetti Lettera 22 typewriter.

With Leo I was different than with the witches, I was more Catholic than ever; it was part of our rules of engagement (we were alone and, in order to be sure of continuing thick as thieves, like insecure teenagers we kept going back to the same obsessions, typically wives or Judaism). I dismissed his lovely collection: "You've got too much time and money to burn."

"Oh, man, give me a break," he said in English. "You know what? I'm a serious guy. I've made decisions in my life, okay? From up on your ignorant pedestal you tell me I'm just a big kid and you hurt me when you say that, but I've chosen this life, all right? I certainly didn't do what you did, running away from your wife without admitting it."

"I haven't run away from my wife."

"I've had my ideas clear from the beginning. I'm one of the few Jews without a shred of a sense of guilt—take note. Just look." He showed me his bald head. "It was, what, the middle of the seventies? In seventy-six I passed my school-leaving exams and I didn't like Italy anymore. After the oil crisis it was a bad scene, believe me, nasty. Bombs, Frank, bombs. And the Yom Kippur War? That definitely scared us. Italy is too far south to feel safe. I told my parents I was moving to America. I was eighteen! I told them, 'We've got a second holocaust on our hands.' I convinced them to send me to New York City and I went to Columbia. So if I want to collect a few little things from a glorious period in our country's history because I'm a nostalgic guy born in the fifties—a privilege you'll never have, you crazy, good-for-nothing millenarian—I don't see why it should be any concern of yours."

Perversely, I asked him whether he made his women sit in the designer armchair and whether he dressed them in the red Pirelli coveralls worn by two wooden mannequins in the big old display cabinet in the antechamber, austerely elegant workers' uniforms with black collars.

"You're an imbecile, it pisses you off that people enjoy themselves and take pleasure in things."

"Oh, sorry, I was talking about people, not things."

"Fine, be a jerk. In my house. Pathetic." He wiped his forehead with a faintly pink white handkerchief. "What was I telling you? Right, some of our relatives had died in the war, obviously. I grew up in the sixties and as soon as I got to high school I found myself in these awful, really awful seventies, and what was there in between? The economic miracle and Gino Paoli—believe me, that's about it. Now, do you know

171

why I can't stand you? Because you're my mother. You're here in my house, drinking my tea, my rum, my purified water, and you ask your prurient little questions, *Who wears the little fifties nightie?* My lovers! My lovers! Idiot. My mother, in twenty-five years of one disgusting thing after another, what does she do? She breaks my balls about everything, about how I must behave and how I must not take this or that girl to bed, how I have to make a commitment and how I have to take advantage of being alive and having all the luck when I could be dead. Now, I kind of did think it was the end of the world, with all those dead Jews and my relatives, and then again with things going to shit, Vietnam on one side and terrorists in Europe, I thought the period in between was some kind of Indian summer, the last days of joy before the catastrophe. And at a certain point, while I was finishing school, I realized that my mother, *even at the end of the world*, would have insisted on maximum self-control and discipline. Understand? Just standing idly by, waiting for the world to end, and to me that seemed absurd, especially considering she'd been lucky and hadn't died in the war, they saved her . . . So that's why I can't stand you, Frank, because you're my mother. As soon as God does you a favor you have to renounce everything and spend your life, your shitty life, thanking God on your knees."

"And the rest of the family, did they survive?" I asked, hoping I didn't have a morbid expression on my face.

But the story of his mother's family had a happy ending, without any women dragged out by their heels, clinging to the doorjamb. Leo's mother, the young Miss Elvira Pacifici, was born in 1934 in Milan to a family with Roman origins that had gone up north a few generations earlier. Her father was an accountant in a textile factory. In Milan during the war they began to carry out evacuations, fearing bombardments: many Milanese families went to stay in the country while the men continued to travel back and forth for work. Mr. Pacifici heard from a friend in the passport office about a massacre of Jews near Lake Maggiore. He gathered up his wife and three children and brought them to the Swiss border, where the authorities sent them back. Returning to the Milanese countryside, they asked a town councilman for help, an honest, middle-aged man, a husband and father. (Leo wouldn't tell me whether he was Catholic, Communist, or Fascist. "This guy was proclaimed 'Righteous Among the Nations' by Israel, you know. With certain people you don't go looking for who they pray to; you might not think so but there's a Good that has nothing to do with Jesus." "No, not nothing to do." "Right, you big imbecile, because you know so much about life? And don't interrupt me.") The councilman welcomed Mrs. Pacifici, Leo's grandmother, into his office, opened a desk drawer, and did something straight out of the movies, placing on the table a number of blank identity cards ready to be filled out. And what he said was straight out of the movies too: "Now I'm going to go out for a moment, and when I return maybe I won't find these documents here anymore." After reentering the office to find the desk empty, he gave Mrs. Pacifici the address of a stamp maker who could turn them into Sicilians. Then he suggested they move to a town even farther from Milan, San Giorgio su Legnano, where the town clerk was a friend of his. They found him there, and he found them lodging as Sicilian war refugees, in an elementary school. They changed their names. They had a classroom all to themselves, fitted out with beds, and received ration cards for food. The councilman's friend was also kind enough to bring them leftovers from the cafeteria of a sewing-machine factory, whose workers had been evacuated to the same school. For religious services a priest hosted them in the parish church where, in a little hidden room, they said their prayers, then left as if they had been at Mass. They spent more than a year there, the children attending classes in the school where they slept; at war's end they returned to live in Milan and then in Rome, in the 1950s, rejoining the rest of the Roman branch of the family.

"So then, they save you and what do you do? Do you go right back to slaving away, to following the Commandments? Now, what I'm saying is, for a couple of rounds, let the *popolo eletto* get some rest."

"And you see them as the *popolo eletto*, the chosen people?"

He attempted a play on words with *eletto*/elections/electoral fraud/Bush, but became flustered and botched the timing. I laughed anyway because the idea appealed to me: the children of God, chosen in a rigged election. However, in the gratuitous warmth of a heated home on one of the first chilly days in an inhospitable city, for love of debate, I objected:

"You're so slippery, Leo. You only consider them the chosen people when you feel like it, when it sounds good."

"What are you talking about? You're crazy."

We squabbled over why he had used the expression *popolo eletto*. He maintained that I had been the first one to use the term and that he had reused it to please me, then I had held it against him.

"You put things in my mouth and then we argue and I end up sweating like a pig." He rolled up his sleeves, brought his slim, hairy wrist to his forehead, then rose and said, "Okay, let me go wash my face."

As he moved away I looked at him from behind. He had a strange walk, placing one foot after the other in a straight line, a bit like models do, and long legs but no rear end, and what little he had disappeared under the well-ironed shirt he always wore untucked. His narrow shoulders and the nimbleness of his movements filled me with pity. Not pity but a sense of fear, fear that Leo wasn't in a safe place. I tried to banish the sensation, which had crept down to my legs because of the drink, and to understand what I was thinking.

The living room was silent and empty; there was only me and the dim light, the 1950s posters, the books; the long glass wall overlooking the narrow street that the entrance was on (in the building opposite an elderly couple in good trim was setting up for a six-person dinner party). Even the house seemed to be in danger—the living room wasn't in good hands—and I finally realized that the problem was me. As soon as I began to see myself as part of the scene—a stranger frequenting this house and this Jew without having come clean about who he is and what he thinks and what kind of people he frequented in his own country—I found myself sinister and untrustworthy: what was I doing in Leo's house cataloging pieces of information as if I had to pass them on to someone, staring at women's coveralls and prints on the walls, memorizing his clothing and his habits?

He returned from the bathroom refreshed, his forehead no longer shiny, with a plate of coconut pastries in his hand ("Do you like these? I love 'em"). He took his place on the couch; then, as one, we reached our hands toward the golden pile.

In another age, I asked myself with a sense of melodrama, almost wanting to find myself sinister and pitiless, would I have reported the family's fake passports? I don't know, because I became an adult at the end of the Cold War and wouldn't know whom to sell the information to. But I knew in what spirit I typically looked upon Leo's bald head and drooping ears, listened to his arguments, and said to myself, "This is 'weak thought'! What Leo proposes is the famous *pensiero debole* that Mario rants on about! Weak thought, beautifully expressed by a Jewish intellectual! The same weak thought as Wojtyła's friends! He is Judaizing me to the core, like Lessing did to Mendelssohn! I'm the young Karol in Warsaw, surrounded by Frankist poets!" Just like in the racist cartoons, in my eyes Leo's features were wicked and grotesque, and in the moments when my pleasure in his company was impossible to hide I also felt guilty toward Mario, who had dedicated his life to flushing out the forces of evil; I was not only running away, refusing to fight alongside him, but had ended up in the arms of our evasive enemy, the cunning Jew from the racist cartoons, and I was entering into relations with him. Relations that I was hiding from and lying about to my wife, to whom I was bound by the sacrament of marriage. I felt like the ultimate conspirator, the one who conspired against everyone, who conspired because this is how his mind was made. It was just that for someone with such a predisposition for conspiracy, I had chosen the wrong field; I should have deployed my talent for intrigue and disguise in a more suitable context, instead of mawkishly devoting myself to these holocausts in a teacup.

13

Not only did he not know what I thought of Jews, but he was also unaware of the fact that his little niece, of whom he had said "She hardly ever sleeps here anymore, I'm so down I'm thinking about going back to New York," spent consecutive nights at my place. There were twelve Métro stops between Pigalle and Montparnasse, but ever since that first week she would slip away to my place for dinner and stay there. Around five or six in the afternoon, after work, I would meet her uncle; then I'd return home, a head full of thoughts, to eat and smoke with Clelia. I had never seen them together, uncle and niece, and as far as Leo knew we were more acquaintances than friends.

Much more than what I was doing to Leo, it was what I was doing to Alice I felt guilty about. Seeing as how I always had the Jewess at home with me, I told my wife I couldn't go down to the new Internet café too often because the neighborhood was dangerous: dealers, strip clubs, unspecified bogeymen; I explained the thing about the cigarettes and the knifings. She told me I shouldn't worry about it: if I kept my eyes to the ground and continued on my way, nobody would bother me.

14

In the evenings, Clelia would read me passages from a book about freaks in the Village in the 1970s: theatrical productions about Siamese triplets "attached at the asshole," invalid children, papier-mâché phalluses, transvestites kicked down the stairs. She told me about the not-so-dangerous part of New York where she'd grown up, the Upper West Side; about Hebrew school. At the age of sixteen she'd bought her first records on St. Mark's Place, but she'd wanted to become a dancer and hadn't ever allowed herself any authentic degeneracy.

After our fourth dinner together, she made use of her trick: she smoked, fell asleep, spent the night on the living room sofa. I shut myself up in the bedroom. Another evening she arrived with a little bag containing contact lens solution and a case.

"The other day I tossed out fifteen euros' worth of new monthly lenses, it doesn't make sense. I threw them on the ground; I was so far gone, I thought they were daily ones. I'm leaving this here just to be safe . . . Why don't you use contact lenses? You're better-looking without glasses."

After the contact lens solution she left a change of underwear in a kitchen drawer. For every similar addition she had an excuse, making an argument from the point of view of convenience. Now I had two vases with flowers in my home, in the kitchen and in the living room; Clelia cooked dishes for us with zucchini or potatoes. She brought over a few DVDs and mascara and an eye pencil, so she could make herself presentable for work.

"I have this problem, I always fall asleep, I know I'm invading your house . . . Sorry."

"I can't kick you out. It's your house. You buy the pot."

The pot and the fresh vegetables. She shopped in the outdoor markets she knew and her corallo beans with tomatoes and hot peppers were a miracle, or better, a form of progress. During those months in the studio apartment I had constant diarrhea. No one teaches men how to live alone; the problem of the adult male who lives alone has been underestimated, and in hindsight I would say that my inflamed colon could have been a factor in my relationship with Clelia. And this improvement in health protected me against the attacks of colitis I would have had due to tension those three or four nights a week in which my numb hands fumbled through the opening of the sofa bed, under the supervision of the placid, half-closed eyes of the Jewish girl, who'd throw herself down, laughing, hair loose (loose like a witch), pulling out her contact lenses and placing them in my hand; I'd head to the bathroom, squirt solution over them, return them at random to one of the two round compartments of their white case.

These, then, would constitute the so-called facts, but you can't do a thing with bare facts. What counts are the discussions accompanying the facts that determine what to illuminate and where to locate the shadows. If I'd spoken with the Teste Parlanti, these facts would have had a certain value, and instead I spoke with Leo, who for instance once lectured me about freedom, including the freedom of a Christian to listen to the imperatives of nature. A line of reasoning perfectly suited to my circumstances, about which Leo remained in the dark, and about which he would not be happy.

To return to the scene at his place, in the living room, with the coconut cookies (he was a creature of habit), Leo seated on the edge of the white couch (dear Uncle Leo always left the leather armchair for me). In the course of our snack we had already touched on the rational definition of Judaism as philosophy ("A concern with right conduct"—Lionel Trilling), the true merits of Catholicism, according to Leo, with respect to the Protestant Reformation ("The providential hypocrisy that allows one to blindly believe while in a group and then sin in private: if you start with the Catholic Church, you arrive at Boccaccio; with Luther you arrive at Bergman"), and the minefield of my heartfelt objections: "But I *promised*, I gave my *word*. I made a promise to God! I made a promise to my wife! Doesn't giving one's word count for anything?"

Moving beyond my problems of fidelity, we arrived then at the theory of his friend the priest—a big deal who had been at the last conclave—for whom the Church could choose between two conceptions of nature and sex, that of Saint Augustine and that of Saint Thomas; so far Saint Augustine's has always won out, but if one were to recoup the latter, "aberrant cases of sexual repression like yours could easily be sorted out." He continued:

"For Augustine, Christ has redeemed you, but we carry the consequences of sin in our flesh: moral and sexual confusion, our attachment to creatures. You need grace at every moment, just so the closed wound won't reopen. You Christians are saved from the start but every day you fall back into sin.

"For Thomas there are two orders, natural and supernatural. Between the two stands human nature, which is nature open to the supernatural. He doesn't have the supernatural forced upon him, he can freely choose. Adam says no, Maria says yes, everyone is free. Nature is an end unto itself, and Thomas says: When you want to, you can raise yourself above nature; when you don't want to, you don't raise yourself and let nature function as it knows how, with its rules. You can raise yourself above nature within the hour, tomorrow, when you want. Thomas is less fearful than Augustine. Nature is not an infernal maelstrom, it's natural. You eat, desire, sleep: nature. You can stay up all night appealing to Jesus, but you can also sleep. You don't always have to remain awake. You don't always have to watch over yourself. It's natural to think about the supernatural, you don't always have to make such an effort.

"For Augustine, grace is given to Adam at creation, grace is intrinsic to man's nature. For Thomas, on the contrary, man's nature can open itself up to grace. It's different. If you're in Pigalle at night with a fortune on you, you try to avoid walking down alleys, you don't want to get it taken off you. For Thomas, on the contrary, grace is like having the money in the bank, and you only have it when you go to the bank. God cannot oblige you to accept grace, because grace is love and only goes where it is requested.

"Let's say that today you don't want to receive grace. You're not up to feeling loved by God, let's say. You want to get yourself a nice blow job. You want to have sex with the camera rolling. You want to betray a friend. That's nature. You betray a friend, find yourself a blow job, and seek out a woman because this is your nature. That doesn't mean that tomorrow, reopening yourself to the supernatural, you can't once again ask for grace and have grace come to you. Besides, one can hardly be a saint every day, every minute. With Augustine, on the other hand, you've got grace, you have to fight to always measure up to grace. Let's say that grace is a tuxedo. It's hard to jack off in a tux, right? It comes much more naturally in underwear. Now, for Thomas, someone jacks off in his underwear; then he becomes a little disgusted at having spent the whole day in his underwear, and that evening he goes to the opera and wears a tux. For Augustine, you're always in your tuxedo, and you're incredibly stressed out by the fact of never taking off your incredibly odious, incredibly starched tuxedo."

This two-bit theologian didn't know that a part of me was totally in love with Clelia, my wife and him be damned, and—I say it in Rosenzweil's terms, not mine—wanted to fuck her. Judaized to the core by Leo, I employed weak thought in the guise of tolerant Christianity in contributing, one night with Clelia, to the staging of a romantic scene perfectly calibrated to end up in bed—a rich and detailed scene, one hundred percent true, in which, almost as if I were more Rosenzweil than Rosini, I displayed ease and naturalness and savored every instant and every single thing: the wait at the station for the last Métro; the tepid metallic wind that rose from the tunnels at the passage of the penultimate train; the throng that dispersed; the delicate sleep of the homeless, for whom autumn means an ambush of sudden cold that obliges them to hide underground in sleeping bags, confined to the smell of piss near the benches, in the worn hoods of once fashionable down jackets; the advertising from the big department stores that stood out in oversize rectangles along the inclined walls behind and above the seats; our silence as we exhaled the remains of the preceding laughter . . . This laughter, I told myself, was really, truly natural, natural laughter, natural sociability and desire for contact that toppled me into her at every new outburst of hilarity; I slapped her gloved hand to scold her, she could tell that I was changed and she pressed against me.

We slipped onto the train, rushed to sit; I threw myself against her, drunk on our natural laughter and her natural odor that every so often reached my nose, the smell of chocolate and underclothes and a studio apartment with kitchenette (Jette's, where we had just been). I tried to think: if in the next hour I abandon myself to nature, if, that is, I do not open myself to the supernatural for one hour, then, after that, could I return to snuggle in the Virgin Mary's embrace, or would I lose the desire for a longer time? Does sin lead us too far from God? For Augustine, on a scale of one to ten, your sin may measure one, but you'll have strayed ten degrees from God. For Aquinas, things are more equitable; you sin one, you stray one.

A few meters away from us a smelly homeless man spoke French in a polished, staccato manner, without saliva. A black jacket, small frame, smooth sagging cheeks, an upright bearing but insubstantial shoulders. He was conversing with a young man in a Windbreaker with his back to me who swayed composedly the entire trip. Farther away, a group of university students with light cotton scarves, souls of reinforced concrete, and bangs hanging over their eyes occupied two sets of four seats and spoke in unpleasant voices about a film. I was undoubtedly in Paris, a bit euphoric at the thought of abandoning myself to nature for an hour. At the other end of the car, behind us, two older couples spoke loudly, the women in beige raincoats, the husbands in unbuttoned jackets—there was something sensual, promiscuous, in the presence of people my parents' age on public transportation.

Outside the Métro, the steps on the escalator unmoving beneath the yellow light, then Rue Notre-Dame-de-Lorette, uphill, with the damp pavement reflecting the lights, the artificially natural landscape of every city. I laughed at everything she said; the poor girl was already at the stage where she would have fallen asleep on the floor or on the couch, but instead she still had six flights of stairs up to my—to our—apartment, and at the top she seemed revived: she slipped the key from the pocket of my coat and inserted it decisively in the keyhole surrounded by light-colored scratches in the wooden door. She penetrated the darkness without turning on the lights, her short, swamp-green jacket above slim dancer's legs, the calves a bit thickened in the green tights. I was free until 2:05 in the morning, an hour, let's say an hour for nature, then I would once again dedicate myself to the supernatural. (Splitting up meant money, money, money, discussions about money in air-conditioned lawyers' rooms between two people suddenly strangers.) She was dressed in brown, both her skirt and the close-fitting top she wore over her broad and not very prominent chest, under a black mohair sweater. When I returned to the living room and saw her lying down, I fell in love with her little feet, so out of proportion to the long body wrapped in tights. She had peeled a red apple as she lay, her head against a pillow; four slices were in her hand, the plate in her lap with the peel and the knife. Her palms were wet and sticky, the smell of apple in the air.

I sat down cross-legged on the lower left-hand corner of the bed. She held the plate toward me; I lost my balance and was forced to put down my left leg so as not to fall.

"How clumsy you are."

I pointed to the plate. She placed it on the floor. Then she sat up to hand me a slice of apple. I ate the tart and juicy apple just to touch her fingers.

"Hey, Tarzan . . . sit up straight."

Without a trace of self-parody, I attempted to straighten my back.

"Straight."

She bent down to the ground and picked up the plate and another apple she had hidden, peeled and divided it into four, and carved out the center and the seeds from every slice. She was much bigger than Alice but had a flatter chest. As she peeled I pretended to yawn and drank water out of a bottle, turning to look out the window at the heavy slate roof of the building opposite.

"Let's take a look at this back now," she concluded, handing me the first slice.

For the second time I brushed her hand. I ate my slice religiously.

"It's not my fault, in a cross-legged position everyone tends to lean forward," I mumbled as I chewed, while my feelings caramelized and weighed on my chest.

She set the plate down in the center of the bed, got up and came around behind me. She placed a palm on my back and pushed in.

"Breathe. C'mon, sit up straight. Move more toward the center of the bed, otherwise you'll fall, Tarzan."

"Wait, wait." I stopped her because she'd placed her hands where my back was bad. "I couldn't breathe for a second, wait."

She returned to her side of the bed and lay down.

"I don't know why I insist on improving you so much."

"In exchange I defend you from Leo."

"My dear uncle? Do I have to be defended from him? From you, if anything."

These are the conversations that lead to unwanted pregnancies.

"Be quiet for a moment." I got up, I wasn't breathing well.

"Go freshen up, go on, stay calm."

In the meantime, she said, she'd roll a joint. I hid out first in the bathroom, then in the kitchen, inhaling as deeply as I could. Under my breath, I tried to move my lips to say "I love you, how I love you." I wanted to see what effect it would have. I recalled a poem and recited it silently, holding my hands to my face in the most theatrical manner.

> *Your tresses*
> *Shine with nameless reflections*
> *Spreading out from the temples . . .*
>
> *Beautiful, useless promises of a gift*
> *Flattering our desire,*
> *As a single unloved woman*
> *Binds us with every bond.*

I stayed in the kitchen for a few minutes, until I felt I had succeeded in breaking the spell, until I was no longer under any obligation to return to her. She wasn't calling me. I slipped off my shoes and waited until the odor of my socks faded.

We are the children of God, the adopted children of God who have rejected the flesh for a new life. Damaged children born to parents in thrall to sin, delivered to the little revolving door of the convent so that we might be adopted by God. Grateful to our adoptive parent, overwhelmed by the distinction we have earned, we remain like children so that we might enter the realm of Heaven. We are not truly free to err because gratitude binds us. Yes, if I had turned off computer and cell phone—household appliances of a moral nature, dimensional doors through which Roman affections could watch over me—I would have been free to err; the microwave oven launched no alarms; no reproofs came from the fridge, just its ineffable drone; the hot-water heater gurgled, obeying orders, not knowing how many of us would use the tub; but the nature of the appliances was irrelevant: I was not free to err.

Chekhov writes to a friend: "A man must enjoy himself, do foolish things, commit errors and suffer! A woman will forgive some impertinence or some cheek, but she'll never forgive your reasonableness."

After an indefinite period of time I returned to the living room and sat down on the little terrace-cornice, to look out at Sacré-Cœur and recite Hail Marys. Clelia, stretched out on one side of the red bedspread, already asleep, gigantic. I saw only the detail, like being in one of the first rows at the movies. The bony prominence on each side of the ankle beneath the green tights, the claylike skin. I had gone to sit on the edge of the bed, on her side, and I could have immobilized her and kept her for myself, tied her down with Lilliputian ropes and spikes, could have had Clelia-Gulliver trussed up from head to toe to keep her still.

I stroked her hip with my little finger. Her hair was spread out all around her head; she slept with her mouth open. I stroked her right arm. My little finger was the army's dispatch rider: the entire body sent it ahead with a message for the giant. Clelia's lips were ridged with wrinkles, at the back of the grotto of her mouth her uvula struggled against the foul air she breathed in. She thrust forth her Americanly white teeth in an orderly row; at times she wheezed like a pug.

The little finger of my right hand moved away from Clelia's

arm. But then I began to stroke her with the back of that finger, as it rested on my ring and middle fingers. Did this count as a caress? Yes.

She slept heavily and I stayed on to watch her, and after that night other nights as well, every time the joint lulled her to sleep, fully dressed, often with her contact lenses still in place on her eyeballs. She was a closed museum, a beach at night, a check under a paperweight on an antique desk in a doctor's office; she was a precious object I wanted to make my own, by what right I didn't know, so I would sneak out to watch her. At night I tried to imagine her naked. I knelt down and sniffed her hair, her clothes soaked with the stench of bars, her sweaty feet, her hips. In a fit of tenderness that first evening, lingering a moment before returning to the supernatural (and before praying for my loved ones and my enemies and the neediest), since I could not crush her in my arms, I said to myself desperately: "The next time, I promise to fuck you, my love." It sounded good, manly, heartsick, like something out of Chekhov. I said it again, this time half aloud to see whether it truly sounded good, whether I wasn't imagining it, whether words like these truly produced the same strong, staccato blow to the stomach as when, suffering from my shortcomings and my sorrow, I pray, *Dear Lord have pity on me, for I am a sinner, and increase my faith*: "The next time, I promise to fuck you, my love, my darling." An hour later, when she got up to take out her contact lenses, I was in my room, still awake but with the door closed and with underwear on under my pajamas.

15

"And this is the bedroom."

"Quite the nabob," she replies, "quite the king, Rosini! What a master stroke! I'm beside myself with envy."

I feel an involuntary and unstoppable smile creep onto my face.

"I knew you'd like it, my love; embrace me."

Alice leans over the bed to feel the mattress, then arches and holds one hand to her back: "*Mamma mia*, I'm getting old"; then she goes to the window and looks out at the roof opposite. "Just look at how the little lord has settled in; you've probably got a nicer place than even I would have found."

A beaming wife is the pinnacle of life. Alice blessed the house and the bedroom, where, the next morning, we even made love, quickly, without preliminaries, without breaking a sweat, with no mention of my rediscovered vigor. As compensation I enjoyed her childlike wonder as she admired my six-hundred-euro dollhouse, and the string of jokes about my good luck, and her admiration for my coup and the courage to have sent the EBac Gestapo packing, another bunch of crazies as far as she could tell from what I'd told her—nor, to ensure her support, did I forget to repeat Robin's monologue about Our Lady of Fátima and pulling the lid back from Hell.

"And it's so clean," she said.

And here not I but Rosenzweil slipped in a lie:

"Yeah, the landlord knew you were coming, so he sent over a cleaning lady."

189

"Wow, that's pretty nice. How old is he?"

"Around fifty."

"He doesn't get on your nerves and he buys you plants— what a change. You've obviously made a good impression on him."

All this took place in mid-November, the first time Alice mustered the strength to leave her daddy behind and come here instead of making me go back to Italy, and now that she was here I was beside myself with joy. She spoke hurriedly, slipped out of my grasp to poke her nose in every room, and would only allow herself to be kissed in the morning, as she opened her eyes; then she would pull back and start talking again—she was anxious to get out of the house and walk all day from one museum to another, from passementerie store to fabric store.

A few days earlier, Clelia had ostentatiously set about getting rid of her shirts and vests and with extreme immodesty had said:

"Doesn't it seem a bit obvious, you and I getting rid of every trace of my presence? Are you sure you don't want to tell her you live with me?"

I would have liked to explain to my phantom roommate, who had convinced herself she was more important than my wife, that Alice and I had a relationship that was, as it were, esoteric, unintelligible to the profane.

"Whatever," she had continued, "to me it seems pretty silly, really, the apartment, the cleaning . . ."

As I silently formulated the words to convince her, Rosenzweil suggested that, for once, I behave myself like a real man and not respond: to keep my mouth closed, to the point of being rude, to refuse to believe I owed everyone an explanation. Clelia had on yellow rubber gloves, her hair tied back; she placed her forearm against her eyebrows to wipe away the sweat.

"All right"—she returned to the argument (we were in the bathroom, she was cleaning the tub with a rag and disinfectant)— "let's disinfect the roommate!"

190

I was capable of not responding to her, and perfectly capable of ignoring the self-pity and the neurosis that moral life has been all about ever since Raskolnikov. Clelia had no rights and should not have allowed herself to consider herself important—and when Alice took over the house, tossing skirts and tops over chairs and leaving her black boots and tennis shoes in the hallway, occupying the bathroom for half an hour at a time, keeping the TV on at deafening volume, endlessly congratulating me, saying that I had "become quite the little man," I found myself on the terrace, bickering with an imaginary Clelia (absent, potentially vanished, perhaps between another man's sheets), saying, "See? Do you get what it means to have a wife?" Meanwhile, from the terrace, inspiring me with an edifying sense of tenderness, I observed my wife wandering around the living room and, in a soft falsetto, speaking to herself as well.

Beyond the big excursions to museums and the timid rediscovery of intimacy (no oral sex, but I was sufficiently moved to lick a wrinkle that had appeared a few months earlier between her breasts), we walked as if on a forced march and talked like conspirators. She updated me on Non Possumus and the Teste Parlanti, saying that in both cases "everyone is worried about you. These people don't do anything *but* worry about their neighbors, everything really worries them. I tell them all you're having a ball."

We were crossing that long avenue with many names that crowns the northeast corner of the city, and crosses Belleville as well, and I was saying, "It's strange to live in another city. It seems like the Non Possumus Rosini doesn't exist anymore. When I'm back in Rome, by God, then he exists a little. But as long as I'm here, no. And I ask myself, all that effort, all that investment, and then . . ."

"You have a tendency to poison yourself, Pié." We weren't holding hands, Alice was carrying two shopping bags with new clothes. "For now you're doing much better here. Stay."

I reminded her that the contract with EBac was up at Christmas.

"Who cares about the contract? If you're unhappy in Rome and you want to wait here for *The Jewish Pope* to come out and all that craziness to blow over, stay here."

"And do what all this time?" I didn't ask what made her assume the book would provoke an outcry, didn't ask precisely when she'd become convinced (taking for granted the foolishness of publishing the book at all) that we'd have to expect trouble from the media.

"If it would just make you crazy to be in Rome, I'd rather have you here doing nothing," she reassured me. "You're much more normal now. You're better. Less crazy. Stay here."

I didn't ask whether she wanted to move. Her authority, the ardor with which she made it clear that she appreciated me, that she thought I was doing well and that she was with me and supported me like a good wife, nipped any possible objection in the bud: I could have provoked a minor crisis by asking how my wife could have no need of her husband for months on end; how she could be so lazy or fearful or paralyzed not to move to Paris, considering her fluid professional situation (for that matter, wouldn't it almost have been an advantage for her to live there with me? I could have put her in touch with some work contacts through Clelia—but this thought was like a broken bracelet that wouldn't close); why she gave no sign of nurturing even the smallest suspicion concerning the open range of time and space at my disposal that remained unknown to her. Either this woman possessed a special grace or I for some reason attributed it to her—for what reason? Because you don't look a gift horse in the mouth? That a woman who leaves you free to investigate parallel lives, so that you might decide which one suits you best, shouldn't be argued with? But rummaging through your own innermost intentions is more nauseating than the foulest-smelling dumpster in Rome in August. You move aside another bag of garbage and up pops another rotten thought: maybe the truth is that *Rosenzweil* was the one not looking the gift horse in the mouth?

And if Rosenzweil had a secret plan, why then didn't a reassuringly textbook marital crisis erupt between us? We had plenty of reasons to argue, and we should have, so that my sins might find me out—but no, Alice was too sweet, too helpful; for all I knew she could have wanted a pair of cuckold's horns on her head: she did everything she could to make them sprout, horns she shared with my sisters-in-law. Or else, *for all I knew*, Alice could have been a contemptible creature who enjoyed confirming just how thoroughly she had defused in me every creative tension, making me a eunuch, preventing me from either having children or enjoying any young Jewish women the international scene had to offer. You push away another rotten cardboard box and through a hole in it come the words of Jesus: "It is not what enters into the mouth that defiles the man, but what proceeds out of the mouth, this defiles the man." At this I felt I had to protest: these were not my thoughts, not those of which I was aware . . . but surely, if I had been dismantled sentence by sentence and spread out on a big table to introduce some order into my jumbled attitudes, these thoughts and other, even fouler thoughts would have appeared. Fouler because buried, and buried well: my love and the faith I placed in Alice were so far from those depths it was impossible to think of Piero Rosini as a hypocrite; such things remained unexpressed, physical, buried beneath our sweet kindergarten chatter.

She dragged me to a fabric store in the Marais, where we went on about all kinds of things. Alice had allowed herself to get carried away by the question of whether you can ever be sure you're not throwing your life away, and what it is that's being thrown away. We wanted to understand whether dedicating myself to the Jewish Pope had been a waste of my time or not, and what to make of my change of heart in the general frame of the history of salvation.

"Do I seem to you like someone acting in good faith?"

Alice shook her head vigorously. "No no no no, that's got nothing to do with it, you're . . ." In her hand she held a lilac stud with a purple bowler hat design cut into it; she was picking out buttons by the dozen. "You're delightful, it's so endearing the way you throw yourself into it . . ." And a half hour later, as she made sure I wasn't eating too much cheesecake at Le Pain Quotidien in the Rue des Archives, between the Centre Pompidou and the city hall, she philosophized, "We take things very seriously, we Teste Parlanti. Too seriously. We're all so anxious. No one from the Teste Parlanti or Non Possumus is willing to waste even a minute being happy for you, for how you're enjoying yourself here." And then, out of the blue, "Do you think death will free us from our fear of mortality?"

I asked her, "But what do you think will really happen when *The Jewish Pope* comes out?"

She took the plate out of my hands, finished the cheesecake, envied the pumpkin-colored coat of a sophisticated forty-year-old who had just walked in, and said, "In Paradise, will we have a sense of humor?"

I didn't understand what was behind her questions. And why, I say now, why couldn't I just have made a clean break and shattered our idyll by saying something like: "And now please tell me what you made of this morning's penetration. Wasn't I more majestic than I've ever been? I practiced hard for you, you know."

We went to the Centre Pompidou to look at paintings and statues.

"Mario wants me back?" I asked.

"Either he wants you back," she said, "or he wants me: he calls twice a week. Maybe he doesn't want you to come back, he just wants to make his way into the empty house of the poor fisherman's wife, taking advantage of my being alone, and make me his."

"Aha! But he doesn't find you there, because you're at your father's!" Here I was stunned once again by how much swing there actually was in our harmony.

"Poor Mario. Going to so much trouble, and all the while I'm at my father's. Do you think those two still do it?" she asked.

"Who?"

"Mario and his girlfriend. Or are we the only poor bastards who haven't done it for generations?"

(Perfect—on the basis of this joke I could have opened a most civilized and loving debate, and instead:) "Mario," I said, "Mario thinks that after a few months of punishment, exile, quarantine, which is what it is, I'll beg to come back. And why not!"

"He expects you to beg for that piece-of-shit job."

"You understand me."

"He didn't even let you change the design of the covers, or the font, or fucking anything."

"He's an autarch, he's too sure of what he's doing."

"One less simpleton we have to discuss."

"That's exactly what he is, a simpleton. Oh yeah, Papa told me the cops are giving out bigger parking tickets now."

"Yeah, you've gotta be careful, you can't park in the no-parking zone in Piazza Esedra anymore . . ." And from Mario we moved on to speaking ill of Mayor Veltroni and then about whomever else, entirely in unison. We chatted away late into the night, after which I usually had to restrain myself from rubbing my crotch up against her if we slept hip to hip. Then, face-to-face instead with the ceiling, to turn my desire into father-daughter affection, I caressed her fine, straight hair and her shoulder, I kissed her head and began to pray for her and her dead mother and Sergio's intolerable solitude. This time I prayed that Sergio might have company and his life not be truly reduced to dinners with Alice and Ada. I prayed for Ada, who for some time had been in my prayers under the heading

Enemies: *Lord, I pray to you for my enemies* (but lately I'd been having trouble distinguishing between friends and enemies). I began to pray for Ada and for her tits that had done me so much harm, and from there, via a thought about Elvis that actually surprised me, I prayed that Elvis's soul might rest in peace under ten layers of fat; I prayed for all my enemies in the Teste Parlanti, for their mothers' tumors and their children's colds, that their supermarket carts might always be full of facial tissue and toilet paper and baby food, and their sheets clean and starched. From enemy to enemy I moved on to Mario, to his leather jacket, to Alberto and his kids, and his wife shut up at home, that neither might she lack for facial tissue and breakfast cereal. At this point our neighbor came to mind, our neighbor and her vexing children, and I prayed for them, that they might grow up strong like their father, and on the weekends always have enough money to fill up the tank of their Renault Espace, and I thought about Robin and his daughter with Down syndrome and about the Virgin, and I prayed for the Virgin and I said to the Virgin, "Try to understand," and here the Virgin revealed herself to be a less bountiful wellspring than my sister-in-law, so I returned to praying for Ada, my greatest enemy, and for her still noneviscerated tits, and then I remembered to pray for Corrado, and this time I was the enemy, I was the one who had betrayed him and I asked forgiveness for having left him in that useless position as factotum for Fassi Events. I prayed for the cheated-on wives of Il Fassi and the Jew Pacini, and after Pacini I prayed for Leo, my only male friend at the moment, and finally I prayed for my friends the witches, for Ana, who was perhaps at that hour being fucked by strangers without ceasing to put on weight, and for Benedetta, who wasn't doing the work she dreamed of doing and felt pressure from her parents because she didn't want to have kids or marry; I prayed for Jette, for her lack of tits, and I asked myself at what level of detail could one pray for God's creatures: for instance, Jette's flat chest was probably a source of frustration to her; could I pray for it and for the suffering it caused her? And on the subject of suffering and girls up to no good, Clelia had to be jealous because she wasn't here and Alice was (Lord, look after my wife, and her beautiful ass, which at the airport after check-in I saw pass through the metal detector and security was able to admire the utter purity of her bones, heart, and stomach, there is no mote in my wife's eye, Lord), and Clelia may have been jealous but she was also sad— could I pray for her sadness?—and Clelia, what she wanted was for her Rosenzweil to be more courageous, and maybe she was imagining that after dinner I would take her in my arms and begin to caress her, to speak as lovers do, and one thing would lead to another until (who knows how she imagined it, this is how I imagined it), until in an excess of passion we ended up against the convex wall in the hallway, she with her open hands spread flat, me standing behind her, Clelia with her bare cheek against the wall, this was Clelia's desire and I prayed for her, and thus also for Rosenzweil, about whom Alice—sleeping right beside me, where Clelia would have liked to be *now*—knew nothing, because Rosenzweil had a right to happiness too, a right to hope, to dream, to seek livelihood and love.

16

One day Satan brought Jesus to a mountaintop. Indicating the boundless prospect, he offered him the treasures of this world. As usual, Jesus refused.

And we with him—*Renounce Satan? I renounce him!* Every offer of worldly goods comes from the Devil: prince of this world, broker of every finite resource on earth, universal speculator, I will not accept from your hands, not even on a silver platter, that Jewish girl, so young and so compatible, because I promised faithfulness, and faith is a coin that never rusts.

Following Alice's visit, Clelia and I suspended our cohabitation. My task was made easier by an unusual show of pride on her part: having perhaps understood that she could not compete with a real wife, without explanation or warning she would disappear for nights on end; when she did stay with me, she no longer engaged in sweet talk or discussions that would bring us together on the couch. At home we behaved like an old couple on the outs, indifferent to each other and much occupied with television programs. When, on the other hand, she wasn't there, I had to be content with her personal effects, which intermittently went from being objects of practical use to relics of a glorious and incomplete past: contact lens case, solution, lip gloss, two men's dress shirts, pairs of white, pink, yellow, green panties, and a few bras—which every so often I would go and look at and touch in the drawer of the old wardrobe.

Sometimes she also left her computer with me, as if to leave a bookmark on my page; what humiliation it was to find the white laptop on the sofa and be under the illusion she was back and call out to her at the top of my voice in the dark house and not receive an answer.

I should have said to myself: "If you're not in a position to have a relationship with a woman you really like, at least go back to Rome." But love isn't everything, and you have to keep in mind the general situation, starting with EBac: at the beginning of December Robin let me know that I would not be participating in the editorial meeting of Monday the eleventh, that I could even stay home. I was glad to accept the offer and took advantage of it to accompany Leo on his visits to tenants. Two days later they wrote to say that if I had other things to do, I could also stop going into the office, and that we could move up my final day to December 15. They didn't specify whether they would be paying me the five hundred euros for the current month. The "terms of the matter" had "completely changed." Robin: "From what I am given to understand, you will not be continuing to work in publishing following this period." I had planned to work at EBac until Friday, December 22, and to return on an overnight train Saturday night; I would celebrate Christmas with my wife and pick up my life where it had been interrupted last Christmas.

To me, all that seemed irrelevant, seeing as how I had already bought the ticket for the twenty-third and thus the final act was already written. Sure, my wife had suggested I stay beyond the expiration of the EBac contract; nevertheless, to remain away from the conjugal bed like this, in one's spare time, seemed to me immoral, and thus perhaps I wouldn't have done it even with the permission of the person occupying the other half of the bed. But, in excluding me from the December 11 meeting and calling an end to our collaboration the following Monday, Robin had permitted me to tour apartments with Leo two Monday afternoons in a row. Enough for the Jew to come up with an idea even stranger than Alice's: that I stay on and work for him as manager of the rental units.

"There's not much to do, this tour of the apartments, keeping the books, paying expenses, seeing how the tenants are doing. Seems like it'd suit you. Everyone thinks you're nice."

"I seem nice because next to you I look normal."

"I'm not jealous."

I told him I wanted to talk it over with Alice. Then I thought it over and, calling him the same evening to thank him, proposed, with what courage I don't know, that he permit me to live in the apartment for free for a few months; I in exchange would help him out as he taught me the . . . hmm, trade, in case I later decided to stay and take the work seriously. Alice was very taken by my enterprising approach with the "landlord" (for her he wasn't Uncle Leo, just as I wasn't Rosenzweil), and said that anything that got me free rent was just great . . . It was very strange to be married and see eye to eye on so many issues, even stranger to agree about the odd choices I'd made. I'd figured out she was happy to see me doing something practical, my mind turned not to conspiracies but to discovering the tactics best suited to ensuring my own personal advantage, and yet her persistence in leaving me here had a power to expand space and time that I didn't know how to handle. Every time I returned home to Pigalle, the apartment seemed to have grown looser on me, more capacious, and every week lasted longer than the one before. Sooner or later Christmas would arrive, but now the plan was to return to Paris after New Year's (to live for interminable weeks in boundless rooms).

A penny for my thoughts: they are the key players here, and I the one kept in the dark—then as now, for that matter. In fact, looking back on all this, I had neither renounced nor refused to renounce Clelia and this little joke of a job. Why did I continue to hover about, without taking hold of anything?

If we stick with Catholic terminology, it must be said that

Leo, with this proposal, risked seeming like a devil to me: a devil in a red velvet mantle tailored to fit his small shoulders and long legs, high waist and thin wrists . . . This comic little devil, willing evil and incessantly creating good, brought me up to the mountain to offer me the medieval lanes around Boulevard St.-Michel; an unapproachable parade of female students in their chromatic combinations of overcoats, shoes, and hats (red and sky blue, green and violet, yellow and fuchsia); bicycles chained to the railings on Rue Ulm; coffee from the big dispenser with his professor friends at the École normale supérieure, in the courtyard of the main building, with its trees, flower beds, and fishpond (I could have come here to read), the weak winter sun glancing off the gum-encrusted wooden benches that never completely dry . . . Understand? He brought me up there and said, "One day all this will be yours" . . . After the university neighborhood the tour continues southeast, back uphill, passing Rue Mouffetard, the Jardin des Plantes, and the mosque . . . "What do you do for work? I walk around until I'm tired and then take a seat in the tearoom of the Turkish baths, orange and crimson, the ceiling maroon and turquoise; then the untalkative waiter serves me tea in a golden cup . . ." Only in episodes of temptation do you find colors of this sort and time so dilated. I did two Monday tours in December, then picked up doing them in January and February. Alice had decided it was a good thing—in any event, I was the one, not she, to go walking with the Devil.

To hear Leo talk, the perfect plan would have been for him to return to live in New York and leave his niece in peace, and for me to stay in Paris and look after his affairs and every so often go to visit him in America . . . "I commute between Paris and New York," fantasized Rosenzweil; the phrase was a mouthful of mint-fresh images, a scenario so precious that Leo's offer (which might even have seemed offensive considering the ambitions I'd harbored in high school and how much money my father earned) glittered with the light of the two metropolises, the streetlights here and the bridge lights there, or better still it reflected the Atlantic that separated them, and in my thoughts the Atlantic became a single, enormous reflection of the sun, a perpetual late afternoon saturating the ocean with light. I saw them all, lost in this light: the transatlantic flights, the landings, the walks over the Brooklyn Bridge, the taxi rides, the Turkish baths in the Village that Leo promised me.

The last apartment on our Monday tours was in the Bastille area, across the river and through the wind lashing the enormous square with the clumsy new Opéra splayed out against the sky, a Swarovski covered in Play-Doh. Approaching the river we had walked along the Boulevard de l'Hôpital past the long facade of the Salpêtrière hospital, where Charcot had reigned in the latter half of the nineteenth century and studied hysteria; standing before the majestic entrance—the pitch black of the cupola and steep roofs, the trees lined up like madmen waiting for pills, the three arches beyond which you could see nothing but blackness—we invariably spoke of sex, and Leo always brought up Freud's joke about Charcot, guilty of concealing the true cause of women's hysteria: "But if everything is sex, why don't you say so? Vy don't you zay zo?"

I have to admit that in a theoretical sense I was lucky: I was meeting people who thrust a finger into my wounds. They probed my motives, were curious about my containment strategy; they provoked me. Some people fade once they've made their choices, once their decisions take on a momentum of their own. They teased me. Benedetta did this in a particularly uncompromising way. One evening she came to visit me after dinner, alone, and thrust a finger deeper than anyone else into my open wound.

After having satisfied our chemically induced hunger, melting a bar of chocolate in a small saucepan and dipping apple slices into it, she urged me to sit down on the sofa and smoke some more. There, comfortable and intimate, she forced me to talk about Clelia.

"She likes you, you live together . . . I don't understand why you haven't fucked her yet . . ."

I asked her why she was so convinced of that.

"Well . . . you're a good-looking man. Older. With a complicated life. You're married, who with no one knows; we've never seen this wife of yours. You've somehow lost your job in Rome. No one knows who you are. You say you're a religious zealot, but you live with another woman, who likes you, and we don't know if your wife knows. It's enough to make you take an interest in a man, I'd say. You have nice shoulders." She concluded, "I don't understand why you don't get this blessed fuck over with. At least you could stop worrying about it."

I explained to her that I couldn't, on account of my wife.

She shot back, "Then kick Clelia out of your house . . ."

"It's her house."

"Chewb, you're pathetic. I want to get into bed, I want to lie down, I'm shattered."

We got up; she waited for me to pull the covers back. I tried to look competent. She stretched out, then asked me to show her how I sat at the foot of the bed when Clelia slept there.

"And you just sit there like an idiot?"

"Exactly."

"Don't be so proud of it. Will you give me a massage?"

She turned over on her stomach and exhaled heavily in my direction. I made a gesture, no.

"It's an order, don't question it."

I climbed up on the bed.

"No. No, I won't do it."

I lay down beside her, on my stomach as well, on my gurgling stomach (I'd been eating mainly kebabs in recent days).

"I can't give you a massage, c'mon."

"What a sad man . . . big and tall . . ."

"Give me a massage if you want, but I won't give you one."

"What a pain in the ass." She jumped up on her knees and climbed on top of me, settling her thighs down on my butt.

"Are you going to take your sweatshirt off?"

I obeyed, awkwardly freeing myself. Now she massaged my back underneath the T-shirt. A pro forma massage, with no technique or delicacy, just crude temptation.

"Can I fall asleep?" I asked.

"No, you still have to give me a massage. Turn over."

Now with more gentle hands she caressed my belly; then she went closer to my jeans and I shrieked until she stopped.

"Sorry, sorry. God, you're so boring. Try to relax a little bit. Try to be happy." She wouldn't take her hands off me, so I said I would give her a massage. She lay down on her stomach; I got on top of her and began to massage her long, narrow back.

"It hurts here." She stuck out an arm to indicate her spine. "Actually, more toward my kidneys."

She lifted her butt up at me: "C'mon, go a little lower." I pulled up her T-shirt just a little bit and massaged her back where it was hard. "No, on the kidneys."

"I can't, don't make me do it."

"Do it, you'll see how easy it is."

"Benedetta," I said melodramatically, "don't make me do it."

"Go down to the kidneys."

Impatient, she pulled down her skirt's elastic waistband to reveal three centimeters of her behind. A strip of tiny female behind, round, like a minor's. With my palms I applied pressure in the vicinity. A plump little rear, marred by a few white streaks, signs of age perhaps.

When she understood that I wasn't going one millimeter lower, she reached back and swatted me blindly, lifted me off of her, and suddenly turned around; she climbed into my lap as I was sitting down.

"Why are you so stuck?"

She asked the question with the innocence of a physical therapist, almost as if I had a problem with my tendons. She was a few centimeters away from my mouth and had no bra on. Seeing that I wasn't kissing her, she straightened up and brought her chest toward my mouth. I kept my lips pulled in as one of her hardened nipples brushed them. I simultaneously tried both to tense my lips, drawing away blood and sensitivity, and to feel those nipples through her T-shirt on my bloodless lips. I felt them well, felt they were alive and wrinkled, conducting electricity and memories.

I stood up, holding her effortlessly in my arms, she was so light. I looked her in the eyes and walked until her back knocked against a wall.

"What are you doing to me!" I laughed, improvising kisses across her forehead, across her cheeks. "I won't fuck you!" I laughed. "Not you or Clelia!"

"You're truly a waste of cock."

I pulled her away from the wall and carried her to the bed, falling on top of her. I sunk my nose into the hollow between her neck and shoulder; we rubbed against each other.

Then I decided I wasn't going any further and stood up. Wringing my fingers, I said, "You make me do things I don't want to do."

"But of course you want to, just look at the face you're making . . ."

"What face am I making?"

"Come on, there's nothing wrong with this. We won't tell anybody. There's nothing wrong."

"I don't want to do anything. You do what you want, massage my back, rub yourself against me, I'm not doing anything. I don't have it in me. I can't do it."

With her lips pressed together, she said, "Waste of cock."

"All right, at most I could watch you."

"You want to watch me? But you won't undress me?"

"No, I won't undress you."

"What a fucking drag."

"Hmm . . . Undress yourself, if you want."

"No way, I'm not getting undressed alone."

"Okay, then nothing."

"Fine, I'll undress . . . but at least let me give you a little blow job."

I said nothing. She said:

"Come on! What do you think?"

"Fine, okay, if you want to, undress."

"Ugh. How humiliating."

She slipped off her electric-blue T-shirt and I saw her tits: broad, low, upswinging, big for her size; she was taking the pill for sure. I cannot, Rosenzweil. Mamma and the Virgin don't want me doing grown-up things.

"Take off your skirt, if you want," I said.

"Still the same deal, alone? Don't you want to undress me?"

"No, I don't feel like it."

"All right, I'll start. But if you don't follow I'll be pissed."

"I told you, I'm not following."

"But you like my tits, huh? You're looking at them."

I smiled at her. "Of course I like them!"

"You're enjoying yourself, huh? You're feeling good now!"

"Yes."

She lowered the skirt slowly down to her feet, watching me the whole time, then she rolled down her white panties as far as her knees. She drew back to support herself better against the back of the bed.

"You want me to touch myself? Do you?"

Having smugly registered my smile, she touched herself there in the middle with two fingers, and I saw her hand, and behind her little hand I saw the inner flesh that usually remains hidden, rolled up; I saw her darker colors, the puckered deep-sea wonder, a new cunt years and years after having sworn I would never look at another.

It was only when she'd finally left, having planted a cousinly kiss on my cheek at the door—"I'm happy I made you laugh"—it was only then that I realized I'd made it. I found myself standing in the bathroom, underwear around my ankles, stunned, addressing the mirror: "There really *are* things I won't do. I'm practically omnipotent." In short this was a veritable renunciation, accomplished, what's more, under torture. A little Jewish story of Leo's came to mind:

> One day the Lord was in a bad mood. He said to Samael, "What are you complaining about?"
>
> Samael responded, "How could I not cry out, when you created me just so you could boast about it?"

In Clelia's absence, with the use of her computer and prodded by the Benedetta episode, I began to explore the pornography on offer on the Web, from the innocent calendars of topless girls on *La Repubblica*'s site to the free sites where people uploaded their own amateur videos. I had quit looking at porn on the Internet pre-ISDN, now I discovered broadband: "Drilled into the floor"; "Tender sex between husband and wife . . ." Neorealism that I hadn't expected, the truth of nonactors who weren't pretending. Domestic scenes, a living room with a glass-paneled bookcase; or a honeymoon in a Mexican cabana; you saw her from behind; his legs, feet, and hands; she's on top, facing away from you, in semidarkness. Between orange and yellow sheets, a well-proportioned ass; he caresses her, she has her back straight and a lock of black hair hanging down between her shoulder blades. Then he enters her, the camera zooms in. The subjects burst out laughing, or stay quiet, or lose themselves in thought, lose each other and find each other again. Often a third person does the filming, and sometimes the girl will look passionately over in that direction as she licks or is penetrated. What's the relationship between the woman and the person filming? Is it a woman? A man? What is this solidarity that is created in a room with a video camera? The friction makes wet sounds. Now she turns and smiles. She's very thin.

The back-and-forth of the shaft in close-up makes me think of those transparent display cases at IKEA in which a robot arm opens and closes a drawer thousands and thousands of times to demonstrate the endurance of Swedish furniture. After a few initial approaches to find the target, he quickly moves on to a frenzied up-and-down motion. The sex here is the hydraulic affair I'd heard about ever since I was a child, which I first saw simulated in elementary school by a classmate who thrust himself up against a weaker classmate from behind as a joke, saying, "I'm a tiger in heat!"

Two at the bathroom window: *morning fuck*. The sounds pull me in and put me in the room with them. I keep it low for fear that Clelia will return, but she would buzz first. Surprised grunts and whimpers, the affectionate zeal of girls in garters. Laughing, gap-toothed women with shadows under their eyes, moles on their tits, flaring nostrils, eyes. The best video features no men: one girl inserts a baseball bat inside the other. The look on her face! She's incredulous and laughs. "Oh oh, yeah, ah yeah, oh that's incredible. You've got to patent it," she says to her friend between falsettos of enthusiasm, "this twisting movement while you push it in, you've got to patent it!" Elsewhere, a woman is tied up and forced to her knees, forehead to the carpet, hands bound behind her in a really uncomfortable way, her rear thrust up like a pear, the split between the cheeks pulled wider, and he pushes in, throwing a shadow over her, gently slapping her. *Doggy-fucked like a bitch.* (Wouldn't it be great to see a video in which two people conceive a child? Maybe I've already seen it, without knowing. When the child asks his parents about the meaning of life, they can show him the film.)

With this jack-off system in place I could resist any temptation: it kept my dangerous organ far from women, helped me not to get obsessed over Clelia or Benedetta, and I could stay far away from my wife—who had in any event relinquished the function of offering relief to my instincts and containing my libido according to the intuition of Saint Paul. The Internet jack-off system is a perfect system, bringing together the oversexed with the repressed, the former happy to flaunt themselves on camera every day of the week, the latter relieved not to have to come up against three-dimensional sins with eye-witnesses.

One afternoon followed another. Sometimes, rarely, I had dinner with Clelia. Benedetta, when we all went out together, would lightly slap my puffy cheeks and laugh, and not mention our secret encounter. I was unsettled and didn't call her—the risk of us doing it *doggy style* was too real, maybe she'd whip out a video camera and I'd find myself on a porn site. But as I stirred the spaghetti or sniffed the ready-made Barilla sauces, waiting for Clelia (who might have shown up unexpectedly at dinnertime, swept in, and then fell asleep in front of the TV, or maybe even taken a taxi back to her place), I felt the weight of the melancholy I had arduously, justly earned.

Sacrifice: why don't certain people know its proper place? It's easier to sacrifice something under the rule of an established law. The awareness of being shut up in my monk's cell of broadband pornography did me even more harm after, at Leo's house one evening, I met his current girlfriend, a young Russian woman, his guest for the past two months, whom I found in the living room sitting at one end of the white couch, busy with a laptop computer. Leo had just given it to her. And she—very serious and way less focused on her own beauty than I was (long hair the color of wheat and skin covered with an amber down that pierced my heart as soon as I sat down beside her to look at the screen)—was trying to work out how to change its operating system language to Cyrillic. Volna—no more than twenty-five, I was sure—knew only a few sentences in English and just as few in French, and made no real effort to communicate. She had come to learn the language and to find work. She had long lashes, two large round cheekbones; she wore clear nail polish and a turquoise chiffon blouse with puffy sleeves. Her small breasts were supported by a gray ribbon that wove in and out of the fabric of her blouse, which also had funny golden admiral's buttons and a big, seventies-style collar. She didn't smile at me once, probably not wanting us two Italian males speculating about her and about what demands could be made of her. Leo, very polite, refrained from making faces or any comments in her presence.

I met him the next day near the Canal St.-Martin, between the mustard and English-green walls of Chez Prune.

"Cute, right?"

"What's she doing here?"

"She lives in Siberia, where it's minus forty-five degrees. Can you imagine?"

"Are you together?"

He swayed his head to the right and to the left, as if he were crooning.

"You met her on the Internet?"

"Yes."

"Who is she, Leo? How'd she come to be at your place?"

"Internet."

"Hmm. From a *catalog*?"

"On a chat line."

"Who is she? Do you pay her?"

"No."

"You pay her, Leo. You gave her that computer?"

"Rosenzweil, Rosenzweil."

"What's the exchange, you pay for her vacation in Paris and she sleeps with you?"

"Completely the opposite," he said, illogically.

"The opposite of what?"

"Can we order something to eat?"

"How old is she? You make me sick."

"I make you sick? Give me back the apartment. You want to sleep with her?"

"With whom?"

"With Volna."

"Leo . . . *No*."

"Good, because I'm not going to let you touch her."

"All the better."

"Good."

"Great," I said, then added resentfully, nodding, "Pure meta-Judaism, of course: 'a general concern with moral conduct.' Yeah, right!"

"Ah, fuck off!" (All the same he paid the bill.)

You could only say one thing to someone like that: "Look, I'm fucking your niece, so you should go back to New York, you're no longer welcome in Paris." But as much as I desired it and resolved to do it, I couldn't bring myself to sleep with her. I approached her as she slept and kissed her forehead, I caressed her shoulder, her arm, her knee, and getting even closer, I breathed her in, smelling fried food and stuffy apartments. I touched my nose to her clothed body and said, "I promise you, my love, next time I'll fuck you."

Clelia was a mannish woman who was particularly male in this respect: she stuck around, she hovered about, she never shut anything down; she was inconsistent and confused and although we only ever talked shit and only ever talked when we were drunk, and she only slept here once in a while, not a week passed without some confirmation of her weakness for and interest in me.

One day in late January I was due to take an early flight to Rome (I may have been scared of flying, but the train cost a lot and this was not a trip I'd planned on, prompted as it was by an urgent need to see Alice again that even I didn't really understand). The alarm didn't go off, or else I turned it off in my sleep. I had to reach the Palais des Congrès by six thirty; the coach to the low-cost airport Paris-Beauvais left from there. Clelia woke me up at six twenty. I didn't know what she was doing, standing there, and in any case it was strange that she slept over the night before I was leaving for Rome. She came into my room in a nightgown, placed the palm of her hand on my chest, and pushed her index finger against my collarbone.

"Don't you have a plane to catch?"

"What time is it?!"

"Six twenty. I'll make your bed." She turned on the halogen lamp.

"I've missed it, I can't believe it, I've missed it." My clothes were on the chair; I grabbed them and put them on in front of Clelia, over the underwear and T-shirt I'd slept in. She watched me as I buttoned up my shirt and pants. The shutters were open, it was dark outside. "I missed it," I said, with unsteady legs, morning breath.

And Clelia: "There's coffee."

"I missed it. I have to go to Rome, I missed the coach."

"You didn't miss it. Take the next one."

I objected that Ryanair only guaranteed to wait for those who took the coach designated for their flight.

"Heading out at this hour, you won't hit any traffic. It's never happened to me."

"Have you missed lots of flights?" Meanwhile I continued to dress.

"Everyone misses them. Shall I bring you some coffee?"

I drank the coffee in the kitchen, placing my cup in the sink. At the door—she had followed me there in silence—I kissed her forehead, standing on tiptoe to do so. I fled down the stairs, putting on my backpack as I went. Paris was slowly lighting up; the Métro car smelled of cellars and sweet bread; the Palais des Congrès was all tunnels and escalators; when I got out it was day; I reached the coach just as it was leaving. On the highway, as soon as the clock beside the driver reassured me that I would not miss the plane and I calmed down, I finally understood: Clelia had made coffee instead of waking me up. She had got up at six and made coffee; she had woken up to an alarm (hers or mine), or else she had woken up spontaneously; and once on her feet, she had decided not to wake me and to make coffee first. Her peculiar behavior made me feel faint, and once I had swallowed (without water) a pair of tranquilizers, Leo's counsel and gift, once the sweet and loony effect of the medicine had made itself felt, I found myself sobbing as I read an article in the in-flight magazine about the death of a famous person, and from there, between sobs, I moved on to thinking about people who die, about human life and what love is, and these thoughts of a sedated neurotic finally tumbled toward the image of Clelia in the dark and silent house before dawn a few hours earlier, in Rue Notre-Dame-de-Lorette, Clelia in a nightgown, wandering through the apartment like an old housewife, making coffee and yawning as she keeps an eye on the pot, a sleepy tear rolling down her cheek.

This thought should have been enough for me to do what I did two days later, but what in fact drove me to it was the turbulence on the return flight. Of my Roman weekend there's not much to report—the essence of Piero Rosini, although with smarter clothes: family, Church, irksome questions from friends about a future I still knew nothing about. My joke of a flight took off two hours late, around ten thirty at night, from Ciampino airport, now hidden by a heavy storm. Rosary tight in my hand and tranquilizers in my body, I sat behind a block of about thirty well-groomed high school girls on a field trip. When the shaking began and worried comments like "Whoa!" and "What the hell" arose here and there and the plane, like a water-park slide, made a sudden jerk, the fifteen-year-olds in front of me started to scream—a theatrical, collective high note for every plunge.

Suffice to say the screams were becoming unbearable, so I leaned forward without thinking, touched one of their curly heads with two fingers, and asked quietly, "Can you all stop screaming? It only makes things worse."

"It's their first time on a plane," said the girl, laughing and turning around slightly. "Sorry."

Raising my voice, I said, "Stop it, for fuck's sake, I'm shitting my pants back here."

The two men next to me, one in a padded jacket, one in a dress shirt, tried to laugh, or maybe they laughed at me.

Twenty minutes later we were still experiencing turbulence, but no more waterslides. More surprises, however, were still to come. The copilot came on the loudspeaker and in brisk, Spanish-accented English said, "Your attention, please, we have to give you some bad news. Beauvais has called to tell us that we are late and that the airport has to close at midnight, so we are being rerouted to Brussels." The passengers who understood English started to mutter and to explain things to the others. The discontent was general, but the fear was greater, and we looked forward to landing. Ryanair would make three coaches available to take us overnight to Paris; it wouldn't take more than four hours.

My seat neighbors knew what was what (they were both slightly on the stocky side, and Roman, Romans in jeans): "That's what Ryan does. They knew full well we wouldn't make it in time. These guys need a plane in Brussels tomorrow, maybe there's another one that didn't make it and so they're bringing them ours. With us inside it."

Our landing was greeted with ironic and liberating applause. When we arrived at baggage claim, an old man in a camel-hair coat said, "These people knew it from the start. They always knew we would be landing here, otherwise tell me why the buses are already here for us." The Italians who heard him muttered and cursed. When we left the building to breathe in the Belgian air in the parking lot, it was snowing.

Everything was white; my upset intestine burned all the way to my rectum. And here emerged the Piero Rosini I would rather not have seen. "We have to write a letter!" I said, addressing everyone. "We have to write a letter because these pilots don't treat us with respect! We have to threaten the company! My sister writes for *La Repubblica*, I'll get her to investigate!"

"Hah . . ." the old man in the camel-hair coat started dismissively, "these people don't listen to us, it goes in one ear and out the other. That's why they're cheap."

"Like hell they're cheap, are you kidding? I paid to go to Paris, don't take me to Brussels. C'mon, let's write a letter, let's stop letting these things happen in silence."

"Oh, calm down, it's pointless to get mad . . ."

"*Pointless?* Excuse me, pointless how?" I didn't even know who had spoken last. I placed a hand on my stomach. "Listen, it's hardly pointless!"

"Yeah, yeah," someone said. At first they had listened to me, but now I was making people smile and move away. I insisted, "We can't keep letting ourselves get screwed. Dammit anyway. It's not right. It's not right! Where does this shitty company's CEO live?"

As I became more upset, ranting and raving to myself, I saw a girl watching me from ten meters away. She wasn't Italian. She took in my gestures and looked shocked. Wrapped up in a hat, scarf, and heavy Windbreaker, no more than sixteen. That zoolike gaze brought me back to myself. We were waiting under a bus shelter in front of the glass facade of the airport. Looking sidelong, I saw myself reflected in the glass as I finished the sentence ". . . shitty company's CEO live?": gesticulating, wild-eyed. Why did I have to be like this? Why was this, exactly, my contribution to the human pageant? I spent my life covering myself with ridicule and screaming like a madman on the street corner, waiting for the Apocalypse. Me, with the physique of a successful contractor: large, statuesque, with a slight hunch that's more a compunction for the excess of health than a weakness. When I sneeze, I move the world like the Atlas adored by the Masons of Manhattan. The girl had no idea of my strength; she would have to just look upon me and drool. I'm rich, I'm tall, I have a cock, I know foreign languages, I live in hiding with a Jewish girl who suffers with love for me. I leave my father's house and come to the city to squander away my inheritance on prostitutes and instead become their protector; I return to my father's house a rich man and build a pool and a solarium. Why haven't you entrusted me with a regiment, a whaling vessel, the offense of a major European football club, a thriving business? If I had just taken a better look at myself in the mirror: hips as tough as guardrails, cheekbones that could take out a housing project. If I had taken a good look at myself in the mirror, I would never have converted; I have excessively broad shoulders, like a Russian oil baron, like a Mafioso, like a sinner; I'm someone who orders hits, who manages a collection agency. When I sneeze, the markets crash.

The coach trip from Brussels to Paris took five full hours, the streetlights along the highway pounding out a monotonous rhythm. The coach pulled up to the Palais des Congrès in the fog. I took the Métro. My building door was sprinkled with cold raindrops. Everything had just been unwrapped for the new day. I climbed the six floors, and when I entered the boiling-hot apartment, Clelia wasn't there.

I recalled the morning of my departure: the alarm clock, the nightgown, the coffee.

I called my father around ten, before he went into church with Mamma, and led the discussion to the point where he was claiming I was courageous and ambitious and would show my sister what I was made of. I conceded every point and let him hold forth on the beauty of Parisian women and the other commonplaces on which he based his judgment. I didn't have a precise plan but yes, I was thinking explicitly about money. I thought I was the best of my father's four children and deserved my share. I had always refused it on principle, while Federica had received help buying a place in Monti and my brothers had built, on the basis of their solidarity with Papa, an entire life in Tod's and station wagons. This time, via telephone, I let my father express his love for me, in words, with promises, with those promises that rich, tenderhearted fathers excel at.

And in the end, with the pride of the last-born, the nihilistic animal pride of a spoiled child, I made a pact with the patriarch: he would loan me a thousand euros a month for the course of my stay. "We're not going to say anything to Mamma about this, obviously, it's our own thing, she wouldn't understand." That it was a pact between men he also made clear by distancing himself from his daughter-in-law: "Alice is hardly married to her father; if you're happier in Paris she should follow you. See how it goes from now until the summer; look sharp, keep your ears open, remember that nearly every young woman doing an internship has a mother and a father in command somewhere behind the scenes."

A few days later the first thousand euros showed up in my account. I checked on the bank website and found the payment memo as annotated by my father: *Paris is well worth a Mass.* The joke, made in good faith by a father anxious to be of help, reminded me that a year ago I had called him Evil's lackey.

17

Rosenzweil. We can say that Papa loaned the money to Rosenzweil, not to Piero, that it was Rosenzweil who had a plan—or, much more than a plan, a dream of taking over my body and making it lead a full life. Did he have the elements required for a full life? He'd made money, and done so in the most reckless way, seducing my father with adventurous talk. Did he know what to do with the money? If it were up to him, he'd have spread Clelia's legs without sparing a thought for tomorrow. And he placed so much trust in his own instincts that he considered it possible somehow, following the example of Rosini senior and not Piero, to climb the social ladder from the bottom by dint of his own charisma. He wasn't sure he could manage it, but counted on creating lasting memories in the process; by, for instance, complicating life with Benedetta; by asking Leo next time to invite over a pair of steppish young women in turquoise blouses; by starting to frequent the art galleries on the Rue de Seine; and, if Paris revealed itself to be too haughty and indifferent to his robust fascination, by convincing Leo to return to New York, where both of us or all three of us, Clelia too, would make a new start in America, as tradition would have it.

It's useful to think about it in these terms, because if it's true that Rosenzweil—a somewhat simple character, assembled with my experience's most recent acquisitions (along with pieces of me that had long been buried), composed for the most part of brightly colored shirts and an attraction to women, moral relativism, and a desire to learn—had before him boundless future prospects, it's also true that, examined from the point of view of this same Rosenzweil, the story of that month of March seems like the story of someone lighthearted and full of hope who found himself trapped in a body, my body, that carried him up and away from his desires; the body of an infant that did not belong to itself, because it was a new fragment, entirely untested, of the rather more complex Piero Rosini, and even Piero Rosini himself, me, even I was unable to exert complete control over my body—and in any case Thomas Aquinas was wrong, given the results of my having abandoned myself to nature and bracketed the supernatural. Thus Rosenzweil had a straitjacket that was Rosini, who was in turn imprisoned in Saint Augustine, who had not freed himself from original sin—and basically Rosenzweil could forget about fucking, forget jeans and a T-shirt, he was going to have to accept a life in the tuxedo of God's grace. He tried, with varying success, to set himself against all this, inviting Clelia over and deluding himself that he could fuck her with impunity.

Of course I'm no idiot. It's not that I'm a lunatic escaped from the asylum with a crumpled tricorne hat; I well know that Rosenzweil is just a gimmick, a contrivance, but this gimmick had a constant hard-on, and in the month of March my gloomy low spirits, combined with Rosenzweil's desire for an independent life, brought the situation to a head.

18

With hindsight I wonder: if Piero Rosini had ultimately returned to Rome, would Rosenzweil have disappeared, or not? At the time the question appeared more clear-cut, and even Rosenzweil, who considered himself daring and shrewd, hadn't managed to remain lucid enough to understand whether he would be returning to Rome with Rosini as a parasite, perhaps initially staying hidden, later venturing out to continue the collaboration with my father, and over the course of months and years to take over from an obsolete Piero Rosini, who was merely spinning his wheels.

As it happened, it was toward the end of winter (in the rain and cold, let's add for good measure) that things took on a more desperate air.

Alice had decided to keep her husband the pawn on the square marked "Paris" for the time it took to burst or drain whatever abscess had developed on the dirty, infected skin of public opinion. It was still impossible to foresee anything, and the waiting induced in us a feeling of nausea, caused us to suffer bouts of the future. The fact that my wife had resolved that for her it was better to protect and do without me than to bring me back to Rome established a constant; it determined the average temperature that the event would have to have; it substituted for the event itself, still unknowable, the stable shape of its anticipation. Rosini was in little or no hurry to return, and Rosenzweil was incredulous to find his most ardent accomplice in Alice.

When the truth comes out and deep-seated conflicts become entrenched, everyone becomes a caricature of himself: Rosenzweil found himself playing the role of soap-opera heartthrob, rekindling in questionable fashion the feelings of the poor young Jewish woman with the nose job.

He invited her to a café overlooking the canal with the excuse that he had lost his keys, whereas he had them in his pocket. It was almost pitch-dark inside; a bunch of young tourists were playing old soul songs on the jukebox. Rosenzweil ordered a carafe of sangria, paying with a crisp fifty-euro note fresh from the ATM. In those days, as evening came on, low blood sugar would make him absentminded and restless, and at times it made his lips tremble. He attempted to pour the wine and fruit into two short, narrow glasses, but it dripped on the table. Clelia whipped out some tissues and laid one over the wine, wiped the inside of her wrist, and said, "I don't have much time; meanwhile, here are the keys."

They clinked glasses, both leaning forward together over the table to drink without dripping on themselves. They spoke of this and that until Rosenzweil went ahead and made the announcement: "I've decided to stay, perhaps until summer. I've come into some money . . . some family money."

"Money?"

"Yes, money. And I have to think carefully. I might be working with your uncle."

"He said something about that."

"Crazy, right?"

But Clelia rose and walked to the bathroom.

Sex and money—these could be Rosenzweil's; and sex and money were areas where I'd decided to have nothing to object to or demand, because in these areas injustices sprout up like mushrooms after a storm every time anything worthwhile is at stake, and the Church's solution for men basically follows principles of efficiency similar to those of Northern European government agencies: every investment in money or sex should have as its objective not personal satisfaction but a further objective; for money, you build a house on a rock; for sex, you fill it with children, and every last one of your desires will vanish in the capillaries of the lungs of your one and only God.

Clelia came out of the closet-cum-bathroom behind the jukebox, pulled the narrow door of ruined wood, and returned to her seat. At her neck she had a red pashmina that covered the top of her chest; she wore a wool sweater and skirt, both black. She sat well away, on a different chair.

Rosenzweil, who had lately come to understand his own capabilities and now wanted to make the most of them, said, "Are you mad at me? Clelia? C'mon, sit here."

She placed a cigarette in her mouth and turned to the next table for a light. The suppleness of that seated twist allowed Rosenzweil to successfully picture her naked.

He rose full of confidence and came down on the chair between them, put an arm around her shoulders like an old friend: "Give me a hug."

Looking down, she caused the cigarette to crackle between her chapped lips. Then she slowly stubbed it out, dragging the embers around the ashtray, blew smoke on Rosenzweil's dark blue sweater as she placed a hand on his back and her head on his chest. The Motown song had words like "ever after," "die," "please," and "your kiss." Clelia's hand rested firmly at the center of Rosenzweil's back and pushed; her hands, with their big fingers, remained ungraceful, but feeling them on his back, without looking at them, was different. From that place on his back a shock traveled down to his pelvis like a liberation army. From his pelvis, the sweet, warm broth of his nerves chanted rhyming couplets down to his toes, up to the roots of his hair, and even the neutral protuberances of his ankles darkened and blackened inside. Rosenzweil exulted, and even Rosini couldn't pretend not to have felt it.

After the embrace, Clelia got up and said she was going home, to the house where she had been staying for the past few weeks. Thus left alone at the table, with nothing to do but cast glances at the tiny bar's other customers in the dark, he gave a shiver of satisfaction for the scene he had succeeded in sketching out, a scene, for all intents and purposes, of passion. An hour later he got up and caught a taxi. After climbing six exhausting flights of stairs, he staggered to the bathroom, started the water running in the tub, stripped and washed his face with cold water at the sink, swallowing, drinking water, water with a bit of soap that had remained on his hands, spitting it out. He ate some bread with Nutella in the kitchen, returned to the bathroom, and immersed himself in the tub, where he thought of Clelia, of how much he would have liked to have her in the tub with him, of how much he would have liked to know her family and the music stores in the Village, of how much in fact he dreamed of traveling with her far away.

Anyone who has lived in two countries simultaneously will have noticed what goes missing in one language and what in another, which parts of consciousness are active and which are dormant depending on the lights in the cafés and in the streets, on the forms of greeting and civility, on the expectations people have of you. In short, Rosenzweil has a right to his say in this affair, and Rosenzweil—this is his opinion—regarded Rosini as a malign or superfluous element. Rosenzweil would gladly have erased an entire series of elements from the memory of the body inherited from Rosini: not his excess fat, that had no negative effects; and not even his knowledge of the Scriptures, an inexhaustible topic of conversation; and, though it may come as a surprise, he would not even have eliminated his somewhat gloomy tendency to pray, which—aside from certain nights when the thoughts would go into a tailspin and his prayer fill up with specters and omens—remained a way as good as any other not to neglect one's neighbor. No, the only elements Rosenzweil would have erased were Rosini's fears, those dogged and spiteful mice that would pop out of a small arch in the baseboard, like in cartoons, and make him jump up on a chair, make him feel alone and exposed. Rosenzweil thought Rosini was wasting his life out of fear of petty little things: Was it such a big deal if Leo gave a computer to a very beautiful young woman and in return she slept with him? Was it such a big deal if his father gave him money and enjoyed imagining his child enraptured by wild, Moulin Rouge–esque entertainments in a Paris of his dreams? (As he sat in the tub, Rosenzweil nodded and played with the lather.) Sex and money: Rosini feared them every time they were not employed for the greater glory of God; and every time that happened, the mice squeaked louder and louder and everything seemed horrible and unjust.

I remember, from romantic attachments in my early twenties, what great pleasure is to be found in the philosophical temper that follows an encounter, whether consummated or not, with a woman. But if you are fortunate, there is a second great pleasure, following on the first: to be called back by the woman in the midst of your reflections. That evening this happened to Rosenzweil in the most exhilarating way: he heard noises in the apartment; Clelia had returned.

Fortunately, the sangria prevented him from remembering that the Jewish girl had turned over her copy of the keys; if he'd had a clear mind, he would have feared it was a burglar. The wonderful thing was that Clelia had had to go to her uncle's place to get the third set in order to come back to him, and not only that: she'd preferred to come up without buzzing first, to enter on her own, and the move made so little sense that it reminded Rosenzweil of the morning she had woken him at dawn only after having made coffee.

He rinsed himself off, slipped on jeans and a T-shirt (even as he knew it would have been better to come out in his bathrobe, feigning concern, and from concern move directly to kisses), and left the bathroom. Awaiting him was a delicious scene that made him feel part of the human comedy: Clelia was out on the terrace and screaming in French to someone down in the street: "I'm not moving from this spot! I'm not coming down! You can stay there all night, if you feel like it! No, I'm not coming! I know! I'm sorry! Go home, you're waking everybody up!"

"Look at this beautiful tearjerker of a scene," Rosenzweil said to himself, and since he feared that Clelia, out of an excessive sense of melodrama, might topple over, he rushed over, grabbed her around her belly, and caused her to plummet backward into the apartment, and there he fell to the ground, with her on top, banging his rear. "Crazy fool." The Jewish girl began to laugh, stretching out and staying put. With the back of his neck Rosenzweil could feel that the floor had not been vacuumed for a week, could feel the cookie crumbs in his hair. She turned and sat up, still on his belly; she leaned her head toward his and submerged him in her unbound hair. From very close up she observed him, caressing his face and his chest. Rosenzweil smiled at her blissfully, letting her press against his stomach. Clelia came closer still, covered him with her long form, and kissed him on the neck. He pulled her to him and caressed her back.

"Will you embrace me again like before?" he asked.

"Certainly, darling."

She nuzzled Rosenzweil's neck and he sat up; she settled herself into his arms, her modest tits right under his eyes; he allowed her to caress his back. This back, inherited from Piero Rosini, was an entire countryside left to wither under the machine guns of the Khmer Rouge. Clelia's ugly, long, yellow hands, pressing and provoking, made of that withered back a great continent of forests and rivers, with thousands of diverse species of birds and reptiles and brightly colored insects and fruit with faintly warm thirst-quenching flesh.

By then it was time to kiss, she made that clear by bringing her lips from neck to sideburns to cheeks—but I, pushing

226

Rosenzweil aside, reclaiming my body, terrorized by this Jewish mouse newly popped out of the baseboard, this long mouse with the snout job who wanted to kiss me, I seized control and said, "No, no, I'm scared! No, please! Not on the mouth!"

Obviously, we're all cheering for Rosenzweil. We all love to think that in the right circumstances we'll be free to choose what we prefer and to ignore our inner old maid. But let him who is without fear cast the first stone; fear is made of stronger stuff than sin.

"Why not on the mouth?" Clelia asked.

"Because on the mouth . . . if we do it on the mouth, then it's like it's happened. Kiss me on the neck, please, I'm scared."

"But it *has* happened."

None of this, thank God, prevented her from continuing to kiss my neck and my cheeks as she ventured threateningly close to my mouth.

"No, if you don't kiss me on the mouth, then absolutely nothing has happened."

"Excuse me? Are we back in kindergarten here?" She smiled with assurance and without stopping. "Come on, don't be afraid, it's beautiful, it's a beautiful thing, try to stay calm, try to relax, Chewb."

"Shit, shit, shit," I said. We stretched out on the floor once again. Against the dusty floor I squashed the fluvial forest and the thousands of species of little palmate animals swarming over my back thanks to that broth of embraces.

"Come on, don't be afraid . . ."

"I am afraid, afraid of losing Alice."

"But you're not losing Alice."

"And if I do?" I planted a kiss on her cheek and said, "I'm dying."

I got up and went out on the terrace to breathe. Clelia remained stretched out like a city and muttered, "Oh man, you really are crazy. No, really."

Later she fell asleep on the sofa bed. I went to say good

night; she offered me a bewildered maternal smile: I had made her feel both insecure and superior.

"You really have some serious problems. You really can't think straight."

"Sorry, I'm sorry," I replied, and ran to shut myself up in my room.

Half an hour later I came out of my room and, lighting the way with the display on my cell phone, rejoined Clelia in the living room. She slept in the center of the sofa bed, on her back, one arm alongside, the other at a distance from her body. She slept in white tennis shorts and my gray IBM T-shirt. I sat down on the bed and watched her. After five minutes of my sitting there on the springs, which creaked at my slightest move, she had yet to wake up. Then, with a lump in my throat, and feeling like a hunchback hidden atop a medieval cathedral, I raised my right hand, which trembled, and placed it on her belly. And if she wakes up, what do I say? I don't know. I kept my hand there for half a minute. Her belly breathed beneath my hand, serenely asleep. My left hand went to see what the right hand was doing, and to help out, picked up the edge of her shirt, while the palm of the other rose up a few centimeters only to dive under the fabric to her naked belly. I sweated between my fingers on her pale skin. I brought my hand up and with the middle finger touched the hollow of her breastbone. Meanwhile, the index and ring fingers spread away from the middle finger and grazed first one breast, then the other. Softness. She didn't wake up, or else she pretended not to wake up. Index, middle, ring, and little fingers chose to head left together, opposite to where I was sitting, and to climb up the left breast, which hung down obliquely, nippleless, a pale, comical, and unresolved mass that had lost its barycenter. Four fingers stayed at the summit of the breast, wondering, "And what will we do if she wakes up?" But Clelia didn't wake up.

The next day the Jewish girl removed her lip gloss and contact lens case; Rosenzweil came out of the shower and she'd gone, gone in a coup de théâtre: leaving the espresso maker going on the stovetop. Its black handle, when Rosenzweil entered the kitchen in his bathrobe, drawn by the aroma of coffee and by the hoarse whistle of the steam being emitted, had begun to melt, and in fact it became possible to distinguish the sinister aroma of plastic.

A joy for Rosenzweil, constantly on the hunt for assurances that he belonged to the human race: a woman was continuing to do silly things on his account. This time there was a telling detail that was only revealed to him once he pieced the scene back together again, in the manner of moonstruck lovers the world over as they compile, usually lying down, their lists of romantic encounters: Clelia wasn't crazy, so it stood to reason that she hadn't rushed out and slammed the door; thus to turn on the flame beneath the espresso maker without telling me she'd done so, she must have waited for the moment when Rosenzweil had turned off the water in the shower, a moment, that is, not long before her lover's probable exit from the bathroom; she could hardly set the kitchen on fire or make an irreparable mess in one of her uncle's apartments. As he removed his bathrobe and began to dress, Rosenzweil had already established that the scene had been rehearsed. And he added to himself that maybe the girl had placed her ear to the bathroom door to hear whether he had finished his shower, eavesdropping on the noise of the water. At this point Rosenzweil wondered whether perhaps the previous evening's scene—those screams from the terrace—hadn't been an act as well, because if Clelia was such an odd character, it could even well be that the lovesick Frenchman did not exist, or was an accomplice. A possibly somewhat exaggerated, but not unfounded, suspicion; the upshot is that someone loves you, Rosenzweil, so put your mind at ease and stop playing insecure.

But this he too had understood. His problem wasn't the degree of his appreciation by adoptive Parisians and their uncles, it was that Rome was pressing in, and predictably, seeing as how *The Jewish Pope* was about to be published, in the days to come there was rather less time for sentimental melodrama.

Alice called to unburden herself—catching him with his pants down, but alone, in the dimly illuminated apartment, without even the computer that Clelia had retrieved some time ago—about the bad blood boiling over between her and her sister, a situation urgent enough for her to call her husband's cell phone from her father's landline. Ada had confronted her, saying, apparently not mincing her words, that she needed to get on a train and get to Paris to claim her husband, and take him home to Porta di Roma. Just hearing the name of the neighborhood made Rosenzweil shudder. A good reason to become Clelia's lover: never again to cross the Grande Raccordo Anulare. "Papa, buy me a house far, far away," thought Rosenzweil, who, as the adoptive son of my father, shared none of my complexes about money. "What makes her think she can say such things to my face?" asked Alice, her voice coming through the flat receiver on a restricted range of frequencies. "Pierino, I'm completely fed up with all this honesty on the part of my sister and the Teste Parlanti. Why do they always say things to my face? Do they think it's easy for me?"

"Did you tell her? That she can only talk once she becomes a nun? Ada's one scheming bastard."

"Come on, how could I say that? I'd kill her if I did."

How could Rosenzweil think of freeing himself from such a sweet woman? From a woman so afraid of causing harm to her neighbor, who treated every encounter as if it were her life's last? Rosenzweil could hate my fears, but this girl, who had always been on our side and supported us in every way, he couldn't hate her. Perhaps this was his undoing; perhaps this was why there was no way he could outclass Piero Rosini. With regard to the book as well, naturally, Alice was on my side. A few nights later she told me the book would be in bookstores in a matter of days, Mario had written her to warn me; it was now mid-March. She asked whether I was afraid, which made us both laugh because we had no idea what to be afraid of; it might be nothing more than a tempest in a teacup or it might provoke a huge debate and end up in Parliament and with an excommunication.

"Public opinion," explained Alice, "is so fucking random. There's no logic to it. After the fact, we see what's become a media phenomenon and what hasn't, and at that point we retroactively decide that there was some profound necessity, that the thing couldn't have happened any other way. It's outrageous!"

She was a fascinating woman who could talk about anything, and Rosenzweil knew this.

Alice also told me that a national Catholic demonstration in support of the institution of the family was about to take place, which had caused a stir among the Teste Parlanti. "It's also aimed a bit at the homosexual lobbies pushing for civil unions. It'll take place in the spring and so you can see, Pierino, how a book against the Pope at the same time as a profamily demonstration . . . it'll be too much for the Teste Parlanti, spiritual collapse. They're absolutely all over Family Day. But when they denounce families that 'don't open themselves to life,' they don't have the courage to look me in the face."

"Do you think we're a sterile family?"

She laughed. "We're a gay family, yes."

"Are you coming to Paris?"

"My dear Pierino, one can't tackle all the issues at once."

Finally, the big day arrived, and it was none other than Leo who gave me the news that the book was out. A breakfast meeting, at the café at the end of the Rue des Martyrs, to talk about work. I had just begun to organize the register of rents and the notebook of needs and complaints, as Uncle Leo called it. I was learning to use some office software on a laptop that he bequeathed to me because he had a new one. The goal was to digitize all the past and present data over the course of a few months; the agreement was that I would do that for the time being, and then, if I decided to settle in Paris, we'd look into how to proceed, to see whether the collaboration made functional sense. A truly odd job. Leo must have been a generous character, or else been aware to an extreme degree of his own needs, to decide that a Ukrainian girl was worth a new computer and that a humble Roman, aimless and adrift but good company, was worth a used computer and even a rent-free apartment, in exchange for almost nothing.

I located him amid the traffic in spare change and fresh-smelling fruit from the Arab vendors who occupied the first stretch of the street. He ordered me a coffee and at the same time spread open a copy of *La Repubblica* on the table, over his empty cup, glasses, and packet of tissues. The street was bustling at nine o'clock; the sky promised rain. Rue des Martyrs, notwithstanding its name and the steep slope and a gray firmament that in Rome would have been enough to ruin everyone's day, was boisterous and cheerful.

Leo opened the paper and then closed it momentarily, meanwhile raising the lower right-hand corner of the first page: "First look at the title."

I read it, incredulous; it was just a paragraph, but it was on the front page.

"What a ridiculous country," he commented.

"I can't believe it." Then, with the bit of nervous energy left in me (only barely did my legs support me; they had become paralyzed as soon as I read "Wojtyła" and "anti-Semitism"), I pretended to receive a phone call and instead called Alice, hiding around the corner from the square, behind Leo's back. "Do you have the book with you?"

"What, did you see *La Repubblica*?"

"Yes."

"No, your name's not there."

"Not even in the book? It doesn't say who the editor is?"

I would so have liked to confide in her, to tell her I was there with Leo, but in order to avoid even mentioning Clelia's

232

name I had never told her my landlord was Jewish, and my friend to boot.

"Not even in the book, don't worry."

"They kept me out of it."

"You're happy."

"Extremely. Dying of happiness."

"I was afraid you'd take it as an insult. I wanted to tell you that I thought it was a good thing."

"It is a good thing."

"So you'll be fine, you see."

"And now they're martyring him?" I asked, looking at the street sign saying Rue des Martyrs.

News of the book spread through the Catholic blogs; Alice told me Mario was becoming an underground hero. "Nobody accepts the book's argument, but they're all against the criminalization of Mario and Non Possumus. A kind of movement has sprung up in his defense. In favor of the freedom of historical research. They're saying we need to have the courage to reject the conventional versions of the facts. They sound like you! Some priests have said that we need to seek out and talk about the secret forces that oppose the Church. Basically they're saying, 'Certain lobbies should be forced out into the open at all costs. And this doesn't necessarily have anything to do with Wojtyła.' It's incredible, Piero, everyone's talking about the stuff you're always talking about. It's strange you're not here. Mario's been invited to go on the *Otto e Mezzo* show."

(Mario wrote me a ludicrous e-mail: short, disrespectful, conspiratorial: "From now on by letter only." Unsigned.)

Rosenzweil reacted to this sequence of events by inviting Clelia over, this time no pretexts. He managed to do so because she loved him and he was savvy and knew how to make a woman who had every right to feel humiliated not feel humiliated. Where had he learned to act like a man?

I tripped him up on this occasion as well, and Clelia, fading fast after two hours spent talking about music and movies and pretending that the handle of the coffeemaker had never melted, smoked a joint and fell into a deep sleep, as though she were a character in a fairy tale and wouldn't wake for thousands of years.

There I was, alone with the body of my adorable Jewess, and as I was in thrall to the inescapable hierarchy of the female body, her breasts were no longer enough and I felt the pull of her pussy.

She was lying on her left side, in a fetal position, knees bent, right hip rising up in an ample curve, one hand beneath the pillow supporting her head. I waited for her to turn over and lie on her back. I waited longer still for her to spread her legs. I went into the kitchen, drank some water, washed my hands, smoked two cigarettes, poured myself some rum.

Another half hour's sleep and the sheet was twisted, pushed aside, lying across her at an odd angle that made me think of a beauty queen's sash. Her cappuccino-colored panties were now visible, contrasting warmly with her yellowish-pink skin, and thus from tits I moved on to thinking about cunt.

She turned her left thigh out forty-five degrees, while her right leg remained straight. She held one arm over her head and one hand half open on her chest, fingers limp.

I set down the glass in the kitchen and went to sit at the foot of the bed. I decided to kneel, so I could get a better view. The crumpled material between her legs, just where her panties (worn, fuzz balls) were at their narrowest, exerted a strange power over me. I rose up on my knees. I gently pushed down on the mattress with my hands, testing the springs. I approached. There was a stretch where the mattress would squeak if I put too much pressure on it. Guiding my head toward the area between her thighs, like a submarine navigating through weedy depths, I brought my mouth to within a few centimeters of the fabric, which, when you looked closely, dipped here and there to trace the contours of the flesh beneath and, elsewhere, molded her from farther away, like asphalt over a hairy thicket. What was hidden behind the fabric was instantly revealed by the pungent odor that reached my nose, carrying information that galvanized every centimeter of my body.

Clelia moved. Fearing that she would close her legs, I quickly pulled myself away and sat down cross-legged between the wall and the bed. I took a deep breath and then held it, trying to force my heart to slow down.

"Chewb," she called. "Is that you?"

"Yes," I said, my voice skipping a step that had formed in my throat.

"Where are you?"

"Down here."

She raised herself up on her elbows and located me. Her face was broad and swollen, her hair still sleepy.

"What are you doing, are you looking at me?"

"Yes."

"What are you looking at?"

There was nothing I could say.

"Are you coming to bed?"

Why could Clelia, why Leo, and not me?

"Come to bed. Come to me."

"I can't do it."

Propping herself up on her elbows, speaking in a sleepy voice: "Why don't we do this: I'll lie here and for five minutes I'll try not to fall asleep. If you can stop being so crazy for a moment, you can lie down here too." She was lying on her back again and was gently talking to the ceiling, and I had the sensation that she was skipping over some of the sentences she was thinking. "You're handicapped. You don't belong to the race of normal men. Even if you do work for my uncle. Maybe it's better if you stop calling me. I come running every time." She sighed. "No?"

"Yeah."

"Who knows what it is you want."

I felt awkward sitting at the foot of the bed, the way I'd done when my parents summoned me to the dressing chair in front of the bed and, lying there with the pillows piled up behind them, minimal effort involved, gave me a dressing-down.

"Are you afraid of me?" continued Clelia tentatively, unsure why I wasn't laying myself open to anything beyond being completely in the wrong. "Are you afraid? Are you mute? Are you afraid to stay here in the dark room with the monsters and your friend Clelia? You're really afraid of everything, then. A woman doesn't tell a man that she wants to fuck him unless she's sure he's up for it."

"Really?"

"Come here, come on, put your arms around me for a little bit; I can't keep explaining everything to you."

From down below I laughed, and she did too, bedroom laughs, the laughs of crumpled white sheets.

"Well? Are you coming?"

"Am I coming?"

"I'll wait five minutes. I'm not saying anything anymore. In five minutes I'm going to sleep."

"You're giving me five minutes to decide."

"Chewbacca."

"Five. You do the counting."

And the Jewish girl, who hoped against hope and decided not to cover herself up with the sheet, counted sheep, and the first sheep was me, and before she could count five minutes' worth of sheep she had given up and she slept once more.

The way people rush to say "History is not made up of *ifs*" is good proof to the contrary.

Now that the time has come to relate what happened next—the minor comedy of errors that finally (without, let it be said, too strong a causal relation) put a major wrench in my plans, whatever those were and whoever I was—I wonder what impact each of the singular events, as well as the entire sequence of events, would have had on me *if*, before those five minutes were up, I had instead gone and lain down on that sofa bed. In short, what I'm curious about is *if* at least that one night, instead of managing to get out of trouble on the cheap thanks to my cold, cold heart, I had suddenly given in before that declaration of love and surrender I had received and promptly minimalized, when many people would have paid to have such ardor and emotion from a woman, to hear "You can lie down next to me"—and I think about crippled people, about the very poor, about the maimed, about people whose skin smells like shut-off refrigerators, about the handicapped who know what love is and can't do it . . . *If* I had woken up in bed with Clelia after having finally committed the great mistake, the mistake that would have truly obliged me to run to St.-Germain with my tail between my legs and to acknowledge before a learned priest, kneeling in a secondary chapel by ridiculously insufficient candlelight, that I belonged to the hordes of weak men who had failed before God and before their spouses . . . *If* things had gone in the way hypothesized here, I wonder whether the no-longer-nebulous but certifiable, definite awareness of having committed an error, or fault, or sin, in imbuing me with humility, would have guaranteed me a resigned and calmer response to the complex events that would shortly take place, in the days following that (penultimate) desperate attempt to convince myself to sleep with Clelia.

When Mario's text message arrived saying "Did you receive my letter?" I became very angry. There was no letter; I asked him whether he had sent it to the correct address; he replied that he thought he had and asked whether I was praying for him. "Of course I'm praying for you, but don't send me letters now, and tell me what address you used." He'd used the correct address, Rue Notre-Dame-de-Lorette. It would not, in effect, have made much difference if Clelia and I had slept together; things wouldn't be much different, namely: the super hadn't given me the letter, it had been sent ten days earlier and—just thinking about it made me nauseated, gave me heartburn, gastritis, bad breath—Leo must have been the one who took it out of the hands of my super, recognizing on the envelope for me, as he collected the bills and the other mail, the full name of the man at the center of the controversy about historical revisionism in Italy. When I asked the super about it, he couldn't remember.

Maybe it would have been better to be Clelia's lover the day Alice sent me a link to YouTube, where I found Mario in a white shirt, unshaven, speaking about the Enlightenment with Giuliano Ferrara, broad and pink with pretty little eyes, and Ritanna Armeni in a suit with a Chinese collar and lots of pink lipstick in the blue studio of *Otto e Mezzo*. Mario was free to speak because Ferrara, in this little controversy about revisionism, which would soon reenter the familiar para-academic context but for a few days at least could be delved into, had decided to play the good-natured provocateur and allow Non Possumus to express its own ideas. It would have been beautiful to make love to a woman while watching Mario, my Don Quixote, finally able to speak to Italians, emerge from his niche and make people understand that even windmills can take your arm off: "No no no, the book's thesis is not the point, however scandalous it may seem; the point is that religions count in history, and not only in farcical ways, as the followers of the Enlightenment would have you believe, but also via more secret paths, paths that are difficult to understand, that are frightening." It would have been beautiful to feel myself fall into the purple pulp of a Jewish girl while my erstwhile mentor elucidated the well-dissimulated and pernicious intentions behind the Frankist windmills.

"Since the end of the eighteenth century you have all believed—they have *taught* you to believe"—he turned to address the wrong camera, but the director accommodated him and the whole of Mario's face was framed on-screen—"you have believed for the past two hundred years that history traces a simple arc, from the dark credulousness of religions—extravagant fools and wells of superstition—to the luminous path of progress and tolerance. Behind your backs, while you drink down this old story, powerful people are building a more fascinating history, an intrinsically spiritual and religious history, that you are afraid to know . . ."

Instead I endured these words alone, not even with Clelia's computer but with the one loaned to me by Leo, without a joint, without a woman; all of this was very paradoxical but not so much that (seeing as how I didn't have a lover) I was obliged to figure out which path to choose: return to being a fisher of men, or become a fisher of women.

As far as Mario goes, I would have greeted the news of his success much more gladly if it weren't for the problem of the letter. So far, in fact, no one had mentioned me: I was a true ghostwriter. The fifteen thousand copies of the book sold (re-printed four times already in just a few weeks) circulated through homes with no mention of who was responsible for the syntax (of a good half of the text—I even considered that it was to my credit if people read it). The only real trouble was the letter. Leo had never looked up my name on the Internet, and I'd published no articles; in the editorial office I was only the one unofficially in charge of matters of language. There was no way he could connect me with Non Possumus; I had done a search and my name didn't appear. What's more, in the books I edited I used the name Pietro Rosini, because it's the name I was baptized with, and it really is a common name.

But now Leo knew who I was from Mario's letter: after a few days of silence he e-mailed me to say he wouldn't need any help for the Monday tour. Two days later, not having heard from him and finding it unnerving to work on the digitization of his paperwork without talking, I was a mess. I was certain it was all over, and after a nearly sleepless night I sent him a message: "Where did you disappear to? If you want to talk about Mario, I'm here." He didn't reply or come to see me for several days. I continued to live in his apartment and to work for him (in a manner of speaking), and he didn't get in touch; I didn't have anything to smoke and had trouble falling asleep; on the other hand, without anything to do, I could wake up whenever I pleased.

This, then, is probably where things would have gone differently if Clelia and I had fucked: now, instead of writing to Leo, I would have taken his niece in my arms and to bed, and after making her come Rosenzweil would have explained about my past and the problem that it was now presenting in my relationship with Leo (in the hope that with her at least it would not present a problem), making her understand that ideally she herself would be the one to plead my case to her uncle.

Regarding this entire affair between these two Jews and me, one thing should be said: this was not the story of my redemption, but neither was it merely a story of depravity; I wasn't a stalker, in other words, and I wasn't someone who had repented of having thought ill of Jews and now that he knew them didn't find them so bad. After all, it's impossible that an ancient civilization like ours, raised to admire brilliantly colored figures in church windows and graceful black forms on clay vessels, could produce rudimentary descriptions and interpretations like "redemption" versus "depravity." *But* (and it's a gigantic *but*, and it's a *but* with which, on a par with *if*, I want to be free to make history) . . . *but if* Clelia had become my lover, I could have told the simplified and progressive version of the story—I know Jews, I redeem myself—and thanks to our embraces, the soothing blow jobs, nights spent clinging together, throats dry and shoulders bare, Clelia's pubic hairs still twined around my uvula, the simplified version would have become the truth.

Too late: I didn't fuck her before the book came out and

now the damage was done, by now Leo knew, and if he still had any doubts—in the unlikely event he hadn't read Mario's name in the return address on a letter from Italy given to him days earlier by the super, or he'd decided it was a matter of two men happening to have the same name—he now definitively knew, thanks to my genius of a sister, who, in the midst of a full-on debate about the possible existence of an anti-Semitic fringe in the Church, published a column on the front page of *La Repubblica*, in which, with the oblique passion that only a woman can have when faced with the great themes of politics and religion, she described how an ideological struggle played out in her family between a progressive woman writer of erotic fiction and her anti-Semitic brother. A piece about the two of us, about our divergence ever since my "postmodern and neocon" conversion, a piece whose aim—as my sister defended herself to my mother for the rest of her days—had been to show that there was no intrinsically public, objective, well-founded debate, because each person's opinions are formed within the context of puerile misunderstandings and quarrels between imbeciles. (She had, in other words, written the piece to make me understand that she still thought of me and that she missed confrontation with me, and in fact, the same day it appeared she sent me a text to tell me that if I wanted to I could write a response and the paper would publish it. Now, poor Fede, since it was only ten days later that things turned out really badly for me, the two events, her open letter and my misfortune, would always remain connected, and for Fede it was a real burden, but at the moment my only problem was being discovered by Leo; *if* I hadn't had this problem—of which she was ignorant, moreover, so how could it be her fault?—the debate about revisionism would have represented a perfect occasion to return to Federica, to discuss everything with her, to admit the error of my ways, maybe even to describe my journey—yes, in this case as well, the simplified version would have worked—of *redemption*, to describe how my own particular paranoid and conspiracy-hunting vision was born of a cloistered and rather colorless life. I could have joked about the fact that I wasn't fucking anyone, my sister and I could have come to a new understanding, and ultimately, at the end of a concise, essential chain of *ifs*, she would have contrived to find me some work in publishing and my life would have been set back on track. But—*but!*—I remained paralyzed by the certainty that Leo had definitively unmasked me, and instead of rushing to Rome to resolve my family problems, instead of writing a piece for *La Repubblica*, I began to wander the streets of Paris, lost in thought, once again incapable of taking a solid crap. Whenever I scratched my head, I came away with a handful of hair; with Clelia I exchanged facetious and painfully escapist text messages—"Apocalypso Now," "Apocalypso Facto"—and with my wife I pretended that in Paris everything was going great and that it was the right thing to stay put—I could hardly tell her I had quarreled with Leo, could I? She didn't even know who he was. Apart from anything else she was furious with Federica, the whole family was, even my two brothers, who had never read a newspaper column in their lives, with the possible exception of Candido Cannavò's in *La Gazzetta dello Sport*.) Whatever the aim of the piece, it had ruined me forever in Leo's eyes.

One morning, on my way to the church, earphones on, I crossed the street on a red: a driver slammed on his brakes. The customers of the café on the corner, who witnessed the scene from the sidewalk tables where Leo always used to wait for me and where, for the last few days, rain or shine, I'd been unsuccessfully looking for him, shook their heads, despairing at my thoughtlessness. The driver took off without even lowering the window to insult me; I took refuge in the church for a quarter of an hour to calm my nerves.

Even Ada got involved. She called and asked me to return to Rome right away. She knew I was afraid of the Non Possumus situation, but I had to go back.

"Pierino, something truly stinks here. I'm smelling something I don't like."

"They're not emptying the dumpsters?" I felt like I hated her.

"You're really missed here in Rome. There's something strange in the air. Your absence is felt. You have to come back."

"Oh please, you mean the absence of my big fat ass."

"That's not true, don't say that; I miss you so much."

"*You* miss me? Do you still see Corrado? Do you go to parties? Have you made out?"

"*Idiot*, that's the farthest thing from my mind."

"I'll only come back if you miss me."

"Alice misses you."

"In my opinion, you only want me to come back for Family Day, otherwise it'll embarrass you that Alice is without a husband."

"What are you talking about, are you stupid? I'm unhappy you're not together."

"We're also unhappy."

"Doesn't seem like it."

"What?"

"No, sorry, I didn't mean that. I know you're unhappy, but then do something, right?"

Since Alice had said she found it impossible to *kill* her sister by responding that she should enter a convent and stop breaking everyone's balls, in the same spirit I said sorry, that I was nervous, and hung up without having made it clear that she shouldn't presume to give me any more advice.

For the next two days Ada made at least fifteen attempts to call me. Contrary to the rule of etiquette that says if any anxious interlocutor covers herself in excessive ridicule, one is obliged to try to break the pattern, I didn't even answer her to tell her to stop. Like the coarsest of men, I thought: "What this woman really needs is a good fuck." Can you believe this came from me?

243

Between one message and another from my sister-in-law came the death warrant—Leo inviting me out to dinner. I showed up nervous and weak-kneed to the art nouveau restaurant on Rue Racine, a historic bubble of pastel colors, French dishes, and raw meat, still girlishly alluring in its pale green stuccowork, curtains, and undulating moldings. Leaving my duffel coat with the waiter, I told myself I should order the tartare, so that even if my stomach was churning with nerves, I could swallow without chewing, but I didn't even have a chance to read the menu. I had my hand on the wooden back of the chair, ready to take my seat, when Leo stopped me: "No, don't sit."

I stood there, the blood running cold in my hand on the hard back of the chair.

"Look, I thought we could eat dinner together and then I could tell you at the end; then I thought I would also give you a speech; I thought about a whole bunch of things, because you know how much we've talked together and I really hate to have to make a big drama of it, or even just to have to treat someone badly, but . . . but . . . but . . . *Pietro, Pietro*, I'm sorry, but it's better if you go back to Rome to your wife, just leave, please, let's not embarrass ourselves, you know it's better if you just go, that's it, don't explain, just go, let the super know when you leave so I can go back and get everything in order, leave the computer in the apartment—yeah, now you think I'll reuse it with a girl, huh?" He laughed, and I gave a laugh that seemed to have been dubbed in over my serious face. "No, I'll give it to someone at the university who needs it, one of my students . . . C'mon, get out of here, go . . ."

The waiter returned my coat and opened the aqua-green glass door. I went out into the coolness of the little street off Boulevard St.-Michel, at an angle and slightly uphill, toward the Senate. I had made an attempt to live. Not a very successful one, but I had all the same driven a girl mad, disappointed a great friend, walked every inch of one of the most beautiful cities in the world, made a miserable impression in front of millions of self-absorbed readers of *La Repubblica*, betrayed my vocation, and left my wife on the outskirts of a city or in the clutches of her unhappy father.

Perhaps Rosenzweil, with his savoir faire, would have succeeded in explaining to Clelia the nature of Piero Rosini's path from anti-Semitism to redemption even as he had been invited to hit the road. The real problem is that he would in the meantime have to move out, to look for a place, and in so doing he would have to spend all the money from his father. Unless he managed to find someone to put him up in Paris— sleeping on a rug would suit Rosenzweil, he didn't even need a couch, as long as he could stay. Stay with, I don't know, Benedetta, or Jette, or Ana. In short, his desire to stay in Paris—a good desire, one that, if expressed years earlier, at the appropriate moment, would have been encouraged by everyone—clearly required him to sleep at the home of one of the women he knew. It's also true that in Paris one seldom makes friends with men, and at this point I hadn't heard from the Belgian from the glider association for months. With no female friends, there's no way you can navigate a situation successfully; this is why very pious men never seem to really exert control over events and they have a disoriented air about them.

Friday morning I received another two calls from Ada (the last one had come Thursday morning) and still I didn't respond. "We have to talk," she wrote then, after days of failed attempts, "and tomorrow we will talk. Your Mohammed." I didn't respond to the message, thinking that tomorrow, like today, I wouldn't respond. Twenty minutes later, she wrote simply:

;-)

The triumphant idiocy of the wink shook me so much that I deleted her messages without taking the trouble to reflect: I should have understood that she was on her way up to Paris because she was Mohammed going to the mountain; and if you're in a complicated situation like mine, you have to try not to be obtuse, and I was, seeing as how my only attempt to explain the unusual sign-off "Mohammed" had merely produced a mental association between Catholics and Muslims—as for example in the case of the alleged Islamic rule I followed of not looking at a woman twice, otherwise there's volition; thus to me it seemed like a plausible term, Mohammed, as if Ada, not taking herself too seriously, meant to say that she knew how to play a bit at saving everyone, at prophesying, at leading lost sheep back to the fold. Mohammed and the mountain never once came to mind.

You can't become a man of the world on a whim. There were only two sensible responses to events: one was to accept the idea, no matter how remote and bizarre, that Ada was traveling in the direction of Paris that very night; to accept Ada with the patience we show to madmen and newborns; to avoid therefore inviting Clelia to my apartment that same evening; the next day, to settle the matter, hold my stomach in, back straight, even offer my sister-in-law breakfast, explain that she had to start paying heed to her own life because others were managing on their own; then to put her in a taxi, accompany her to the Gare de Bercy, and make sure she got on the train to Rome (a true gentleman would have bought her the ticket right there); and, once I had seen the train leave, to pick up my Parisian affairs where I had left off. The second sensible response would have been to give priority to my own life in Paris, with the implicit recognition that this life had become more real than the Roman one, had thereby become my life: either not to accept the idea of Ada's missionary trip and invite Clelia over, finally sleep with her, and then, surprised by Ada's arrival, ignore the intercom, go to the window, and shout: "You're not coming up! I won't let you!" Or else, even more courageously, to understand that Ada was coming, intentionally invite Clelia over the evening before, kiss her and undress her and love her as a deliberate ritual of exorcism against this sister-in-law withered by good intentions, and on seeing her appear the next morning, shout, "You're not coming up! I won't let you!"

I could have done one of these two (three) things, and it would have worked. But inside me reigned a confusion of powers.

If: If I had made love to Clelia, I could have counted on an accomplice and made the arrival of my sister-in-law a key moment, a diriment impediment. *But*: But wasn't that precisely the point, that I refused to have women accomplices behind my wife's back? Here was the *ubi consistam* of fidelity: you are bound jointly and severally, you must sink along with the ship.

If the first time with Clelia had been the time before, her last entry into my—her . . . her uncle's—apartment would have had an entirely different energy. Not that the Jewish girl hadn't responded with her usual solicitude and absence of pride—when I sent her my invitation via text message she didn't even give me time to suspect it might not be the thing to do, responding within minutes, "Give me an hour." (*If* Clelia had taken a bit more time, would I have crumbled?) She came and I made her some pasta, from one of the three open packages on shelves more and more desolate-looking by the day, no sauce, just garlic, some extremely yellow oil, and a packet of chili powder; then she had me smoke pot from a tiny azure-blue pipe because she was trying to stop using tobacco. She talked to me about Ana wanting to go back to Spain and how the news had devastated Benedetta. She gave no sign of whether she knew about me from her uncle. *If* she knew, then did that mean she wanted me still and forgave me? *If* she didn't know, was it the moment to confess all and ask for her to intercede with Leo?

She insisted on sleeping, saying "I'm wiped out." In hindsight I could have guessed what she was getting at, but one can't simply turn oneself into a man of the world, Rosenzweil. As Clelia prepared for bed, having produced a T-shirt and shorts from where I don't know, she begged me to leave the living room, she was dying to sleep. I was only capable of thinking in biblical terms (rather than taking the situation in hand or at least looking the other way while Rosenzweil exhumed his romantic character, neglected for days on the basis of the evident superiority of my past to his foolish aspirations for the future), and in particular I said to myself: "Look, Piero, you're like the prodigal son from the parable, who asks his father for an advance on his inheritance so he can go spend it in bouts of debauchery, but you stand like a no-hoper at the brothel door."

But Rosenzweil was not convinced by my speeches in the least, in fact they bored him, such that as soon as I'd closed the door to my room, without even brushing my teeth or taking a piss or pouring myself a glass of water, putting on some pathetic blue sweatpants as pajamas, Rosenzweil went back into the living room still in jeans and T-shirt, and after whispering by way of summary, "How have you managed to put up with me all this time and how have I managed not to give in to you? Will you ever be able to forgive my foolishness?" slipped into bed with Clelia, murmuring another couple of sentences that made her laugh and convinced her to reply, "All right, then, now just leave it to me, because you must be all confused; I'll kiss you to calm you down, and when you're calm you can kiss me too, okay?"

And Rosenzweil responded, "I can't hold back any longer, it's going to kill me."

Along my spinal column the tropical forest once again took over and extended over the places the Jewish girl kissed, until Rosenzweil's smooth pink body became a verdant planet crossed by playful streams, tickled by the little paws of strange animals.

Instead I woke up a few hours later in a state of anguish

and decided to go look at her. I found her curled up on one side beneath the sheet and purple bedspread.

Would I wake her or not? I didn't know. I leaned over her. She had her mouth open, a foul odor of sleep and digestion already issuing forth. Kissing both her lips was technically difficult. I now drew back, slowly; I went to the foot of the bed and rubbed my hands together. I got down and ever so slowly, bending low like a cat, approached her on the side she slept on and, pushing aside the sheet, nosed my way to within twenty centimeters of the place that, between the age of eight and first contact, children and adolescents dream about, Treasure Island, whose exotic name they learn thanks to the password: mons veneris, the enchanted peak with a river at whose source lies in eternity the goddess of love, about whom everyone knows how to write and sing in eternal frightful awe, except the Christians, who read the Song of Songs and are proud of it, but there's quite a gap between that and saying it's okay to contemplate the pussy. Anyhow, Christian or non-Christian, I could have looked for as long as I wanted, but I would never have had the courage of Rosenzweil, who just then got up and took his place on the thin strip of bed next to Clelia, and turning his back on me began to whisper sweet nothings; these not waking her, however, he covered her with kisses, until the Jewish girl woke up and after backing away a few centimeters widened her eyes and without saying anything gave him permission to kiss her—then, when they were already out of their underwear and still wearing shirts, a bit like Donald and Daisy Duck, Clelia looked into his eyes (she had her legs spread wide and knees bent, a Meccano robot covered in milk chocolate) and said, "Uncle Leo told me and I know everything, but now you go ahead and fuck me all the same because I know that you're good, that you're just a great big befuddled Chewbacca."

Clelia woke up, maybe because I was looking at her and thinking about her too much, there on my knees beside the bed.

"What'd you do to me? Chewb, tell me, what have you been doing?"

I didn't move.

In her still sleepy voice she asked me questions she must have prepared.

"What'd you do to me? What have you been doing to me at night? For how long? You're crazy."

"No, I swear, Cle . . . lia!" protested Rosenzweil, the Latin lover. "I'll explain everything, just give me a minute!" He understood that now he either kissed her or got himself in serious trouble. "Don't move a muscle, stay where you are. I'll explain everything, and afterward you decide if you believe me."

Instead I tried to stand up and the Jewish girl ordered me, "Don't move a muscle, stay where you are. Explain what you were doing."

On his own initiative, Rosenzweil had already set out to explain the entire affair, from Non Possumus to the Jewish Pope, to the Teste Parlanti, to his desire to kiss her, and Clelia replied that she didn't believe him anymore and that she knew that he touched her in her sleep, that he was a pervert . . .

Both Rosenzweil and I asked her then, "Have you spoken with Leo?"

But my question was posed idly, playing for time, whereas Rosenzweil's was expressed, to use a Catholic image, in sackcloth and ashes, and to Rosenzweil Clelia responded, "Yes, I spoke with Leo, and if you don't come to bed now I'll report you for molestation," but she said these things with her eyes open wide, bright and dull at the same time, inviting eyes, then, and Rosenzweil began to laugh and to pick himself up off the floor, and, perhaps after a sigh, he delivered his last words as a technically faithful husband: "It's true that right now such a charge would come at a really bad time." And his gaze too was lucid and simultaneously dull, a gaze, what's more, focused on the eyes of the Jewish girl, who replied as his equal (involved in the rhetorical game in which one hesitates for an instant once the deal has effectively been struck and awaits only the final touch of a mouth wet with saliva on another mouth equally moist and slightly open), "Can you imagine if I were to report you now that your sister has ruined you in front of all of Italy, if I were to go and say that you molest poor Jewish girls? Ho ho ho . . . can you imagine?" and, strangely excited by the thought of those *ifs*, Rosenzweil placed a hand between her legs at the first contact with those chapped lips—and both of them stretched out on the bed, responsive to every touch, and included that *if* among the ingredients determining the taste of those first kisses, kisses providing an audaciously friendly conclusion to an unhealthy affair.

I was less fortunate precisely because my question had something entirely dishonest about it, leading her to respond, "That's none of your business."

"It is, a little bit, actually, it is."

"No, it's not. Tell me what you were doing."

"I was looking at you."

"No, you weren't just looking at me. You were doing things you shouldn't have."

"That's not true."

"You touched me."

"No."

"And yet you did. And it's not the first time. How many months have you been doing it? You're a sorry piece of shit."

"Don't say that, that's absurd." I moved away, setting my back against a cabinet.

"Come back here or I'll call the police," she said, sounding paradoxical to be sure, but with no trace of warmth. "Why do you act this way, Chewb? You scare me."

"I don't know." I was on my knees, hands on my chest.

"What are you doing to me in my sleep?" she asked. "Make me understand."

"I'm certainly not torturing you, I swear."

"Oh Lord, just listen to how he tries to get out of it."

251

"I look at you."

"You're a maniac."

"No, no . . ."

"Chewb, it doesn't bother me one bit if you look at me. But you understand that the things I know about you now make me stop and think a bit?"

I stayed calm, joining my hands together, and said, "Yes, I understand. Maybe." I decided to simplify: "Maybe with you and Leo I was trying to leave that world, that's why I got out of Rome." I told her a good, reliable version: "I didn't want to be with those people anymore, we no longer had anything in common, I got myself fired."

"Piero, I don't give a fuck if you got yourself fired, it's that Uncle Leo said you have to leave and now what are we going to do?"

"We hardly see each other anymore anyways."

The surrender in my voice sent a rush of blood to her head: "What? Are you serious? We hardly see each other anymore? And you're touching me in my sleep!"

"I don't touch you, I swear."

"I felt you last time."

"Hmm. Then why did you come back?"

"I wanted to be sure."

"No, you came back because you're crazy."

"Ah, I'm crazy."

"Yes."

"Ho ho ho," she said.

And I aped her laugh.

"Come to bed."

"No."

Her silence, sheets pushed aside; then she rose and went to the other end of the room to get her bag on the chair.

"Let's play a little game."

"Not a sexual game."

"No, let's play the game of truth."

"Okay."

She jumped up on the bed and sat down opposite me; my knees ached and I returned to leaning my back against the cabinet, a meter or less away from her.

In her hand she held a tiny ziplock bag containing white powder, plunging me immediately into a state of anxiety. It was MDMA.

"Let's play the game of truth. It's only a few hundred milligrams, we'll share it; I promise you that just by looking at me you'll understand what you have to do." She shook the bag and kept her back very straight. "Just looking at me, you'll know if you love your wife. You can't go wrong."

"No. What you're trying to pass off as a truth machine is really just a love potion."

"No, it's not a love potion, it's a truth machine. Or even better: you might kiss me out of affection, or give me a hug, or more likely you'll touch my arms and shoulders a little, but this just makes you accept the state of things. If you love your wife, you love your wife. The drug is conservative—it'll help us to see if you really want to live with your wife, and if that's the case"—she forced herself to be impartial and optimistic— "that's fantastic, because you're about to go back to Rome anyway . . ."

Confronted with such optimism, Rosenzweil did not know how to resist and finally gave in: he dipped a finger into the bag four or five times and licked it—the most bitter and penetrating flavor ever to touch his tongue. Clelia refilled a two-liter Coca-Cola bottle with water, took her own dose, leaving a little for later, and finally began to prepare the room (turning off the chandelier in favor of a little lamp covered with my orange shirt, turning on the music) so that our senses might delight in the hours to follow, gently stimulated by lights, sounds, and the revelational textures of everyday objects.

Which after an hour or so swelled up like the paint on walls next to radiators: the purple bedspread became a vast panorama, rich with scenery; Rosenzweil had put on a red T-shirt and now that the temperature of his shoulders had gone up, those shoulders were very large and swollen, and Clelia touched them, saying, "You're getting really hot, Chewb, really hot." She had connected her iPod to the speakers and they listened to beguiling, hip-swaying melodies, voices and xylophones, which put Rosenzweil in mind of an old video game for Game Boy where a marble rolled along surfaces without walls, inifinitely suspended in space.

The voice, for what seemed like hours, managed to stay on course and never once fell into the void—a marvel; and Rosenzweil, contemplating the possibility of landing on the ceiling and planting a flag to establish a colony among the trapezoidal shadows cast by the orange light, and making these astronomical calculations while Clelia touched his shoulders with her hand, giving him to realize that never in his life had his miraculously warm arm received such a soothing, benevolent caress, said, "I have never been *so absolutely happy* in my life."

Then he looked at her and Clelia's face was composed of a few flourishes, well assembled, and her mouth had the timid air of a little fish pressing itself up against the aquarium glass, and he said again, "No, no, don't you get it? I have never been *so absolutely happy* in my life."

They were stretched out on the bed and got up to dance at Clelia's suggestion, but Rosenzweil was afraid of not being able to and she said slowly, "If you don't want to, we won't get up; if you want to, we'll get up," an equation with extremely relevant implications.

"Clelia, you're like your uncle. You're so nice. I've never been so happy, never like I am now. And it's really strange that I'm realizing this, that this isn't a memory. That this isn't a memory is really the strangest thing." Then: "You and your uncle are always so nice—you're always going back on things. The other day, Leo, a bit more and he would have been apologizing for having asked me to leave."

"That is, you see, even in . . . discord . . ."

"It's as if it were concord . . ."

They rose without much effort and began to follow the voice-marble, swaying softly.

"Uncle Leo is so, so good . . ." said Clelia, who was now holding his hands, "and he'll understand that you're good and we can stay here. Because from a certain perspective, Paris is an extremely simple city."

Rosenzweil thought about the Métro map, about Boulevard de Sébastopol, about the Grands Boulevards, and he slapped his forehead with the palm of one hand: "Yeah, I really don't know how they managed to make it so simple." He noted that the eviscerations were well intentioned. He understood that the road to Hell is paved with good intentions. And he found this unspeakably touching.

"What are you thinking? What are you thinking?"

"Clelia, dear, can I kiss your nose?"

He kissed her remade nose.

"I understand, Clelia: the truth machine and the love potion are the same thing . . . the same thing . . . because truth is love, and so they correspond!"

"Ho ho ho."

"That's it precisely! Listen, I believe I'll have to start kissing your arms."

"Yes, yes, good idea."

They were warm arms, generous arms that had worn themselves out for him month after month, making his life happier, and now they ought to be kissed all over in order to regenerate them, even if there was in fact nothing to regenerate, because these arms were safe and warm. After a while, Rosenzweil knelt down and kissed her ankles and her legs, then he looked up from below: "I thought I would kneel down, but now I've figured out where this reconnaissance mission of mine is leading."

"Ah, you've figured it out."

"Yes, maybe you haven't but I have. It leads directly to your cunt."

"I sort of suspected as much."

"Now I believe we'll have to make love."

"Aim for the cunt in the meantime, then we'll see."

He looked up: "What does that mean, 'we'll see'?"

"No no no, stay calm. It's just that, if we heat up too much, it might not be good for us. We're really hot. Can you keep kissing me all over my skin? Then we'll fuck tomorrow."

"Ah, right. Right. You're afraid of overheating."

"It's not fear, it's molecular consciousness."

"You possess molecular consciousness?"

"I'm the microscope. You can possess molecular consciousness when you look at me, but not me, I can't, because I'm only an instrument."

"It's true . . . you are the instrument of truth. You are the truth machine."

"Keep looking at me."

Clelia's features were very original.

"Always look at me, okay?"

And he did virtually nothing but look at her and kiss her for hours, standing and seated and on the terrace to cool off, and at nine in the morning they went to bed, but sleep was interrupted by continual trips to the bathroom to piss; they got up in turns and sometimes together; that night they had drunk liters of water, their hands were dry but smooth, their teeth on edge. When the intercom buzzed, around eleven, they were headed to the bathroom together.

"This will be Mohammed. Poor girl. She's come all this way. Should we open up? If we open up and I have you in my arms she'll understand. Let's take her to bed."

"But she can't understand. Because she doesn't follow our religion. Who are you talking about?"

"Fuck, that's true."

"Who is it?"

"It's my sister-in-law, come to ask me to go back to Rome. Because I wasn't going to Rome, so she decided to come herself. Mohammed. Let's take her to bed."

"It's not important, Chewb. We mustn't proselytize by force. Sorry, but otherwise it's ugly, otherwise it's coercion."

"It's true. Oh Lord, it's really true. With these words you have practically insulated your new religion from all criticism."

"I know, it's fortunate. Let's go back to bed. Ah, not yet! I have to piss."

"Then let us piss," concluded Rosenzweil, immediately turning his back on the intercom, heading toward the bathroom door. A considerable portion of human destiny, it seemed to him, was the presence of people outside the doors of buildings while others are warm in their homes and in their beds, their bodies made of matter, of flesh, thick shoulders and smooth thighs. We spend our lives waiting, right? Right. What a sight. The big door was covered in dewdrops at dawn (no, it was eleven, the dew was gone), and an eager girl was standing before it. That scene would help Ada to grow up and to understand; that is, that waiting outside the big door, for this still virginal girl, was a very valuable lesson.

The other Rosenzweils had more or less collapsed after spending the night between Clelia's legs. The intercom surprised them, a pair in the bedroom, another in the living room. Two said, "This must be my sister-in-law"; the other thought instead of Leo, but they all went to the window to see and, discovering it was Ada—a head of dark hair turning from side to side, avoided by passersby whizzing up or down the street—decided to go back to bed, where, awake now, they started kissing again and were soon back where they were, between Clelia's legs, determined to ignore first intercom and then cell phone, too stupefied by the miracle of fucking and incapable of denying themselves the privileges obtained during the night. Meanwhile also the fourth Rosenzweil, head rinsed

257

by the MDMA, posteuphoria but still in that pulsating calm that precedes depression, having pissed away the umpteenth load of transparent pee, returned to bed, took his place next to Clelia, and said; "Don't forget to fuck me."

Predictably, then, the only one to get up to respond to the intercom was me. I pissed and came away worried. Clelia and I had slept in each other's arms on the bed; she'd expected I wouldn't agree to try MDMA and had only suggested it as a provocation, and she'd been such a good and sweet person, just like her uncle: all night long, sleeping in the intervals between a hundred reawakenings at the strangeness of the embrace, she'd showered one side of my chest with tiny kisses and hadn't insisted I kiss her in return. At that point there was no plan, but when the intercom buzzed and we were in bed, and I realized that Mohammed didn't mean prophet but was a reference to Mohammed and the mountain, I said to myself, "The latest Freudian slip! My neurons are capable of avoiding anything!"

I walked over to the receiver and picked it up; at the sound of the click, a spirited voice sprung to attention: "Pierino! It's Ada!"

Losing his temper, Rosenzweil launched a counterattack: "You realize we're all adults here, right?" ("I thought you knew." "No, I didn't. I'm busy now, I can't let you in." "Then we'll see each other later?" "I'll see how things go. Call me after lunch and we'll talk." "Okay. Sorry, I didn't mean to give you a fright." "Don't worry about it. Call me later," concluded Rosenzweil, and went back into the living room in better spirits and with a newfound sense of courage brought out by Ada's cheek, such that in less than a minute he and Clelia were already mixing saliva once more.) I on the other hand, as if surrendering, said, "Mo . . . hammed."

"I've come to visit you!"

"I see."

"Let me in?"

"I was in the shower."

"But it's eleven o'clock!"

"I'll be down in five minutes, wait for me."

"Piero! Paris is so beautiful!"

"Just wait."

Clelia had risen and looked out at me worriedly from behind the bathroom door. "Is it Uncle Leo? Is he coming up?"

"No, it's my sister-in-law." I explained to her about Mohammed. "Wait here for fifteen minutes, I'll get her out of the way. Then you take off, head down toward the Boulevards, and if we see each other don't say anything."

"You're kidding, right?"

"No, please." I pulled my sweatpants from where they hung on the clothes tree, slipped them and my tennis shoes on in the hallway, and turned to make for the door. My breath stank.

"C'mon, you can't let her have it her way." She came toward me.

"But what if she's sussed us out? She already knows everything. She's come to tell me off. She's always said she would. She thinks marriage leads to sainthood—to sainthood!"

"You think so too."

"I'm going down." After five steps I realized Clelia was following me down the stairs. I stopped. "What the fuck are you doing?"

"Let's walk down together. You can introduce me."

"No, stay here."

She laughed in my face. "You're incredible." She was two steps above me; we looked each other in the face with our dragon breath. "I don't even know where to start . . . Take a moment and locate your balls, then we'll go down together, tell your sister-in-law that she's not your father and should mind her own fucking business." Having said this, she tried to overtake me, but I stopped her and embraced her.

It was kind of a scuffle. I held her tight and must have hurt her chest. Clelia wanted to walk down at all costs, but I blocked her way, and when I saw that she was about to scream I covered her mouth with my hand and went up one step and kissed her forehead. At that point she jumped into my arms and I carried her inside—every minute that passed was a confirmation of the wicked thoughts of my sister-in-law unable to understand passion. I closed the door and carried Clelia into the bathroom. How ridiculous we were in that tiny space, pressed together; how lovely it was to hold her wrists still as she squirmed, just like sex scenes in the movies, when the tension is so great that only copulation can provide a half hour's respite from the general mayhem. However, there was a virgin waiting for me in the street, and I knew that in all the world there was no one to whom I felt a greater duty to account for myself than my sister-in-law. She was the only person I knew who had taken purity as seriously as I had done; the only person to decide not to break anyone's heart and to help her neighbors instead.

This is how our little struggle ended: I shut the Jewish girl in the bathroom with a blitz, that is, I gave her a violent pinch on the forearm that forced her to stare in astonishment at her tingling limb, allowing me to grab the key and slip out. (Rosenzweil, rather than meting out a pinch, looked at himself in the mirror in this wretched hour and realized how close their bodies were, how explosive, achieving for the first time a true understanding of their corporality, a truer understanding, under the ungenerous bathroom lights, than the ethereal vision of the Rosenzweil-Clelia duo reflected back at him in Paris's shop windows as they walked all over the city—and thus forestalling any need to give her a pinch, he transformed the conflict into a mawkish finale and they found each other for real, she with her coccyx against the flat bottom of the sink, he looking in the mirror at the outlines of his own body filled with Clelia's back, a hint of her bottom, her spine beneath the T-shirt, shoulders arching up, covered with long, dark hair, and on top like a half-moon the face of Rosenzweil entering and leaving the mirror to the rhythm of kisses, every so often the irresistible Jewess raising a hand that popped into the mirror at an oblique angle to caress the half-moon face of her new lover.) Immediately she began to bang on the door.

"Bastard! Let me out now! You're insane, Piero, don't be an asshole!"

"I swear I'll come back up, just two minutes and I'll send her away."

"No, you're going to let me out. Piero, you're getting yourself into the biggest mess of your life, I'll make you pay, I swear!"

"I swear I'll come back up!"

"Swear to God!"

"I'll come right back; don't freak out or you'll have a panic attack!"

As I walked down the stairs, one of my legs gave out and I grabbed onto the handrail. I breathed in, drew myself up, and continued my descent. Eyes narrowed, brows furrowed, a network of muscles shrinking my cheekbones.

I opened the little door in the big door onto a day with a typically disappointing Parisian climate. My sister-in-law was typical Ada with her hooded sweatshirt and jeans not cut too low, an American Indian–style jacket with a fringe, a large, full yellow-and-blue Invicta backpack with snap fasteners. She had her hair pulled back and had washed her face somewhere; she was chewing gum. (This nondescript spectacle was enough to make Rosenzweil say to himself, "From this? This is what I'm running away from? I'm afraid of being judged by this pitiful creature? Then I must really be in bad shape. Really bad shape.") Surprising his sister-in-law, who was certainly not expecting a welcome, he took her in his arms, drew closer to his former obsession, Ada's Tits, then began a long speech with the words "Ada, I'm not in love with my wife." He pointed out a café twenty meters down the street, told her to choose a table and order, he was now going to go back up and get a sweater and jacket, put on some socks, then come down and explain everything. He raced up the stairs, his heart pounding as he reached the top, feeling like God was observing him through the transparent cupola that surmounted the stairwell; he inserted the key into the lock.

Before opening the bathroom door, he said to Clelia, "I told her I don't love my wife anymore." Clelia didn't respond. "I told her I don't love my wife anymore; now she's waiting for me in a café and I'm going to go tell her I have another woman."

In a weak voice Clelia said, "You don't have another woman."

"Of course I do," shot back the romantic Rosenzweil, who had just ruined his reputation and his future in the Church and therefore had a right to be melodramatic. "I do indeed have a woman, I've had her for months now but didn't even realize it!"

"Stupid," she said, "you're just a stupid Chewbacca, you retarded, incapacitated man."

"Incapacitated, not retarded."

"Are you going to let me out?"

"Yes, but don't hit me . . ."

A brief kiss, and then she accepted that he'd be speaking with his sister-in-law at the café—an extremely sad conversation that quickly reduced them to tears—and that the couple, Clelia and Rosenzweil, would make love only in the afternoon, after they'd cheered up; then Clelia suggested they share some MDMA in order to achieve greater understanding, and Rosenzweil declared himself open to the possibility. Seeing Ada slowly chewing her gum at that hour, that gum and my empty stomach, my sleepiness and too palpable, too unambiguous sense of dissatisfaction, added rockets to my feet. I turned right, uphill, saying, "I have to get some coffee," and without another word to my sister-in-law started up the street toward Place Pigalle.

We exchanged generic information en route, concluding

with a "But you're all right, Pierino?" from Ada as she plodded around the inclined square of Rue des Martyrs, among the telephone booths and the carousel, a little girl riding Bambi, a horse, a goose, all out of scale, a woman waiting impatiently in line for a booth (I heard her fart). The drowsy city, without coffee, without sugar, came at us from all sides, stores advertising "*Transactions Immobilières*" and "*Couleurs et Mèches*," the greengrocers' stretch of Rue des Martyrs, the cars climbing the hills, the *bobos* on their Saturday stroller excursions, creating shallow shapes in the gray; at the corner of another square, outside a pharmacy, a homeless man in slippers. In the wedge of horizon between two buildings I could make out Montparnasse, from this distance a black medieval tower; a cloud had parked itself atop the tower, in the form of an overturned sofa. Ada kept at me from behind: "I only wanted to talk, I only wanted to ask if you needed, maybe we could pray together. You seemed alone to me." Was she referring to something we were talking about? On the avenue were music stores, samplers, keyboards, and mixers, fifteen-year-old music lovers at the windows with poor eyes; Pigalle, XXX theaters, and McDonald's, the great big black sign for Folies Pigalle flashing red, the neon signs of Le Théâtre: "Live show/Peep show," the fountain gushing in the square, spurts of water that drove the dogs crazy, the buses bending into curves, the sky overcast to the south, clear to the north, Ada still walking behind me, unwilling to approach.

I took Rue Pigalle, heading down toward the Boulevards: Arab women in brown veils out walking with their children; the city without sounds, save the low ebbing rumble of a passing car as it slowed to a stop at the light; every street sloped down to the Grands Boulevards and forked, split by the acute corner of a triangular island block; from a store selling electric basses came the sound of boiling resin. I was horribly tired and this . . . what, this sort of pianissimo pursuit had already come to seem odd to me. Were Ada and I talking? Her presence was so overdone. I knew she was behind me, I heard her panting, her saying "You're walking so fast, stop running!"

A homeless man sitting on a black suitcase, a chunky young Arab boy on a kick scooter, three girls with golden curls from good families. I turned back onto my street and we came to my building, but I walked straight ahead, fiddling with the bathroom key in my pocket. A prim-looking fag pedaled a bike up the hill; a homeless woman in sunglasses with a cart full of rags, practically in the middle of the street, beat time with her foot in a flip-flop with the Brazilian flag. On the cover of a magazine in the glass case of a tobacco kiosk, the yellow "*avec DVD*" seal was printed over the pussy of a fourth-rate model—small, pointy tits, holding back her red hair with one hand, revealing her shaved armpit. The brown back of the church, the idlers at the café, the Arabs in their spice shops, the men behind the newsstands, the traffic cop directing the cacophonous orchestra, tomatoes, cucumbers, mint plants at the vegetable stand, the water glimmering in the gutter on the way to the sewer mouths, the *centre de bronzage* with the sign "Smile, you're tanned."

"Are you taking me somewhere? Do you want to show me something?" I must have said something, to which she responded, "Forgive me, Pierino, but you weren't talking to me." She tried to take my wrist, I yanked myself free.

Yellow inflatable lanterns swinging in the wind outside a Japanese restaurant, exhaust fumes, various sweet stenches, covers of gay monthlies, in Place Kosuth signs for "Opéra" and "Concorde," a squat, knock-kneed punk kid, the exit for an underground parking garage, blacks smoking outside the PMU where they played the horses, houses being renovated, their windows spotted with white paint, an old restaurant, Au Petit Riche. On Boulevard Haussmann, in front of the headquarters of BNP Paribas, the smell of rotten eggs, employees outside smoking. I walked out onto the Boulevard des Italiens. Ada followed me and spoke to me from a few steps behind. I continued to mumble. I read the signs for Madeleine, Opéra, Concorde. I'm out of breath and that's why the lights change first and the city has a single sound subsuming the steps and the triple steps of the lame men on crutches, who rattle the coins in their hands and take up their chant again with *"Pardon, monsieur, une toute petite pièce."*

One Rosenzweil is trying to sleep and not give into his urge to piss; one Rosenzweil is banging Clelia up against the fridge; one has made her his in the hallway; another has said yes to the drug and his taking a shower with her; another is comforting his sister-in-law as she cries in the café; another is about to make love for the first time, concerned about his lack of familiarity with it all; another is in the bathroom with an attack of nervous diarrhea: Paris was swarming with busy Rosenzweils, while I, most unlikely of hypotheses, stalked the city like a man possessed, shadowed patiently by the virgin, who most likely had no real sense of the enormity of this event, as we walked through the Parisian streets. Certainly, however, someone equally patient but a bit more sensible than Ada would have just let me go, would have waited for me at the café, following the Gospel's example (don't run to the tomb in search of Lazarus, wait patiently for him to rise again). With this I absolutely do not wish to blame my sister-in-law, also because while the abomination that was about to occur appears to the foolish as meaningful and judicious, it might have happened to me in a less tension-filled moment—without Clelias, Jewish Popes, virgin sisters-in-law, or unofficial evictions— a moment that would have laid itself open neither to theological readings nor to those marked by vague theories of fate, providence, or destiny (and yet how difficult it is not to attach such readings to events), a brief moment of extreme banality, a very serious accident that befell someone dear. And *instead*—because history is made even with *instead*s—the manner in which the accident happened on that precise morning lent the event something intolerably rhetorical, just as, for that matter, the life of Piero Rosini had always been rhetorical, because he was the last-born and a bit of a special child, and he had always made proclamations, before as well as after his conversion, and even if I can no longer do anything (it's not as if I saw the car coming—I was crossing the Boulevard des Italiens with the flashing green, distracted by the white-and-yellow panels of a boulangerie on the far side of the crowded street, distracted by the life-size model gravely sizing up the ugly people in the street from an advertising poster on the adjacent newsstand— the car arrived and took me out, I rolled across the windshield and fell back to earth, under the flat and impassive gaze of the model as well as that, incredulous, of Ada, who all of a sudden felt as alone as if she were at the center of an iceberg), allowing oneself to be run over like that, on the Grands Boulevards, under the eyes and tits of Ada, could seem like a stupid, un-asked for, perfectly avoidable manifesto.

19

But let us not think of sad things, let us think of good things.

My move to Paris had marked a turning point in the life of Corrado Paloschi as well: if for the entire summer he had tormented himself with thoughts of his friend Piero, pushed into losing his job out of idealism and misplaced faith in his book, in September he found out that I had omitted to tell him about my writer sister. The revelation, slow in coming (reading the name Federica Rosini in a newspaper; an Internet search; discovering photos of her; the attempt to establish whether this woman with such a common last name didn't perhaps, unlikely as it was, resemble an editor at Non Possumus; vague hopes in the face of her biography: date of birth, place of birth; staking out a position outside a bookstore after a public appearance; absolute certainty regarding the resemblance: shoulders, nose, eyes, gestures, nasal voice; and, to conclude, the infallible approach and the "Hi, I'm a friend of your brother, I didn't know he had such a cute sister . . . I mean, a sister who's a writer . . ."; "Oh, tell me, I'm curious . . ."), proved remarkably significant: for starters, it rendered obsolete his fruitless friendship with me, and indeed I was not informed of his discovery or their meeting. Above all else, it made available to Corrado a much more pleasant and influential person with whom to establish a literary alliance. As a matter of fact, just as I took to him, so did my sister. Federica for him, at the beginning, was above all a bizarre optical effect: a Piero transformed into a big-haired woman, agnostic into the bargain, a pleasure-seeker and bon viveur, shapely and genuinely connected in the publishing world. This new, bewigged Piero, with the silky voice and scheming eyes, invited Corrado over the evening of the first day they met; not only was he cute, and with cute young men Federica moved quickly, but he was also, unexpectedly, the only secular friend of her younger brother, about whom he knew some not-at-all-well-known particulars that had excited her curiosity—like the fact that, according to Corrado, I had tried to get a novel about gays published, to the point of quarreling with my ultra-Catholic employers, or that, among other things, I had a secret passion for my sister-in-law's tits.

There had, therefore, been no reason not to continue their first conversation at Federica's house in Monti, after three hours spent talking outside the bookstore and in a restaurant with publishing people, then in a pub and through the narrow neighborhood streets, on topics of enormous relevance to them both: Corrado's manuscript, the true life of Piero Rosini, the Ada's Tits affair, and so forth. To cap off this auspicious beginning, while denying him intercourse, Federica let him feel what experience and two full, fleshy lips might achieve.

Afternoons at her place, speaking of me and of books and partially undressing, became a habit both nerve-racking (she had a serious boyfriend) and delightful (she could no longer bear to be with a man whose handicapped son was a form of living moral blackmail, that idiot little face, always aware, perpetually needy), a vice from which both extracted a great deal: Federica found recreation and also recovered a certain affection for her faraway brother; Corrado, who would get back home ready to work into the night correcting his manuscript, was now taken seriously by a real writer, as they chatted about Russian and French novels in the hopes of arriving at a literary collaboration via oral sex (Federica declined to have full intercourse, only blow jobs and cunnilingus; one time she muttered "I hate penetration" and Corrado wondered what the hell kind of family were the Rosinis).

Corrado Paloschi's prayers were answered. Little by little Federica varied the programming of their domestic encounters and began to ask him what he wanted to write about; until one afternoon she sat down to read the manuscript about the gay couple who dreamed of having a traditional family. In less than half an hour, making her way through the first chapters, she laughed spontaneously four times, emitted a few "ahas," "nices," and an undecipherable "hmm." The next day, approaching the middle of the book, she removed her reading glasses—the sole object capable of revealing her forty years—and as if speaking to herself said, "No, there's no novel here." She had liked, she added, only certain descriptive details, minor characters. She went on to catalog the defects of the plot as well as instances of what she considered my ingenuousness as an editor, then finally laid out the three fundamental merits of Corrado's writing and encouraged him to concentrate on the secondary characters (drawing inspiration from those of Nabokov and Arbasino): "Yours have a lot of life, I'm envious. But"—and here she laughed with satisfaction—"the main characters really don't hold up."

The grammatical, logical, philosophical finality of her judgment (the non-here-ness of the novel) mortified the aspiring writer, who for a few days proudly considered not allowing himself to be sucked off. He had yet to find out how much participation being panned by Federica might entail: having pronounced her verdict, she committed herself to making sure that Corrado, "a talent," toss out his pretensions to social commentary—which served only to reveal a lack of in-depth knowledge as well as culture—and concentrate on the secondary characters in his manuscript, bowed and weary figures who were at the same time vital and shameless, almost like something out of a Neapolitan-style nativity scene, making them the heroes of individual stories.

One of the first rewrites soon appeared in a notable literary review. It was the story of a middle-aged man from Naples who has lost his brother, and when he arrives in Rome to visit the cemetery, he prefers not to stay in his brother's widow's house: "A woman alone, a young woman. It doesn't seem right to me." Admirable despite the excess of parataxis; embellished with rare diseases, local slang, "faded florists" and the precise names of flowers . . . A few writers read it, and at the parties and literary aperitifs that Federica took him to he managed to pass himself off as a legitimate guest. In preference to the dusty charm of the counterculture, Corrado—a Roman Bel-Ami in whose eyes the milieus of success were impossible to deconstruct or put on trial, being none other than indisputable flashes of the highest human condition, the condition of those on whom fortune has smiled—reveled in cocktail parties with white-jacketed waiters on hotel terraces or in foreign cultural institutions, having the names of friends in the newspapers, phrases like "They were talking about it at Frankfurt" or "They caught them in the bathroom at the American Academy." Perhaps it was ignorance, or his social background, but for him it was as if the last fifty years of antibourgeois cultural critique didn't exist, and for that reason he was able to enjoy scenes and ceremonies that Federica and her friends, even as they frequented them, gave to believe were trivial.

Perhaps, as a writer, he had this to say: he honored the things that fell to him with enthusiasm and a sense of the epic.

One night her boyfriend, furious after a rebuff from Federica, showed up at her place; Corrado, there at the time, was obliged to shut himself up in a walk-in closet for half an hour. The crystalline banality of the situation sent him into raptures: a young lover among mothballed coats and plastic garment bags, sweating in a T-shirt, his limp black-and-yellow checked underwear in his hand, his naked ass on the parquet. An additional benefit: since this episode happened to a writer, it would soon be immortalized in a book, such that what he was living through already took on something of the shape of a novel. Another glorious moment that autumn (Why do I know these things? Am I dead? Am I writing?) was a stay in Ravello, in a villa overlooking the glittering sea, a weekend as Federica's companion among literati and their Neapolitan fellow travelers, at the end of which, on the Naples–Rome Eurostar, looking back over his own notebook like an instant archaeological artifact, he was overcome by emotion almost to the point of tears. They were shining words; no Paloschi had ever achieved so much, no one had ever been able to describe the circumstances of his own life in these terms: "Seated in a circle beneath apricot leaves attached to the branches by thin red veins. / Wicker divans in the shade of a pergola, drystone walls and bougainvillea. / The villas clinging to the mountain, looming over the sea. / A fat fag in black canvas shorts charged with telling jokes and simpering. / A woman past seventy, her broad, flat chest and two nipples under a dress the color of hydrangeas. / The son of a notary from Catania on his second marriage, to an Ethiopian princess. / Vines climbing the little colonnade outside the living room, white stone benches with long blue cushions. / Olive trees; pool; sailors' knots behind glass; the blue towel draped languidly over a low wall. / By eight o'clock the clouds had thickened . . ."

Without counting the fact that Federica had cut quite a figure showing up with him (the message: she was getting older, her lovers growing younger), something that would have earned Corrado all kinds of favors. Between them, however, penetration never figured; even after leaving her boyfriend, Federica had decided to defer such hydraulics a bit longer ("It creates more problems than it solves").

. . . I wasn't upset; a few years later I published my first novel. One day, at an event for debut authors, an editor said to me, "Listen, you have the luck of the, I don't know what! You're invited everywhere, you're always finding free places to sleep!" and "Look, Paloschi, you have to make fortune understand that she has to keep smiling on you. Tomorrow for dinner . . . you have to buy something, a gesture so that fortune understands. Bring some twelve-year-old Scotch. No, better: bring a widow. Tomorrow, bring a widow to dinner, put her in the fridge, you mustn't even say that you brought her. Fortune will know anyway, fortune will understand." In a society short on initiation rites, the unexpected request to "bring a widow" sounded decidedly esoteric, and above all forced me to think again about Alice, the widow of Piero Rosini, and about the relations between us (first between me and Piero, then between me and Alice, both while Piero was in France and after his death). I entered the world of initiates the following morning, when the owner of a wine store explained to me that *widow* stood for Veuve Clicquot, a relatively prized brand of champagne. The next evening I did as requested, hiding the widow in the fridge without looking for credit; someone found the bottle with the orange label and poured it out to a small section of the thirty guests. Neither I nor the editor tasted a drop of it and thus fortune was honored—from that day on, if a wish of mine comes true, I spend thirty euros on a bottle: from the foil capsule on down, the illustrious widow continues to invoke for me the favor of the gods.

There in the future of wishes come true, Corrado had broken off oral sex with Federica Rosini, but in his life he could expect to find naps in airports, German and French friends, his name printed on a large place card among those distinguished speakers, sumptuous free dinners in those restaurants along the state highways. Federica Rosini proved herself loyal. After my Parisian accident she found it natural to break off her adventure with Corrado Paloschi and to elect him substitute brother without so much as an explanation. Which meant his never having to go without her support, her wangling jobs for him with magazines, publishing houses, cultural organizations, in short guaranteeing him an income, satisfactions, a social life.

Let's go back to just before my death: Corrado, a well-organized man when it came to pursuing his diverse and even contradictory desires, had begun, alongside his secret relationship with Federica, an equally secret but chaste friendship with my wife.

The discovery that I had a sister provoked an immediate angry telephone call from the deceived to the wife of the deceiver. Alice was ashamed in a way she rarely had call to be and instinctively agreed to meet him alone to clear up the matter. They saw each other for a raspberry cremolato, with a double portion of whipped cream, just down the street from Sergio and Ada. It was the end of summer, Alice in her usual sleeveless dress, Corrado in his usual polo shirt. She was there solely out of embarrassment for having covered up a stupid joke made by her husband, with whom she would have discussed this, that same evening, if she hadn't arranged to meet, later that afternoon, three old friends she hadn't seen since I'd left. They had never liked me and little by little, thanks to me, they had drifted away. As if seeing in Corrado a candidate for their anti-Rosini party, an intelligent, good-looking man, well suited for the campaign, they were enthusiastic about the news that Alice had gone out with someone, abusing me and asking about the when, what, and where of the date. The thing blew up on its own; soon it was no longer a cremolato they'd had but a gelato. And her "having a gelato" with Corrado Paloschi was turned into "having gelati," and entered into their private argot, halfway between *La boum*–style delicacy and the Italian eroticism of gastronomical metaphors: "Having gelato this evening?" The result: Alice didn't tell me she was spending time with Corrado, and prepared herself for the big sideshow sure to ensue if ever I caught her: "It's all you and your secrets' fault!"

The relationship between the two of them—if you leave out a series of text messages discovered by Ada one afternoon as she searched through her sister's cell phone, which put it in her head to go up to Paris to warn me—remained without consequences or further action: my death stopped them before they found the courage to betray me. The only time they came close was when my deadbeat of a wife finally decided to reconnect the electricity, a dozen days after an ACEA employee had placed a seal on the meter (I didn't know anything about this, either). Alice lived at her father's, in the same room as Ada, and was lazy about certain things. She told Corrado about it; he told her it had happened to him once and it was just a matter of going to the headquarters in Ostiense.

"Ostiense? That's so far away!"

He took her there on his moped, one morning in December, having requested the day off from Fassi Events: he had decided to give it a go. His relationship with Federica was in any case highly secret, and one with Alice would have been even more so. So he reasoned. They paid the fine and the three outstanding bills (so perhaps I was also in part to blame for this), after which, the woman behind the counter having informed her of when to expect the technician's visit, four o'clock that same afternoon, they traveled back through the city to Porta di Roma, a journey so long as to seem like a pedantic philological operation, a slavish reconstruction of the original trip.

They waited in the house for the electricity man; waited on the terrace, actually, smoking on their feet due to the cold, without music or TV or lighting, and when they went in to warm themselves up by the radiator at the entrance, each wondered whether the time had come to embrace. Alice needed it, and even if convinced she would remain ninety percent faithful to me, experienced a certain relief in finding herself with the extremely common problem of having to choose between two men. What's more, rapidly addressing herself to her mother, she even thought, "You can see that I'm about to go crazy, that I'm not doing well; in a little while this young man will kiss me and I'll feel better." The young man, who was at that point spending several nights a week at Federica's house and had in fact silenced his phone to avoid unwanted rings, felt guilty about my sister and not about me. Alice continued to postpone the decision because she realized that she liked Corrado, that she thought about him all the time, and thus passed from craving a therapeutic kiss to wondering seriously whether it was not time to leave me. After my death, everything was suspended indefinitely.

There is no pleasure in rudely interrupting people, particularly people we care for; fortunately, nearly everyone is spared the awkwardness of announcing his or her own death. If I'd had to do so, for example to Leo, I would've hated provoking in him the inevitable impression that I was throwing something in his face, as if between our estrangement and this affair there were a connection and some type of blame. (Leo hadn't at any rate had anything to do with the disappearance of Mario's letter and hadn't snooped and hadn't found out that way that I was part of the Non Possumus project. Mario's letter had never reached me because the address was wrong: Rue Notre-Dame-de-Lorette, but with the street number of the apartment on Rue Notre-Dame-des-Champs, provided by Alice. It had been my text message that prompted Leo.)

The distressing tearful call in which my sister-in-law asked Leo whether he was a friend of mine, because his number was in my cell phone memory and among my last calls—rare, dated—incoming and outgoing, surprised him in bed in his apartment in the Bastille area, hosted by a new tenant of his, a talkative and well-fed American researcher he'd fallen for—this was the reason he'd excluded me from that Monday tour. He replied that he was my friend and that was enough for Ada, already in tears, to practically scream as she gave him the news that, after an accident, I was undergoing "critical" emergency surgery.

Upset, immediately prey to a pair of premature ventricular contractions, Leo slipped out of bed, naked as a hospital patient, and went into the bathroom to wash his face before going out. Holding the phone between neck and shoulder as he tightened his belt, he tried to let Clelia know that her friend, the one in the apartment, was in the hospital. He didn't know about Clelia and me beyond that we had the same group of friends, but when for the sixth time his niece failed to pick up the phone, Leo grasped the situation immediately: Clelia and the anti-Semite had a connection. She had never in fact asked her uncle about me. And her disappearance from Leo's house coincided with my arrival in Rue Notre-Dame-de-Lorette. And when he'd told her Rosini was anti-Semitic she'd been a bit too upset. Well, Leo was an intelligent person. In the meantime, even Ada had established that Clelia was my lover; she had seen the strange name in the list of calls and messages, which, if it hadn't been for the accident, would have made her furious: she'd gone up to Paris to beg me to get back to Rome to defend Alice from Corrado's courtship and now, ambulance trip notwithstanding, a slightly autistic part of her reasoning, the part authorized to state the obvious even in the most difficult and confused moments in life, was saying, "Hold on, am I the only one who cares about this marriage?"

As for Leo, he tried Clelia once again but the phone continued to ring; five minutes later he called her emergency number, Benedetta's, the name Clelia and Leo had agreed on that would allow him to find his niece in case of need. He hoped to obtain a denial with regard to a thought of his that already as he descended the stairs he was dismissing as irrational: Piero Rosini was in the hospital, Clelia wasn't picking up, I want to know whether there's something between the two of them, I want to know whether the fact that Clelia doesn't pick up, when who knows what's happened to Rosini, means something. He opened the street door.

Benedetta, incredulous and ready to rush to the hospital,

confirmed this and added that Clelia was definitely with Chewb—"Who?"—because last night she'd slept there and today was her day off. Leo was afraid and, collapsing on the faux-leather seat of the minivan taxi, feeling his energy drain out the sleeves of his jacket and out the broad bottoms of his crumpled pants, gave the driver the Rue Notre-Dame-de-Lorette address rather than that of the hospital. Since Benedetta had confirmed his wildest fear, that Piero and Clelia were sleeping together, Leo felt grimly authorized to believe every one of his own thoughts. He began, then, to view himself from the outside, protagonist of the worst of Saturdays, to imagine himself having to telephone his sister to report a racist crime of passion, a homicide-suicide with two victims, an anti-Semite and her *kleine* Clelia. Overcome with concern for his family, he began to curse me. But it was all his fault, he hadn't known how to judge whom he brought into the house. Now he was accusing me of a crime. The nerves in his cheeks and his fingers were trembling, his knees were two universes in contraction, enormous and painful, his heart pirouetting outside time. Such that he began to doubt whether it was not perhaps better to go to the hospital after all, in order to have doctors and defibrillators at hand.

Getting out of the cab was a genuine clown act. Leo clung to the door, then to the body of the minivan, then sat down on the hood of a parked car, setting off the alarm. The prospect of climbing six flights of stairs seemed like a real undertaking; his niece didn't respond to the intercom; he decided to go on up. He realized that if he'd really believed it possible he would shortly be finding "his niece's corpse" in the bathtub or under the bed, he would have asked the super to accompany him. So then, he said to himself, "Maybe I don't really believe it." And yet his body very much seemed to believe it. Even if in reality Clelia was probably in the hospital with this horrible man, me, in the same ward; maybe it wasn't my fault and something (car, lamppost, madman's pistol, mugger's knife, terrorist's bomb) must have struck us both down in the same way . . . He called Ada's number, sitting on the overstuffed divan at the foot of the stairwell, asked her breathlessly, "Is Piero alone, or . . ."—impossible to want truly to know the answer—"or is there a girl with him?" This was for Ada final confirmation of her already obsolete suspicions (at that point I'd already fallen into a coma), while Leo, hearing her reply—"No, he's alone . . . it's just him"—hung up, refusing to sympathize with the tearful stranger. They were playing a game in which everyone must only look after his or her own family in order to restore order. Leo was full of cares and fears. His heart threatened him: *Don't you take a step toward those stairs or I'll climb up into your mouth and take a diving leap off your tongue onto the green carpet.* What strength could he summon to climb those stairs, stairs that months earlier he'd climbed with his new friend, that repugnant, diseased individual, who *the entire time of our friendship, including my asking him to work for me, had carried on a devious hidden relationship with* kleine *Clelia? Rosini, who criticized me for my Russian girlfriends and then orchestrated this sick little game just to experience the thrill of a Jewish lover. A fine young girl full of* . . . Impossible to climb the stairs. He called Clelia again; no response.

Now let us imagine a man who, in slippers and without breakfast, climbs a snowy peak. It was following an effort of such magnitude that Leo reached the floor directly beneath the glass cupola. Seated on the doormat, exhausted, he pushed open the door and Clelia's voice now flooded through: "Chewbacca you piece of shit what the fuck got into your head you damn impotent faggot impostor open this fucking door I'm going to kill you."

From these words and from their quality of unmistakable aliveness, Leo learned that his niece had not been killed by a Roman Nazi; and probably not even raped, she didn't have the voice of a person who'd just been raped; in this way, however, Leo also learned that his umpteenth exaggerated intuition had some truth to it. He had these thoughts as he sat on the ground, against the open door, distracted in so many ways from the scene of his niece—a shrieking voice muffled by one of the doors, but which one? There was some truth to it, there was the improbable: his niece a prisoner (ah, she was in the bathroom) in one of the houses supporting the two members of the family living abroad in France. He said nothing; Clelia was railing against Rosini ("Chewbacca"?), "I hate you, you piece of shit you'll never see me again . . . what the fuck are you waiting for? Open up, asshole."

With shreds of breath Leo announced himself in English: "Uncle Leo. It's Uncle Leo. Uncle Leo."

And Clelia, as if responding in rhyme: "Uncle Leo?"

She silently faced the first barrage of questions to appear in disorderly, riotous file at the reception desk of her intellect. Leo left her inside to think, lacking the energy to spur things on to the next stage. Then another telephone call from Ada (which he didn't respond to for twelve rings, actually one ring and eleven silent vibrations because he pressed the button cutting the ringtone) brought him back to the present, still plagued by all the potential worst-case scenarios he had carried with him from the home of his forty-year-old lover to this top-floor apartment in Pigalle. He interrupted Clelia's thoughts—she had meanwhile been racking her brain to find a way to ask forgiveness for having trusted a lunatic—saying, "Sorry. It's . . . my heart. I'm, sitting down. Oof. Now, I'll let you out. Oof. How . . . are you?"

"F-fine. Uncle Leo, are you okay?" (It crossed her mind that her uncle might have beaten me up . . . Such a simple tragedy, so many misunderstandings. Clelia imagined her uncle beyond the door as having survived something terrible, spit out by a drooling monster, in agonizing pain.)

On the phone, which Clelia had heard ring once from the other side of the door, was Ada, who wanted to tell Leo to hurry because she couldn't manage alone, an elliptical way of announcing—to herself preparing the phrase, more than to the abstract three-letter entity discovered in my cell phone, L-E-O—that her brother-in-law, Piero Rosini, was dead.

And so when the bathroom door was finally unlocked and the captive princess liberated from the ogre's lair and able to cautiously throw her arms around the hero's neck (her uncle was still having trouble breathing), these two friends from my final days came together again, after so much misunderstanding, and gazed tranquilly into each other's eyes without being troubled by the fact that I was dead. And there was no need for Clelia to explain why she'd believed the scoundrel Rosenzweil. Afterward, Leo sent Benedetta to the hospital and it was from her that he learned what followed, that is the absence of anything following as far as Piero Rosini was concerned. An unclassifiable piece of news, he didn't communicate it to Clelia immediately and asked Benedetta to do the same. Clelia was shielded from the crushing evidence of seeing the corpse, and from meeting Rosenzweil's mother and brothers the day after (his father, suddenly taken ill, remained behind in Rome, in the care of his daughter); and when the time came to go down to Italy for the funeral, she had already landed in New York to stay with her parents and deal with her grief, while Benedetta entered a church in Rome on Leo's arm—and here I am, solemn, lying in an expressionless coffin . . .

We all know what Italian funerals are like: no one plays your favorite music, no one reads passages from your diary, you are remembered in only the most generic fashion. One presumes either that the Eichmanns charged with administering purgatory have little interest in personal qualities, or that the loved ones in black prefer not to summon up memories of the departed, at least while a coffin is present. Let's say for the sake of brevity that my father wasn't there, a precaution following the attack; that my wife was curled up like a conch, her head glued to her knees, and it was impossible to lift her from her black skirt. Let's say that Mario, freshly entered on the Anti-Defamation League's list of dangerous anti-Semites, experienced a deep feeling of the power of God and thought about the time Jesus burned a fig tree that failed to give fruit, and he also thought "Good heavens, Piero, I even paid your fake EBac salary out of my own pocket!"; and that the chorus was performing Gregorian chants accompanied by neither organ nor guitars, marking the time of the Mass, and many of them, even the drummer (who that day as on other occasions directed the cantors beside the altar with his left hand), could not dismiss the horrifying thought that I had died just as I had distanced myself from the Church—was God so jealous of His flock as to sacrifice a lamb He had failed to bring back into the fold? Elsewhere, throughout the pews, people were meditating on the meaning of life, their thoughts ranging across a broad spectrum of possible philosophical positions and finding their opposite extremes in the Teste Parlanti and the reflections of Lavinia. She sat next to Corrado, with whom she was no longer sleeping, even after her sudden return from Paris; Il Fassi was four pews back on the right . . . Lavinia had Corrado explain who the various relatives were and, once Chewie's famous virgin sister-in-law and writer sister had been pointed out and she'd caught a glimpse of Alice, she thought with regret, benumbed by tears, that if she'd had the opportunity to meet the beautiful women in my family, she would have taken it upon herself to explain to me how lucky I was; she would have run to us, to our house, to our bed . . . Here she had Corrado take her hand and she imagined herself in Porta di Roma, where she had never been, in a mentally reconstructed apartment, using the house of a pair of married friends as a model; she saw herself in our double bed under a down quilt, intertwining legs, arms, and tongues with me and the two orphan sisters (she had a passion for big breasts) . . . It was a fantasy she wistfully developed in the days to come, to the point of inventing dialogues with me in which she urged, "You choose, who do you want first? Ada, or Alice?"

Be that as it may, I had forever become a tragic figure,

something I had never been in life for anyone. When the funeral was over, with no chorus to break the silence, my brothers and a quartet of Teste Parlanti members hoisted up the coffin on their shoulders; the others saw me paraded past toward the light of the street, solemn and bouncing, a sturdy president in jacket and trousers of lacquered oak, so puffed up as to proceed horizontally. Alongside the coffin, relatives, friends, and coreligionists all crying, all played for fools.

Seated in the space left empty by my father, next to my brothers and my mother, posing as a little old lady, Federica declared that she would never write about it, never profit from it; there would be no tearjerking novels or stories. And a mother in mourning: how to describe her for the benefit of a son who had never understood anything about her, who considered her virtue incarnate, victim of an egotist husband, but who'd never truly noticed that she was small and hunched and that there were wrinkles beneath the hairs on her upper lip and little scabs at the corners of her mouth, and that she always pressed her lips together, and that she had always disguised herself as nothing more than a wife when, in fact, her heart wasn't in it? How to describe for my benefit the ruse I'd never understood, by which Papa was the normal one and Mamma the crazy woman who played the good wife against her will, who was always the captain going down with the ship, even when the sailing was smooth? How to describe to the dead man this woman at her son's funeral without her husband at her side? Would you tell him that she wore "black pants and a feathery shawl"? Would you describe her white hair "and an expression on her face that looked like . . ."? *No, my dear Pierino, I won't tell you what Mamma's expression was like.*

Federica put fiction aside and for a time scraped a living as a correspondent for the glossies, interviewing actresses, women in politics, designers and Chinese engineers from Milan to Australia. Fausto and Carlo were simpler and more straightforward, they would have known better how to handle Mamma, and she had explicitly asked this of them. Once Federica had finished mourning for her brother and for her father, who died two years later, more from heartbreak than old age, she began taking notes for a new novel, the basic plot of which revolved around thoughts about her family and was easily and conveniently poured into the symbolic receptacle of yin and yang symbology.

For at least a year after breaking up with her boyfriend she had allowed herself to be penetrated only by inorganic, unthreatening, sterile objects. She turned over in her mind this anxiety with regard to penetration. Family problems. Were there similarities between her case and Piero's? Just as she, at the center of her black yin (feminine, nocturnal, terrestrial) held this tiny white dot (fear of consequences, responsibilities, all the connections born of intercourse), so Piero—thus did the urban planner of her fictional world deliberate—had to have, within the white flourish that was the yang (the masculine principle, luminous and aspiring to Paradise), a tiny black dot of darkness. What was it?

. . . I found my answer as I reflected on Piero's flight to Paris— there was no reason for him to move to France. Piero had fled for love, he had met someone. This clichéd scenario quickly bored me, but it was transformed into an exhilarating idea that was doubtless true: whatever his motive for fleeing to Paris, Pierino did indeed have a lover, but she was Italian, and was none other than his sister-in-law Ada the incorruptible, the woman whose virginity he had often bragged about vicariously. By dint of singing her praises he had fallen in love, and through twisted Catholic legerdemain they must have believed themselves to be made for each other, soul mates, Abelard and Héloïse, tragically repressing—or else consummating, or consummating and repressing together—their own passion.

This explains Ada's presence in Paris, about which no questions had been raised given the dramatic outcome of their walk (Ada told Sergio and Alice that she hadn't been clear, before embarking on her supposed trip to Milan, that she was in fact going to Paris). It was the desperate march of two lovers at their wits' end; putting five hundred kilometers between them hadn't extinguished the flame of their passion blah, blah . . . It was impossible to make a plot congeal around these elements and the novel I published was completely different. Neither did I wish to be so pitiless toward my mother as to have her find out that in my view her son—my brother—had killed himself for having become like his father and in so doing betraying her.

If obliged to identify precisely when I gave up on the idea, I'd say it was after having written the note "Piero = Anna Karenin!" and thinking no, it really wasn't worth continuing.

It's a mystery that Federica had chosen not to speak with Ada, who, by this time, had entered a convent in the Marche region (without taking a vow of silence). The most likely interpretation is that, in seeking the poetic truth about her own relationship with her brother, Federica Rosini didn't want to risk discovering what she suspected—that Ada had not, could not have been Piero's lover. Who knows whether in that conversation she never had with Ada, during the muggy visiting hours at the convent Ada had shut herself up in while her sister still wore mourning (a season of black skirts that, graphically underlining the exceptional circumstances of the shadows beneath Alice's eyes, made sure she wouldn't wither on the vine, conferring on her an exciting glamour about which more anon), who knows whether Ada would have spoken to her with the vague optimism of the newly ordained or whether, sheltered from the pitiless judgments of the world, she would have felt free to let slip some details of her recent life. Because, if she had reacted this last way, both secular interviewer and vestal interviewee would have made quite a discovery: Ada, of the relationship between Corrado and Federica; Federica, of the brief, inconsequential moment of intimacy between the future nun and Corrado Paloschi, shortly after which Ada had resolved to take vows.

It was a kind of blitz on Corrado's part, improper to say the least. He invited her into his own house, his mother absent, to take stock of the situation, to talk about me, to talk about Alice, to drink tea, wine, or beer. Ada still felt guilty about the accident but only admitted as much in confession. Corrado maintained it had been my dream to lead "a simpler life." He revealed that I had begun recently to question the presumed necessity of "restraining myself" and "not yielding," of spending immense amounts of energy in order to "hold still that which is constantly in motion, passion." As Corrado spoke, the presence in the room of Ada's Tits was perceived by him with all due gravitas; Ada's Tits were legendary, even dangerous characters, bearers of misfortune like Helen of Troy or Marie Antoinette. He thought of me, he thought "eviscerations"; he thought how once those tits were something one could laugh about. He wanted to touch them.

. . . And I decided to open up. I was struck by what I'd come to know about my brother-in-law after his death, that Piero had desired me, thought about me. Corrado realized I was upset. We embraced on his mother's sofa, the two of us each living with a single parent, I with my father and he with his mother, two people who had yet to amount to anything. It was May and it seemed like summer, I had on I don't know what shirt and an ugly bra. I let him do it, let him unbutton my shirt, let him unhook my bra and he practically came running to support my breasts in his hands. The bra wasn't padded, and when he undid it, it came off in his hand. First, for a few seconds, I didn't look him in the face, concentrating on the sensation I was feeling, on the heat and the intimacy, then I pulled away from him a few centimeters in order to see what expression a man who supports your breasts in his hands has. He was engrossed, staring at what lay in his palms, massaging them in a pleasantly stubborn manner until my large, stippled nipples sprouted. He had ceased to speak of Piero and I didn't know how we ought to behave; he gazed at me in contemplation. As soon as he leaned forward, bending his neck down to kiss them, I drew the curtain of my shirt and moved him away with a nunlike smile.

Well, it wasn't really such a big deal. I entered the convent soon after. No one had really wanted me around, and as soon as I left Rome everyone was free to do what he wanted: Papa invited the woman whose existence we'd always suspected to live with him, a certain Giovanna; Alice returned to Porta di Roma to leave them in peace, but she didn't want to live there alone and had a friend move in with her. The house became like a hotel. Alice didn't tell me about it, just made out how she needed not to think. She made torturous speeches about her presumptive deep needs. She got together with . . . and brought him home with her to Porta di Roma, which enraged me, but then I had to acknowledge that the bond of holy matrimony no longer applied.

Two years after the funeral, Corrado shamelessly (let this be said as objectively as possible) called Alice again. Not long after, over a quick cremolato she deemed a greater source of unhappiness than nostalgia, she told him in so many words, "You're not the right person for me. This cremolato wasn't a good idea."

. . . letting it out lifted something from my heart, as if saying it to Corrado compensated for my never having been able to say it to poor Piero. On this occasion I exploited Corrado for my own ends, but maybe that isn't so very important—he's capable of looking after himself, and, in turn, perfectly able to be exploitative himself when the right person comes along.

I wouldn't have known what to make of him. At the time, I'd already started seeing my son's future father, and he had a way of keeping me entertained that was quite different from those chaste cremolati or gelati on Via Nemorense. I don't know when I became pregnant but during the stretch when it happened we were making love practically every day, except when I had my period. With this man—what does it matter what kind of job he has, what his origins are, the kind of socks he wears? Men like him are to be found in every age, in every class and nation. He wasn't the answer to my prayers, it just worked at the time—I had my habits and routines, he knew how to fuck me (from behind), and I knew that I was beautiful dressed in black. On Sundays, for example . . . one summer Sunday we walked to the shopping center, now well and truly inaugurated and already showing signs of wear and tear given the steady stream of families who, like me, preferred a trip to IKEA or Media World on Sundays than to the beach or the countryside. He said, "You have an hour. Be in front of Fnac at three forty-six. One minute late and I'll make you pay."

"Okay."

I was late, so he poked a stiff index finger into the small of my back, through my shapeless, short-sleeved T-shirt; then, without making a scene, escorted me out to the street, past people pushing shopping carts, maxi-scooters balanced on their kickstands, hair curlers and dangling children, all the way home, then into the elevator . . . He can tolerate the shopping center on Sundays only if he gets to punish me in return. Nothing serious or elaborate, he uses a cotton scarf as a blindfold and pink plastic handcuffs. When he's blindfolded me he leads me to the sofa; I kneel when he tells me I should, and with his help I arrange my head on the sofa, unloading the weight of my body onto one cheek; the blindfold smells of his dried sweat. It's sweet. He orders me about, he asks me questions, he tells me things.

"You were late, huh? You could have saved yourself a lot of trouble . . . You're in trouble now . . . Next time you'll think twice before being late . . ."

So, yes, my cheek is squished up against the sofa, my hands are behind my back, and my knees are pressing into the brown rug. I could say "I was only five minutes late . . ." but I always say "Yes."

"Yes, what?"

My knees hurt (Do his? Where does he put his knees? Does he rest them on the pants he's slipped off?), I can't see a thing, I feel the rug and I feel him behind me, his sweaty palms grabbing my hips; my back hurts too, and tomorrow my kidneys will be sore.

"Yes . . . the *next time* I'll be *on time*?"

"Yes."

He caresses me and two big drops of sweat fall on my back; his forehead is always sweaty because he's big, bigger than Piero, and he sweats so much and knocks himself out for me. In the summer he sweats on his pillow, he leaves damp footprints on the floor when he's barefoot, the hair at his temples is always wet, his hairline's receding faster than Piero's . . .

It didn't take him long to get me pregnant.

The day my son was born, in terms of life lived, I felt I'd outdone everyone. Sweatily enraptured by my son (tiny, ugly, not handicapped, and all mine), during one of the blessed quiet moments at the clinic, I had the extraordinary sensation of having lived a long, almost eternal life: my husband never knew my mother, and my son never knew my husband, or my mother either. Three generations in a flash, a sensationally long life—all I do is start over.

•

Leo thought similar thoughts, but turned on their head. He reproached me for having stubbornly gone in search of death, for having shortened my life in order to simplify it. Desperate, affectionate thoughts. "You came to the end you wanted," he said to me, "and that was death. You went straight to death, Rosenzweil. You really didn't want to give life a second chance. You and Saint Paul."

Ungenerous conclusions, like those of Federica, who decided I'd committed suicide—not exactly lucid thoughts. Why suicide? Why think I'd seek out death? Why would I do that? I was hit by a car!

"You lost out on New York," Leo reminded me bitterly in the spring of 2008. He'd flown to America with Clelia; his niece had gone back there to live with her parents and no longer wanted anything to do with Paris. Rumor circulated that Benedetta had slept with Chewbacca, and this thanks to the disclosures made by the interested party to Ana: "The last pussy Chewb ever saw was mine." Clelia had taken off without seeking clarification.

With the passing seasons, Leo forgot the monstrous image he'd constructed of me from the articles in *La Repubblica*. He too was seeking a poetic truth (What other truths are there, after all? And yet they feel so incomplete) and his poetic truth was that, actually, I loved the Jews: "You lost out, could have been a guest at my sister's enormous house. You would've been immersed in Jews . . . I know you liked the Jews, you wretch. I would've taken you on a tour of Jewish things, my old Hebrew teacher would've made your sidelocks grow out right there on Thirteenth Avenue in Brooklyn, taken you to sniff the eucalyptus balm at the Russian baths, to go see the Mets, to a synagogue, wherever you wanted, Frank . . . I would've taken you to get a massage, Rosenzweil, *you schmuck*, I would've taken you to get laid . . ." He walked uncertainly down Columbus Avenue, dodging garbage cans and people and newspaper boxes, accelerating into longer strides, more illustrated than alive, and at the thought of the massages a big cartoon strip without corners (from a panel by Crumb, Spiegelman, or Katchor), a giant dusty lightbulb—"Idea! Idea! Eureka! I would've taken you to a masseuse who'd give you a *happy ending*! Rosenzweil! The happy ending!"

He stopped in a diner and ordered breakfast. "And you call this breakfast of mine an existential failure? Midmorning, Upper West Side, around the corner from the Museum of Natural History, huevos rancheros and corn cakes? Actually, now I'm going to go for a massage and I'm going to get myself a happy ending and to hell with you, Rosini. We would've had a good time, stupid apologist idiot; all you had to do was not get fixated on Augustine . . . You never even managed to sleep with my niece . . ."

But what's the point of these internal struggles? Of getting bogged down in arguments with dead people?

"You're spilling your seed," said a faint, disembodied voice he took for Rosenzweil's.

"Ah, so I'm spilling my seed, according to you? Here you are, then, let's scrap a bit over the parable of the sower. Let's get on with polemicizing about the parables in the Gospel—me, my eggs, and the voice of Rosenzweil. Excellent. *Midmorning.* Let's hear it."

"It's just that you're spilling your seed. The seed that doesn't fall on good earth doesn't bear fruit."

"Now you listen to me carefully, I'm going to explain what happens to the seed . . ."

. . . I'd like to tell a joke about it. Jesus walks into a bar. But it doesn't work, I don't know how to come up with jokes. Let's be theologians, come on (Oh God, just think if I end up having conversations of this sort with Jiminy Cricket for the rest of my days; by what right has Rosini turned into my Jiminy Cricket? It makes no sense). The farmer is there with his sack, and he's throwing seeds everywhere; the seeds are the word of God. Jesus says, "A seed falls on the road, the birds come and devour it." This means the Word of God has entered ears that do not understand, and the Devil gulps it down in a single bite. A seed falls on rocky ground: the plant grows, but it doesn't put down roots and it withers away. These are the hearts easily moved to enthusiasm, and there the Word is not fruitful. Okay. *Next.* A seed falls among thorns. The thorns are the cares of the world, the temptations. The little plant is snuffed out by distractions and dies. (It's the dilemma of the rich young man who won't give up his riches. I'm thinking just like Rosenzweil.) *But* a fourth seed—still the Word of God—falls on good earth: the little plant grows and yields fruit. Good. These are worthy Christians like yourself. Congratulations. I have a question for you: What credit do you deserve for being the good earth? And another: Who cultivated you? What fertilizer did they use? Your natural goodness? Fear? Intelligence? And what credit would you deserve? Let's say you were the good earth.

"Let's say I was," responds the petulant voice that appears to be that of my dead friend, from some quarter of the packed diner, somewhere around this table with my leftover corn cakes and a magazine and my little notebook. Huh, if you were the good earth, do you know what I'd say to you? "Tell me." None of this even matters to Jesus! What he said was just an observation. There's good earth, there are thorns, rocks, and the road, so goes agriculture; the farmer knows that some of his seeds will be spilt, but not all of them. You know what I think? "I never said I was the good earth." What are you doing, circling me? I'm trying to tell a joke and you're circling? "I never said that." Look, if there was some earth where the seed took root, it was you . . . since it was so important to you . . . "Whosoever loses his own life will find it." Oh, no doubt. Can I order you some coffee? A muffin? Oh, no, sorry, I forgot, you don't have a digestive system. "I was the rocky ground, or maybe the

291

thorns." No, look, sorry, but it would be even more unjust if you hadn't been the good earth and you still died—let's say that you're the good earth that yields fruit . . . "No." Let me tell the joke! "You're no good at jokes." I miss you, Piero, we had fun together. "We gave each other a hard time." I only wanted to say that the good earth is made up of chumps like you! You messed up my timing. "Right, like the chosen people with their rigged election. You don't know how to tell jokes." I have other redeeming qualities. I wanted to say: You thought you were fertile soil and you were just a stinkin' chump. I hope the joke came off this time. The fourth category, the good earth, is made up of chumps. But I have other redeeming qualities, sooner or later you'll have to admit it.

That afternoon, lying on the massage table, being worked on by a short woman who was most certainly not Aryan, who was very focused on the task at hand, I asked for my happy ending and, as the woman began to play with my cock I tried as hard as I could to come up with a joke about "seed," or about a "happy ending," and still it wouldn't come off. And the fifth seed landed in the hands of the masseuse. *The End.* And the fifth seed landed in the sperm bank and thence was born the Messiah. And the fifth seed gushed from the good earth. It's hard to be funny on command. And the fifth seed . . . I continued to think about it in the melancholy aftermath, hesitating at first to get up from the table, empty, happy, depressed, light, anxious, anxious . . . Back out on the sidewalk after having paid, in the sun, amid odors organic and inorganic, taking my place in the froth of pedestrians, handbags, and cell phones, and the beat of women's heels reverberating beneath the scaffolding of buildings being repaired, I hastened to draw a line between spiritual life and good sense. Dear Rosenzweil, here we bid each other adieu, because I don't talk to dead people.

ACKNOWLEDGMENTS

For the hospitality: Mico and Rosalinda; Ferro and Francesca; Piero; Cristina and Marco; Neme, Chou, Emma and Daniele, Andrea Decovich, Samy; the Carpios; Tamsin and Matt; Mattia, Francesca, and Luisa; Giulietta; Alessandro and Veronica; Matteo and Carlotta; Martina; Summit Street; Andrea De Marco; Via Sicilia; the Pacificos.

For the help: Kylee Doust, Anna Stein, Marion Duvert, Mitzi Angel, Chantal Clarke, Stephen Twilley, Lorin Stein, Mark Krotov, and Brian Gittis.

He just wanted a decent book to read ...

Not too much to ask, is it? It was in 1935 when Allen Lane, Managing Director of Bodley Head Publishers, stood on a platform at Exeter railway station looking for something good to read on his journey back to London. His choice was limited to popular magazines and poor-quality paperbacks – the same choice faced every day by the vast majority of readers, few of whom could afford hardbacks. Lane's disappointment and subsequent anger at the range of books generally available led him to found a company – and change the world.

'We believed in the existence in this country of a vast reading public for intelligent books at a low price, and staked everything on it'
Sir Allen Lane, 1902–1970, founder of Penguin Books

The quality paperback had arrived – and not just in bookshops. Lane was adamant that his Penguins should appear in chain stores and tobacconists, and should cost no more than a packet of cigarettes.

Reading habits (and cigarette prices) have changed since 1935, but Penguin still believes in publishing the best books for everybody to enjoy. We still believe that good design costs no more than bad design, and we still believe that quality books published passionately and responsibly make the world a better place.

So wherever you see the little bird – whether it's on a piece of prize-winning literary fiction or a celebrity autobiography, political tour de force or historical masterpiece, a serial-killer thriller, reference book, world classic or a piece of pure escapism – you can bet that it represents the very best that the genre has to offer.

Whatever you like to read – trust Penguin.

read more
www.penguin.co.uk